MW01000512

WHERE THE LIGHT FALLS

Where the Light Falls

SELECTED STORIES OF

Nancy Hale

Edited by Lauren Groff

A LIBRARY OF AMERICA
Special Publication

WHERE THE LIGHT FALLS: SELECTED STORIES OF NANCY HALE

Introduction and volume compilation copyright © 2019 by
Literary Classics of the United States, Inc., New York, N.Y.
All rights reserved.

Published in the United States by Library of America.
Visit our website at www.loa.org.

No part of this book may be reproduced in any manner whatsoever without the permission of the publisher, except in the case of brief quotations embodied in critical articles and reviews.

All stories published by arrangement with the Estate of Nancy Hale.

Interior design and composition by Gopa & Ted2, Inc.

Distributed to the trade in the United States by Penguin Random House Inc.
and in Canada by Penguin Random House Canada Ltd.

Library of Congress Control Number: 2019935124
ISBN 978-1-59853-642-3

1 3 5 7 9 10 8 6 4 2

Printed in the United States of America

CONTENTS

Introduction by Lauren Groff ix

The Earliest Dreams 5

The Double House 9

Midsummer 17

To the North 28

Crimson Autumn 52

That Woman 75

A Place to Hide In 95

Book Review 100

Those Are as Brothers 110

The Marching Feet 122

Sunday—1913 129

Who Lived and Died Believing 148

Some Day I'll Find You . . . 171

On the Beach 186

Inside 197

The Empress's Ring 202

The Bubble 208

Miss August 220

How Would You Like to Be Born . . . 238

Outside 250
A Slow Boat to China 262
Flotsam 275
Rich People 290
Sunday Lunch 316
The Most Elegant Drawing Room in Europe 328

Sources 349

INTRODUCTION
by Lauren Groff

IN THE LATE 1970S, Nancy Hale—then in her sixties and white-haired, elegant, queenly—toured the National Gallery of Art in Washington, D.C., in preparation for writing her biography of the Impressionist painter Mary Cassatt. Hale later described herself moving silently and in growing excitement as the galleries opened into each other, each successively framing a new movement in the artist's work, until at last, upon leaving the exhibition, she turned to her guide and exclaimed, "This show *is* a biography! There is nothing to say about Mary Cassatt that isn't here." She did in fact go on to write Cassatt's biography, but her point was, as she later said, that an artist's work "was not *like* his life, it was his life."

Nancy Hale was the daughter of two Impressionist painters: her father, Philip Leslie Hale, a scion of an old Boston family who had known Monet at Giverny during his dissipated youth, and her mother, the successful portraitist Lilian Westcott Hale, a beautiful, warm woman whose entire focus was her art. In the same pages in which Nancy Hale spoke of her revelation about Mary Cassatt, she wrote of her mother's paintings that "it was not that the pictures told about her, so much as that they *were* her, just as the other side of the moon, hidden, is still the moon."

This collection of Nancy Hale's short stories, *Where the Light Falls*, is the result of a long and joyous immersion in this immensely overlooked twentieth-century writer's work, not only in her more than one hundred published stories—ten garnering an O. Henry

Prize, over eighty published in *The New Yorker*—but also in her novels and memoirs and assorted other writing. These stories, which span the greater part of Hale's long and productive literary career, can be read as a dark-side-of-the-moon biography of the writer's life, her obsessions, and her growth as an artist.

Hale acknowledged the nimbly semi-autobiographical nature of her own work in her memoir, *A New England Girlhood*, saying:

> My pieces, although their background is the scenery and characters that bounded my childhood, are intended less about the real and ascertainable past than about the memory of it; and memory as a mode of thinking tends to burst spontaneously into fantasy at every turn. Some of the events in the stories are true to fact, some not. What interested me in writing them was to try to catch the reverberations from childhood that sometimes make it seem as if the first few years of all our lives constitute a riddle which it is a lifework to solve.

I would hesitate to draw biography from the work for most writers—I have a horror of the biographical fallacy—but for Nancy Hale it feels appropriate to sketch a biography out of the stories, to solve the riddle with what we hold even now in our hands.

Here it is. Nancy Hale was born on May 6, 1908. Her Bohemian mother and father never seemed quite acceptable to her; she wrote later that as a child she wanted different parents, "orthodox ones, against whom I could properly rebel and for the proper reasons." In her first story in this collection, 1932's "The Earliest Dreams," she writes in a strange and breathless second person—long before Jay McInerney and Lorrie Moore popularized the conceit in the 1980s—about the experience of lying in bed as a tiny child and hearing guests downstairs as they arrive for a party, the sense of coldness and vibrating wonder at being excluded from the warmth and laughter of the adults. The writer Ann Beattie says of this story that the effect of it is "like a buzzing in the ear emitted by something that won't go away." The paternal side of Nancy Hale's family, relatives of the Revolutionary spy and soldier Nathan Hale and the writer Harriet Beecher Stowe, were genteel, formal, and moneyed, like Uncle Paul in the story "A Place to Hide In."

The larger, refined Boston world of Hale's youth was pedigree-proud, and practical-verging-on-parsimonious, like the Yankee sisters in "How Would You Like to Be Born . . . ," who restrict their meals to cheap organ meat they don't even enjoy so that they can give money to their progressive causes. As a child, she felt that she was destined to admire but never own the beautiful things of life, like the little girl in "The Empress's Ring," who is given a precious antique gold and turquoise ring which she loses in her sandbox and which haunts her in her adult life as a symbol of her own unworthiness to be the possessor of treasures. The effects of living with parents who were turned inward toward their artwork are made visible in "Outside," in which artist parents overlook their daughter's dangerously high fever in their self-absorbed preparations for an afternoon party, ignoring the girl's brave minimizing of her pain to the point of her own collapse, then the girl's deep sense of abandonment that ensues when she wakes up alone in the hospital.

Lilian Westcott Hale's fine and vivid portraits were in high demand in Boston society, but Philip Leslie Hale found more success as a critic and teacher of painting than in his own art, which caused him great disappointment. He would trudge off to his classes in deliberately bourgeois clothing—a bowler hat and a banker's suit—pretending to go with a light heart, but an older Nancy Hale understood that his cheerfulness was only a façade. She mirrored her father in her fiction as the parent in "The Double House," whose wearisomely feigned adult solidity is the only thing allowing his deeply sensitive young son to hope that life will be less dark and difficult and confusing when he grows up.

Though money was tight, and the Hale family lived for most of the year in Boston, they managed to spend their summers on the chill and rocky New England shore. Her story "Flotsam" sketches with love and economy the town of Rockport at the end of its season: "stout middle-aged women in shorts and halter, usually surmounted by a Jazz Age shingle or an imposing pile of marcelled hairdo. Several children of less than school age ran, on little bare brown feet, down to the beach in summer-ragged, summer-faded bathing suits. Here and there an artist had pitched his easel near the sidewalk and stood scowling past his canvas at the cobalt waters of Sandy Bay." And "To the North," my favorite story from *Where the Light Falls*, and one that I find a world-class achievement, even after a dozen rereads, speaks achingly of a place called Graniteside, where the summer people meet but hardly notice the hardy Finnish working class who live there year-round. The main character, Jack, loves

> the wild, brilliant sea and the long slabs of untouched gray stone, the miles behind the sea of rough moorland, full of low, stunted growth, smelling of wild rosebushes and bayberries and sweet fern; the high, clear, strong air, full of sun and salt. He loved the heavy purplish clouds that came across the sky suddenly, the ocean turned lead gray and whipped up into little points, the abrupt violence of the wind and then the downpour and hurricane of the northeaster screaming in from the sea. He loved the land in its particulars, in its small unique things—the thorny locust trees that blossomed in white too early for him ever to have seen; the red spiders no bigger than pin points that ran in thousands over the rocks in the sun; the deserted quarries back in the moors, jagged holes filled with blue fresh water that reflected the rotting, rusting derricks above them; the way the

> wind rose imperceptibly day after day after the first of September, rising a little, steadily, as if toward some terrific crescendo still months away.

The family spent the rest of the year in the far more cosmopolitan Boston area, and in her late teens, Nancy Hale became a debutante, which both fed her hunger for society and glamour and made her chafe against the straitened futures such young and wealthy girls were expected to enter into. Her story "Crimson Autumn" paints with a brightness borne of nostalgia the manic life of youthful Boston society of the twenties, with its Harvard football games and Bugatti rides through the cold to the ballroom at the Copley Plaza just as the orchestra is warming up. (This story is also a first pass at a long passage in her third and best novel, *The Prodigal Women.*) In "Rich People," the debutante main character's puritanically healthy mother—described as an adherent of cold baths even in winter, hearty Scotch tweed, breakfasts of "whole oranges, whole-wheat porridge, and whole milk," and all dinners alfresco, no matter the cold and wind and chilling mist at their summer place on the shore—remarks not unkindly that coming out was not a success for her daughter. Nor was it for Nancy Hale, especially, who had not-so-secret artistic ambitions and who spent two years studying the fine arts before marrying at twenty the socialite and writer Taylor Scott Hardin in 1928. The marriage, too, was not a success, although Hale did have a son, Mark, with Hardin; and when the little family moved to New York City, the new, bright, exciting city gave Nancy Hale the second of her three great locations for her fiction. "The Bubble," one of her best-known stories, in which a very young and pregnant new wife is put up in the grand and elegant Washington, D.C., house of her mother-in-law, is a study of maternal and marital and socioeconomic ambivalence. The young mother, when her baby is born and her body has become sleek again, flees to New York and picks up her flashy, exciting life there as though something as momentous and earthquaking as childbirth hadn't just happened to her.

There are surprisingly few short stories of motherhood in Nancy Hale's body of work, but among the best is the deliciously alienating and moving "On the Beach," in which a mother watches her plump little son on an outing to the shore. Hers is a child with whom the mother feels a great and wordless sympathy, who, she muses, "used to look up even from his play pen, the light in his face reflecting her exact mood." But on this particular morning the mother feels the close affinity with her son broken as Cold War–era anxiety slowly overwhelms her in great waves; only with difficulty, at the story's end, does the pragmatic little body of her boy bring her back to the moment. Later in the collection, in "A Slow Boat to China," an angry mother is ambushed by her grief and loneliness when she drops her son off at college.

Although the Hales of Boston boasted of a long literary heritage, it was only when she moved to New York City that Nancy Hale's life in letters began. She worked for *Vogue* as a bright and beautiful young creature, freelancing at night, and almost immediately started publishing in places like *Harper's*, *Vanity Fair*, and *Scribner's*, where she was edited and championed by the legendary editor Maxwell Perkins. By twenty-one, she was publishing in the newly founded magazine *The New Yorker*, and by twenty-six she had published two novels and divorced her first husband.

In the last of her ground-shaking deracinations, Nancy Hale married her second husband, the journalist Charles Wertenbaker, in 1935, and moved with him to Virginia. The shift from the prim North to the bewildering South brought out a satirical side in Nancy Hale that hadn't showed itself in her work before. In the story "That Woman," Hale shines a bright light on Southern women's hypocritical attitudes toward sex and the way they often unquestioningly uphold the patriarchy. The stories "The Marching Feet" and "Book Review," both written in 1941 during the thick of

World War II, describe how Southern ideas of white supremacy are subterranean, uniquely American flavors of fascism. "Those Are as Brothers" pulses with anger, a searing denunciation of the way wealthy people often feel free to diminish the poorer, less powerful, suffering people whom they hold in their thrall.

Yet the Virginia landscape's beauty also brought out a sense of romance and wonder in Nancy Hale, best seen in her story "Midsummer," with its breathtaking Gothic overtones:

> There was something terrible about the hollows, deep-bottomed with decaying leaves, smelling of dead water and dark leafage and insufferable heat. The sound of the horses' feet was like a confused heartbeat on the swampy ground. They both felt it. They used to get off their horses, without having said a word, and helplessly submerge themselves in each other's arms, while the sweat ran down their backs under their shirts. They never talked there. They stood swaying together with their booted feet deep in the mulch, holding each other, hot and mystified in this green gloom. From far away in the upper meadows they could always hear the cicada reaching an unbearable, sharpened crescendo.

There are years of intense rupture and renewal in all lives; 1941 was one such year in Nancy Hale's. During this year, she divorced her second husband—with whom she'd had a second son, William, in 1938—and published her magisterial novel *The Prodigal Women*, a book that she'd struggled to write for seven difficult years. Shortly after she finished her novel, she had a nervous breakdown, for which she sought psychiatric treatment at a sanitarium. A number of stories in *Where the Light Falls* come out of this and subsequent harrowing experiences of mental instability and attendant vulnerability, including "Miss August," "Some Day I'll

Find You . . . ," "Sunday—1913," and the excellent "Who Lived and Died Believing," a story in which a woman's madness washes through her in vivid pointillism until, eventually, shock treatment washes it out of her.

In 1942, she married her third husband, Fredson Bowers, a renowned textual scholar and a professor of English at the University of Virginia. This last relationship turned out to be the happiest and most stable one in her life: she and her husband would remain married for forty-five years, until her death. Although the final story in this collection was published in September 1966, she never stopped publishing or writing her memoirs, nonfiction, short stories, and novels, including a never completed novel-in-history of a Hale relative, Charles Hale, who had been a U.S. consul general to Egypt and the publisher of the *Boston Daily Advertiser*. In 1971, she cofounded the Virginia Center for the Creative Arts, which currently offers residencies to over 350 artists per year, a magnificent gift of time, space, and silence in which artists can dream and fail and, eventually, create. In 1980, Nancy Hale was slowed down by a stroke, but according to her friends, she still wrote and thought about her writing until the very week of her death in 1988.

How sad it seems that, in the thirty years since then, Nancy Hale has been almost entirely forgotten, even by the writers who consider themselves to hold a library of American short stories in their skulls. I am a rabid fanatic and practitioner of this literary form, but I confess that my only exposures to Nancy Hale before this project were in a few late-night insomniac forays into the online archives of *The New Yorker*, and in Lorrie Moore and Heidi Pitlor's magisterial *100 Years of the Best American Short Stories*, which includes her 1941 story "Those Are as Brothers."

I said earlier that her slow forgetting was sad, but in fact it makes me riotously angry that such a brilliant and important writer as Nancy Hale could fall out of public consciousness. Over these months of living with Hale's voice in my head, I have asked myself over and over how we could have turned our eyes from her, and I find that I have no decisive conclusions, only a few hypotheses. These include internalized misogyny and the quiet, deadly, constant devaluing of women's work; the sheer quantity of her stories, some of the later and more purely autobiographical of which *do* feel a bit slight and sweet, like too much meringue at the end of a meal; the fact that Nancy Hale's aristocratic Boston lineage and her later adopted role as a Southern gentlewoman unfairly lend to her imagined person a stale, old-fashioned whiff of dust and starch; the false presumption that the short story form, the one in which Nancy Hale excelled, is a lesser creature than its big and blustering sibling, the novel; the work's straightforward realism that can tempt the reader into thinking it easy, at least until you come up for air at the end of a story and are struck still by the work's precision and emotional muscle; and William Maxwell's point, in his tribute to Hale after her death, that she was a writer who really cared about feeling and that "the intellectual content of fiction has been more valued than the emotional." Though each of these devaluations is knocked out cold by reading even a few of the stories in this collection, the paradox is that one has to read the stories to understand how wrong we have been to let Nancy Hale slip from our memory. It is in this way that the circuit of forgetfulness endlessly repeats itself, to the detriment of the literary canon, which, through forgetting, pares itself down to seem like a monoculture of educated, white, upper-middle-class men.

I hope, very much, that this volume will serve as a necessary correction to Nancy Hale's slow slide into oblivion. The more time that I have spent with these stories, the more invaluable her work appears to me. During the era in which she was writing, it was taken for granted that the stories most worthy of being told were those of the heroic or well-off white man, like those by Hale's contemporaries and fellow Scribner authors Ernest Hemingway, F. Scott Fitzgerald, and Thomas Wolfe, but Nancy Hale insisted on the importance of the lives of ordinary women and children. She saw the turmoil and drama of a little boy so driven by despair at the revelation that he would carry his melancholy into adulthood that he would run into a basement and put a noose around his little neck; she saw the profound loss incurred when a woman, in order to live in the wider world's stark reality, has to give up her treasured belief in a wild and all-consuming love. She saw how rigid ideas of propriety can so warp a good and gentle woman who has lived a long life under the thumb of her severe sister that even when she has broken free from her sister's constraints, and wants to exult a little in the life of the body, she finds herself unable to do so.

What I love in Nancy Hale the most is that her shining surfaces hide that she was a ferocious critic of the time in which she lived. William Maxwell, her editor at Scribner (and himself a vastly underappreciated writer) wrote of Hale that "though she had much of the personality of a poet, her style remains firmly anchored in prose—lucid, unobtrusive, well-shaped, and with an implied voice. Only when the reader detaches himself from the emotional hold that the story has on him is he likely to become aware of how flawless the writing is . . . she is at home in, though not actually committed to, the world of good manners." One can be lulled by the hard and brilliant glaze of the prose into believing that Nancy Hale *subscribes* to the good manners and the elegant world that she's so adept at *describing*; in truth, though, she was quietly yet ferociously committed to undermining them. She never announced herself as a particularly feminist or political writer, yet it was a profoundly political act for her to focus her steely gaze on women's internal lives and pay them the fullest attention, to write about botched South American abortions, mothers who don't want their babies, promiscuous young career girls, the way men take their dominance for granted and crush those they consider weak, and the hideous and simmering misogyny and racism of the South, the very place in which she made her home for decades. Her criticisms are so quiet that their power only reaches you later, when you're washing the dishes or lulling yourself to sleep and thinking about her work, and then they reverberate into your following days. Nancy Hale speaks beyond the twentieth century, into our current moment, when it is still a political act to acknowledge the equal status of women, to talk about abortion, to make plain that the ignorant tribalism of some parts of the South is, in fact, deeply fascistic.

And it would be most apparent to any reader who came by chance upon this volume that Nancy Hale was impeccable in her craft. She was sensitive to the precise emotional pitch her stories needed to hit before they come alive, always attentive to structure and pacing and the slow and building momentum of her lines. The child of two skilled Impressionist painters, she was a feeling and interested student of Impressionism herself, and I think it's safe to say that her own writing at its best borrows many of the ideas and techniques of her parents' school of art. Nancy Hale's work is a sort of slantwise realism; one peers for so long at a thing that one pushes through one's initial judgment and all the freight of taught expectations, until form separates into daubs of color, and so in the end shows itself more purely as what it truly is. For Nancy Hale, these daubs of color were often the subtle, just-barely-mappable emotional currents inside the hearts and minds of people, for the most part women, who, from the outside, could hardly be considered interesting subjects: a casual reader may in fact consider them too well-bred, too moneyed, too privileged to reveal such deep and dark and changeable currents of feeling that they hold inside themselves. At the end of her study of Mary Cassatt, Hale muses about

> The Impressionists' way of looking at dividing lines. They were much concerned with what they called the edges; getting the edges right. Even color mattered chiefly in terms of what one color became when placed against another. The understanding of form, for them, lay in seeing

> where the light fell, where the edge of the shadow came. As for line itself, one great Impressionist teacher used to say, "Line is the study of edges." . . . Line . . . is not so much what separates different spaces and tones as it is the relation between them.

I found it impossible to discover who exactly that great Impressionist teacher was, but I suspect that the voice here was that of her father, Philip Leslie Hale, whose great gift was in the criticism and teaching of other artists. We took the title of this collection from a similar saying of his, from her memoir *The Life in the Studio*: "Where the light falls is the light. Where the light does not fall is the shadow. Chiaroscuro, the clear and the obscure. Don't go mucking your drawing up with half-lights." Nancy Hale listened to her parents' early lessons, discovered the profound relation between different spaces and emotional tones, and mucked nothing at all up with half-lights. Her work lives on, brilliant literary chiaroscuro.

Nancy Hale's voice has become a quiet and internal intelligence that over the past months I have begun to rely on; finishing this book gives me a gentle, bittersweet tang. She once said, according to her granddaughter Norah Hardin Lind, that the work of a great writer makes it feel as though we are "sitting on some cosmic front porch together, rocking, exchanging long, gratifying accounts of our happy or unhappy lives. At any moment the writer is trying to make it seem that the reader can break in upon the writer's stream of discourse crying, *Why, that is just the way it was with me!*" Many times in reading for this volume, I had that same slippery sense of connection with a keen and perceptive mind that saw pieces of my life more clearly than I could. A small, ignoble part of me even wants to keep her as my own brilliant friend without having to share her with the rest of the world; a joy held secretly within the heart can illuminate a dark time or a difficult day, and there have been plenty of these for all of us in recent months.

Yet even my worst self knows that, given the choice between keeping a beloved writer as a prized secret and shouting her brilliance to the world at large, it behooves all of us to shout, to make noise, to throw parades for the writers of the past who merit rediscovery. Consider this introduction to be the loosening of my grip on this extraordinary writer. Please feel the weight of Nancy Hale's brilliant stories in your hands, open to the first page, and let yourself be seduced. Nancy Hale will continue to be mine; I am so happy that she will now also be yours.

Where the Light Falls

Selected Stories of Nancy Hale

"Where the light falls is the light.
Where the light does *not* fall is the shadow.
Chiaroscuro, the clear and the obscure.
Don't go mucking your drawing up
with half-lights."

—Philip Leslie Hale

THE EARLIEST DREAMS

THAT WAS long, long ago.

Your bed was maple, the color of brown sugar, and upon the small round posts of it in the darkness some moonlight danced in the hush, in the quiet. Your mother had rustled away, far away and bright and legendary, and your window stood open to the great stars and the wide dark snow. It was so quiet, and the air of the night and the snow came through the window and smelled so cold, so sweet, and of faraway sad promises. What was it you wanted so? From miles and miles away you heard a late train breathing across the countryside, hurrying distantly through the white winter night to the yellow lights and the little quiet towns. Its whistle blew, so far far away, three times, Ah, Ah, Aaaah. . . . You longed for something, lying still between two smooth slices of sheet, but you could not think what it was, and now you will never know what it was.

Downstairs they were all laughing in the dining room, and you could hear both the two sounds, the waves of cool mythical laughter underneath your room, and from the back of the house, coming up the back stairs, the comfortable low clatter in the kitchen. Bridie and Catherine, moving about in the hot yellow light in the kitchen, over the dry brown boards of the floor, between the white table and the sink, from the pantry with all the cups on hooks, the bags of flour and the crocks of potatoes and the jugs of molasses and vinegar that stood in a black cupboard under the marble slab, up a little creaking step to the stove. You thought of the stove, as black as your hat with strange wonderful things to eat steaming in covered pots, and the piles of plates heating up on the shelf at the back. You could hear the footsteps heavy and busy across the old boards, and your heart caught in your throat when they opened the door to go in to wait on the dinner-party, and all the laughter came upstairs suddenly in a gust.

Outside the house a car drove by up the dark road, with a broken chain around its wheel, rapping as fast and muffled as a heart-beat upon the frozen snow, louder and louder, and the lights came in the window and ran along the wall until they came to the bed. For just a minute your bed was blue-white and bright, and then the lights scraped along the other wall, bobbing up and down along the pictures and over the book-case, and ran out of the window so fast. Far up the road the broken chain beat on the snow on the road, farther and farther and then it was gone away. It was enormous and still outside, deep in the breathing snow, with the stars a million miles deep in the high sky.

They were laughing downstairs. It rang like bells, like the wind running in and out among little bells, fewer and fewer and then all at once another and another until the bells were all tinkling and singing in different keys. You heard the important clatter of plates, fragile, impossible, fairy plates. What were they all laughing at? Something you knew nothing about, something beautiful and exalted. You wondered why they always laughed so much in the evenings after you had gone to bed. In the lovely evenings, in the pale candle-light shut in from the white night, they were all so beautiful downstairs in their dresses and their little colored slippers. They knew about strange things, places, and shining people, great singers, and dancers from Russia, balls in Vienna and cities in China, and they knew slender little jokes that nobody but they could understand. You never knew what they were laughing at when they laughed so long in the evenings.

II

You lay very still in your bed and listened to something, perhaps a dead leaf, perhaps a twig from the top of the house, fall with the gentlest pat upon the surface of the vast, murmurous snow. Forever, all over the round smooth world it was dark and still and beautifully cold, fatefully and eternally hushed; under you only was a house full of lights and the sound of people laughing. Lying there you felt yourself rising higher and higher into the dark sky where the stars shone; where the stars burned like heavenly secrets, high and coldly radiant.

You were suspended in a dark tower above the world. Planets and great winds, chimeras and islands lost under the sea, and archangels striding among the stars. And a great bell tolling.

You heard the peal of the front-doorbell sing through the house, and some one opened a door and all the laughter came up to you in a clear sudden burst. And then they closed the door, somewhere, and the sound clapped shut, and you could hear them laughing faintly, far away.

You thought about the little animals in the woods beyond the snow, the rabbits packed together in warm clusters in holes, and little mice among the roots of trees. You thought about the unheard fall of cold leaves at intervals, among the trees upon the drifted snow. You thought of the silent woods, where there were no lights and no sound, with perhaps the infinitely small track of an animal running momentarily under the trees in the dark. Beyond lay the meadows rolling over the hills, with the moon shining blank white and pure upon the snow, with the wind sliding like a skimmer over the crust, and the great stars in the sky above the world.

You held the pillow up to your face and fitted it to your cheek, and lay still in the room you knew so well. You alone were alive in this still, unbelievable world, in your own room with its long window.

The moonlight lay along the glass of the pictures and across the bookcase, and you thought about the books in their shelves and the three white chairs and the black table and your desk, all ranged in the darkness around you.

III

Then downstairs some one began to play the piano, and you listened to the muted music. What was it that you did not know about, what was it that the music had known and wept for, something that was over and could never be forgotten, but for you it had never been begun. You felt so sad, so happy and so sad, because something that was all the beauty and the tears in the world was over, because something lovely was lost and could only be remembered, and still you knew that for you the thing had not yet started. Perhaps you were sad for the regret you knew you would feel some day for this sadness. The music was bitter and sweet and sorrowfully reckless, very fast and resigned and gay in a minor key. You wondered what it was that had made the music so sad, that made you so sad.

Then they stopped playing and it was all still again. The moon moved as slow as a cloud into the frame of your window, and stood still in the sky outside, and you lay in your bed in the dark and watched the moon. Outdoors the quiet snow and the sky beat like a pulse, and then you heard a leaf scrambling across the crust of the snow, scratching minutely with fingers of wire; it slid, and ceased.

They were all laughing in the drawing-room below. You wondered what they were laughing at, that made the laughter sound so wise, so gay, so confident and foreign. You never knew what things they laughed at when they laughed so long in the evenings, and now you never will know.

1934

THE DOUBLE HOUSE

The little boy, whose name was Robert, used sometimes to think how horrid their house would be if his father did not live in it. It was half a house; nobody lived in the other side. In the middle of the house as you came towards it there were two front doors set side by side. There were shutters on the windows of their side of the house, and the door was painted green, but the empty half had blank staring windows and a rusty-colored door; the low cellar windows, flush with the ground, were broken, and Virginia creepers ran into the holes and disappeared.

Robert used to think, as he came home from school, how ugly the house looked, and how hopeless and sad. He tried not to let his father know he knew it was not a very nice house because he had an idea that it was the best house his father was able to get for them and his aunt Esther, his father's sister, to live in. He imagined that his father did not think it was very nice either; at least it was so different from that house in the stories his father told him of the days when he had been a little boy. But he did not want to speak about it, because it might make his father unhappy, and at the possibility of his father's unhappiness Robert felt a sense of terror. It was only because his father was such a happy man that life was possible at all.

Aunt Esther was always weary and gloomy. She was kind too, but she wept if she listened to the stories of the days when she and Robert's father were children, and that was why the stories were never told when she was around, any more. She wanted to be good to her nephew, but Robert tried not to be alone with her since the time, about a year ago, when he was ten, when she had looked at him with tears in her eyes, and shaken her head, and said that he was lucky to be a child, for childhood was the only happy time. At that Robert's heart had stood still with fear, for if it were true that he would never be any happier than he was now, then he was lost.

So when he came home from school every afternoon he could not bear to go directly into the house, but cut off at the side of the house and went around to the back, on the empty side, where a cellar window was so broken that he could get himself through the hole. He would come walking down the street in the late afternoon sunlight, in the crisp autumn air, with a strap around his books and the end of the strap in his hand, alone, small and thin, with his coat buttoned up the front; he would turn and walk up the unsodded ground to his front steps and put his books on the steps and then go around to the back and slide on his back through the broken cellar window that was the way into the empty, silent, cold half of the house.

He had brought in some of the books his father gave him, and he would sit on top of the old deserted bureau in one of the dead musty bedrooms, in the late sunshine of those afternoons and read the books, wearing his coat buttoned up in the cold. He had brought in his paintbox, and with some water in a jelly-glass and a brush he sometimes colored the illustrations in the books, or made pictures of his own on the flyleaves or on a pad of school paper. He did not like his pictures. He knew that they were all wrong, and he hoped it was true that, as his father said, people got better at doing things as they grew older. If that were not true then, he thought, he was lost, for he was weak, and different, and the other boys hated him, and he could not even paint nice pictures. But his father had told him that it was true, and that things got much better as people grew older, and Robert believed him, for he could see that his father was a happy man.

He knew that this late-afternoon life in the empty half of the house was the only life he lived on his own resources, and he saw that it was not much of a life to make for himself and that it was lonely and pathetic. He detested himself for his shyness and his queerness and unhappiness and unimportance, but he could not do anything about it any more than if it had been a sickness. He used to think, I must just hang on and get through things until I grow up and then everything will be better.

When the sun went down he would go away from the darkening upstairs room where he had been playing and go down through the cellar to get out. The cellar would be pitch-dark and frightening, and sometimes one of the cobwebby ropes hanging from the cellar beams would sway against his head as he passed; he was in a hurry to crawl through the broken window and get out of that dreadful cellar, although he loved the place too, because it was the only place he could think of to himself as being his own.

He would go around in the early chilling dusk to the front of the house, and sit on the steps watching the men come up the street from the train. After a while his father would come along, and Robert used to notice that although he walked heavily and stoop-shouldered farther down the street, as soon as he saw his son he would straighten up and walk faster, waving his rolled-up paper at Robert and smiling through the twilight.

"Hello, Robbie, old boy," his father would shout at him. He was a stoutish, thick man with a moustache, and he wore a black overcoat with a velvet collar. He would give Robert a little slap on the back and they would walk up to the house hand in hand, his father already starting on stories of what had happened at the office. Robert would squeeze his father's hand and look up at him, and his father would squeeze his hand back and say, "Don't look so glum, old man. Everything's all right, isn't it?" and Robert would say, "Sure. Fine."

The rest of the day was always happy, once Robert's father had come home. They all had supper in the warm yellow light of the kitchen, and his father would eat a lot of everything and make jokes and josh his sister Esther along, while Robert ate his supper and listened, and felt safe and gay. His father made such a lot of noise and was so cheerful that everything they did in the evening seemed exciting and successful. Sometimes he read poetry aloud, and at those times Robert could see that he was moved, but there was nothing miserable about it, but a kind of glorious, joyful sadness, and his father would say, "Gee. That always gets me," as he laid the book down. Everything was all right; the house was nice, the light was warm, the fire crackled, and the evenings were long and happy, because Robert's father was there. Robert used to kiss his father when he went up to bed, although he knew it was supposed to be sissy; his father's moustache felt big and bristly, and his father would give him another slap and say, while Robert's ear was still very close, "Good-night, old man. Everything's fine. You're just like me, you know, and all you have to do is just keep plugging along."

Robert's father always used to walk to the station via Robert's school, a little out of his way, and leave him at the corner of the school street. It was a nice walk that led through the little graveyard next to the stone church, and along a broad sunny street. It seemed sometimes to Robert that his father walked very slowly, and he worried about that; it made him feel terror to think that perhaps his father was getting old.

One morning as they were going along one of the paths of the graveyard, Robert's father saw a small red flower growing inside one of the iron-fenced inclosures. Robert was in a botany class at school, and his father had been interested in the specimens the pupils were supposed to collect, and had given him tips about where to go to look for them. Now he stopped short. "Let's rob a grave, Robbie, shall we?" He made it sound wicked and exciting. He lay, stout and awkward, down upon the ground and reached in for the flower, and brought it out and got up, red in the face. "There, now, you take that to class and knock all their eyes out," he said. "That's a rare one. They'll all be jealous." Robert took it in his hand, looking at his father and unable to say anything. He was so touched by his father's helping him, and yet he knew so well that he would not knock their eyes out, that if anything they would only find his new flower an excuse for laughing at him.

They walked on again. At the corner of the street they parted as usual, with a slap on Robert's back. As soon as he was alone Robert could feel the old fear and desperation come into his heart, and he looked back for one last sight of his father. He saw his father's heavy back going down the street, and for a minute he imagined that there was a slump, a tired look to his father's walk now that his father had left him. Then he went on to school, with his face set, holding onto his book-strap tight, and with the flower in his other hand.

School was a sort of nightmare broken by little intervals of hope. When he went into a classroom he always half-imagined that some one might call out for him to come and sit next to him. But no one ever did, nor was this day an exception. His find of a new flower was praised in botany class by the teacher, and for that half-hour he felt a little rise of pride, and of the interest that his father had made him feel for the subject. The teacher asked him to stay a minute after class, and talked to him about botany in appreciation of his response.

That class was followed by recess, and as Robert walked out into the big dirt yard he passed one of the other boys in his class. The boy stared at him. "Hello, Daisy," he said. Two minutes later another group of boys called him "Daisy." "Shut up," Robert said to the boy nearest him, who was grinning into his face. "Make me," the boy said. Robert hit him in the face, and a minute later he felt hard, gritty dirt in his mouth, before he realized that he had been knocked down. The other boy was on him holding his shoulders down. “Daisy, Daisy, Daisy,” he chanted. “Robert brought a Dai-sy to Tea-cher.” Robert struggled wildly, crazy with rage; then the after-recess bell rang, and the other boy jumped off him and ran off without a word. Robert got up and went in to class.

It was one of the worst days for him. When he came out of the cloak room at the end of school to get his coat, he could not find his cap on its hook. Then he saw that two boys at the end of the hall were throwing it between them for a ball. “Let’s have the cap,” Robert called, walking over as he put on his coat. They stared at him for a moment, and then, suddenly laughing, ran out of the door and into the yard with the cap, and Robert ran after them. It seemed to him that he ran and ran and ran, round and round the schoolhouse, hopelessly, never catching up to the two boys, who at length dropped it on the dirt, stamped hastily on it, and ran off. Robert picked it up and started home.

He seemed to feel a little lonelier than ever in the cold, secret playrooms of the empty half of the house. He sat on the old bureau and wondered dully when things would begin to get better for him. He felt a tired, hopeless acceptance of his own queerness, his weakness and difference from other boys. Sitting there, his mind drifted off into one of its dreams, of being strong and powerful and brilliant, of being safe and unassailable. From that it was all the more bitter to come back into the dim, lonely reality of the barren room, with his books, his paintbox and efforts at making pictures scattered dismally about the floor. There was nothing in him that was a reason for his being alive in the world. After a while he went out, and down to the dreadful, black, unthinkable cellar; as a loop of the dusty ropes that hung from the beam slapped against his cheek in the dark he started and his heart stabbed with terror; he hurried out through the broken window and went around to sit on the front steps, wanting his father more than ever.

But his father seemed to be longer in coming than ever before. The other men all came up from the station in a straggling procession which dwindled and ended. His father had not come. Robert felt a kind of panic. He felt burning, wild tears behind his eyes. He felt sure that something horrible had happened to his father. He imagined that heavy, tired form run over by a truck, even run over by a train or fainting in the street, and the visions were too terrible to think of. After a while he could not bear it, and wandered down the street in the darkening twilight, staring and staring ahead of him for the sight of that familiar approaching bulk. But the street was empty. People were having their suppers in their lighted houses on either side of him, but still his father did not come. Suddenly he turned and ran home as fast as he could, holding back the sobs in his throat. He fell, and scraped his hands on the dirty pavement, and got up and ran on, into the house, into the kitchen, to Aunt Esther. "He hasn't come," he burst out. "Something's happened to him." His aunt looked at his wild little thin face. "Oh, it's all right, Robert," she said. "He's missed his train, that's all. He's done it before." He sat down on a chair and kept still, listening and listening.

When he heard the front door open he dashed out and hurled himself at his father in the dark hall. "Oh," he sobbed, unable to keep from crying, "I thought something had happened to you." He could not speak any more. His father switched on the light. "Why, you poor old boy," he said in his big, safe voice. "There. There." He cleared his throat, curiously. "I missed the silly old train, that's all, Robbie, old scout. Buck up. You poor old man. Now, then, go upstairs and wash those black hands of yours and come down and we'll have supper." But Robert clung to him for a moment longer, his arms around that large, solid bulk, his heart pounding in him. Then he ran upstairs.

He washed his hands for a long time while he let his heart stop pounding, and his great relief rolled over him in a lovely warm wave. His father was here, and so everything was all right. His father, whom he loved, and who was happy and strong, and his only promise of safety. His father, who said they were just alike, and so held out a reason for living to Robert. Everything was all right. Just keep plugging along. Everything will get better as soon as I get older, Robert thought, in sheer relieved joy. My father says so. He wandered downstairs, and started back toward the kitchen.

But the voice he heard was so horribly like and unlike his father's that it stopped him short in his tracks. He could not move, he could only listen to hear that dreadful sound again.

"My God, I could almost give up," this voice said.

"But I thought everything was getting along well enough at the office," his aunt's voice said, trembling. "Was this the first you knew, that they were going to let you go?"

"Yeh." Robert heard a long, heavy sigh. "Sometimes I'd wish I were dead, if it wasn't for that poor old boy. Oh well." There was a pause, and then Robert, shaking outside the door, heard one more sentence. "My God, Esther, how I wish we were children; we were happy then."

Robert turned, with his hands before him as if he were blind, and without will went to the front door, opened it, and found himself in the chilly night. He walked around to the back of the house and looked up at the sky as he walked, and saw it filled with brilliant and meaningless stars, and shut his eyes against them. He started to get into the hole that went into the empty cellar, and then sat for a moment half in and half out, with his mind throbbing like a wound. It seemed to him that this was the end of all happiness, of all hope. He began to cry, hysterically, and let himself on through the hole into the black, frightful cellar. Terror, and hopelessness, beat upon him like oceans, overcoming him. He stumbled in the darkness until his clutching fingers felt one of the dangling ropes. As he fumbled at the loop he was sobbing crazily.

1934

MIDSUMMER

THEY WOULD RIDE through the hot, dim woods that sultry, ominous August. From the hard ground, littered with spots of sifted sun, on the hills their horses would carry them in a minute to the hollows. There was something terrible about the hollows, deep-bottomed with decaying leaves, smelling of dead water and dark leafage and insufferable heat. The sound of the horses' feet was like a confused heartbeat on the swampy ground. They both felt it. They used to get off their horses, without having said a word, and helplessly submerge themselves in each other's arms, while the sweat ran down their backs under their shirts. They never talked there. They stood swaying together with their booted feet deep in the mulch, holding each other, hot and mystified in this green gloom. From far away in the upper meadows they could always hear the cicada reaching an unbearable, sharpened crescendo.

After a while the queer possession would grow too much for them, and, dizzy and faint, they would mount the horses again. The path carried them up to a long field where they would kick their horses and gallop wildly. The meadow grasses were dusty gold in all this heat, and when they galloped a hot wind pressed by them and all the million flies flew away from the horses' necks. Streaming and throbbing, they would pull up at the end of the field, and could laugh and begin to talk again. Dan would pull the squashed package of Camels out of the pocket of his wet blue shirt and they would each light one, with their horses' wet sides pressed together, and ride along at a walk. Then it would be time for Dan to go back to the stables to give his next lesson.

The country-club stable-yard was bright and normal, hot as thunder as they rode in, with the water in the trough near boiling and the brown horses looking out of the boxes into the sunlight. Dan put the horses away in the dark strawy stalls, and then he would walk back to Victoria, standing at the precise point where she had got off her horse. He would walk toward her in his blue shirt and brick-red breeches, his black hair mounting damp and thick from his red forehead, and his eyes as blue as an alcohol flame, lighting another of his Camels. He would offer her one. Then they would walk over to the stable-yard well and he would pull up a bucket of cold water. He would say, "Will you have some water, Miss?" and hand her some in the glass that stood on the well's edge. She looked at his shoulders and his big red throat as she drank, and pushed damp ends of hair away from her face. Then he would have a drink.

When Dan rode out of the yard again, with some group of children perched on the high horses following him, she would wave at him as he turned the corner into the road, and he would make a little bow from the neck, the bow of an Irish groom. Then he and the children would trot noisily down the macadam, Dan riding so beautifully and carelessly half-around in his saddle, with one hand on the horse's rump, telling the children to keep their heels down. Victoria would climb into her big green roadster and drive out of the stable-yard as fast as she dared, skidding the corner and going up the road in the other direction with the ball of her foot jammed down on the accelerator.

Victoria Jesse was sixteen that sultry summer. She lived on White Hill in her parents' Italian villa with the blue tile roof, so gruesomely out of place in the New England landscape. Her parents were in France, but the servants and old Nana were in the house and the garden was kept up by the disagreeable gardener, always on his knees by the rose bushes, which dropped thick petals on the turf. The water in the cement swimming pool was soup-warm and dappled with tiny leaves from the privet bushes around. The tennis court was as hard and white as marble, and the white iron benches drawn up around its edge were so hot all day that they could not be sat upon. The Venetian blinds in the house were kept drawn, and the rooms were dim and still, with faint sweat upon the silver candlesticks and the pale marble of the hall floor.

Victoria was sixteen, and sometimes, at the end of the afternoon, when she sat in a rattan chair on the shadowed lawn, when the grass grew cooler and a breeze sprang up and the exhausted birds began to sing, she thought she would go wild with the things that were happening inside her. She wanted to stand on the edge of the pool and stretch upward until she grew taller and taller, and then dive violently into the water and never come up. She wanted to climb the huge pine tree on the lawn, throw herself upward to the top by some passionate propulsion, and stretch her arms wildly to the sky. But she could only sit around interminably in chairs on the lawn in the heat and quiet, beating with hate and awareness and bewilderment and violence, all incomprehensible to her and pulling her apart.

She could only drive her car as fast as it would go, wrenching it around corners, devouring the ribbon of road with it, driving for hours with the unformed hope of adventure; she could only be cross with Nana and so passionately disagreeable to her old playmates on White Hill that she was not asked to play tennis or picnic, which gave her a melancholy satisfaction. She took a dizzy pleasure in going to the dances at the club with nothing on under her dress and a belt pulled tight around her waist, and dancing with the fuzzy, pink-faced boys of her age, pulsating in all her muscles to the jazz music, and then suddenly walking out and leaving as she had come, alone in her roadster, streaming along the white moonlit roads in the middle of the night, until she was so tired that she had to go home and fall into tossing sleep on the slippery white sheet of her bed.

She could not imagine what was happening to her; she had never imagined such violent sensations as beat at her; inside she was like the summer itself—sultry and fiery, and racked by instantaneous thunderstorms. At the end of the day the air relaxed into moist, nostalgic evening, but she had no relaxing, only a higher tension in the poignant secretness of night. She thought, with defiance, that she must be going crazy.

She had grown thin from her own fire and the unrelenting fire of the weather. She was white, and her green eyes burned unhappily in her pointed face; her bright, thick hair seemed thicker from being always a little damp.

Superimposed on all this ferment was the incessant preoccupation with Dan. She began to take riding lessons in June, to work off a little of this torturing energy, since she wanted to be away from the infuriating "younger crowd," and felt it might satisfy her to ride as violently as she drove a car. Dan took her out, and within half an hour, with this tropical immediacy with which she was feeling everything, she uncomprehendingly desired him and wanted to touch him, and could not take her eyes off him. She gave herself no time to be frightened at such unprecedented emotion. She got off her horse to get a drink at a deserted well in the middle of a field, and he got off to help her. With some kind of instinctive simplicity, she went and stood against him, facing him, touching him, waiting for him to do something. He acted; he put one arm around her, holding the horses' reins with the other hand, and leaned and kissed her hard. For a moment she had the first relief she had had in weeks, and from that moment she wanted him more and more to touch her and to kiss her. After his first reaction, Dan became very stilted, with a recollection of his "place" and his job, but by this time the turmoil inside her had concentrated itself on him, and she would not allow him to remount his horse or help her mount hers; she threw her arms around him with a wild relief.

He had no sophistry to combat her abandon and no way to reason or cope with her obvious passion. He had a conscientious feeling that he had no right to let her have her way, that it would be much better if he somehow put a stop to things, and he saw how young and bewildered she was. But he had never seen anybody as strange and as beautiful as she was, or had the sense of being so dangerously loved, and he saw her lack of reserve and her lack of coyness, and the vulnerability of her youth, and all his vague Irish mysticism made him respond to her as something akin to his horses and the wide countryside he loved. He had the simplicity to sense her quality of being lovely and lost, and different from the fat-legged Irish maids who were his normal social lot.

He left the extent of their relationship up to her, at first because he was impressed by the difference between their stations in life, and later because he loved her, too. He was nearly as bewildered by the queer, sultry passages between them as she was; he was nearly as lost and puzzled as she was, for different reasons. He thought she was a strange little thing, and sometimes when he lay on his mussy bed in the room off the tackroom where he slept, he felt a conceit that he was so irresistible to her, and that she had started it all; but in those submerged, lush hollows where they kissed, he was as bemused and possessed as she was.

None of it was leading to anything. Nothing in the world seemed to be leading to anything. Victoria had no idea of making Dan run away with her, or of young dreams of happiness—she was conscious only that her relief was in him. She got the nearest thing to peace in those dim hollows. The rest of her life had a fabulous, dreamy aspect to her; she lived through these days minute by minute.

One evening she had a telegram from her parents. She was

having strawberries for dessert, and sitting limply at the end of the table while two white candles flickered in the wind from the west window. Her fresh yellow dress clung slightly to her shoulders, and her hair felt heavy. The telegram said that they would be home the next day.

She heard the mail plane to New York muttering its way through the evening sky. She heard the servants talking and rattling the dishes out in the kitchen. As long as she might live, she could never forget the immediacy of the streaky pink strawberries and cream before her, the wan look of white wax trickling down the candles, and the little wind stirring in the short hair at the back of her neck.

She got up and opened the door that led out into the garden, and all the renewed scents of evening flowed in like sweet liquors. She walked out on the grass and the dew wet her stockings above the tops of her slippers. The vicious sweetness of the summer night was intolerable and she leaned against a lilac tree, thinking, What is going to become of me? What is all this beauty and this desire that I cannot touch or take within my hand, and what shall I do? They will try to take me back, and I will never be happy again. What shall I *do*? Oh, my God, what is the matter with me? Why do these desires for I don't know what run through me like hot and cold? I don't want to see my mother and father. I couldn't face them, because I am not their child any more, I am nobody at all, I have become only these desperate desires that drive me wild. Why am I so lost?

Her mind went round and round and helped her no more than ever, but seemed to be submerged by the smells, the touch of bark under her fingers, and the taste of flowers on the air. As usual, her vague desperation resolved itself in a need for action, and she went out to the drive and got into her car, whose seat was wet with mist. She roared out into the road and down through the town and tore out along the country roads. The bobbing glare of the headlights showed up the leaves of the branches that hung over the road, and the white road, and the grass along the edges. Outside this, the night was immense and breathing and terrible. She could only cut a white hole through it. She had worn no hat, and the wind scraped her temples and raked her hair.

She drove for two hours as fast as she could, at the end finding herself headed for the stables and Dan. As she turned in the drive into the stable-yard, she thought, How ridiculous! I must have known I was coming here. Why didn't I come at once? She stopped the car and went around to the back, where the little room off the tackroom had a light in its window.

She knocked, and Dan came and let her in. He was surprised and very much embarrassed. He was dressed in his riding things, but he had taken his boots off and his breeches fitted to his bare white legs. She came in and sat down on his narrow bed. Several moths whacked against the chimney of the oil lamp. Dan had been reading the *Rider & Driver*, and it lay on the bare floor with his boots.

"You mustn't be here, Miss," he said. "It's not the place for you to be coming."

"My family's getting back tomorrow," she said.

"Will you have a cigarette?" He held his crumpled package of Camels out to her. Their little ceremony of lighting took place, with them looking at each other over the flame, solemnly.

They sat and smoked. There had never been any real attempt at verbal communication between them, and now they said nothing at all, but sat by the oil lamp and listened to the sawing of the crickets in the marshes outside. Far away somewhere, some one was playing a harmonica.

She made no reply to his telling her that she should not be there, and he said nothing about her family's return. They both forgot. They looked at each other gravely, with concentration, and said nothing.

"What am I going to do, Dan?" she asked after a long time.

"I dunno."

"What is life all about?" she asked, not really caring about an answer.

"I dunno," he said again. "I like the horses, but I dunno, if you mean about dyin' and all." His face was beautiful and simple, cut in the sharp, lovely planes of the Irish.

She had nothing to talk to him about, really. She wanted to be with him. She felt a relief now, she was almost perfectly happy, in a dazed, numb way. They simply stared at each other for a long time. She could not take her eyes from his face. All the wild, furious bewilderment in her seemed to leave her as she looked at him, and she felt she wanted to go on looking forever. Then the lamp flickered and faded. Dan got up and turned it up. The queer magic broke like an eggshell.

There was a lot she could have begun to talk about—her family, and what he and she were going to do about seeing each other when they returned, and a dozen other thoughts in the back of her mind—but she felt no real desire to.

"I wish I could stay here with you," she said, breaking the long silence.

"Ah, you couldn't do that, Miss," he said.

He came back to the bed where she sat, and sat down stiffly beside her. She lay down and pulled him down beside her. It was the first time that they had ever lain side by side. She felt calm and peaceful.

"My little darling," he mumbled suddenly into her hair. He had his arms quietly around her.

"Oh, Dan, I love you so."

After that they did not speak. They did not move. They both lay in drowsy stillness. She was plunged into a dreamless daze, wanting nothing, in a deep well of content. He felt the same strange, unreal sense of peace. Neither of them thought at all.

Finally they slept, with their cheeks together. The lamp went out after a while, and soon pale day streaked along the floor through the little window. Victoria got up, and Dan stood up too, and they moved and stretched themselves without saying anything. He threw open the door, and the fresh smells of the morning flooded the close air. On the other side of the wall, they could hear the horses champing and moving their feet.

They went out into the stable-yard. Hens were making a lot of noise and some birds flew low to the ground. The green car stood there in the early mist, bulky and practical. Victoria got in and closed the door. It made a heavy, solid sound. Dan stood beside the car and they looked at each other for a moment, vaguely. Then she drove slowly out of the yard. He walked back to his room, still in his bare feet, with the breeches-ends about his calves. Victoria drove home along the country roads as it grew lighter, and threw herself into bed and was instantly asleep.

She did not wake until eleven, and then Mr. and Mrs. Jesse had returned and were waiting to have it out with her. They had had four letters from fellow-townsmen informing them that their daughter was carrying on with the riding instructor at the club, a common Irishman. The Jesses were the richest people in the town, and before Victoria was even awake they had arranged that Dan should be discharged immediately, with wages in advance. The club steward was having him packed off on the noon train. They had done everything they could. Now there was nothing left but the talk with Victoria.

They sat in the dim library, and she came in to them. The heat was already at its height. They talked and talked. They told her how common such an affair was, over and over. They tried to find out just how much she had actually done. They were furious and hurt and outraged.

Nothing they said made any impression on Victoria. She heard their voices far, far away, and she got a sort of detached impression of what they were saying. She sat in a big chair, languidly, while her dress wilted and clung around her, and watched the leaves outside make the light flicker between the slits of the Venetian blinds.

Finally, bewildered at her detachment, they told her that the instructor had already left, had been fired for his conduct. They told her four times before she understood what they were talking about. She looked at them vaguely and without saying anything for a few minutes, and then fainted and could not be brought to for some time.

Doctor Russell, with his little mustache and long tubes of colored pills, told them it was the logical result of the protracted heat wave. She was as thin as a bag of bones, and as white as a sheet, and gave every sign of physical and nervous exhaustion. He prescribed two tonics, and said she must stay in bed for a day or two.

She lay in bed all afternoon, trying to concentrate. She couldn't get anything straight in her head. She would remember that Dan had gone, and then she would remember that she loved Dan, but by that time she had forgotten that he had left, and it was impossible for her to assemble things to make any picture of what her life was. She was not very unhappy. She was hot and tired, and the only things she could think about without an effort were the sombre hollows where she and Dan had gone, with their curious green gloom and the smell of submerged decay. Her mind rested in those hollows, dim and steaming.

Her mother came in to see her late in the afternoon, with a plate of strawberries for her. She sat down on the edge of the bed and kissed Victoria gently.

"Darling," she said. "Poor little child. I shall never forgive myself for leaving you alone this summer. You mustn't be too unhappy. Daddy understands and I understand, and we want you to rest and be our happy little girl again. It's really our fault that you fell into the power of this dreadful man."

"He isn't a dreadful man," Victoria said, and closed her mouth tight. It was an effort to talk. She turned her face aside and pretended to go to sleep. After a while her mother went away, leaving the strawberries by the side of the bed. Victoria turned over and looked at them lying on the white plate.

It grew dusky in her room, and then it grew dark. The little breeze of the evening came faltering through the window. Victoria got up and went to the window and breathed the terrible sweetness of the garden at night.

In her nightgown, she climbed down the honeysuckle trellis below her window, and dropped to the grass. She had used the trellis for running away when she was small, and she stood at the foot and thought about that for a while, how impossible that that small girl was the same as herself now. She gave it up.

Barefooted, she walked along the terrace to the lilac tree where she had stood last night, and stood there again, swaying a little, remembrances and thoughts swirling in her head.

Suddenly she pulled her nightgown off over her head and threw herself down on the wet turf. The smell of it filled her nostrils. She pressed her body violently against its softness and fragrance; and ran her fingers desperately into the damp earth. Dan, Dan had gone and all her heart had gone, too. Everything had gone. If life was to be as terrible, progressively, as it had come to be at sixteen, she wished she might die now. She wished she were dead, and felt the exquisite touch of dew-soaked grass against her breast.

1934

TO THE NORTH

THIS IS the way the Finns live at Graniteside. They live in simplicity and extreme poverty, in honesty and serious, innocent ambition for their children. More than the severe New England soil to which they came they are fertile; every year during the long fecundity of the Finnish wives there is a new child born with the light blue eyes and fair hair of North Europe, to burn brown and bleach under the violent sun of the American summers, to grow tough and stringy through the months of hard winter beside that frozen sea.

They are stonemasons and truck farmers and fishermen and laborers in the nut-and-bolt factory beyond Graniteside. In the summers they make a little money from the people from New York and Boston who come to swim in the ocean: moving their furniture, carrying their water, cleaning their houses, cooking; but it is the children who do that through their months of vacation; the parents are always busy. They make the money last through the winter for shoes, for school paper and pencils, for contributions to the Finnish Lutheran Church, and coal for the stoves that warm those houses that they painfully bought from the bred-out, contemptuous native Yankees years ago; when the Yankees, Woodburys and Tarrs and Savages who had their land by Indian grant, saw this chance to quit the long years of gainless lobstering and planting rocky ground, sold out with scorn to the foreigners, and moved into the snug streets of Graniteside. In those houses, that are small, white, wooden, weathertight within double lath and plaster walls, the Finns live with their own customs and their own ways that nobody knows. The Yankees are above caring and the summer people never thought to wonder in forty summers, none of them but Jack Werner.

The Werners took the same house every year, the green house with porches on the cliff above the rocky beach, and so Jack's first summer in Graniteside was when he was less than a year old. He had a Finn girl, Vera, for a nurse. When he was one, and two, and three, she used to take him down to the beach and sit him on the stones; she watched him while she knit the socks her brothers needed. He wet his fingers and toes in the shallow pools of salt water and played with starfish and snail shells and dried seaweed through the long clear days of June and July and August. He watched the wet formless bodies of the snails issue from their holes and wave about in the sun; when he touched them they shrank back instantly and sealed their doors with a purple seal. He popped the black bladders of the harsh spiny seaweed. His body burned light gold under the Northern sun. On any day there were ten or fifteen babies playing like him, turning red and gold, on the beach, while the quiet, serious Finn girls watched them.

Jack's mother said the Finns, Vera and the others, made excellent nurses. They were so much calmer than city nurses and made the children calm. Except at the end of the summer; Jack screamed himself purple in the face when he had to leave Vera, when he understood that that was happening to him. He was a different child at home, Jack's mother said; he gave trouble and disobeyed and did things like biting his Irish nurse. Of course, she said, the beach made such a wonderful playground; the children could stay there all day long and there was so much room, and they found so much to play with they didn't even want their pails and shovels. The other summer mothers agreed that it was wonderful (as they turned in their wet bathing suits to tan the other shoulder); they, too, liked the Finn girls, although there were those that said the Finns were so *silent*, they didn't really *play* with the children. None of them, either, had Jack's mother's trouble about leaving in September; their children went docilely, were glad to be going somewhere new. Jack's mother said it was funny the way that child carried on about the place.

He loved it. From the first moment of his consciousness he loved the wild, brilliant sea and the long slabs of untouched gray stone, the miles behind the sea of rough moorland, full of low, stunted growth, smelling of wild rosebushes and bayberries and sweet fern; the high, clear, strong air, full of sun and salt. He loved the heavy purplish clouds that came across the sky suddenly, the ocean turned lead gray and whipped up into little points, the abrupt violence of the wind and then the downpour and hurricane of the northeaster screaming in from the sea. He loved the land in its particulars, in its small unique things—the thorny locust trees that blossomed in white too early for him ever to have seen; the red spiders no bigger than pin points that ran in thousands over the rocks in the sun; the deserted quarries back in the moors, jagged holes filled with blue fresh water that reflected the rotting, rusting derricks above them; the way the wind rose imperceptibly day after day after the first of September, rising a little, steadily, as if toward some terrific crescendo still months away. But that, too, he never could see, because soon after Labor Day all the summer families went home.

Such a passion in a young child gives its mother very little trouble. When Jack was small he had tantrums in September, but when he was an older boy he went away quietly and said nothing about how he felt. His mother was amused at this passion of his when occasion made her notice it; all children, she said, get funny crazes. He had a brother and two sisters who liked Graniteside quite calmly and had their own crazes about other things: machinery, swimming, dogs. However, the other children with their enthusiasms remained what Mrs Werner thought normal. It was when she began noticing Jack's feeling about the Finns that she started thinking of her oldest boy as curious, a queer child. After a while the other summer people thought of him that way too; he was more and more different from the other summer children that came to Graniteside.

Because Jack Werner never played with the other, the summer, children. As soon as he was old enough not to need a nurse he went away from them and the beach and made his own friends among the Finn children. That meant working with them, because they had so little time to play. The strong, brown-haired little boy with his firm, pointed jaw; his quiet green eyes and impassive mouth: without making any sort of point of it he simply began pitching the hay with the Finn boys his age; getting in the boat when they went out for butterfish and Old England haik; carrying the pail of fish and ice up to the back doors of his mother's friends and taking out the fish while his Finn companion took the few cents of payment; going to the Sauna on Saturday afternoons with the Finnish men and boys.

The Sauna, the weekly steam bath of the Finns, was behind the beach, back of a rocky field where cows were pastured. It was a small shack of weathered wood. There was one door for the men and one for the women, and inside a men's dressing room and a women's dressing room. The steam room was occupied in turn by each sex for perhaps twenty minutes. The group that was waiting sat naked on the benches in the dressing room and shouted cheerfully over the wooden partition at those who were inside, hurrying them on; the old people spoke Finnish, the younger ones English.

Perhaps there would be a couple of boys Jack's age waiting; four or five men. The little boys, skinny and immature, sat together and didn't talk too much. The men had fine bodies, with light hair on white skin. They talked, a little Finn, a little English, about their affairs: what fish were running, the price per dozen lobsters, the cut in pay at the factory; not much talk, slow and quiet. On the other side of the door the women splashed the water about, talked.

The room was not so steamy as it was hot, when the men would go in. It was a damp, strong heat that lifted the palate and made breathing different. It was a small room. On one side was a square block of stones with a fire inside that had been burning since early morning. Next to it stood two barrels, one of cold water, one of water boiling hot. The cold water was slowly heating from the fire; as it got hotter someone in the room dippered it into the other, the hot, barrel. Below there was a spigot that ran cold water.

There were three tiers of shelves across the length of the room where they sat. It was hottest at the top; Jack didn't like sitting higher than the second shelf, nor did the other boys; it made them cough. The men sat up high. They all sat for a time and the sweat ran down their bodies fast; the men's white bodies showed sharp blotches of red under the thin skin. Then someone would get up and run himself a wooden pail of water from the spigot, adding hot water from the barrel with a dipper; he would go back to his shelf with it and a piece of soap from a big dish, and wash himself all over, rubbing and rubbing. In a minute or two they would all be washing. Afterwards they threw cold water over the bodies to wash the soap off, holding the filled bucket high over their shoulders, throwing cold water at each other's backs. Jack caught his breath deliciously as the cold water struck his chest, ran down his stomach; almost at once he began to sweat again. In a big basket were bundles of twigs tied together; the older men beat themselves with the switches, all over, until their bodies were red.

The room was dim, lighted by two tiny windows. The white bodies glimmered in the half light, moved past one another, climbed up to the top of the room. The thin little boys moved quicker than the men, playing in the buckets of water until it was time to go out. Each one had brought his towel, his ragged, mended swimming trunks. They dried off in the dressing room and ran across the field, across the stony beach, in their trunks and cast themselves into the ocean.

Jack loved it. Obscurely he felt something stirring in it—the deep cleanliness, the strong white bodies in the dim room, the run across the rocks into the sharp salt water. He never missed a Saturday, he was there as regularly as any of the Finn boys with his towel, his fifteen cents. Wherever they were, he was. Besides his love, he had some kind of sensitiveness to them; he adopted their ways, their mannerisms. He kept quiet, as they did; talked briefly without raising his voice. Every day, all day, he was away from his house except when he came to snatch lunch, and sometimes not then. It began when he was about six and went on, year after year. He hardly saw any of the other summer children besides his brother and sisters, with whom he never played in those summers. His mother was amused, then occasionally annoyed. In the end she accepted his passion, his insistence, and simply waited for him to grow up and get over it.

After a time the Finns accepted his presence too. At first the older people were tentative, shy. After a year or two they came to take for granted his presence with their children, the restrained eagerness with which he worked along with them. His friends' mothers spoke to him in their natural way, in a few words of Finnish: told him to clear up that bit of hay in the corner, to round up a straying cow; gave him a sip of the strong coffee with salt in it that stood simmering all day long on every Finnish stove.

When it was September and he had to go, Jack would say good-by to his friends one afternoon, as if it were any day; walk off down the road past the sea, away from them, having accepted their convention of impassivity, but with his heart sick inside him at having to leave them. He would walk slowly along the hard road, strewn with granite dust, looking up at the blue, late-afternoon sky, smelling the sharp salt in the chilling air; looking at each house, each tree, each field, as he passed, as if he would never see any of them again. And he never felt sure that he would see them again. His love was so sharp and immediate that in this repressed wrench of leaving he felt such pain as he would feel if it were forever.

He could not bear it that he must go away now, when everything was turning—the leaves to red, the ocean to dark sapphire—when everything was heightening and sharpening into some kind of rising excitement. He wanted terribly to stay, to spend the winter here. He wanted to see it happen, whatever it was. He found out every bit he could from the Finn boys. The rising storms that grew bigger, wilder, longer. The ocean, that changed its nature and turned dark gray and surging in winter, reaching up on the shore yards above its summer high-water mark. The morning of the winter's first snow, the drifts across the road, and the day that did not come every winter, when the inlet beyond the beach froze over solid and you could walk across.

Walking down that road that last time each summer, he thought beyond the winter into the spring he had never seen here, the chilly, fragile, Northern spring that came late and with hesitation. Slowly the ocean would turn its gray into blue, and the faintest gray-green would turn the ends of the branches into a mist. The snow would retreat a little, retreat a little, stubborn against the delicate push of the spring, until there were only streaks of it here and there, under the cliff, at the margins of the quarries. The lemon-colored winter sun would turn yellower a little every day, and soon, soon, those twisted, stunted branches of the locusts would break into a fog of white, the white locust flowering that Jack had never seen.

That way he imagined it, and every year he felt that pain, that sickness, that it was only in his mind and probably he was wrong about it all. It must be different, better, beyond his powers of imagination. He could not bear it that he must go away now, or that in the next year and the next year he would also have to go away. When he was a man . . . Of course, when he was a man he would live here all the year, watch the long year through its tumultuous, brilliant changing, and never go away at all. That would be when he was a man. That was a long time off. . . . Now the deepening blue waves smashed up against the rocks of the shore; the sound he tried to hear in his ears all winter long. He walked along the road in the early twilight and heard the gulls screech out over the water.

In the winters he lived and went to school in a big town in New York State. Later he began to go to a boarding school in Pennsylvania. In both places the air was inland air. He studied and played football and sat around with the boys and lived the life of the place he was in. He was strong and intelligent and enough people liked him. He was a part of the things he did. It was only when he went to bed at night and before he went to sleep that he indulged himself in the thing he liked best to do in winter.

He turned over his knowledge of Graniteside and the Finns very slowly, tasting each fact. It was like turning over a collection of very beautiful things that he loved beyond anything.

He was not a Finn, but carefully and over a period of years he learned as much about those people as anyone could who was not one of them. He knew the parts of Finland that they came from. He knew about the forests there, the terrible winters, the frozen rivers, about the reindeer that the grandfather of one of his friends had driven. He knew the years when the different families had come to America. He knew about their national epic poem, the Kalevala, and repeated over to himself those few Finnish lines which he had been able to learn. Lying in bed, those inland nights, he even used to count to himself, slowly, in Finn.

He knew the Lutheran pastor had been a missionary and that his children, older than Jack, had been born in South Africa, in Dakota. Uno Hildonen, the Finn who lived far up in the moors, had been a laborer at the factory and one after the other had had both hands crushed in the machinery. He had eleven children.

His wife and Mrs Ronka, who had fourteen children and lived down near the sea, were sisters; they both had the same beautifully boned, stark, thin faces that had dignity and form even after all their teeth were gone. They visited each other alternately every Friday night, after the work was done, every Friday night whether there was snow or storm. Friday night was visiting night among the Finnish women. Then they stopped their long days of work for a few hours and sat with each other and drank salted coffee and ate the Finnish coffee braid.

At the grammar school there was a teacher, a Miss Kelly, who pulled the children by their ears and beat their hands with a ruler. Jack said he thought it was awful and his teachers at home didn't do that. The mother of his friend who told him looked at Jack with her bony, impassive face. "They must learn good," she said. The Finns didn't mind, even the children themselves. All of them were thirsty, avid, for learning. They worked hard, studying and doing hard work at home too. Sometimes it was impossible for them to be spared from home to go to high school. Their parents wanted them to, but sometimes it was simply not possible. They wanted to go to high school as they wanted to go to heaven. And later on—college. As Jack grew older he heard his Finn friends talking about college with the nearest to emotion he had ever heard in their voices. There was just a chance, just a tiny chance, that they could make the money to go; enough to pay the tuition and leave some at home so that their absence would not harm the family security. Most of them wanted to go to technological college; they wanted to be electrical engineers, mechanical engineers.

Ana Savenin was an artist. He drew pictures everywhere, on the rocks with a piece of water-washed brick. The Olsen children could not go to school last winter because their shoes were not good enough. Mrs Olsen had twins that fall instead of one, and it took more money for clothing than they had expected.

Every year Jack knew more, he had more to turn over in the

nights before he went to sleep. And every year he went back there; the family moved into the green house as soon as the children's schools were over. The next morning Jack would disappear, and for the rest of the summer his family hardly saw him.

The summer after Jack's last year at boarding school he was eighteen. There was a big crowd of young people about his age at Graniteside that summer. There were Ted Cleaves and the Grandin brothers and Betty Grandin and the rest of them—all the children, grown up, that he had known and never played with when he was small. And there was a new girl, Leonora Tait, whose family had taken a house down the road from the Werners'.

She was new to Graniteside and she was different from the other girls there: taller, more bizarre. She was only seventeen; but she wore rubber bathing suits, pink and pale green, that clung and molded to her ripe, flexible body; her hair was bleached nearly white and her skin was dark brown. She used to lie on the rocks in the sun, her chin propped on her thin, lazy hand, her full young breasts swelling over the edge of her tight bathing suit, pushed up by the hard rock under her chest and her stomach; singing jazz tunes in her low husky murmur and speaking abruptly, mockingly, to the avid boys who hung around her. She had long brown legs that tapered from the rich, developed flesh of her thighs down to hard, whittled ankles.

Her family were nice people and Mrs Werner played bridge with Mrs Tait. She liked Leonora and approved of her self-assurance, her control over the boys who followed her round. One morning she saw her son Jack looking at those long legs stretched out on the hot rocks; Mrs Werner looked amused and glanced away, went swimming. She liked what she saw. She was proud of her eldest son, and she would have liked to see more of him in his vacations. She saw he was tall and big, good looking with his slow green eyes and strong jaw; she had the feeling that he possessed more unreleased violence, more heat and passion and emotion, than her other children. He had always been a queer child—an attractive child. Mrs Werner foresaw a full, moving life for him, but in order to begin it it was time to wean him away from his Finnish friends, she thought. She believed that Leonora was the person to wean him, at this moment of his life.

That was in early June, at the beginning of the summer.

As always, Jack looked up his Finnish friends as soon as he got to Graniteside. He simply joined them again; smiled shyly, in their own way, at the mothers and said hello to the girls, the sisters. In a day, in less, he was back in the life he loved. He was haying with the stocky, muscular young Finns; going out at dawn to fish with them and to empty the lobster pots; going to the Sauna with them and scrubbing his body beside them in the steamy dimness of the hot room; swimming with them after work. He was with them all day long.

But the nights were longer at eighteen. He liked to go out in a dory with the Finns and row about in the darkness while one of them played a harmonica, queer, thin music. He liked sitting in their houses with them on bad nights, drinking their coffee, sitting in long silence, talking with them a little about their plans, their hopes for college and afterwards, while the mother and the sisters sewed. But he was not with them every night. As a child he had always gone home at dusk, and the evenings had never belonged to the Finns in the same way that the days had. In the evenings he saw his family and, with them, the other summer people.

They had always bored him. They played bridge and talked and went on moonlight swimming parties, and they bored him. The young people swam at night and drove around the countryside in cars and went dancing at a roadhouse, and they bored him too. He did not understand all about why. It seemed as if he were more serious, but not that either; as if he were more violent for actualities, for motion that went somewhere; their perpetual running about and laughing and aimlessness left him uninterested. He felt that he was slower, more directed perhaps; he liked to work, to do things that moved towards an end; he liked the Finns and they lived that way.

When he saw Leonora, when he looked at her and felt the physical sensation she gave him, he felt differently. She made a reason for staying away from the Finns in the evenings. He took it for granted that she liked him; he had never been unconfident. She looked back at him differently than the way she looked at the other boys, and so he sat beside her and talked to her in his own way, slowly with long silences, looking at her steadily with his quiet green eyes.

One night he took her driving in his family's car. He drove fast through the salt-smelling darkness and they talked a little. He could feel the heat from her body sitting beside him on the seat, and inside himself he could feel the sensation she gave him rising toward something, moving in the direction of something: wanting her.

"You think we're all pretty silly, don't you?" she said. Her voice was very lazy and faint.

"I've never played around much with the summer people here."

"What else are you? . . . I hear you like the Finns."

"Yes."

"Social work, or do you like the gals?" she asked. He knew that was like her, to be mocking, to try to say the unsympathetic thing, and not to care what was thought of her for it.

"I like the people," he said.

"Yes, some of the girls are good looking," she continued in that smooth, lazy voice. "Good thick hair—so blonde. And good bodies but not for clothes exactly; too stocky, I think. Do you make passes at all of them?"

He felt a sudden sense of outrage, a childish anger. He only pressed his lips together in his own way.

"You don't? But you leave all the summer butterflies alone, pining for you. Who do you make passes at then? . . . A big boy like you . . ."

She laughed, and he thought he could feel an actual heat from her laughter, that was so low and lazy and thick. She made him angry, and he stopped the car there, where it was under a long row of willow trees. The top was down; he could see some stars between the meshes of the willows.

". . . You're old for your age, aren't you?" she said, and the last word was pushed out between her lips as he put his arms around her and held her hard.

She felt the way he knew she would, different from all the girls he had ever kissed in the winters, at dances and on the way home. This time it felt right, the way he wanted it. Again he was conscious for a minute of his feeling mounting toward something, moving, the sensation he loved, had always loved, of movement toward a crescendo, in all things.

He did not talk at all, and she was not able to. He felt alive, he felt absorbed and powerful. He held her hard against him and felt the mass of her breasts pushing his chest, her hollowed sides where his hand lay. He put his other hand on her thigh and liked its being big and firm. He did not talk; he pulled the top of her dress loose and pulled it down; he slid his hand down along her smooth, soft back. . . .

Then he heard her talking. "Stop it! I mean what I'm saying. You stop it at once. You've got things all wrong."

He was dazed, and drew away and looked at her in the flickering light from the far-off street light.

"You're the damnedest boy. I don't know what's the matter with you," she said, buttoning her dress. "Do you think I'm crazy too? Look, I'm actually young, and I'm certainly not a fool; I'm not going to do this sort of thing, oh, for a long, long time, do you see? No one is, with any sense. You are queer, aren't you? Actually queerer than me. Older for your age or something. Nobody else is so serious about all this, sort of like a grown-up animal. Necking, yes. But it's fun—don't you see?—fun, not great animal stuff. Don't you like fun, or what?"

He drew a deep sigh, deep into his stomach, and started the car. Now that she had stopped him, now that the long slow swelling toward a crescendo had been broken in him, he didn't think of her beside him any more. She wasn't anyone he cared anything about. He had his own friends, people he loved. . . . He took her home, and she jumped out, stared back at him and caught her breath as if she were going to say something, and ran into the house. He put the car away and went into the house and went to bed, thinking about something Leonora said. He wondered if he didn't like fun. He had a good time with other boys, in the winter too. It was only fooling around in a circle, going nowhere, that bored him so. He supposed, then, that he didn't like fun, and went to sleep.

Mrs Werner was disappointed. Jack stuck fast to his Finnish friends all summer, as he always did; she saw no more of him than ever. She could not understand it about Leonora. He never looked at her, attractive as she was. . . . Perhaps he was not old enough to fall for girls? . . . But as far as that went, Leonora never seemed to look at him either. Except that she seemed a little, rather specially, nasty to him.

The long golden summer wound out, through July, through August. There were plenty of lobsters, plenty of delicate-fleshed fish; the hay was cut twice and piled and taken away to the lofts. The summer went by in short glittering weeks and at the end of each week Jack and the Finns sweated themselves red and burning and scrubbed themselves clean and beat each other with switches across their backs and their strong hairy legs. In the next room the women shouted to them to hurry, in Finnish and in English; the young voices called in English. Jack was conscious of the women's voices, and the women, now. When they had finished and run across the rocks to the ocean, when they had swum in the cold salt water and lay on their backs lazily under the hot sun, he would turn his head and watch the girls run across the field, across the beach, from the Sauna. They ran fast, laughing a little. He watched their breasts move as they ran, the muscles move in their round, full thighs. Vera and Ailie and Ida, Hilma and Alexandra.

Alexandra was his good friend. She was one of the Hildonens, the poorest of the Finn families, the hardest working. He had worked with her and swum with her all the summers of his life in Graniteside. They were friends and smiled at each other when they passed, working. She was his age and had finished high school. Now she was working, all the Hildonens were working, so that perhaps she could go away to business college. Jack liked her best. But he liked all the Finn girls. He thought about them this summer.

Sometimes he touched them, although, with their strict bringing-up, they never invited it. Swimming with Hilma Savenin his hand came on her leg. They played roughly, laughing and spitting water; he held her leg above the knee and would not let it go. She hurled her body against him, breaking his grip, and for a minute he felt her whole strong, soft body pushing against him.

Once he kissed Ailie, Hilma's sister. He was walking home in the dusk and she came up in the other direction, driving the cows. The big slow animals rolled by him one by one in the twilight, their heads low, their heavy bags swinging. Ailie came up to him after the cows and stopped a minute to talk. In the faint light he stood close to her and then took hold of her and kissed her. Like Hilma, Ailie was strong, solid; her arms were soft and big under his hands that clenched them. He stood, kissing her; then she went on up the road behind the slow cows and he walked on toward the sea.

The gulls screamed over the water and the moon was already out; the air was sharp with salt. Jack held his head back, looking at the sky. He felt so happy, so desirous. He thought of the Finnish girls, how they were strong upon the columns of their legs and how their chests were set straight, firm, upon the block of their hips. He thought, I want them all. I want to kiss the Finn girls, all of them, I want them. . . . He walked along the road by the sea, feeling wonderful and young and full of inexhaustible power.

Then it was late August. Now the evenings were getting colder, the beginning of that tightening, that day-by-day tensing of everything, the heightening wind, the rising sea, that had always seemed to him to be building, moving toward something great, some wild crescendo that he must miss. He did not want to waste these evenings at home. He walked up the road into the moors again one night, looking up at the white half of the moon. He thought he would go to the Hildonens' house and sit with them in the kitchen. Uno Hildonen was going away next week to the technological college. The family had achieved that. Perhaps next year they would be able to plan for Alexandra too.

Behind the house, out by the well, he came on Alexandra pulling up water. He pulled the bucket up for her and then leaned across it and they talked a little.

"Let's not go in," he said. For a second he felt surprise, because she put out her hand, took his.

They walked across the wide yard, through the gap in the old stone wall and into the scratchy undergrowth of the moorland; they walked slowly. The moor was flat and mottled white and black under the cold moon; he put his arm around her waist and pulled her in tight and kissed her. He kissed her, still pulling, feeling his arm sink hard into the soft flesh of her back. . . . This was different from anything, from any girl, ever. They were lying on the ground, pushing down the sharp twigs of the bushes under them, and Jack's hands were full of her body, heavy and warm and strong. His face was deep between her neck and her shoulders; he felt her lips kissing his hair; her flesh was in his mouth. . . .

". . . Get up, you."

Weino Hildonen. He stood right there, waiting in the moonlight.

Weino, who was good at mending lobster pots, who won a prize at school when he was thirteen, who had a scar from a fishhook in his right palm. . . .

". . . Get up, Alexandra. The water goes in the house."

She had gone, and they were fighting in the bushes, stumbling on the rocky ground. Weino had hit him in the jaw, and Jack hit back, the cheekbone; they were stumbling in the moonlight, grappling and swaying for a long time, then punching again. . . . Weino hit him again in the jaw and he fell and lay, feeling weak and faint and blank.

". . . You summer people. You keep away from us Finns."

Then Weino went away and he lay there in the bushes. The wind was rising and the bushes all over the moors whispered with the wind in them.

After that his old life in Graniteside was over forever. He started in college that winter; in early June he came back to the sea; he went toward the field where four of the boys, his friends, were planting a second crop of corn, and none of them turned around. He stood at the edge of the field. One of them was Weino Hildonen. After a while Weino straightened up from planting and stood looking at Jack. He kept on looking for a minute or two, and then he leaned over again. None of the others even looked up. Jack turned around and walked away. The next day was Saturday and he wanted to sweat, get clean, sweat hotter and hotter until at last he threw himself into the sea. But he knew he could not go into the Sauna, into the room with the other naked men. He saw that and all the rest of his exile in the minute or two that Weino looked at him in the cornfield.

The older people, though, nodded to him when he passed them on the road. One day he passed Mrs Hildonen.

"How is Alexandra?" At last he could ask somebody that.

"Fine. She got a job now. She work in New York."

"Everybody else all right?"

"Fine. Good-by."

For a month Jack stayed at Graniteside, swimming and playing tennis, and his mother saw a lot of him. Then he went back to summer school. He was going to college and so he might as well get through college. He went to summer school every summer after that and got through college in three years. He took premedical courses in college and planned to enter medical school the next fall. The night he graduated from college he got drunk, with two other men. They sat at a table in a bar drinking rye whisky and talking very seriously and very slowly.

"You'll make an excellent medico, my friend. Hard-working buzzard. You'll be a fashionable medico. Not to mention the nurses."

"Not obstetrics," Jack said. His green eyes were very slow and his voice was thick. He ordered another whisky.

"And practice where?"

"New York. Chicago. Paris. London. Constantinople."

"Not the home town? Only Constantinople? Not cure your old friends?"

"I haven't got any old friends," he said.

"Me. My cirrhosis of the liver."

"All right. Your cirrhosis of the liver."

"Not deliver your old girls' babies, Jack?" The other man was the tightest.

"I haven't got any old girls," he said.

"Not any old girls at all? Not even a little one?"

"No."

"How about new girls then?" The man hung over the table, persisting. His glass was tipping so that some of the drink spilled.

"Sure, new girls. Any number of them."

"More and better new girls," the second man said, and they all drank.

Jack went to Europe that summer because his mother wanted

him to go with them. They went to France and Switzerland and Germany, and Jack had a girl in Paris for about three weeks, but he didn't mind leaving her when his boat sailed. Two weeks later he started medical school.

His second year of internship in the New York hospital was five years later. He had the pneumonia wards that week, and a call came through to his room at two in the morning to go on duty for one of the bad cases. He walked down the half-lighted corridor, empty in the middle of the night. The doors to the ward swung open and shut, and a nurse came out carrying a bowl. The nurse was Alexandra.

"I thought you were going to business school," he said. He could not think of anything else to say, but inside himself he was so glad to see her that it was pain.

"No, I went into training instead." She smiled at him. It was a firm, impassive, Finnish smile. He looked at her by the dim reddish corridor light. Her face was white and strong and her hair was thick yellow under her cap and her eyes were light blue. She was all Finn.

He took a long quivering breath.

"Where's the patient?"

". . . In here, Doctor."

He saw her in the wards after that, and in the corridors they would smile back at each other, in the same still, quiet way that they had smiled at each other when they were children, when they passed each other hoeing corn, or when she came down to the rocks to take the fish out of the dory. But he did not even ask her when her night out was. His days seemed all different to him now because he saw that face, that strong, impassive Finnish face nearly every day; but he could not ask to see her. All the years full of nights when he had lain awake and gone over his collection of knowledge of the Finns, of knowledge that was now stopped, finished; those nights when he had heard Weino Hildonen's voice say over and over, "Keep away from us Finns . . . keep away from us Finns . . ."; those nights, the sum of them all, were too much for him. It had ceased to matter very much why he had been cast out by his old friends, his only friends; what he had done to bring it on himself. What mattered and made him rigid with diffidence was the fact of his exile, the fact that they did not want him, did not need him, that he had long ago ceased to be of any importance to them as anything but one of the summer people. Being one of the summer people, having them think of him as that, was too much, it was unbearable to him; he had not even been to Graniteside for years, because he would not go that way. . . . Anyway, he had girls in New York. That wasn't what he wanted. He didn't think about girls much. He worked himself to the limit of his strength at the hospital. He often wondered what he was working toward, what he would do when internship was over and he was all alone to live. It was a bitter thing to work toward nothing very sure, not to feel a mounting crescendo in his work that he could feel was rising to some height. . . .

More than girls he liked drinking on his nights off. There was a crescendo, even if it was only a fake one. He liked the feeling. He liked working toward the very limit of his capacity, feeling the liquor mount inside him, getting a little drunker and drunker. He would begin early so that at midnight or one o'clock he could quit. It took that much sleep to function properly in the hospital the next day.

One of those nights he got back to the hospital between one and two. He moved very slowly, carefully, toward the elevator, holding himself stiffly, his eyebrows lifted as if a part of keeping his balance. . . . A nurse passed him. He could not be sure, but he thought it was Alexandra, so he tried to smile. He tried to make the shape of the kind of smile they gave each other always; he bent his stiff, thick-feeling lips and tried to make his eyes look quiet. The nurse passed on. Perhaps it wasn't Alexandra.

The next day he passed Alexandra in one of the wards. He smiled, but she did not smile, she stared at him. It was the same stare, the stare of all those nights; Weino's stare, the same thing. Then it had been Alexandra last night, and it was now because he had been drunk. Suddenly he was angry.

He stood in the corridor outside the doors to the ward as she came out.

"Why don't you speak to me when I speak to you?" he asked and then felt ridiculous.

"I'm sorry, Doctor," she said. "I didn't hear you speak."

"You know what I mean, Alexandra," he said. "Is it because you saw me when I was tight last night?"

"Yes," she said impassively.

He felt hot.

"You Finns are too goddam stiff-necked," he said abruptly. He was surprised at the words that came out. "Any man gets drunk. All your own fathers get drunk."

"Any man isn't throwing away what you're throwing away," she said.

"What are you talking about?"

"You shouldn't waste yourself when you're needed so badly."

"What do you mean, needed? I'm not injuring myself as a doctor by drinking. You ought to know that."

"You aren't working toward anything, are you?" she asked, nodding her head. She walked on down the corridor with quick, silent steps. He watched her strong figure, the sharp flip of her starched skirts; he caught up to her further down the corridor.

"When's your night off?" he asked.

"Last night was," she said.

"You wouldn't have dinner with me, I suppose?"

"Why not?"

It was unpleasant, like fighting. He said he would meet her on the corner next week, and let her walk away again.

It was very curious, having dinner with Alexandra, who came from Graniteside and long before that, before she was born, from Finland, in a small smoky New York restaurant. It was all wrong, he thought, sitting opposite her; she didn't belong in her green silk dress, her green felt hat; she ought to wear an old cotton gown, her hair be loose; the wind off the sea should be blowing. . . . Then he thought, No, quickly. It was the wrong way to feel, sentimental. She and her race belonged wherever in the world they found themselves; in cities and factories, in any countryside: strong, self-reliant, using their power and making something of the conditions that were at hand, building their lives into something, toward something.

He looked at her. She was a good nurse; she was in her own way at home in this place; she had the grain of self-sufficiency in her, and all things, all places, were hers to use; she could never be overcome. He saw all at once that it was only he that needed Graniteside. He needed that land he loved and the people there, the Finns, to make him whole and happy. They didn't need Graniteside; they didn't need him; they didn't even need each other.

While he was talking to her, ordering dinner, he thought about this. Instead of depressing him it gave him a sudden new hope, a kind of explanation. When he was a little boy he wanted to be a Finn, he tried to be like a Finn and know the things they knew. He still did, in a new way. This was the thing to aim for, the direction to build. That way he would never be aimless and he would never feel that he was working toward nowhere. To be like a Finn. To hold your own world inside yourself. Not to need special places, special people, to make you whole, but to use what you could take from the places life put you in. Then you would be without fear always, safe and sturdy; he understood why the Finns were impassive, why their mouths were quiet and content.

That way you held intact your own plans, your own mountaintop that you were climbing for. The thing you wanted to make out of your life, the work you meant to do, the children you desired and begot: this way you were free to go ahead and pry them loose from the world, take them. No fear. Safety and intention and persistence within your own soul. . . . He thought—and went on talking with his mouth about the hospital—Now I know how I want to live; only I still need them, I still need them to teach me more how to do it. I still need them. He broke off sharply in what he was saying.

"What did you mean, I'm needed?" he asked her.

She sat opposite him. She was big and white and strong. Her face was beautiful with strength, sure and impassive.

"The Finns." He noticed with an old thrill of pleasure that Nordic rise of the voice in speaking.

"Not them, they don't need me. You know that."

"Yes. There has never been a good doctor there in the winters and they need one. That's where you are needed anyway. Other places perhaps, anyway there. I thought you would have seen that."

"I know the old ones never wanted any doctor, they didn't believe in doctors."

"The young ones do. And the old ones are dying now."

"Not me though. You know that," he said again.

"You are the only one who would be right. You know all about them, Jack. You were there all the time, just like us, all those years. Nobody else who would possibly go would know all you know about them. They do need you."

"You can say that. They wouldn't let me come back, be with them, after . . . that."

"After that night with me," she said quietly. "They would if they knew you wanted to be one of them. That, Weino—you should see now that was because it made them think you felt outside, one of the summer people, coming in and taking things away. . . . If they knew you were one of them, if you were my husband, that would all be forgotten, it wouldn't be true any more."

She sat perfectly still and grave, looking at him. He could not say anything. His lips were together and he looked at her with his slow green eyes.

"If you would like to marry me," she said. "I would like to marry you. I have always loved you, of course; you know that because of that night."

She spoke with such calm.

He put his hand out and took hers. She held his tightly for a minute, looking at him, and then let go slowly.

Her hand felt big and firm and warm with vitality. He drew a long breath, looking at her strong face that would be beautiful through all the years of hard work of her life; her round neck set firm on the soft, wide shoulders. Below there was the powerful structure of her body that could work and endure, the body that could bear and nourish from its bone and its deep flesh so many children.

He looked on and on into her blue eyes. Hard work, and hard passion, and many children, and saving and helping good struggling lives. The long years lay ahead. Every year began with spring and the flow and push of life into the short hot summer, into the rising winds, the stormier ocean of the autumn. The winds rose higher, and the sea swelled as if it were tossing in full, pregnant birth; up and up to the great profound crescendo of the winter. They would see, live through, the drawn-out crashing of each winter's height. All the long years lay ahead. One upon another, heaped up and up toward the full roar and pounding of a life's completion. Jack felt in him the old surge, the old beginnings of movement that would build and build, in the sharp salt air, beside the deep gray sea; but this time it would be for life.

"That's all I ever wanted," he said to Alexandra.

1937

CRIMSON AUTUMN

After the second half had begun, the light would begin to fade; the red autumn sun would drop beyond the western end of the stadium and the sharp air turn chilly. Overhead the airplanes that flew over the game, and the blimps that drifted over, trailing advertisements, were still bright with the last of the sun; but the stadium and the field were in shadow. The figures in white trousers and crimson sweaters, the cheer-leaders, still jumped up and down before the stands, threw red megaphones away, hammered the air with their fists, jumped high in one last paroxysm; but the roar that came in answer seemed faint and unreal in the twilight. The light grew fainter; across the stands little pinpoints of light flashed out like fireflies for an instant; thousands of people lighting cigarettes, throwing the match away. Somewhere in the heart of the cheering-section the band broke into brassy music that sounded thin and remote now: "O'er the stands in flaming crimson, Harvard's banners fly." The music died away, disappeared, and a hoarse roar rose, and a little figure trotted off the field far below; another figure was running in fast. In those late afternoons there was a queer sense of hush, of hurry, in the stadium. The light failed steadily; the white figures of the linesmen stood out in the dusk; a thin stream of people going out, early, through the exits, walking around the edge of the field in fur coats, red hats, carrying rugs; and the long, subdued roar of thousands of voices, rising a little, rising. The two teams would fight steadily down there, moving a little down the field, up the field, turning into a muddled chaos of bulky bodies.

Suddenly it would all be over. The tension would break; the stands poured themselves down on to the field. Everything was moving, departing in the growing darkness; the band sounded faintly from somewhere; the crowd moved slowly out of the exits, across the Anderson bridge, where already the arc-lights were lit.

These were the long fall afternoons when Melissa, sitting beside Richard Bruell, watched Davis play half-back on the Harvard team. All the Saturday afternoons of October, and then of November, she sat beside Davis' best friend, his room-mate. In the ruddy glow, in fading sunshine, in twilight, they sat and watched the person they both loved best: a tiny figure, a spot of dark red and brown, with only a white figure on his back to know him by. Melissa loved those afternoons; they were full of a queer excitement, a queer beauty and magic and nostalgia.

It was not till fall was over and it was winter, that she ever wondered about the magic; whether it came, as she thought then, from watching Davis, whom she loved; or whether the magic was in watching with Richard, seeing the long dramatic decline of the afternoon from brilliance and sunshine to that strange tense twilight—the whole panorama of the game that she and Richard saw together in those afternoons, and that Davis knew nothing about.

After the game was over, she and Richard would walk arm in arm across the bridge into Cambridge, moving in the slow push of the crowd. Thousands of 'coonskin coats, red felt hats, banners fastened to canes, maroon chrysanthemums, and occasionally a face they knew, a voice calling to them across heads. Boys walked on the concrete parapets of the bridge. Harvard Square was a whirlpool of hats, crimson and one other color that was different each week. The little green Bugatti Richard and Davis owned was parked behind Dunster House; it roared and spluttered like a thunderstorm as they moved along Memorial Drive into Boston, hurried along faster, faster, by the special traffic policemen.

Melissa was Davis Leith's girl; everybody knew it, and she was conscious of it all the time; it was like a great diamond star pinned on her breast, or a halo of light-rays. Everybody who passed that car, going into town, knew who was in it; Davis Leith's room-mate parked the Bugatti back of the Copley-Plaza, and they went in to where both ballrooms were opened up in a blaze of white light. Hellstorn's orchestra was playing jazz, and girls were dancing in black velveteen dresses, in little bright-colored hats, sitting at tables and eating cinnamon toast with freshmen, sophomores, juniors, seniors. Richard and Melissa took the table that Davis liked, at the end of the long ballroom, and settled themselves in peace and understanding to wait for Davis. Waiting, they danced; in all the times that they were together, waiting for Davis, they had learned little special dance-steps together, so that they were very good; they danced in accord, in silence, their contented, smiling faces close together. Back at the table, Melissa drank tea, Richard drank coffee, and they talked together very little, understanding each other, content with each other, waiting for Davis. Melissa was very happy.

When he came, the peace exploded, turned into the dazzle and restless excitement that Davis always brought with him.

They would both see him coming. That was part of his unbelievable, spectacular vitality; everybody else in the two great rooms saw him too. And yet he was so restrained; the control over that fire of his energy made it more electric. He would walk across the floor from the door at the far end of the rooms: tall, big, with thick brown hair and blue eyes that you could see long before you could see the color of anyone else's; with his curious, controlled walk, measured and smooth: you felt that without that control he would be running, tearing across the ground in a rush of tremendous, eternal strength.

When he saw Melissa, his face turned into brilliance like a light, and his eyes smiled in that way that brought her heart up into her throat. Nobody else in the world could smile like that, so simply but like a released charge of electric power. Now the quiet, the expectant peace she had alone with Richard was over and snuffed out like candle-flame; everything was a blur of glory, red and yellow and breathless. When he came, he turned the table into a throbbing nucleus of excitement; now she had forgotten that there were other people, that they were looking at her and knowing she was Davis Leith's girl; she had forgotten Richard and everything except that one presence that absorbed all of her, took all of her. She could not look at anything but him, and she knew Richard was looking at him too, as much absorbed as she. He was Davis' best friend, and she was Davis' girl, and the world was Davis' too, not because of the way he looked or because he was a football star that year, but only because he was the way he was.

Then he would take her hand and pull her up and dance with her. She could feel her heart pounding in her chest, pressed against him. He was an erratic dancer: he did impossible, fantastic things with his feet that were sometimes awkward, and sometimes wonderful and accomplished. Sometimes, suddenly, he seemed to be impatient with dancing at all and stood nearly still on the floor, or moved slowly, almost walking. Then he would look down into Melissa's face, smiling like a child, a happy, sweet, wicked grin. His blue eyes seemed to burn; his mouth was tipped at a crazy one-sided angle; he hunched one shoulder and grinned at her, and Melissa knew completely that he loved her. Then abruptly he pulled her in to him and began to dance fast. She could feel her heart pounding. When he took her back to the table, she was as exhausted, for a second, as if she had been running; but she could not stop looking at him, and quickly she had pulled herself together into alertness again. She was never walking on the earth, sitting on a chair, when Davis was there; she was suspended in the midst of heaven, or flying through the sky.

She loved those afternoons, too, after the football games that fall. It was not till much later that she began to wonder when she had been really happiest: dancing with Davis, sitting at the table with him and feeling breathless, ecstatic excitement; or, after all, with Richard, in the peaceful time they spent together, waiting for Davis. . . .

Melissa Cranleigh was nineteen that year. The year before, she had come out in Boston, and she could never understand why in that year of nightly parties she had never met, never seen, Davis Leith. He had been a junior that year, and going to the same parties, but they never met. It was as incredible as if you spent an evening in the same room with a comet without noticing it, Melissa thought; but somehow that had happened. They met at the very end of the summer that came between.

That was at one of the early pre-season parties, a dance in a house on the North Shore, at Hamilton. Melissa liked being a post-débutante. She felt gay and experienced, with her own train of beaux dancing with her, with her hair done a new way, a new dress of voluminous poison-green net. The little débutantes looked so tremulous and unsure in their pink taffetas, white tulles. . . . She was dancing slowly, and talking, gesticulating with one hand; some one cut in and introduced Davis.

In that second this new overwhelming life began for her. That feeling of self-assurance was a short-lived thing. This new man, this Davis Leith who was a "big man" in college, who came from New York, who was so rich and run-after—suddenly, almost at once, she was in love with him, and not for any of those things, not for any reason, simply overcome and swept into the excitement, the magnetism of his vitality. Never as a débutante, not even as a schoolgirl, had she been so eager, so pitifully anxious, as she was now. She was almost beside herself with the strange emotions that tore at her heart, choked her. Only one thing was clear: that life wasn't worth living unless Davis was in love with her too.

It was only two weeks, but it might have been months, after that party that she found herself sitting on a velvet sofa in the lounge of the Somerset Hotel, listening to the music drifting out from the ballroom. She sat between Davis and Richard Bruell. She had met the room-mate a few minutes after meeting Davis himself; where Davis was, Richard was too: quiet, dark as a Spaniard, smiling a little; taking girls off Davis' hands, getting whatever Davis wanted, or just standing with him. Those two figures stood everywhere together: one tall and alive with restrained violence, the other shorter, slimmer, calm. And it was clear that there was nothing unfair about that friendship; if Richard worshiped Davis and looked after him like a child, it was equally true that Davis needed Richard, depended utterly upon him.

They sat in a row on that green velvet sofa, with Melissa in the middle; because Davis was there, she had forgotten that she looked lovely with her light hair brushed smooth and shiny against her head, in her mulberry satin dress. Davis was talking—he was always talking; the other two looked at him as if they could not look long enough, watching the electricity of his eyes, hearing the quick, broken, enthusiastic sentences of his speech. He talked to them, smiling at them; his lips spoke, and then he would smile his crooked, tipped-up smile; he absorbed them and took everything they had. . . . The glasses they held in their hands had been emptied of champagne; Richard went to get some more.

Davis smiled at her, and Melissa took a quick breath, as if this were the first smile of his she had seen, as if she were bracing herself to endure more of this overwhelming, heart-catching excitement. He dropped his hand between them and took her hand and squeezed it; thrills that almost hurt ran up her arm.

"Melissa—darling—" The words hammered into her mind like blows. "I'm in love with you, darling." He laughed with happiness and excitement, and his eyes were as innocent and delighted as a child's. He was absolutely simple, absolutely honest. "Do you love me too?"

"Oh, of course I do!"

All that evening they danced together, getting off into corners to avoid being cut in on, laughing and looking at each other, not talking, with this terrible tension of excitement Davis made. Richard stood back against the wall, and when some one did walk over from the stag-line and cut in, Richard cut in on him directly so that Davis would not have to cut back on the same man. Richard was, in a sense, the instrument of their staying together all the evening. He stood against the wall, quietly, and watched them, smiling a little with his dark eyes.

After the party they climbed into the little Bugatti and thundered out into the empty spaces of Harvard Square; they left Richard there. Davis drove far out into the country, fast; they shifted into the fourth speed, and the motor purred deeply, and the autumn trees dropped leaves on their heads as they rushed down the country roads in the darkness. When they stopped, it was beside a pond in the woods, shining in the cold moonlight. Davis put his arm around her and kissed her, over and over. She loved him so that her throat ached, her heart ached; all of her ached.

It was turning into dawn when she got into bed that night. She lay for a long time while the tension, the excitement of being with Davis, wore away little by little, little by little, and she could go to sleep. Just before she fell asleep, she thought how happy she was. She was happy then, thinking of Davis, but she hadn't been happy before; she had been too charged with his electricity, too tense and stimulated, to feel anything at all but his presence. She had never in her whole life been so tired. But she didn't think of any of that till much later.

That was how it began. All autumn it went on, this new life that was completely overwhelming, racking, dazzling, exhausting, quite incredible and unlike anything Melissa had ever known she could feel, anyone could feel. This was being Davis Leith's girl, that he wanted to marry after college was over, the only girl he danced with any more, the girl he loved and gave all of his emotion to. He took her to all the parties he went to, being in training. His room-mate took her to all the games, to watch him play. Everywhere she went that fall, she went with Davis, or with Richard, and being with Richard was to be thinking of Davis all the time. The fall was full of big parties, week-ends, football games, tea-dancing; Davis' girl went everywhere.

That last afternoon of tea-dancing at the Copley-Plaza, Davis drove her home in the Bugatti in the sharp November air of early evening. Richard sat in the little dickey-seat behind. They pulled up in front of her house, under the bare dark trees of Marlborough Street. Davis held her hand tight before he started to get out. His head was close to hers.

"Darling," he said, "you know I've given you all of myself. I love you so. . . . Do you think you can take it?"

"Of course—darling," she said, holding onto his hand. She loved him so terribly; of course she could take everything he had to give—all the tremendous burden of excitement, intensity, that passed from him to her—if it killed her. She was amazed at her thought. Later that evening, in bed, she thought about it.

All autumn she had been growing more and more tired, until now she knew she was going entirely on her nerves. She adored Davis with every nerve in her body; but he was taking everything she had, exhausting her; in the mornings she had to drag herself out of bed, and at night she was too tired to sleep; it was only when she was actually with Davis that a flame was set on fire inside her, an unreal vitality that burned and made her, then, alert and brilliant. . . . And with Richard, too; when she was alone with Richard, waiting for Davis, she felt more rested; something in Richard, a deep calm, rested her. It was queer, quite wonderful.

She was so tired. She did not know what she could do about it. There was nothing to be done about the excitement that flooded her at the instant of seeing Davis, that roared inside her like a tempest and a flood all the time she was with him. That was what Davis did to her, and she knew he always would; that was his special thing, the thing that made her love him, his superhuman vitality, electricity. She did not want him different; that was the Davis that she loved with all her heart and her belief in his future as a great man—without question he would do something fine in the world. He was good and honest and loyal, and he loved her; but he exhausted her beyond all words.

There was nothing to be done. The thing went round and round and round in her head. She would simply have to take it—until it killed her. She would have to summon up every last reserve of her strength, everything she had stored away in the years of childhood, and give herself with all of it to enduring the turmoil of loving Davis. Because there was only one escape, and that was impossible, automatically ruled out: leaving him. That was not to be contemplated ever; that was a sort of nightmare of impossibility: never to see him again, to feel his lips, to know that he loved her and wanted her to marry him; to have to know that some other girl was receiving that precious, unbelievable thing, Davis' love.

Nothing for it but to take it. She lay in her bed in the darkness, with the cold air and the quiet street-noises of Boston coming in through the window, and thought about it soberly. It was a sobering prospect. She wanted to spend the rest of her life with Davis: that meant years of straining every nerve of her body to keep up with his vitality, giving herself extravagantly. . . . But it was worth it.

"And besides," something in her tired young mind kept saying, "it can't always be like this. He's going to grow older, quieter. I'm going to get more used to him. There'll always be times—like this—when I can rest."

On the last week-end in November was the Harvard-Yale game, played at New Haven. Davis had gone down ahead with the team. Richard drove Melissa down on the Saturday, leaving Boston early.

It was pleasant thundering along the shore road in the little Bugatti, with the wind of that cold, brilliant November morning slashing their faces. The road was full of cars southbound, going fast. They stopped once or twice for hot-dogs, and then climbed back into the low seats, settled themselves comfortably. Richard was quiet and companionable beside her; his arm felt solid and warm against hers. She wore her soft, heavy tweed coat that was voluminous around her knees, and loaded with thick fur; her maroon cap clung to her fair head. . . . She was very happy.

It was fun coming into New Haven through the press of cars: seeing a few familiar faces, snatching lunch, parking the Bugatti, making their way out through the jammed road to the Bowl on foot among thousands of young faces, thousands of fur coats, banners; the sounds of calling, laughing, "Pick your winning colohs!" the insistent honks of thousands of motor-horns. Inside the Bowl was one vast roar of sound; the sun had gone under a cloud, but all the reds, the bright blues, the motion, made the stands glitter.

Now the Yale band was marching down the field, the baton of the leader twirling in the air like quicksilver. The big drums, the shining brasses, "March, march on down the field, fighting for Eli," and in a minute the roar from the stands was rising, drowning the thousand voices singing, and the teams ran out on the field and threw a few balls around. Lost in the cheering-section, the Harvard band played fast before the game could begin, and the music seeped in little snatches through the long vast roar—"*For Harvard wins today, And we'll show the sons of Eli, that the Crimson still—*" Now the roar had reached its peak, and the game began. The cheer-leaders, blue ones and red ones, all in white pants, leaned on their long megaphones and watched the kick-off.

After hours, years of slow fighting, up the field, down the field, of quick cheers, short snatches of band-music, wild concerted yells of excitement from thousands of throats at tense moments—it was the end of the first half.

Richard and Melissa pushed down the concrete steps under the stands with the crowd. They had a drink from his flask, and stood arm in arm, pushed about, smiling at friends, talking little.

"Are you warm enough?" he asked her suddenly, in his low, companionable voice.

She looked at him and nodded, smiling. All at once she saw him with a new clarity, for no special reason. His dark calm face, his brown eyes, the firmness and clarity of his mouth. . . . She squeezed his arm a little with hers, in sudden pleasure. He was the best friend she had ever had; she was happier with him, in long, quiet, speechless happiness, than anyone else.

They went up the steps into the stands, and it was beginning to rain. The drizzle increased a little, moment by moment. The teams ran out into the muddying field, and the second half began. No score yet, and no one was scoring. The rain increased. The opposite stands were a grayish blue through the rain. The cheer-leaders were jumping like jack-in-the-boxes, slipping in the thin mud. . . . The teams were down by Harvard's goal-posts. Some one shouldered, pushed, stumbled, slipped, and the ball was over the line.

Now the stands were on their feet in the rain, and from the Yale side came a wild, endless roar, and the little blue-and-white figures jumped up and down on the sidelines like mad. Melissa watched the big 6 slipped into the board at the end of the Bowl. She moved her wet feet restlessly.

That roar never ended. It had turned into a long whine, a droning "Ah-h-h-h-h-h" that went on and on, as Yale kicked the goal, as the game went on and on. The most persistent, most interminable and oppressive of all sounds, that long whining drone, the Undertaker's Song.

It grew nearly dark. The points of lighted matches glimmered for a second in the stands across from them, went out in the dragging rain. The linesmen's white clothes were a dirty blur against the field. On the field everything was mud and a mass of bulky bodies whose numbers were indistinguishable, bucking and scrambling in a heap, and moving, a little at a time, a little more. . . . In one second the game was over, and the Yale side was pouring down into the field in the rain, in the dusk. The Bowl was chaos.

"Poor Davis!" Richard said beside her. Melissa got up, and they went quietly out through the exits, an inch at a time. . . . The Harvard posts were shaking as they went out; one post had come loose, and the crowd was pulling at the other; the long snakelike procession was dancing in spirals down the field in the rain.

They pushed along the jammed road into New Haven. In the hotel they dried themselves and drank hot tea and ate cinnamon toast. They were the only quiet spot in the whole of racketing, roaring, screaming, cheering New Haven. The hot tea felt good. Melissa felt wet and disappointed and miserable, and she thought suddenly how glad she was to be with Richard.

They sat and waited together for Davis to join them. . . . The strangest thought shot through Melissa's head: she wished he were not coming. It was almost more than she could bear. If she were to be alone with Richard, they would be quiet and happy and have dinner somewhere, and then she would be able to go to bed early. But Davis was coming, and then everything would be excitement, motion, hurry somewhere, a big party that night, and bed at dawn. And besides that, Davis himself, wearing her out, taking her strength, exhausting her. . . . She was shocked, violently, by her thought.

She pushed it away and drank another cup of tea. She wished people would stop yelling, stop shouting, that the turmoil in the street outside would stop. It seemed as if this noise had gone on for years.

They waited and waited; after a long time Davis came pushing through the crowd toward them. He was wildly excited; instead of being depressed by Harvard's defeat, he seemed stimulated, gay to a point that even Melissa had never seen before. The other two were immediately caught up, as always. Davis was intent on breaking training: they each had a Martini, and then another round.

"If we're going to get to New York through this bedlam in time to go dancing tonight, we'd better get started," Davis said. Even his voice was pitched a little higher. His eyes sparkled; he laughed all the time; his face shone with his spirits, and he could not sit still for an instant. He took Melissa's arm and hugged it, and they all pushed out into the rain and found the parked Bugatti.

Driving into New York was a long purgatory of traffic and confusion. It was night now, and the street-lights were foggy through the rain. . . . A long time later they came into New York. They dropped Melissa off at Hope Blagdon's, where she was staying, and went on to Davis' home—they would call for her again in an hour.

Hope was dressing to go out herself. She sat on a stool in the bathroom while Melissa took a bath.

"You look worn to a frazzle. That game must have been hell," she said.

"It was," Melissa said. She lay inert in the tub, feeling the hot water soak into her eternally tired body, and wished she need never get out.

But when Davis and Richard came back, when she heard that voice in the living-room, she was keyed up back into excitement again. She joined them, in her glittering dress made of tulle and silver spangles, and they ran out into the cold wet street, hailed a taxi, started out on their evening.

It was fun being in New York, wet and nasty as the night was, tired as Melissa felt underneath this surface armor of stimulation made up of dance-music, champagne, and Davis' electric presence beside her. They danced everywhere: they went to big shining places with huge orchestras, and little places with tiny floors and orchestras that did stunts. They took taxi after taxi, trying the night-spots of the town, uptown and downtown. At two o'clock Richard said:

"Anybody feel like bed? We've all been up since dawn."

"Certainly not." Davis put out his hand and covered Melissa's on the table beside him, among the champagne-glasses and the flowers she had unpinned from her shoulder. His voice was a little thick; he was drinking quantities of champagne, and his dancing was more erratic than ever, but his wild spirits were undimmed. "We haven't even begun on Harlem. I can't cheat my girl out of Harlem." He smiled down into her eyes with his own, blue and gay and restless.

They went to Harlem. They went to a big colored dance-hall, and another like it, and they went to a small place where a woman sang in a voice like a pipe-organ. Melissa ached all over.

"Day, it's late. Let's go home now."

He stared at her with a queer, childish look.

"Don't spoil my evening," he said. "Think how long it is since I've had a drink."

He was strange now, unable to be still a second, quivering with nervous vitality; Melissa looked at him, loving him hopelessly. She was unable to refuse him anything. But she could not believe he was real; such energy was superhuman. It was incredible that any human being could spend a day and a night such as he had spent, and still be throbbing with unreleased energy. But there he sat in his chair at the table, smiling his quick sweet smile at Melissa, looking around the room, applauding the music, laughing and turning suddenly to kid Richard about something. Richard was quiet and composed; he drank a little, slowly, and smoked a cigarette. Melissa noticed how he watched Davis, a queer, almost paternal manner.

"Day, it's five," he said. "Haven't you had enough?"

"Not nearly enough!" Davis cried. He whirled around in his chair to look straight at Richard; then his elbow slipped off the table, and his head dropped, quite suddenly, onto the cloth and stayed there.

"We'll get him home," Richard said, practically. He smiled at Melissa, a steady, encouraging smile.

Melissa was very quiet all the long way home through the Park; they stopped before a door in the Sixties, and she waited while Richard went up the steps with Davis' limp length leaning over his shoulder; he went in, and she waited until he came out again. He gave the driver Hope's address, and their taxi went on, bowling along the black wet empty streets of New York. They stopped, and Richard got out to help Melissa step down.

She caught her heel in the metal strip under the doorway, and fell out onto the wet sidewalk, a crumpled heap of velvet and white tulle and spangles.

"Are you hurt? Melissa darling, are you hurt?" Richard and the cab-driver were helping her up.

"No. . . . No. . . . I just—" She could not talk at all, she was crying so desperately. She could not stop crying; she knew she would cry, now, forever and ever, never stop. She was lost in a black wilderness of tears.

She was back in the cab, somehow; they were driving somewhere; her head was on Richard's shoulder, and his arm was around her, warm and solid. He said, "There, there!" at intervals.

She cried, helplessly, for a long time. Then for a long time she could do nothing but let the great sobs rise that shook her all through. Richard's arm was firm and close.

"What is it, darling?" he asked at last. Through a blur she saw the trees of the Park as they drove by.

"I'm so—tired." Another great sob shook her voice.

"I know. There."

"Oh, *Richard!* I can't stand it."

"Tell me all about it."

"Oh. . . . I love him so, and I just can't do it. He's too much. . . . He's not real. He's made of—I don't know. Oh, Richard, what am I going to do? I just can't go on any longer like this."

His hand patted her shoulder, a slow, deeply comforting feeling. But he didn't speak.

"Richard, you understand, don't you? I'm just not made like that, or something. I *can't* go on and on and on. . . . I'm so tired. I'm always tired. I can't stand it—all my life."

"Tell me something: Is it the things we do—going out so much and staying out late, and all that? Is that what tires you?"

"Oh, no! I've always done all that—last year—I always expected to. It's just him. I can't stand it. It's something shaking you all to pieces. He's not human. You do understand, don't you?" (She thought: "He always understands." She leaned against his shoulder in a great wave of relief and sudden love for Richard.)

"I know," he said. "Day's like that."

"Oh, Richard, why do I have to be in love with him? Why can't I be safe and happy? Why can't I be in love with you? . . . I do love you, Richard."

She heard him catch his breath.

"Melissa." His voice was very slow. "I love you like hell. I suppose you know I've been in love with you since I've seen you. But you were Day's girl. You know about us—he's been my best friend since I was four, or something. Anyway, I wouldn't have a chance with him around—even if I wanted to take something away from him. But if it's like this, really—if you're miserable, and he does this to you—well, it seems different to me somehow. I'm probably wrong. I do love you so damn' much, Melissa!"

"Richard!" She could not think at all now, about what any of this meant; she could only feel the perfect comfort of Richard's arm around her, his quiet, strong presence beside her. She looked up at his face through the last of her tears: his face was so calm, so reposed; its thin dark cheeks, its quiet eyes, were everything there was of safety and rest.

Then he kissed her. She kissed him too, but that didn't seem to matter, to mean anything to her; what was important was the comfort of his arm, of him there beside her. She leaned her head back and sighed with content. She was always so happy with Richard.

When he helped her out at Hope's door, he hesitated.

"Melissa—I don't think you'd better drive back with us tomorrow. Day's going to be in bad shape, and he ought not to drive—I'll do it. Anyway, I think it would be a mistake. It would be a bad idea—now."

"You mean you're going to tell him about—this?"

"I don't know."

"You mean we can't all do things together any more, of course." She bit her underlip.

"I don't know. Good-by, darling. I'll call you in Boston day after tomorrow."

"Good-by, Richard."

She went in slowly, in the growing dawn. There was too much to think about, too much. Tonight meant more than she had realized; it meant the destruction of so many things, perhaps, things beyond herself. Richard, she thought, dear Richard who had comforted her! But as she fell asleep, she thought of Davis; she loved him with all her heart.

All next day, coming home on the train, things continued to revolve dizzily and pointlessly in her head. She did not know what she was going to do. She felt a curious, definite relief with part of her mind: that she had made some kind of break, however unknown to Davis, but with him. She felt freer, more relaxed, than she had for a long time. Even the very fact that Richard had kissed her seemed to release her to some degree from that iron-bound slavery to Davis that she had felt. But with the other half of her mind, she knew, just as definitely, that she was still hopelessly in love with Davis; she did not see how she could ever be anything else. He was the only person she wanted.

It was a desperate sort of mess. What she wanted was Davis, still. But Davis wore her out, demanded more of her strength than she had to give. As an alternative, there was Richard, who loved her. She did not love him; but in some curious way he was at the same time just what she needed—strength, repose, calm, rest, love. Sitting unhappily, restlessly, in the green plush Pullman seat, she thought that she needed him now; if he were here, he would make her calmer, settle things, somehow. It was a choice, she thought, between the love of her life and that life itself. For if she stayed with Davis, married him next year, if it did not kill her it would wear her down to a point where life would not be worth living. She had been near that point already.

But—she went into the dining-car to get some hot tea—if it were not to be Davis, why must it be Richard? She saw what that would mean to that friendship that had lasted so many years: if she turned to Richard, if next year she were to marry Richard, that would destroy most if not all of the old, great friendship between him and Davis; for Davis was not the man to endure the transference of the girl he loved to the man who was his best friend. It would ruin something that had existed long before she ever saw, heard of, Davis; and did she have the right to do that? If she must, then, leave Davis, why not leave him for no one, go back to a life without a love, and wait for something that some day might express some part of the emotion she had felt with Davis? . . . She was very unhappy.

She finished her tea and wandered back to her seat, sat down, stared out at the severe brown landscape of New England. Her chin was in her fist, her feet propped on the radiator that ran the length of the car.

She would rather that it should be Richard than no one else, than anyone else but Davis. Her mind was so definite in this that she wondered about the reason for it, considering that she was not in love with Richard. . . . The train pulled into Providence, stood still while the station filled with hot white steam from the engine. . . . She saw why, suddenly: because for her Richard was a part of Davis; he partook essentially of Davis' presence, because for her he had always been associated inseparably with his friend. If she married Richard, she would be marrying something that was very like Davis. She put her hand down into her lap, clenched it with the other. She saw no way to make herself happy but to turn, now, to Richard. He gave her what she needed, everything; and with him she would always have the scent of that glory that being in love with Davis had had. Perhaps it was unfair; that friendship would be impaired. But Richard said he wanted her; that the friendship was less important; and for Davis no one such thing could ever be too bitterly important. He would be safe, happy, all his life. She thought for a minute of his invulnerability, his high, tearing spirit that would always wave above him like a flag, and her heart shrank up and pounded inside her, as always, because she loved him so.

She was having dinner with the family, giving them a modified version of her evening in New York, speaking of Hope, when the telephone rang. Instantly she thought of Davis, and sat still at the table, tense, while she heard the maid's slow steps going to the telephone.

"For you, Miss Melissa. A gentleman."

She ran, and her breath was quick as she answered: Davis, Davis, Davis!

"Melissa? This is Richard."

"Yes, Richard."

"I waited till I thought you'd be home."

"Yes. Got in at six."

"Melissa—Davis is in the hospital."

"Richard, what's happened? Richard—"

"It seems to be pneumonia, the doctor said. . . . He had awful pains in his chest when he woke up this morning, but he *would* drive back. By the time we got here— He's pretty sick."

"Can I see him?"

"No."

"I can't?"

"They said nobody could, for a while. He's at Stillman Infirmary. The doctor said nobody could see him. Till later. That spot on his lung—"

"What spot?"

"Nothing that's bothered him. He was sick when he was a kid. You can see it's never bothered him. But he never would take care of himself—you know."

"But Richard—tell me—"

Not being able to see him, not knowing really how he was, was awful. Richard gave her the reports on him every day; he had a high temperature, was out of his head, and had not reached the crisis of the disease. Melissa could not bear to go to any of the parties in those days; she stayed at home and took long walks in the dreary leafless Fenway; and in the evenings Richard came to see her. He was very delicate; he said nothing about that early morning in New York after they took Davis home. He was only very quiet and very comforting. A week went by. Richard telephoned that Davis had passed the crisis, that the doctor said he would be all right now, with care. Three days later he telephoned her in the morning.

"You can see him now. He asked to."

"See me?"

"Yes. The doctor said this afternoon, for a few minutes."

"And he asked to see me?"

"Yes."

The long waiting became a turmoil of trembling excitement. She had worried so terribly. And the worst thing, the thing that lay at the bottom of her worry, was that fear: that Richard had told Davis about that night in the taxicab, and that that, somehow, had made him sick—her fault, her disloyalty, he would think. She had not dared ask Richard whether he had said anything—she was too afraid he would say yes.

They drove out to Cambridge in the Bugatti, in the white December weather. Richard hardly talked; once or twice he turned his head and smiled at her, with a look that had a question in it; that look made her remember that she still owed Richard something, some sort of statement of her feelings. He had not touched her, or spoken, since that night in New York. She had a feeling he was waiting until she had seen Davis, to tell him how she felt. As always, she felt a wave of warmth toward him sitting beside her in the car, so solid and safe and good. It was nice, comforting, to have some one like this love her.

They walked down the long white corridors of the infirmary, and a nurse met them; Richard left her at the door.

Davis lay still in bed, his face white and tense, his brilliant blue eyes alert.

"Hello, baby," he said. His voice was very faint and husky.

She went and sat beside his bed, trembling. The old tension enveloped her. It was awful, panicky. There he lay, sick and still, and yet his old aura, that atmosphere of excitement, nervous vitality, assailed her and left her breathless. She clenched her hands together and stared with love and helplessness at Davis' face, that was like a white flame on the pillow.

What they talked about was trivial. He was very weak. But for the five minutes or so that she was there, she felt the old quivering tension seizing all her body; at the end she went to the door, and Richard was outside; the nurse closed the door. Melissa was almost crying.

"Oh, Richard," she whispered. He took her hand and squeezed it.

"Richard, I can't stand it," she whispered. She felt completely spent and without hope. If Davis, *sick*, could drain her like this, then there was no hope for her. She would never be able to live up to him. Instinctively she held Richard's hand tighter, clinging to him.

A man came hurrying along the corridor, the doctor. Richard introduced him to Melissa.

"May I speak to you a minute, young lady?" the doctor asked.

They went into an empty room, closed the door.

"He's all right now, isn't he?" Melissa asked.

"Yes, he's all right. . . . I believe you're the young lady he does all the talking about, when he doesn't know what comes out. You've got a big responsibility with that young man; and I hope you realize it."

"What do you mean?"

"He'll kill himself if he goes on wasting his energy the way he does, for many more years. You see, I know him a little, outside. . . . He's in love with you. It seems to me you could do a pretty good job on restraining all that vitality of his, making him conserve it. Because if you don't, he'll burn himself out."

"But—"

"Don't tell me you thought he had plenty. He's got no more strength than any of the rest of us; he just gives it out more. Bad things happen to people like that—things like this pneumonia. People like that need to be held back—by people that love them and understand about it—so that they can use their energy to some useful end. This is too good a young man to squander all he's got in his early twenties. You do something about it."

The doctor bowed and hurried out. Melissa sat down on the edge of the hospital bed, alone. The thoughts were going round in her head, slowing down into sense. She had never thought of any of this before; it put a new face on life for her. More than he wore her out, Davis wore himself out. He needed her to protect him from that.

She loved him so much, so terribly; and now everything was different. It was as if she had been lifted on a magic carpet and put down in a different relation to Davis. How could he ever exhaust her any more? It would be her work to keep him from exhausting himself. He never showed his exhaustion, was unaware of it himself; thus it could be too much for him and destroy him, if she did not take care of him. She loved him so; she was very happy. She smiled, unconsciously.

Richard was still waiting, out in the corridor. She smiled at him, and went back to the door that was Davis'. She opened it softly; he was moving restlessly about in bed, and his eyes started like flickering blue flames when he saw her.

"Darling," she said, "get lots of sleep, and I'll come and see you tomorrow." She said it quietly, softly, without that usual nervous response to his vitality that had always made her voice, with him, high. He looked at her with his blue eyes as if he loved her. She looked back at him, and closed the door again.

They walked down the corridors again. All the nervous fatigue had dropped from Melissa, and she felt calm and steady. She had a job to do. She looked at Richard beside her.

"I can't wait for him to get well," she said.

She saw he understood what she meant, but he smiled as quietly, as surely, as ever. He would always be there, loving her and loving Davis, and helping her with him.

They came out into the high cold New England air. She took a long breath. She knew all about the rest of her life, now.

1937

THAT WOMAN

MEN OUTNUMBER WOMEN by a considerable percentage in the United States, it is reported, and this sounds splendid except that in actual practice in many places there just aren't enough extra men, and a girl has the very devil of a time getting a beau for her exclusive use. This is particularly so in the small proud towns of the South, like Bremen, where the fact of being a woman implies a long battle to get escorted to entertainments, and getting married represents a victory over practically insuperable odds.

When I lived in Bremen there were only three unattached males you could consider having in your house, no matter how pressing the necessity to make an even number, and of these one was sixty, one was twenty-four, and the third had fits; all three were insufferably conceited. Before moving to the South I had heard that Southern women were brave, capable characters while Southern men were often boors; I soon found that there was truth in this allegation. The men of Bremen were a pretty infuriating lot principally because since the cradle they had known themselves to be in crying demand.

It is a beautiful, oak-shaded, graceful, honeysuckle-scented little town, Bremen. Old country houses with beautiful names—Lutesville, De Courcy, Music Hall—mark at intervals the romantic, rolling countryside. In town the houses are set back from velvet lawns; magnolias and crêpe myrtles shade the porches where friends from families that have visited each other since Queen Anne's day gossip and sip juleps. The hours are gently passed in pleasant ways, as though these Southerners had long ago given up thoughts of effort or strife and were making lovely each hour on the way to the grave.

If there were plenty of men, surely all would be peace in Bremen. But in Bremen an old maid is an object of pity and shudders of self-congratulation; a girl with a date is one with a considerable triumph to her credit; an engaged girl is one on tenterhooks, who will not be able to relax until the words of the marriage service have mercifully been spoken; a married woman is a successful woman; but a woman like Alida Norris, who has been married four times, is a serpent and a menace and a slur on Southern womanhood and worse than that. I said a woman like Alida; there are no other women like Alida in Bremen. To find another husband after one's husband dies is a definite *coup*, and hardly to be expected. But to have the gall to divorce a perfectly good husband, and another, and another, and end up with a fourth, even if he is the town drunk, is cosmic impertinence due for punishment from the gods.

I heard about Alida soon after I moved to Bremen. Her name was not long off people's tongues. I was sitting in Sally Davis' living-room drinking a highball in the late afternoon; there were four or five women sitting about having a drink, smoking lazily, unhurriedly, as if there were an eternity for seeing one's friends. The minute Alida's name came up there was a sudden edge in the air. Sally explained for my benefit.

"She was Alida Maupin—as good blood as any in Bremen. First she married Dick Wells, back up country at Perryville, owns a racing stable. We didn't know what to think when she divorced him. Thought he must have tried to kill her, the way Maizie Hankins' husband is always acting up; couldn't think of any other reason; thought she was a fool for throwing away a husband like that when heaven knew where she'd get another. She was always a right pretty girl, went to dances at the University and all when she was young and had plenty of attention; but sort of vague; used to say the craziest things, still does. Well! If she didn't marry Duke Enters, who is,

I reckon, the most famous Bremenite we've got; you know, consul or something at Paris, real distinguished man. She married him and went abroad to live, and first thing you knew she was back here in Bremen at her mother's, divorced again. She got Duke while he was young and not famous yet, but he was getting famous by the time she left him, and would you think . . . Well! We naturally thought that finished Alida for good and all. We thought she must be just naturally crazy, throwing away husbands. And what should she do but marry again. Armistead Butts, the head of the school board and principal of the high school and a most scholarly man, really old family, never looked at a girl before, although of course every girl had been after him for years. We had to hand it to Alida," Sally said grudgingly. "She certainly fooled us. But when she divorced Armistead too we really had had enough of Alida. Didn't have any use for her. Didn't know a good thing when she had it, just flighty and unprincipled and *common*, throwing husbands around like pea pods. And so then she married again, Billy Norris, the most good-for-nothing wastrel Bremen ever had, drinks, sits around all day, not worth the powder and shot to blow him to Kingdom Come. Serves her right. What does she think she is anyway? Cleopatra?—I suppose we're just jealous," Sally added to me in a tone designed to make it clear that she was not any such thing. The one thing sure was that she was good and mad just from talking about Alida.

"What has she got that we haven't got?" The question was unconscious and heartfelt; it was put by Miss Letty Coxe, who had never got married and, you could see it in her face, knew now that she never would.

"If she had gone away from here, picked herself up husbands somewhere else, it would be one thing," Virginia Staige said. "But every—single—one—of those husbands of Alida's was a Bremen boy. Now how did she do that, Sally? How do you reckon?"

"Well, she is pretty, you have to give Alida that. She's still just as pretty as she can be, though she must be forty-three, if she's a day.

Maybe forty-four. She's got a right pretty figure, and she's funny to listen to sometimes, if you don't go stark staring crazy trying to follow what she's talking about. I don't know how she got them, Virginia. What is it that men want anyway?" There was real, stark tragedy in that question, I thought. There was all the long, frenzied, anxious asking of all the women of Bremen.

"Well, she can have her four husbands but she can't come into my house," Helen Randolph said, and all the women nodded. "I'm through with Alida. I don't care if her grandfather was my grandfather's colonel; she has gone too far and behaved disgracefully and I can't receive her in my house where my children are, just growing up. She's a bad woman," Helen said viciously and took a big drink of highball. I suddenly saw fear in her eyes, in her voice. They were all afraid, all these women. They were terrified of this woman, Alida Norris. She had done the impossible; she had married four separate and distinct times; surely it was not inconceivable that she might at random pluck a husband from some other woman. Terror was in their hearts and distrust in their minds, and deep down inside of all of them they hated her. They were all nice women too; but they knew what trouble was and the frantic search for a husband, and to them Alida Norris could only spell danger.

"I'd like to meet her," I said.

They all looked at me and I could see the same look in all their eyes. You haven't got a husband, they were thinking; you don't have to be afraid of her.

"You won't meet her here," Sally said firmly. "I don't know where you would meet her these days; I don't know a person that doesn't feel about Alida as I do. She just isn't received, she or Billy either, although I may say I feel sorry for him, even if he does get falling-down drunk, which my father always said no gentleman could do no matter how much whiskey he had inside him. Bad blood somewhere, that's what it is. Of course Billy, his grandmother was in Staunton and his great-grandfather went over to the Yankees." Sally looked at me sidewise. "But I don't know where it got in with the Maupins. But it's there. Bad blood. You can always tell."

"I'll point her out to you someday on Jefferson Street while we're marketing," Virginia Staige said. "Or you'll probably meet her, sooner or later, at one of the club dances. You can't keep her out of the club after all; she is a Maupin, whatever. But I can't invite you to meet her at my house because I just won't have her in it, and that's all there is."

"Of course I understand," I said. But I was obsessed with a desire to meet Alida Norris. The potentialities were enormous. In this quiet town of conventional women, hag-ridden only by the difficulty and necessity of getting married, I had discovered the existence of what sounded like a guaranteed *femme fatale*. She must be something to see indeed, a sort of super Southern belle, all beauty and lure, or else brilliant and witty, or—something. Bremen was no place to be a *femme fatale* in; there wasn't anything to work with. But here was a woman who had done it anyway.

Quite a lot of time went by after I first heard of Alida Norris, and I didn't meet her. There was a real blockade against her in Bremen society. I thought of her as so fascinating that she kept her husband contented with her sole company; but I wondered, in view of her record, if she wasn't perhaps wearying of him, approaching towards the time when she would divorce him too and accomplish another impossibility, marry a fifth husband. I could not imagine what she would be like. She was my mystery woman. Someone pointed her house out to me, a perfectly ordinary house in need of paint. The house told me nothing.

One day in October I went to a cocktail party a little way out in the country. Sally Davis drove me out in her car. It was a characteristic Bremen party, lots of whiskey and soda, or water, to drink, more women than men, and the men behaving the regular Bremen way. At a Bremen party all the men go off and talk among themselves, leaving the women to drink and gossip. The women don't seem to mind a bit; only the unmarried women, looking a little like anxious loose horses, keep drifting in among the men who receive them without enthusiasm. The doctors flock together and talk medicine; the lawyers form groups; the horsemen likewise. It all seemed so uncivilized and boorish of the men, and so meek and resigned of the women, that I was that day especially exasperated. One likes to see women putting out sparkle and magnetism, men making an effort to be charming to the women; here the women sat and drank together and the men stood and drank together.

I was sitting with Sally and two or three other women, when Bourne Davis, Sally's husband, walked past with a fresh drink in his hand. He did not even glance towards us; he was making for the back room and his friends, but Sally called to him, and he turned.

"The children are at Janie Bray's birthday party," she reminded him.

"You'd better go and get them. It's getting late. Come on back here for me after you've picked them up," he said and strolled off.

She began gathering her things together quite unconcernedly. I was suddenly in a rage. I was furious at Bourne's spoiled selfishness and at Sally's acceptance of it, and at the fact that men all treated their wives like this in Bremen and got away with it. The wives ate it up. It was as bad as the Middle Ages; the wives put out everything, ran everything, and the men took it as their right, and there was nothing to be done about it because of the incontrovertible fact that men were at a premium. In Bremen there seemed to be no ignominy too great for a woman to take in order to get and to keep her man. I thought that Southern men were even worse than I had heard. I was too mad to speak.

After Sally had left I decided to walk home alone and work off my temper. A couple of men offered to drive me home, but I wanted to walk and, besides, I knew now how much my acceptance of an offer I should have once thought quite an ordinary one would disturb the wife of whoever made it.

It was exquisitely beautiful outside in the dusk and my rage evaporated almost at once in the cool exalted air. The broad land lay in the twilight, large and generous, rolling in great swells back towards the lights of occasional houses riding on the hills, towards the lights of Bremen shining up from the shallow valley ahead.

The side of the road was deep in fallen leaves and I scuffed along through them; scuffing leaves is a very soothing thing to do. At least, if the social system of Bremen was all wrong, the physical aspect of the place, its sights and smells and sounds were divinely right. I could smell apples and grapes and the indefinable sweetness of the fields, and I could hear cow bells from the pastures and the sound of a church bell tolling the hour faintly, away in the town.

I rounded a curve and there was a car standing on the side of the road. As I got nearer I saw that there was a woman sitting on the running board. I came abreast of her.

"Hello," she said, in one of the most beautiful, liquid voices I have ever heard.

"Hello," I said.

"Isn't it lovely this time of day?" she remarked casually. "I've been sitting here for hours looking at that hillside. It turns a different color every few minutes. It's been orange and then yellow and then blue and now it's dark purple."

This was a most unusual way for anybody to talk in Bremen. You felt that every one loved the beauty of the country passionately but quite inarticulately; it was a part of their blood, their bone, that they felt without outwardly perceiving.

"I don't think I ever saw such lovely country," I said. I could not see the woman's face clearly. She just sat there, leaning forward with her arms crossed over her knees.

"I'd like to stay here all night," she said.

"It would be fun," I said. I started to walk on. I wanted to talk to the woman, but she seemed so absorbed, so really unconscious of my presence and talking almost as if to herself, that I had a feeling of intrusion. I had got a little way down the road when she called after me.

"I forgot. Do you know anything about cars?"

I walked back.

"Not much," I said. "Is something the matter?"

The woman got up from the running board.

"I was forgetting why I stayed here," she said, and laughed a laugh as lovely and musical as her speaking voice. "I stopped the car to look at the view and then I couldn't get it started again. So I just got out and enjoyed myself."

She got back into the driver's seat and I got in beside her. In the glow from the dashlight I looked at her profile. It was innocent and like a child's, although I could see now that she was in middle age; she had a tipped-up nose and a high smooth forehead. She put her foot on the starter and the engine whirred.

"You see?" she asked triumphantly. "It just won't go. I'd better walk back to town with you. My husband will do something about it. He knows all about cars."

"You haven't got the ignition turned on," I said.

"Oh." She sounded slightly crestfallen. She turned on the switch and the car started at once. I thought of Mrs. Peterkin and all the vague and impractical ladies of fiction.

"I think you'll be all right now," I said and started to get out.

"Oh, but you must let me drive you back to town," she said, and I thought of a little girl exhibiting her best company manners. "I'm Alida Norris. I'm Mrs. William Norris. You must let me take you home."

Wild horses could not have dragged me from that car. I introduced myself.

"You're from the North," she said. "Mr. Wilson at the drugstore told me all about you. He says you buy lots of sodium bicarbonate.

I hope you don't have stomach-aches. You live in the Marbin house, don't you?"

I have never felt such tangible, irresistible charm radiating from any one. She was facing me now eagerly, and I could see her face. It was a child's face, alive, unconscious. Its most beautiful feature was the mouth. The mouth was large and soft and mobile and as delicate and sensitive as a young girl's.

As we drove into the outskirts of town she suddenly turned to me, breaking off a conversation in the middle; it was a charming, impulsive turning, but it nearly killed us because two cars were passing just at that moment, and as Alida Norris turned her body she turned the wheel too. I did a moment's intensive praying.

"My," she remarked when the bad moment was over. "There are so many crazy drivers, aren't there? I was going to say: don't go home, come and meet my husband. He'd just love to meet you. You aren't a bit Northern and I'd like to prove it to him Northern women can be real nice. You see, I know it anyway. I've travelled. I've lived in Paris, Le Havre, New York and Washington, D.C.," she added.

"I'd love to come," I said fervently.

"I want you to see Billy. Billy's wonderful. He could be anything he wanted to. He can fix cars and electric lights and plumbing, and even the stove. I never knew any one like Billy. And I ought to know; I've been married three times before. I suppose you've heard that," she said, more mournfully than anything else. "They were all perfectly wonderful men. *Wonderful* men. But there's never been anybody like Billy. He's so nice to me," she said in an ecstatic voice. I could not imagine any one not being nice to her. Also my preconceived ideas of Bremen's *femme fatale*, the caster-off of husbands, were being badly confused by this ingenuous, enthusiastic, affectionate creature. She was more a mystery woman than ever to me.

She stopped the car.

"This isn't the house," she said. "The house is three houses back.

But I always stop the car here. It spoils the view out of my front windows, and I'm perfectly sure the Carters—they live in this house—don't mind having their view spoiled."

We got out and walked back. We went up an untidy front walk and through a front door that opened directly into a large shabby living-room. Although it was in disorder, the room had charm. It looked like a room in an antique store. Nothing was in place; a pile of Wedgwood plates stood on the floor under a Hepplewhite desk; a lovely old flower print lay flat, face up, on an end table; a screen that looked like a Coromandel stood meaninglessly in the middle of the room. There was a man sitting by the open fire with a glass in his hand; he got up as we came in.

"This is Billy. He's just having a drink. He drinks too much," Alida Norris said proudly. Again I thought of a little girl, this time showing off.

The man laughed and shook hands. He was not an attractive man. He was short and sloppily dressed and he had a bad, grayish complexion. But he had gentle, intelligent eyes. Alida put her arms round him and kissed him. It was quite obvious that they were both very much in love with each other.

"You'll have a drink, won't you?" she said to me. "We'll all have a drink. Billy, you get them."

"There aren't any more of the glasses," he said, getting up.

"Oh, gosh. So there aren't. Well, there are the other glasses in a basket under the table in the hall, darling. They're awfully dirty. But alcohol sterilizes things," she said to me.

Billy Norris got us drinks and we all sat round the fire. It was somehow very happy. You feel it when you are with happy people. We were all rather childish and laughed a lot. I liked them both enormously. They were both absolutely simple.

Alida with her charm and beauty was perfectly irresistible. Her violently illogical remarks, her trains of thought made me laugh and they made her husband laugh too. He was the first man I had met in Bremen who didn't act like a lord of creation. He was just himself. He was extremely pleasant to me and attentive to his wife. I never saw a man with better married manners. But there were no two ways about it, he was a nondescript, unimpressive little man. As time went on it was apparent that he was feeling his liquor.

"Billy's getting drunk," Alida said to me. "Aren't you, Billy?"

"Unh-hunh. Gettin' drunk now," he said cheerfully.

To someone who does not know Bremen this interchange of remarks may not seem significant, but I had been living in Bremen for some time by then, and I had seen too many husbands asserting with a proud and didactic air that they never got drunk when they were obviously reeling, and too many wives not daring to take the wheel of the car when their husbands were quite incompetent to drive safely, not to realize that in the South ability to hold his liquor is almost the ultimate point of a man's pride, and that wives are taken to task for far less than questioning that point.

I thought it was time for me to leave, and I said good-bye to Alida. I asked her if she would not come in to lunch on the following Tuesday.

"Tuesday," she said reflectively. "Tuesday—let's see, that's Thursday. Yes, I'd love to."

God knew what she meant. I left. When I got to know Alida better I realized that in her funny mind were all sorts of special systems for things. Tuesday unquestionably was Thursday by some personal mathematics of her own, and black was white and the moon was green cheese.

I thought, in view of the opinions I had heard expressed, I should tell the women I invited to lunch on Tuesday that Alida was coming. As soon as they knew that they promptly declined in no uncertain terms. Sally Davis hauled me over the coals for even suggesting that she come to lunch with that woman.

"You might as well understand that none of us are going to tolerate Alida for one moment," she said over the telephone. "She's ostracized herself permanently in Bremen by her carryings on. I won't come to lunch with a woman who's been married four times, and that's that. And I'm surprised at you asking her. But of course you're a Yankee," she said condescendingly. "I know people are right broadminded up North. But you can't be too broadminded down here. I'm just warning you, darlin'. I mean people just aren't going to put up with Alida. You can't have her and us. She's a hardhearted, fickle, common woman. Four husbands!" Sally went on about it for some time; people talk for hours on the telephone in the South.

And so Alida and I had lunch alone on Tuesday. By the time we left the dining-room it was impossible not to feel that I had known Alida long and well. She had the gift of intimacy without effrontery. She had charm and style and a wit of her own. She was by far the most attractive woman in Bremen. I understood, all right, about how she had found herself four husbands, and why the hand of every woman in Bremen was against her. She was a real honest-to-God charmer.

We sat in the little drawing-room. Over the mantel was a painting by a friend of mine of the Ile St. Louis.

"I know that place!" Alida explained. "I told you I'd lived in Paris. That was when I was married to my second husband. He was a vice-consul. Named Duke Enters. My, he was handsome." She said it with frank admiration.

"Duke was the handsomest man I ever saw, ever. I used to love his ears. I remember I told the consul to look and see how beautiful Duke's ears were. He was awful mad at me that time. I wish you could have seen him then! You've probably seen his picture. But then! Oh, he was so tall and dark and kind of American looking, it gave you a thrill to look at him. Like looking at the American flag. He looked so handsome in his clothes. He looked handsome out of them too but he never liked me to say that. He liked his clothes himself, I do think. Liked to have them kept pressed and all that. I was so awful, I never remembered. Somehow I never can remember about clothes. Once we were staying at the George V and I threw his tailcoat out of the window. He was good and mad that time."

The picture she was calling up of herself was irresistible to me. I could see why men would be mad about her, even more than I had before. A young Alida, fresh and gay and irresponsible, as natural as the wind, vague and bat brained and lovely—no wonder she had had a success with men. But with her outspoken admiration of Enters I wondered what had made her divorce him. There are some things one can't ask, and since she was so frank about everything else and volunteered no information on that point I concluded that it must have been for a very good and very personal reason. Perhaps her third husband had won her away from her second. I asked about the third husband—what was he like?

"Armistead? Now, you would have adored Armistead. I did. Except I wasn't good enough for him; I mean I don't know anything and Armistead knew everything. I guess Armistead had read every book that ever got printed. He loved books. Really loved them. It used honestly to hurt him when I did awful things, like leave books open face down, or bend the corners of pages back. I ought to have learned but I never could somehow. And when I was cross one morning and threw a lot of books around the room it just about killed him. I used to feel so guilty. Afterward. It used to humiliate him awfully how dumb I was when we went out. I never knew what he was talking about and he did talk about such fancy things."

I thought I could guess why Alida had divorced that one. The pedantic grade had been one she couldn't make, and I didn't blame her. Armistead sounded terrible to me. One of the most disarming things about Alida, I thought, was the way she always told the bad tales on herself and never blamed any one else. She hadn't said a critical or unchivalrous word about either of the husbands she had discussed; she had loudly sung their praises, and, seeing that she had found it necessary to get rid of them, I thought it was very sporting of her.

A few days later I went to see Alida at her house, stopped in on my way back from a luncheon party. As I walked up to the house I saw a man in painter's overalls sitting on the doorstep, occupied in some curious way not connected with painting. Alida came running out as I approached.

"Hi! I'm so glad to see you!"

"Would you mind telling me what that man is doing?" I asked. I could see what he was doing now. He was picking up silk stockings from a pile of them next to him, running his hand up each one and scrutinizing it, then rolling them up in pairs into neat little balls.

"Oh. He's the man who's painting the kitchen. I asked him if he'd mind sorting my stockings and he said he'd love to. I can't see why. I just hate to sort stockings. They accumulate for months in my bureau drawer."

She led the way into that strange antique shop of a living-room. We sat and smoked together in the pleasant atmosphere of being old friends. Alida looked perfectly lovely. Her soft, red, sweet mouth was all quivering with smiles and her eyes beamed. She sat at the end of a sofa with her pretty legs hanging over the arm, playing with a china zebra that stood among green china grasses.

"I was married to a horseman first, you know," she said. "This zebra makes me think of it. I guess that would make Dick pretty mad if he heard me say it, as if zebras had anything to do with horses. But they have, haven't they? I don't know why horsemen are so fussy about names. You mustn't call hounds dogs, you know," she said like a little girl repeating a lesson. She sighed. "Dick was my first love. I fell in love with him while my hair was still down my back. He was such a marvelous horseman and he looked so wonderful in his pink coat—you mustn't say red—and his top hat when he went out hunting. I was just crazy about him. I don't suppose you can ever feel like that again when you get older. He sort of had so much glamour. He could ride any horse that ever was born; he used to ride steeplechases—my, that scared me; he used to get so mad when I'd scream right in front of people. I used to try so hard to get interested in horses because he wanted me to. But I just *can't* make myself get so excited about an animal. I mean that way. Of course I always was interested in the wrong animal. The fox. I used to feel sorry for the fox, and you mustn't feel sorry for the fox; it kills chickens or something. I hate chickens. Once I was out in the pony cart when they were hunting and the hunt came by me and the huntsmen asked me which way the fox had gone and I told them the opposite way. Wasn't that awful? I don't think Dick ever forgave me. He was good and ashamed of me. I couldn't seem to learn to ride right. I fell off so much. My, I hated it! But I did try. Honestly I did. But I've always been scared of horses. They look like wild animals to me, with those big mouths, and I always feel as if they were going to put their heads round and bite me when I'm on top of one. I mean mounted. I always think a horse would look better behind bars—like a lion—than out loose there in the fields, don't you? Dick used to tell me that they were scared of me, but I didn't believe him for a minute. I was awful. I don't blame Dick for being mad at me most of the time."

I had come to deliver an invitation. I wanted Alida and Billy to have dinner with me at the dance at the club the next Saturday. Alida said they'd love to.

"But you ought not to be seen with me," she said quite cheerfully. "People think I'm awful, you know, on account of all those husbands and everything. You mustn't get criticized for going around with me."

Her humility, her gentleness and frankness touched me deeply.

"I like you better than any one I've met in Bremen," I said. "And I'll see you all you'll let me."

She gave me the most beautiful smile.

When I first came to Bremen I thought perhaps club dances would be a cut above ordinary parties—that the men would stay with the women perforce, since surely a dance is designed for the glorification of the female. But they were only a little bit better, or, rather, better for only part of the time. People sat in parties at tables and danced during the early evening. The music was rather good, and every one of course knew every one else, and the stage seemed set for gaiety. But along about eleven or midnight the blight would strike. The men would drift off into the smoking-room and the bar, to talk to one another, and the women would be left high and dry at the tables to twiddle their thumbs. I had grown increasingly enraged at a succession of these dances, and it was a relief at this one to have my own table which I hoped to be able to run as I pleased. It was a table for four—the Norrises and one of the three extra men—I think it was the old one—and myself.

The extra man, I remember, annoyed me by acting as if he were seated at table with the Scarlet Woman of Babylon. He kept his eyes downcast and replied to Alida's amusing sallies in mumbles, or else leered at her in a manner I considered offensive and which she ignored. She was at her most dazzling that night. She had on a gold dress that showed her pretty shoulders, and if ever I saw a woman intended to be surrounded by adoring and competitive admirers, she was the woman. She seemed to have an inexhaustible stock of vitality which struck off like sparks in gaiety and her own characteristically ridiculous remarks.

Her husband was not much of a conversational addition but he did seem to appreciate Alida. It was plain that he was crazy about her. When he danced with her he looked down at her with the look that men have for women who enchant them utterly. He was a funny, drab little man for Alida to be married to, I thought, especially after the romantic or impressive characters she had described her other husbands as. But she loved him, you saw that.

She seemed perfectly satisfied with him, and with his drinking, of which he was doing plenty that evening.

Alida had hardly anything to drink, but she seemed more than ever intoxicated with the fact of being alive. She played absurd games with the silverware on the table, a sort of involved tiddlywinks to pop a spoon into a glass of water. I was aware of disapproving glances thrown at our table, but she either did not see them or did not care.

"There are a lot of the horsy people here tonight," I said at one point.

"These ones are mostly Yankees," Alida said, squinting her eyes up and looking round the room. "That's the way to get somewhere down here. Buy a big place and a lot of horses and then climb the social ladder dung by dung."

Billy Norris laughed uproariously. The extra man looked a little shocked and I could have slapped him. The hour was growing later and the men in the room were beginning their customary thinning out. More and more women sat unattended at their tables, gossiping of this and that and of, no doubt, us. Billy Norris was getting good and drunk. The fact seemed to amuse both him and Alida. Billy kept propping his elbow on the table and letting it drop off, at which both of them would laugh. I have seen few wives who do not become either acid or morose when their husbands get drunk.

Finally he got up in a sort of diagonal way and excused himself. We waited, and he did not come back. It was well on to two o'clock.

"I suppose he's joined the masculine circles in the bar," I said bitterly.

"I don't think so," Alida said. "They bore Billy. He's probably just off finishing up his drinking. He does love to drink."

We waited for a while longer and still he did not come. My earlier approval of him was being dissolved by annoyance at this treatment of Alida.

"Do you think we ought to send some one to look for him?"

I asked her, glancing meaningly at the extra man who had been looking wretched for hours. I knew he wanted to get away and I was not going to let him go. For this once let him behave like a civilized being.

"All right. Go and look for Billy," Alida said to the extra man with that special Southern intonation and rise of the voice at the end of the request which makes unnecessary the word "please."

He went, and he did not come back. Nobody came back.

"Well, what do we do now?" I said after a long time.

Alida looked quite happy. She was drawing a picture on the tablecloth. It seemed to be some cats with their tails curled under them sitting on top of an elephant seen rear to.

"You take me home," she said. "What's-his-name will never turn up if he hasn't turned up now. And Billy's probably gone long ago and taken our car."

"And left you here?"

"He likes to go back in the mountains towards Sugar Hollow and wake up the mountaineers and drink with them," she explained. "It reminds him of his youth in Prohibition when he had to buy corn liquor back up there. He's all right. I don't mind a bit, you know."

We left and I drove her back into town to her house. I waited while she went up the path, for her to get in safely. But she turned and came back to me.

"I forgot. Billy's got the key. I can't get in. It just shows how silly it is to lock doors anyway. You just lock yourself out."

"You come right home with me and spend the night," I said.

"That's right sweet of you. I'd love to," she said contentedly, and climbed back into the front seat.

But I was really indignant now. Billy Norris was just another insufferable Southern male with no consideration for his wife. Leaving her stranded at a party, and going off with the key so that she couldn't even go home. . . .

When we got back to my house I showed Alida her room and got her a nightgown and a toothbrush.

She curled up on the bed; so many of the things she did reminded me of a very small girl.

"Don't go away yet," she said, smiling coaxingly. "Let's talk. It's fun spending the night out."

I sat down in the armchair and put my feet up. The feeling of intimacy and affection I had for Alida was extraordinary; she gave out warmth and friendliness and love.

"I'm beginning to feel like one of those women with a Cause," I said. "All I do is get madder and madder at the men down here in the South. I think they really do behave too abominably. Billy just going off and leaving you in the lurch is the last straw. I should think you would be furious at him."

Alida lay on her back with her hands behind her head and looked at the ceiling.

"I don't mind one bit. Billy really loves me. And I just love to be loved. I don't mind anything as long as I'm loved. I like to love people and have them love me back. Billy loves me back, lots, and he doesn't mind the awful things I do. He thinks I'm funny."

"Well, who would mind? You know you're a perfectly fascinating woman and your vagueness just makes you more amusing."

"My other husbands minded," Alida said mildly. "They minded terribly. I made them just as mad as the devil."

"The saps. I suppose that was why you had to divorce them."

"Oh, I didn't divorce them!" Alida said in a tone of childlike surprise. "They asked me for a divorce, all three of them. They couldn't stand me. Billy is the only man who has ever been able to stand me."

I have never been more astonished.

"You mean to tell me those men *wanted* to be divorced from you?" The whole picture was changing violently.

"They certainly did want to be divorced from me. I reckon people fall in love with me sometimes, but nobody except Billy has ever been able to stay married to me."

"But . . . why? You're the most attractive woman in Bremen."

"You're sweet to say so. . . . But I haven't any whatyoumaycallit, dignity, *you* know. I spoiled their dignity. Bremen men have an awful lot of dignity. They want their wives to reflect to their credit, and I was so undignified. They all ended by being ashamed of the things I did, ashamed of me. I loved all of them, you know; I guess I would have been happy with any one of them. But they just couldn't keep on loving me after the way I would disgrace them. You know the way I act. I can't seem to help it. Billy loves me the way I am. Billy doesn't worry about dignity."

"It's the most preposterous thing I ever heard. Why, in the North the amusing things you do and say would just make you all the more sought after, would make a Northern man all the crazier about you. It's just these damned, pompous, spoiled Southerners . . ."

"Oh, but I love it here down home. I like it lazy, living." I was so stunned by what she had told me that I didn't speak for a long time.

"I suppose you know every one thinks you just tossed your husbands aside. Nobody has the faintest idea, nobody could have the faintest idea, that they were the ones who wanted a divorce," I said finally.

"Honestly?" Alida's childlike eyes were large and astonished. "Isn't that funny! Imagine any one thinking I would want to divorce wonderful, attractive men like that! Aren't people funny?" she said.

1940

A PLACE TO HIDE IN

When I was a child we used to go two or three times a year to lunch at my Uncle Paul's. We always went on my birthday, because it was his birthday, too, and he always remembered it and asked us. The birthday came early in June, and for dessert we would have ice cream and, on top, the strawberries that Uncle Paul raised. He raised them as one of his hobbies. They were the biggest strawberries I had ever seen, dark red and juicy, as big as small plums.

My Uncle Paul had never married. My father said that he had always been too shy even to call on girls. He was born about 1870. When I knew him, he was sturdy and plump and very well dressed. He had pink cheeks and his gray hair was cut very neatly. He was very hospitable and gentle. He lived in a house in the country just outside our town, with two Irish maids. The cook cooked very good food and the waitress wore a white cap and used to smile at me when she passed the things.

Uncle Paul had studied to be an architect. He went to the Beaux-Arts in Paris and stayed over there about ten years, all through the nineties. He lived on the Rue des Saints-Pères on the Left Bank, in a house with other students at Julian's and the Beaux-Arts. He must have had a very good time in his own gentle way, because long afterward, when I knew him, all his little stories were about Paris.

One of them was about an American who had just come to Paris to study and lived in the same house with Uncle Paul. This American had asked the concierge to bring him up some hot water to shave with. The water didn't come, and the American went to the head of the stairs, and bawled down, "*Voulez-vous apporter moi l'eau chaude ou voulez-vous non?*"

In Paris, my Uncle Paul used to see most of the famous artists who were there in those days. He used to see Whistler and Monet, and once he saw Wilde, who was then in the evil days before his death. Uncle Paul said that later in Paris there was a society formed of people who had admired Wilde's work and who claimed that he was not dead but living somewhere still. They claimed that no one had seen him in his coffin and that what Lord Alfred Douglas said did not count. When I knew my Uncle Paul first, it was at least 1915, and he used to say then and later that perhaps Wilde was still not dead.

Uncle Paul had never practiced as an architect. The only thing he ever designed which was built after he came back to America was the house he lived in. This was a white, shingled house of an Early American type, very neat and trim outside, and inside very comfortable. The house was just like him. There was a lawn in the front and a big lawn in back that you looked out on from the living-room, with a fishpond in the middle. Beyond that lay the vegetable gardens. My Uncle Paul had a gardener to help him, and he raised strawberries and green-flesh melons and other specialties that won blue ribbons at the Grange fairs. He had enough money, so he had never needed to work, and he just lived there in his nice house that exactly suited him.

Beyond the gardens were the pinewoods. They ran back for a long way, and it was very dark in among the pines and the roof of the treetops was far up above. When we went to lunch with Uncle Paul, I would go out into the woods and play, building a tepee out of pine branches leaned against a tree trunk. I only got a little done each time, and we did not go very often, but nobody ever moved the part I had done, so I would go on with it the next time I went.

The others would stroll around across the lawns and through the gardens while I was in there in the secret pinewoods. Once, when I was about thirteen, my Uncle Paul came into the tepee, where I was, and stood and watched me fixing the boughs. (I always imagined at home that it was much more of a structure than it really was, and I was always disappointed when I got there and found only some branches leaning against a tree, letting in light and air, when I had thought of it as a tight place where I could go inside and be as snug as if I were in a house.) I felt some one standing behind me and turned around, and it was my Uncle Paul. He had a little gray mustache on his pink face and he was dressed, as always, in a nice, warm brown suit of tweeds. He showed me a way to fix the branches so that they would interlock and stand much more firmly against the tree.

"I want it to be so I can get inside and be safe," I said.

"You always have to leave a door," he said. "You can have it all shut in except that."

After a while he walked away. He never bothered people. He had these pleasant lunch parties that gave pleasure to the guests, with splendid, rich desserts the children liked, and everybody had a good time. He never asked you too often—just often enough so that you were glad to go again.

During the World War, my Uncle Paul gave a good deal of money to the Allied Relief, my father said, and he used to knit washcloths for the soldiers. When we went to lunch there it was just the same, except that the gardener had gone to the war and Uncle Paul knitted washcloths after lunch. The food was a little different, because we all had to do without wheat and sugar and such things. But it was still good, plentiful food and he always had the same cook and waitress.

I used to think that my Uncle Paul had the best life of any one I had ever heard of. He had been born just at the right time to be out of any bad trouble in the world. He had never married anybody and he lived alone in just the way that he chose and he did not have to work or be with people except when he asked them to come. He was very shy and I understood about that. Once there was a dinner for old Beaux-Arts men and my Uncle Paul had to go to it. He was in a panic for fear he might have to speak, and he could not eat any dinner. But in the end he did not have to speak at all. Nothing had ever happened to him, nothing, nothing. He was able to live his life and enjoy it without being troubled by all the things that tortured other people—debt and worry and misunderstanding and fights. He could live his life and enjoy it as it passed day by day and nothing happened.

But later on, when I was grown up, my Uncle Paul began to have heart trouble. He would have frightful attacks of pain quite suddenly when he was going upstairs or even sitting in a chair.

He was beside himself with terror. I don't know what he was afraid of, whether it was the pain itself or whether it was the fear of dying. He got a doctor to come and live with him in the house. His name was Dr. Alexander. He was a short man with an olive complexion and smooth black hair. He called my Uncle Paul "Paul," but Uncle Paul, who was a formal man, always called him "Dr. Alexander." Dr. Alexander lived in Uncle Paul's house from that time on.

My mother and father still went there to lunch a few times a year, but I had gone away from home then and I did not see my Uncle Paul for a long time. I still thought of him as having the best life I had ever seen lived. I was sorry that his heart had gone bad, but when I thought of him I saw the smooth, green lawns and the specimen strawberries like great ruby blobs among the green leaves, and the comfortable chintz-covered chairs in the living-room, and everything beautifully neat and orderly and nothing happening.

Once, though, I went to lunch there again when I was visiting at home. It was different. It did not seem to be Uncle Paul's house any more but to belong to Dr. Alexander. Dr. Alexander was a sociable man and he did all the talking at lunch and my Uncle

Paul sat silent. Dr. Alexander talked about operations he had seen performed. After lunch we walked out on the lawn in back of the house, where a putting green had been arranged so that Dr. Alexander could practice shots. Of course, no one could have said that Dr. Alexander was anything but nice to my Uncle Paul. But he was an active man and he liked things to happen, and so he kept the conversation going gaily and kept jumping up and lighting cigarettes and everything was different. He kept talking about his days in the hospital, and when he started saying anything about the present, he would begin, "You know, we lead a very quiet life here. Poor Paul . . ." Uncle Paul hardly spoke during the time we were there at lunch. He looked frightened. It was not his house any more and he was frightened about his heart and he could not do without Dr. Alexander.

About a year after I lunched there, my Uncle Paul died. I was told he had had a bad attack when he was lying on the sofa after dinner and it was so agonizing that he was screaming; he rolled off the sofa in his anguish and it was on the floor that he died. He left all his money to Dr. Alexander. I do not know what Dr. Alexander has done with it or where he is living now.

1940

BOOK REVIEW

ON THE WAY BACK from the trip to Williamsburg, they stopped for the night at a large house in one of the northern counties of Virginia. It had the cedar-bordered avenue, the portico, the fan-light, the dogs rushing up through the red mud in the twilight as they drove up to the door. The colored man in a white coat came down the steps, smiling, as they got out of the car.

"It's run as a club," Fred Wilkins said. "They do you damn well, make you feel like a guest and all that. I fork out dues each year, but it's worth it for a place like this, eh?"

Elizabeth Mayo and her husband, Pete, did not really know the Wilkinses very well. This trip had been one of those ideas. Pete made drawings for the advertising agency where Fred worked; they had cooked up the idea for a trip to Williamsburg over the rising friendliness and enthusiasm of a few drinks in New York. It had worked out pretty well. On the drive the men had talked advertising steadily, and the women had stuck to clothes. It was somehow like a trip you might have taken fifteen years ago, Elizabeth thought, when you were young and nobody really talked, but laughed and kidded.

Inside, the house was too luxurious to be really old Virginia. The Mayos were given a large bedroom on the second floor with a bathroom fitted with turquoise blue plumbing. When they came downstairs they went into the long drawing-room, with a fire snapping at the far end, and a beautiful polished floor that reflected the lights. The Wilkinses had joined the group of people having cocktails. There was only one other party staying at "Midmont." It was a party of six; they were middle-aged, substantial looking people from New York, apparently all old friends, who had driven down to visit the sons of two of the couples at a Virginia prep school. The man who ran the place was with them, a plump, old-maidish man of forty, very hospitable and gracious. They were drinking Old Fashioneds; Elizabeth remembered that Fred had stopped in the last town to buy a couple of bottles of Bourbon, explaining that you were supposed to supply your own liquor. The men wore their business suits; the women had on dark afternoon dresses. The Wilkinses were very much at home with the other party, talking business and the market and new plays; Pete, with his gaiety and charm, was taken in at once. They had three rounds of cocktails together, and it was nearly like staying in the country at a house-party to which you had been invited.

When they went in to dinner Elizabeth was put on the left of the host, with the man they called 'Commissioner' on her other side. There was a bright fire in the dining-room too, and old silver on the table, and a tall centerpiece of ivy that dripped over gracefully on to the white cloth. The host was chattering in a high, Southern voice to the wife of the Commissioner, who was on his right. Fred was next. Pete was somewhere down at the other end of the table.

"Well," the Commissioner said, "I hear you've been visiting Williamsburg. A gem, isn't it?"

"Yes, indeed," Elizabeth said. "I thought it was almost too perfect to be real."

He looked at her. He had a brown face, like a monkey, with broad thick lips, and thick hair parted in the middle.*

---

* Likely allusion to acerbic and influential critic H. L. Mencken (1880–1956), who famously covered the "Scopes Monkey Trial" in Tennessee, in which John T. Scopes was prosecuted for teaching students about Darwin's theory of evolution. Like Hale's Commissioner, Mencken was no fan of Hemingway's writing. Newspapers of the day often commented on the fact that he parted his hair in the middle.

"I hear your husband is an artist," he said. "But he looks like a nice fellow."

She laughed.

"Quite a lot of artists are nice fellows."

"Yes . . . yes . . ." he said. "Are you an artist?"

"No," she said. "I used to write before I was married."

"Oh, *write*. Writers. . . ." The soup plates had been taken away by the colored man and a maid. "I have no use for the stuff that's being written now," he said. "Have you read this book by this fellow Hemingway?"

"Yes," she said. "I think it's magnificent."

He put his knife down from cutting a piece of dark brown ham.

"You do? Well, I hope you will do me a favor. I hope you will be so kind as to explain just what there is to admire in that book."

"You mean you didn't admire it?"

"I thought it was filth. Just filth."

Elizabeth took a long breath.

"You must have a dirty mind," she said lightly; she had to say it, but she hoped her manner would make it all right.

"I think not. I sincerely think not. But if you can tell me what there is besides filth in that book. . . ."

"There are some of the most splendid characters ever written about. Some of the noblest."

"I don't call characters splendid that can't open their mouths without filth, and nothing else, coming out."

"They talk that way, Spanish peasants," she said, painstakingly. "If a writer hopes to make his characters true, he's got to make them talk as they really do. The words they use they take for granted, as you might say damn. You don't think what damn means when you say it. It isn't what they say; it's what they are."

"Just name me one character in that book that's what you call noble."

"Pilar. The woman."

"The woman! Look here, she was nothing but a prostitute. I'm sure I can't imagine what you find noble in a prostitute."

"I can see I can't make you understand," she said. She was very angry. She glanced at the host, but he was still chattering to the Commissioner's wife.

"And as far as that goes, every one in the book was just one of those Republicans. Just Communists. That's another reason I think the book ought never to have been written."

Elizabeth stared at him.

"You don't mean that you were for Franco?"

"I certainly was."

"I didn't know *anybody* was for Franco!" she cried. "I never met anybody before who was for Franco!"

"I don't know what kind of people you know," he said stiffly. "You must be a Communist."

"I'm not a Communist. They weren't Communists. They were the people. Are you against the people?"

"No, I'm not against the people. But even this fellow Hemingway admits the Russians were fighting their battles for them. They were just a lot of dirty Communists."

"Then you're for the totalitarian governments, is that it? You're for Hitler."

"No, I'm not for Hitler."

"He helped the other side. He boasts of his Spanish campaign. He and Mussolini. I suppose you like Mussolini."

"I don't think he's so bad. He's not a Hitler. Let me tell you I was in Italy before Mussolini and after he had been in for a few years, and he's done a lot for that country."

"I know," she said. "The railroads run on time. There aren't any beggars. So you are for the suppression of the Spanish people, when all they wanted was to be free. Haven't you read any of the books? Don't you know how they were oppressed? It was like the Middle Ages."

"Look here, my dear young lady. I was in Spain before the Revolution and it was a happy, prosperous country. The people were well off. It was a constitutional monarchy. The Revolution was brought about by Communist agitators. The people were well off as they were."

"Nonsense," she said.

"May I ask if you were ever in Spain?"

"No, I never was."

"Well. . . ."

"But I've read books about Spain under the monarchy, and apparently you haven't. How long were you in Spain?"

"Well . . . nearly a month. But I got a lot more accurate knowledge from my own observation than I could have through reading Communist propaganda."

Elizabeth had been aware for some time that the rest of the conversation at the table had ceased, and that every one was listening. She did not care. She was more outraged than she had ever felt, and she could not let it drop now.

"Listen," she said. "You approve of the French Revolution, I suppose?"

"Yes."

"And you approve of our own Revolution?"

"Of course."

"Then why do you disapprove of the Spanish overthrowing their king and setting up their own Republic?"

"It's an entirely different thing. The French were under a despotic king and suffered great oppression. We were oppressed too. I'm telling you, the Spanish people were not oppressed. I was there."

"Oh, pooh!" she cried. "You were there for a couple of weeks as a tourist and you think you know all about it. I tell you the Spanish peasants were ground down, they were starving, they'd starved for centuries, between the monarchy and the church they had been stripped of everything. . . ."

"We won't discuss the church," he said. "Surely you will grant that in their Communist revolution the Spanish were guilty of throwing over God himself?"

"He'd never been very good to them. You can't blame them for wanting to get rid of a church that had systematically bled them for generations."

Fred Wilkins was leaning across the table, with his genial, good fellow's, advertising grin.

"Going it hot and heavy, aren't you? How about breaking it up and giving the rest of us a chance? I didn't know you were such a Red, Liz."

Her face felt hot and flushed.

"Fred, do you mean you were for Franco, too?"

"Well, I'll tell you how it is, Liz. America can't afford to open itself up to Communism. Sure, some of those Spanish suffered—both sides suffered, I guess, but it's not American, you know, to go over on the side of those birds from Moscow."

"But it's all right to open ourselves up to Fascism, I suppose."

"No, we've got to guard against those boys too. We just won't have any truck with either of them."

"You don't realize . . . you don't realize . . . the Spanish were fighting just to be free."

Fred went on leaning across the table, his handsome, ruddy face smiling. The Commissioner was eating his salad and not talking to anybody. Fred was being his most winning.

"You see, Liz, some of us Americans had that idea, that the Spanish were fighting for freedom, and some American boys went over there to fight in their war for them. And you know what happened to them? They got shot."

"Naturally. In a war."

"No, I mean those dirty Communists that were running the war shot them. Lined them up and shot them. Now, it's not very nice for a boy from America to go over and get shot by one of those birds from Moscow."

"I don't believe it," Elizabeth said. She felt her heart pounding.

"But you see, Liz, it happens to be true.—Guess we've got her hanging in the ropes, eh, Commissioner?" Fred's smile radiated across the table, making everything all right. "But I'll hand it to you, Liz, you're a gallant little arguer.—Isn't this wonderful pie? I'll bet the cream is an inch thick, and all off the place, isn't it, Vincent?" he said to the host.

"I'm *not* hanging in the ropes," Elizabeth said. "I'm in the right. Don't you know I'm in the right?"

But Fred was talking to the host, and all down the table she saw amused or curious or hostile eyes being turned away from her and conversations being resumed. She turned around in her chair and faced the Commissioner. She could tell that he was ready to start in again. But from across the table his wife spoke.

"Ray, dear, aren't you going to drink your coffee? It's such good coffee."

Then there was a fluttering of napkins and they were all leaving the table. They wandered out into the great hall that ran from the front of the house to the back. The host was speaking to Elizabeth.

"Let's go on out on to the porch, shall we? It's real mild this evening, like a spring night."

The others were going in groups into the drawing-room. The host and Elizabeth and Fred's wife, Vera Wilkins, went out on to the broad porch and sat down.

"My, it's pretty," the host said. "Would either of you like a coat?"

He called to the colored man and sent him for Vera's coat. Elizabeth felt burning hot. She stared blindly at the great dark sky full of winter stars. The broad countryside fell away from the house in easy swells. Vera and the host talked. The night was soft, peaceful and vast, and there was no sound in it. Everything was peace, everything was comfortable, everything was pleasant in this place.

After a while the front door opened and Fred came out with some others.

"Got to make an early start," he said. Vera got up.

The Commissioner came out of the light-flooded doorway. Elizabeth saw his silhouette; he was coming straight to her. But his wife stepped out of the group on the porch and laid her hand on his arm. She laughed. Her voice was very feminine.

"No arguing, now, Ray!" she said. "Bedtime."

She steered him away to the railing to look at the stars.

Every one drifted upstairs. Elizabeth and Pete went into their room and Pete shut the door. The beds were turned down, the curtains were drawn.

"You certainly got into a row tonight," Pete said pleasantly, taking off his coat. "You ought not to do that, you know. With strangers. Every one thought you were a Communist. Practically. This isn't like staying with friends, where they know all about you. And you were pretty mad, there."

She turned to him passionately.

"But did you hear what he said? About Hemingway's book? About the Spanish Revolutionists? Why, he's a Fascist. I didn't know there were people like that, here. Don't you see how important it is?"

"Sure, sure," he said. "But you want to go easy with strangers. It was sort of embarrassing for Fred and Vera, you know; they brought us here. I mean, *I* know what you're talking about, and you know how I feel about the Spanish thing. But there are lots of other points of view, and you heard one of 'em tonight. The Commissioner just doesn't feel the way you and I do, that's all. I lost over four dollars," he said, emptying his pockets, "playing backgammon with him, tonight. Thought I better kind of soothe him down."

"You did?" she asked. "Pete, do you know what kind of a Commissioner he is? I don't."

"One of the Commissioners of Education, he said."

"Oh, Pete! It's shameful! What's going to happen if people like him are running the education in this country? What's going to happen?"

"Hey, calm down," Pete said. "He's kind of a nice guy when you get to know him. Personally. Of course I agree with you. But, see, this is a club, place where you've got to get along with the people you meet. That's all I mean. Keep the soft pedal on when you're with people who don't share your opinions."

"I know," she said.

When Pete was in bed she opened the window and looked out into the soft, infinitely still, Southern night. No sound anywhere. 'No war or battle sound Was heard the world around.' But that was not true. On the other side of the world it was not true. There was no silence there.

She got into bed and lay in the darkness trying to make her mind a blank and go to sleep. Twice she smoked a cigarette in the dark, and put out the stub quietly. She could see the calm stars in the square of night made by the window. After a long time she got up and fetched herself a glass of water. Getting back into bed she knocked over the ashtray and it clattered on the floor.

"Aren't you asleep yet?" Pete said sleepily.

"No, I can't seem to sleep."

She heard him turning over in bed.

"Not still stewing about the Spanish, are you?" he mumbled.

"No, not that."

"We've got to get off early. Better get some sleep. It'll all come out in the wash."

No, not the Spanish any more. Her mind had raked feverishly all through what she had said, what the man had said, and all that mattered now were the things she had not thought of to say. They mattered terribly. She would never have a chance now to say them to him. But what mattered more was what she had not known to say. She sat up in bed drinking the water in the dark, thinking, I don't know anything. I know I'm in the right, but I don't know anything. If I had known dates, and places, and facts, I could have annihilated him. I could have made him see. I know I'm right. But I don't know enough about it.

1941

THOSE ARE AS BROTHERS

The long, clear American summer passed slowly, dreaming over the Connecticut valley and the sound square houses under the elms and the broad living fields and over the people there that came and went and lay and sat still, with purpose and without but free, moving in and out of their houses of their own will, free to perceive the passage of the days through the different summer months and the smells and the sun and the rain and the high days and the brooding days, as was their right to do, without fear and without apprehension.

On the front lawn of the white house on the river-bank the two little boys came out every morning and dug holes and hammered nails into boards and pushed the express wagon around filled with rocks; their skins were filled with the sun, with the season, and they played all day, humming tuneless songs under their breath. In June their mother came out and watched them from the hammock under the maple tree, but in July the tension was easing out of her muscles and she began to laugh at the things they did and when they came across to her to show her turtles they had found, or delivering rocks at her station, she got up freely and without looking behind her and played their games with them for a little while. Up the road at the gardener's cottage of the big house where nobody lived, the gardener, who was unmarried, a short stout man who was a Jewish refugee, tended the borders of the garden and painted the long white fence and worked on the driveway; in the summer morning sun he sang too, in German, as he did his neat work.

In the evenings after supper when it was dusk and the only light was left in the red sky on the other side of the river, he would come walking down the road to the house on the river-bank, to call on the German governess who took care of the two little boys. His footsteps could be heard walking, hard and quick, down the road. Fräulein would be sitting on the stone front steps. He would stop short in the road in front of her, dressed in his clean clothes, his body round and compact and his black hair brushed down, and bow. "Good evening," he said. "How are you?" Fräulein said. Then he would come and sit beside her on the steps and the conversation would continue in German, because although he could understand sufficient English, Mr. Loeb could talk hardly any.

Fräulein was friendly to him because she was a friendly woman, but always a little superior because he was a Jew and she belonged to a family of small merchants in Cologne. She was sorry for him because he was a refugee and because he had been in concentration camp in Germany, and it was necessary to be kind to those who had suffered under that Hitler, but a Jew was a Jew; there were right German names and wrong German names; Fräulein's name was Strasser. She did not mind speaking her mind to him on the subject of the Nazis who were ruining Germany. There were no other Germans about, in this place, as there were in the winter in New York, who might be on the other side; to them she had only praise to speak of Hitler, for after all her family were still in Cologne and people suffered at home for what was said by their relatives in America—if it came to the wrong ears. But Mr. Loeb was a Jew and safe to talk to, to tell exactly what she thought of those people, those Nazis. He never said anything much back, just listened and nodded; his face was round and florid.

In the evenings Mrs. Mason sat in a garden chair out on the lawn and listened to the crickets in the marshes and watched the red fade beyond the river. Or, if it was one of the nights when she could not enjoy the evening sounds, the smells, when a little of the tension and fear clung to her mind and twisted it about, she would sit inside in the living-room, on one of the chintz-covered chairs under a light with a book to read. She read all sorts of books, novels, detective stories, and the papers and magazines that were full of the news about Europe. On the bad nights, the nights when peace was not quite at her command, she noticed that whatever she read seemed curiously to be about her, always to fit her situation, no matter what it was meant to be about. And especially all the books, the articles, about the Nazis. She did not know if it was morbid of her, but she could not help always feeling he had stood for the thing that was the Nazis, that spirit, and she had been a country being conquered, a country dominated by those methods. It was so like; so very like. When she read of those tortured in concentration camp, of those dispossessed and smashed to the Nazi will, she knew, she felt, how those people felt. She had been through a thing that was the same in microcosm. Her life was a tiny scale-model of the thing that was happening in Europe, the ruthless swallowing the helpless. By a miracle, by an overlooked shred of courage, she had escaped and was free here. She was a refugee like that man out there talking to Fräulein who had escaped too, by another miracle, for only miracles saved people from that spirit. In refuge peace and assurance were coming back slowly like strength to a sick body, and the fear, the terror that was once everything, was draining away drop by drop with the days of safety. The same thing must be happening to him, the man out there; confidence and a quietly beating heart, in this calm summer country where there was nothing any more to fear.

Only the habit of fear; only the uncontrollably quickened pulse for no reason any more, the fear that came out of nothing because fear was a poison in the blood and passed in and out of the heart again and again and again before it was finally worked out, if it ever was. Perhaps, she thought, it never was. If you were infected virulently enough with that poison perhaps it never left you, but recurred forever like some tropical fevers, forever part of you and in your blood though you were a thousand miles away from the source of infection. He was nearly a thousand miles away, too, and there was no reason why she need ever see him again; but perhaps the fear would stay with her though there was nothing left to fear.

As the summer wandered by the young man from across the river came over more and more often to see Mrs. Mason. He came in a boat with an outboard motor; she would hear it buzzing across the water, and the sound of the motor cut as he came up to the dock; then there would be silence while he tied up, and then he would come walking up the lawn, very tall with his fair hair cut short all over, catching the light from the sunset in the quiet dusk.

"Hello, Fräulein," he would say as he came up the steps. "Hello, Mr. Loeb."

Mr. Loeb always got to his feet and bowed smartly. Fräulein said "Good evening, Mr. Worthington." Then he would come in and the screen door would slam and the sound of German being spoken quietly would begin again and he would walk into the living-room and grin at Mrs. Mason.

He used to sit in the chintz-covered chairs with his long legs stuck out in front of him, smoking cigarettes. Sometimes he took her out on the smooth dark river in his boat. Once they struck a log in the darkness on the water and she started violently and cried out. "What are you afraid of?" he asked her. "You're so lovely, I don't see why you should ever be afraid of anything." It was impossible to explain to him that she was not afraid of the log, nor of the water, nor of anything; that it was only a reflex that she was helpless to control, without reason; just fear. "You know I'd take care of you, if anything ever happened, don't you?" he said. "If you'd just let me." And she knew he would, but that did not make any difference. Nobody could help because nobody could possibly understand the irrationality, the uncontrollability, of fear when it was like this, in the blood. Any help had to come from within, the self learning through days, perhaps years, of peace that nothing of all that that was over would ever happen again. Talking to it was no good; no young man's protectiveness penetrated to it; it had to learn slowly by itself.

The young man was falling in love with Mrs. Mason through that long summer. But it was inconceivable that she should fall in love with him. No matter how kind and strong he was, no matter how much more each day she saw him she saw how good he was, how there was none of that spirit in him, it was inconceivable that her muscles could ever grow slack enough for her to look at him quietly, a man, and fall in love with him. She had been naked once, and vulnerable to everything that had happened to her; now, and perhaps forever, something in her clutched the coverings of tension, of reserve, of aloneness, having learned what happened when they were dropped. Her mind could say that it would not happen with this young man, who was all gentleness and generosity; but the inner thing did not believe that, it believed nothing except what it had learned.

When they sat on the lawn smoking in the twilight, or inside in the big cool living-room, the German talk went on quietly on the front steps. Mr. Loeb was a quiet man, and Fräulein did most of the talking. She told him when she had said her say about the Nazis, about the children, how Hugh was as good as an angel and Dickie was just as different, a sweet child but always up to something, just a busybody. The big June-bugs and the moths banged against the screen door behind them, and the light from the house came soft and yellow through the door and lay upon the stone slabs of the steps.

After a while, when she knew him pretty well, Fräulein told him about that Mr. Mason, what a bad man he was and how glad she was that they did not live there any more.

"That poor lady," she said. "She took plenty of unhappiness from him, I can tell you. My, what a place! I can't tell you what a man he was. You wouldn't believe it. She never said anything, but I knew what went on. I don't mean maybe beating her, I know husbands get mad sometimes and beat their wives, that's all right, but that man! I tried to keep the children from knowing anything about it, and they certainly saw him little enough; and she helped me to do it. Not that I ever discussed it with her. She's that kind of a lady, very proud, and I never saw her cry, only heard her sometimes, nights when he was very bad. She had such a look in her eyes in those days; she doesn't have it any more. I can tell you I'm glad she got rid of him. In this country it's very easy to divorce, you know."

"Yes," Mr. Loeb said quietly in the darkness.

"Well, she's got rid of him now and I'm glad. It would have killed her, a life like that, and my poor children, what would have happened to them? She's got rid of him, thank God, and now she can just forget about him and be happy."

Mr. Loeb said nothing. He didn't smoke because he was saving money out of what he earned as a gardener. He just sat there in the darkness, and he smelled a little of sweat. Fräulein made allowances for his smell, knowing that he was a laborer and a Jew.

In the middle of the summer Hugh had a birthday and there was a big cake with seven candles, and one to grow on. Mr. Worthington came across the river for the little party, and both children were allowed to sit up till ten. After supper Mr. Loeb came walking down the road as usual, and Mrs. Mason called him in.

"Won't you have a piece of cake?" she said, holding out a plate to him. "Here's a piece with a candle in it."

Mr. Loeb made his bow and took the plate. Mrs. Mason smiled at him and he smiled at her and they did not say anything.

"We're going to play games in the living-room," Mrs. Mason said. "Do you know any games, Mr. Loeb?"

The children were wild with excitement and ran round and round the room. Mr. Worthington showed Hugh a game with a piece of paper and a pencil, where he could guess any number of a total if he knew the right hand numbers of the other lines. It was very mysterious. Dickie didn't understand at all, and stamped and yelled to make them stop and do something else.

"I show you," Mr. Loeb said and hesitated. He asked Fräulein how to say something in English.

"He shows you a card-trick," Fräulein said. Mr. Loeb's face was round and red and smiling. He took the pack of cards Mrs. Mason handed him and took out two aces.

"You see," he said to Hugh. "This is the farmer's cow." He pointed to the ace of hearts. "And this is Mrs. Sisson's cow." Mrs. Sisson owned the big place where Mr. Loeb was gardener. The card was the ace of clubs.

"Now I put them back again," Mr. Loeb said, shuffling the pack. "Now. Which cow you want to see? The farmer's cow? Mrs. Sisson's cow?"

Hugh deliberated, standing on one leg.

"Mrs. Sisson's cow," he decided.

"Then go to the barn and look for it!" cried Mr. Loeb.

The children were enchanted. They screamed and rolled on the floor; Dickie kept crying, "Go to the barn and look for it!" Everybody was laughing.

"That was a very nice trick," Mrs. Mason said.

The children, after a while, fell to playing with the cards in a corner on the floor. Their two little round butts stuck up in the air, and their two little boys' heads were close together. From time to time they would break apart and shout about something, then go back to their game.

Mr. Loeb finished his cake and took out a folded handkerchief and wiped his mouth. He put the plate down carefully on the desk near him.

"Thank you very much," he said to Mrs. Mason. He was still standing up, politely. Now he moved towards the door.

"Don't go away," she said. "Stay and talk. Sit down, please. You're part of the party."

"Thank you very much," he said.

"Understand you had a bad time with those Nazi fellows," Mr. Worthington said gently. "Were you really in one of those concentration camps?"

"Yes, I was. It was very bad."

"I was in Germany once," Mr. Worthington said. "The thing I kept noticing was, they were such damned bad losers. One night I went out drinking beer with a lot of fellows, me and a Frenchman I knew. They seemed all right guys. But about two in the morning when we'd all drunk a lot of beer one of them said, let's have a foot-race. Down the main street there, it was all quiet. Well, we started, and in a minute or two this Frenchman was way in front, and I was just behind. They just quit. Started walking along. Wouldn't admit they'd been racing. But if they'd been ahead you can bet they'd have rubbed it in. They want to be on top, that's it, and they take it out on the fellow underneath. If *they* get licked, they won't admit they were playing at all."

"Yes," said Mr. Loeb.

"You'd see fellows pick fights all the time, late at night, but you never saw them pick a fight unless they thought they could win. I played a lot of tennis over there, and of course, you know, American tennis. . . . They just wouldn't play again. Fellow over here would say, 'Let's play a return match and I'll lick you.' Not them."

"Yes," said Mr. Loeb.

"Those concentration camps, now. Just the fellows on top doing it to the fellows underneath. It must have been a job keeping your courage up."

"I did not keep my courage up," Mr. Loeb said.

Mr. Worthington looked embarrassed.

"I don't blame you," he said. "The things you hear about those places, they just break your spirit, I guess."

"Yes," Mr. Loeb said.

Fräulein sat under the light with her hair parted smoothly from the middle. She looked from Mr. Worthington to Mr. Loeb with self-assured eyes, not entirely understanding nor especially interested. Mr. Worthington twisted his long legs around one side of his chair.

"Anyway," he said. "It's all over for you and I bet you're damned glad. You can just forget about all that stuff. This is a free country and you can do what you please and nobody can hurt you. It's all over and finished for you."

"For many it is not," Mr. Loeb said after a minute.

"Yeah, that's right. Poor devils."

"But," Mr. Loeb said hesitantly, "I have thought, I do not know how you say it; the more and more that are all the time—surrendered?"

"How do you mean?"

"He means oppressed," Mrs. Mason said. Mr. Loeb bowed to her.

"The more and more that are oppressed all the time, the more there are who know together the same thing, who have it together. When it is time and something happens to make it possible, there is something that all of these have had together and that will make them fight together. And now Frenchmen too, Belgians too, Flemings. If you have been in a concentration camp it is more together than that you might be of different countries. I speak very badly," Mr. Loeb said.

"No," Mrs. Mason said. "A common cause."

"Please?" Mr. Loeb asked. Fräulein spoke to him in German.

"I do not think that it is what you call cause, just. But knowing the concentration camps together. And what happens. That they were all crying together and no—courage. It makes them love."

"I don't see what you mean, exactly," Mr. Worthington said.

"I do," said Mrs. Mason. "They all remember the same thing together."

"Yes," Mr. Loeb said.

It seemed to her for a minute that she saw a sea of faces upturned, with the same look in all the thousands of them, the anguish, the terrible humiliation, the fear. It was a vast and growing sea, a great host of the tortured and the outcast, who had known ultimate fear instead of death and had been together into the valley of living hell. Separately each of them had known fear, had felt it burning inexorably in their veins, but now that they were all together the common fear became something larger, because there were so many millions of them, because they were not alone; it was set in dignity like a brand of brotherhood upon their lifted faces, and there were more of them, and more of them; if there were any more it would be so large a part of all the people that there were at all, it would become strong by its numbers, and unshakable because of its suffering shared. This was something that she had never thought of before.

The children were sent off to bed at last, and Mrs. Mason went up to say goodnight to them. They lay in the two cot-beds holding still while they said their prayers and then releasing into a last wild activity before the light should be turned out on them. She pushed them back under their sheets and kissed them. When she came downstairs again Mr. Worthington was sitting alone in the living-room and the German voices were coming in softly through the screen door, from out in the warm darkness.

"Hello," Mr. Worthington said.

"Hello," she said. He reached out and took her hand as she passed where he sat, and kissed it. She stood still for a minute, and smiled at him.

"I love you from now," he said. She went on looking at his face, bent over her hand but with the eyes looking up at her. After a minute the consciousness of what he said, where she was, the consciousness of herself, came back over her and she drew away her hand. But for a moment she had lived in freedom, without watching herself.

In August Mrs. Sisson came back from California and opened the big house, and Mr. Loeb was much busier, doing all the things that Mrs. Sisson wanted done. Mrs. Sisson was a woman of fifty with black hair and a big strong figure, who was very particular and liked her big place tended to perfection. Mrs. Mason did not know her except very slightly—to wave to when Mrs. Sisson drove along the road in her big black car with her initials on the Connecticut license-plate, and to speak to in a neighborly way when they met in the village. Sometimes now Fräulein started to tell her things about Mrs. Sisson, how badly she treated all her servants, that she didn't even feed them properly, and had had three different waitresses in just the time she had been back.

"Nobody wants to work for a woman like that," Fräulein said.

But Mrs. Mason thought she ought not to listen to gossip, and did not let Fräulein talk about it much.

One afternoon she came out of the house on to the lawn. Mr. Loeb was standing at the gate, talking to Fräulein. The two little boys were playing at the end of the lawn. Mr. Loeb was talking very fast in German, his voice much higher than usual, and Fräulein was looking at him and from time to time saying something calmly. Mrs. Mason walked down to the gate.

"Hello, Mr. Loeb," she said.

Mr. Loeb made his bow, but he looked distracted. His eyes were contracted and his face was even redder than generally. Mrs. Mason thought he looked almost as if he were going to cry. He looked at her and began to speak in English but stumbled and was silent.

"That Mrs. Sisson," Fräulein said. "She says to him she will report him to the Refugee Committee in New York so that he will never be able to get a job again."

"What did he do?"

"Nothing! She talked to him the way she talks to all the people who work for her, she bawled him out, he doesn't paint the fence quick enough, she says he's too slow. He's a foolish man, he pays attention to what she says. I tell him he ought to shrug his shoulders, what does he care, as long as he gets his pay."

"I cannot have her speak to me that way!" Mr. Loeb broke out. "I cannot have her call me those things she says. I cannot . . ."

"He pays attention," Fräulein said. "He gets his feelings hurt too easy. I tell him, what does he care what she says? She's nothing. But he says to her, she can't speak to him that way, he cannot have her speak to him that way, he cannot stay and work for her if she talks like that. So she says all right, she's going to report him to the Refugee Committee."

"What can she say?"

"She was terrible angry," Mr. Loeb said. "She will say I do not work. She will say I am a no-good worker. She will say I speak to her fresh."

He looked at Mrs. Mason with his frightened eyes, and she nodded at him. Their eyes met and she nodded again.

"I'll go up and talk to her," Mrs. Mason said. She did not feel at all afraid to do that, suddenly. She was not thinking about how she felt.

Fräulein shrugged.

"I don't think it makes any difference, you excuse me, Mrs. Mason. That Mrs. Sisson, she doesn't want Mr. Loeb to work for her any more because he talks back to her, and she writes the letter anyway."

"I'll write to the Refugee Committee too," she said. "I'll tell them that I know all about Mr. Loeb and he's a good worker and a nice man. But I'll go up and talk to her now anyway."

Mr. Loeb leaned against the fence and looked at her. She came out of the gate into the road.

"Thank you very much," Mr. Loeb said in his foreign, formal voice.

She smiled at him. The tension had gone away from his eyes, the look of fear that she recognized had gone.

"You don't have to worry, you know," she said. "I wouldn't ever let anything happen to you."

1941

THE MARCHING FEET

We sat in the garden behind one of the Palladian brick houses on the lawn of the university. It was early summer and red rambler roses and white hung dripping over the serpentine wall around the garden. There was a mockingbird in the crêpe myrtle by the gate. You could smell honeysuckle already, spreading everywhere through the soft, warm Virginia air. The ladies smoked, and knitted for Britain, and sipped long drinks made of iced tea and ginger ale, flavored with mint, and a strong stick of whiskey.

On the other side of the house, out on the lawn, the three companies of the Naval Reserve unit of the college were drilling. They would march up the lawn and then you could hear nothing but the mockingbird and the ladies, talking. Then the men would march down again and you could hear the rhythmic beat of their marching and the hoarse, barked commands.

"I can't say I approve," Miss Mayson said. "Drilling on the lawn."

"I wonder what Mr. Jefferson would think if he could see this place now," Mrs. Gregory said.

"He'd approve," Mrs. Leith said. "After all, what you hear now is just preparation to defend democracy. Reckon Mr. Jefferson would approve of that."

Mrs. Gregory's man Marshall came out into the garden in a white coat, carrying a pitcher full of the iced mixture. He filled up the glasses.

"'Do Marshall," Miss Mayson said.

"How you, Miss Mayson," Marshall said.

"How's that brother of yours? Still in jail?"

Marshall grinned and his white teeth flashed. "No, Ma'am. He's been workin' down to Miz Templeton's."

"Well, you tell him to behave himself or I'll tell Miz Templeton all about him, hear?"

"Yes, Ma'am!" Marshall carried the pitcher back into the house.

"This is a heavenly combination," I said, shaking the ice in my drink.

"Isn't it?" Mrs. Gregory said. "Sue Carney's Lucius showed Marshall how to fix it when he came to help out for the party I gave Garden Week."

Mrs. Leith laughed. "How'd you make out with Lucius?" she said.

Mrs. Gregory laughed too. "He was pretty uppity when he came. Saying he wanted this and he wanted that. I let him know he couldn't behave like that in my house. He is a real good cook, though, practically a chef. If he didn't have the Hampton in his system, he'd be all right."

"One thing I have no use for, it's an educated niggra," Mrs. Leith said.

"I thought Rosalie was coming this afternoon, Judy," Miss Mayson said.

"She is," Mrs. Gregory said. "She's bringing her house guest."

Miss Mayson exclaimed, "Oh! That Beatrice Steinberger? Well! I heard she was coming."

"Have you read her book?" Mrs. Gregory asked.

"Certainly have," Miss Mayson said. "It's just as good as the reviews said it was."

Mrs. Leith nodded. "Rosalie says she's a great woman. She's Rosalie's celebrity."

"One thing I always say about this place," Mrs. Gregory said. "If you wait long enough, you meet all the celebrities without budging away. They all come here."

"Isn't she a—well, a Jew?" Miss Mayson asked.

"Well, yes, with that name," Mrs. Gregory said. "But most superior, I'm sure. Not everybody could have written the things she's written."

"No, I expect not. Of course, there are Jews and Jews," Miss Mayson said. "My sister in New York says you meet some you'd hardly know were Jews. Cultivated, well bred, dignified—"

"Reckon we don't get to see the best type down here. Just that riffraff that's ruining the college," Mrs. Gregory said.

"Why can't they stay up North and go to their own colleges," Miss Mayson demanded, "not come flocking down here?"

"Because they know they can do here cheaper, that's why," Mrs. Leith said. "They pare down to the last dollar and get all they can for as little as possible. Never knew a Jew who didn't try to get something for nothing."

"I wish you could hear Lucy on the subject," Miss Mayson said. "After she had let her rooms to Jewish students for a year. She said she had to have the place completely fumigated."

"They're so scheming; it makes me mad when they take the scholarships that are intended for our own boys," Mrs. Leith said.

"Of course, they're apt to be brighter," I said.

"Brains aren't everything," Miss Mayson said, staring at me. "There's things like honor, and decency, and a traditional way of life."

"I heard the Givney place was being sold to some Jews from up North," Mrs. Leith said.

"Now, there I draw the line!" Mrs. Gregory cried. "I mean, I haven't any prejudice against Jews, but why can't they stay where they belong? With their own kind? Buying our places and coming to live in our country is one too many."

"They're going to restore the place, I hear, back to what it used to be," Mrs. Leith said.

"I know, but money isn't everything." Mrs. Gregory took a sip of her drink. "Our forefathers settled this place and it's our inheritance. We don't want people just as different from ourselves as—as Chinese settling here. I'm all for the Jews being treated properly, and of course it makes you perfectly sick to hear of the atrocities that have gone on abroad, but they *are* treated properly over here. I just don't want them coming down and taking over our country."

The gate in the wall opened and Rosalie Jackson came in with a tall, slender, dark woman.

"This is Miss Steinberger," she said, introducing her guest to the ladies.

"What a beautiful garden," Miss Steinberger said. She sat down in a canvas chair. She looked like a Persian princess: the long, olive face, the dark, almond-shaped eyes, the nose like a delicate scimitar.

"It *is* lovely," Mrs. Gregory said. She called to Marshall and he came out with two fresh glasses.

"Have you been seeing our country, Miss Steinberger?" Miss Mayson asked. "Have you seen Monticello? Of course, we think the university is really the gem."

"I think I do, too," Miss Steinberger said. "It's a perfect monument to Jefferson."

All the ladies looked pleased.

"We've been reading your new book, Miss Steinberger," Mrs. Gregory said. "We think it's wonderful. It's so interesting to meet you."

"Thank you very much."

"It was a pleasure to read the things you said about that man Hitler," Miss Mayson said. "I can assure you we all agree with you one hundred per cent. I hope the things you said make him writhe."

"We all care especially about democracy down here," Mrs. Leith said, "as this might be said to be the cradle of democracy."

"You know," Mrs. Gregory said suddenly, "I've always thought how nice it was that this is such a relatively small place—if they *did* come over here, you know, and there actually was bombing. I mean I always felt they'd probably overlook us. But Henry says this would be the first place they'd bomb. They'd want to destroy this place because it is a symbol of democracy. Isn't that awful to think of?"

"Imagine the Rotunda bombed," Miss Mayson said in a low voice.

"The Rotunda's burned down twice in its history," Mrs. Leith said vigorously. "I reckon we could build it up once more. Look at the British. We've got the same spirit they've got. You can always put a building back."

"Yes, you can," Miss Steinberger said. "And I am sure you would."

The marching out on the lawn was growing louder. They were marching away from drill towards the house. The ladies fell silent and listened as the marching feet came nearer, nearer, and the hoarse voice called, "Hep-two-three-four. Hep-two-three-four." The voice grew closer; the tramp grew louder and harder, coming down the lawn.

"You know, there's something unpleasant to me about hearing marching get nearer like that," Rosalie Jackson said. "It's silly. It almost upsets me. Once, when I was about fourteen, Daddy and Mother took me to South America—do you remember, Judy? Daddy was going down to Chile about nitrates, something. And you know, when they cross the line—the equator—they put on a kind of show, have a court of trial, with Neptune and his consort and a whole lot of passengers dressed up like devils, and they drag all the passengers who've never crossed the line before into court and sentence them—they smear them up with paint, and throw them in the ship's pool. All in fun, of course. It's a big party. But living down here, I'd never learned to swim. I didn't tell anybody, but I was terrified when I was told about what was going to happen. I knew they would throw me in the pool and I would drown. Isn't it silly the way you are when you're a child? I shut myself in my stateroom. It opened right on deck. Then I heard them coming. I could hear the marching feet coming nearer along the deck. At each stateroom of a passenger who hadn't crossed the line before, they'd stop, and there'd be a great to-do while they dragged out the victim—laughing, of course. They came nearer and nearer. That was the only time in my life I've ever been terrified. I felt sick with it. Well, they got to my door and I went with them, knowing I was going to die, and they brought me before Neptune and he sentenced me to be ducked in the pool, and just at the last moment I gasped out, 'I can't swim.' They all laughed, and one of the devils reached down and scooped up a handful of water and sprinkled it on my head and said, 'I christen thee an old salt.' And that was all there was to it. But I still get that feeling of absolute panic when I hear marching coming nearer and nearer. Like this."

The marchers were leaving the lawn now and coming down the narrow alley between Mrs. Gregory's house and the one next to it. The tramping came closer and closer to the gate of the garden. Every one sat still, in silence, listening.

Miss Steinberger glanced at the faces of the ladies around her.

"It sounds like something else to me," she said. "It sounds the way they would sound when they came. The marching getting nearer, and then the halt outside the door, and the knock on the door. Coming for one."

"What?" Mrs. Leith said. "What coming?"

"The Storm Troopers," Miss Steinberger said, and smiled. "Or whatever they would call them here."

"Here!" Miss Mayson cried. "My dear Miss Steinberger. As if Fascism could ever come to this country! We'll never have Storm Troopers here, I can assure you."

Miss Steinberger shrugged her shoulders delicately. She smiled again and said nothing. The marching feet had passed down the alley now and were growing fainter, in a moment had gone.

Marshall came out of the house with a fresh pitcher of drinks and began to refill the ladies' glasses, walking on the grass behind them, leaning over and pouring neatly into their glasses so as not to interfere with their conversation.

1941

SUNDAY—1913

THE VERY FIRST thing when Laura awoke in the morning was that terrible, queer burning in her feet and ankles—almost too much to bear. It was as if she had walked miles and miles yesterday, when really she hadn't to do anything at all; darling Morton always said, if she mentioned the burning feeling, "Now, sit on a cushion and sew a fine seam, Puddykins." It wasn't anything she did. But it was so—disappointing, to wake up and not find it gone, to feel the soles of her feet like fire and the fire running up her ankles. It was four weeks, no, almost five; five on Tuesday it would be, since it had begun. And Dr. Palfrey said, nothing; no rheumatism, not a pretty young lady like you.

It was wicked to go on feeling sorry for herself. The most fortunate girl ever. The thing was, when you woke up in the morning and started to think wrong, horrid wicked thoughts, to count your blessings. Laura had heard an old lady say, when she was a child, that the thing to do on awaking in the morning was to count your blessings. It was wonderful how things you had heard long ago suddenly came to have meaning for you. Counting blessings was such a tremendous help in the mornings. What was it that was so *terrible* about the mornings? It must be that she was a wicked girl, somehow.

Tonight she would pray to God to make her a better woman, with better thoughts. And darling Morton would pray too. In the meantime. . . . She opened her eyes to begin on the blessings.

This beautiful big room. She had always wanted a room with

a fireplace, in the days when she was poor, before Morton came riding like a knight to rescue her from making her own living. Once, when they were engaged, he had said as they sat on her little sofa, he holding her cold hand in his big hot one, "I'm your knight, come riding." That was a beautiful way to think of it and often she would close her eyes and try to see Morton in armor on a horse. Yes, she had always dreamed of a big beautiful room, and darling Morton had given it to her. Blessing number one. This room had turned out to have a big, a huge bed in it so that they could always, always be together. Mamma Gorton had bought the bed, so it was black walnut, but of course the house belonged to Mamma Gorton and everything in it was really hers. And there was always the fireplace and the lovely highboy. Laura looked at the highboy and spurred herself to forget her feet and enjoy it. It was such a beautiful, a pure, a crystalline, classic highboy.

Oh, a kind mother-in-law, and two Irish servants to do everything, and new friends here in Bleecker anxious to make things pleasant for Morton's bride, and plenty of money somewhere behind everything—oh, she *was* such a fortunate girl; she was, she was. And first and foremost and overwhelming everything, her big, loving, indulgent husband, such a wonderful good man and still like a boy about so many things, just a romping boy. "The love of a good man." That was another saying she had heard long ago and whose meaning had now suddenly become quite clear to her. Greater than any blessing for a woman was the love of a good man.

Laura lay still making the thankfulness form a kind of grateful arch in her mind. The trolley-cars clattered by on Tomkins Street—a morning sound, busy and yet sad to her, a sound that told her that she was in Bleecker. She heard the Billings' automobile being backed out of their garage. Oh, and an automobile to be thankful for; who would ever have thought when she was just a young poor orphan giving drawing-lessons in the city that she would ever have an automobile? It was as improbable as a balloon.

Only very well-to-do people had automobiles. She, Laura, was a well-to-do young bride. Just think.

Suddenly she was smothered, stifled; it was Morton waking up beside her, and he loved her so that his first thought in the morning was always to turn directly to her. It was so lovely in him. He was just like a big bear hugging her. He had thought of that too: "I'm just your teddy-bear," he liked to say, burrowing his tousled head. Laura lifted her face and gasped for a little breath of air, because he was *so* big and he loved her so much.

"It's Sunday, Puddy," he said now into her ear, mumbling her hair in his mouth. Puddy was short for Pudding. He said she was his sweet fat little Pudding. She was getting a little fatter, too. He didn't want his wife to look like a half-starved little crow; he wanted a plump little wife; he wanted . . . "Are you a happy little Mrs. Gorton this beautiful Sunday morning?" he breathed into her ear.

"Oh, *yes*," she said, trying with all her might to hug him back really hard, really appreciatively. "Just those old feet. . . ."

Now what made her say that? She knew it made darling Morton unhappy. He slackened his grasp around her. It made him unhappy because he hated to have her unhappy, and it made him feel he ought not to try just then to have a baby with her. Because after all Dr. Palfrey didn't know everything, and any time, any time, she might start to have a baby. Only Dr. Palfrey did say that after a year and a half it probably meant she couldn't, not ever. . . . But they could always keep trying. She had tried really, so hard, and prayed about it. And Morton said maybe it was only that God didn't mean for them to have a little baby quite yet. So if they kept trying. . . . But Dr. Palfrey said it; he said it. Never, never. . . .

Morton always jumped out of bed with a great bang and whirl of covers. That was one of the ways he was just like a little boy. He stood in his blue striped nightshirt and smiled down at her boyishly with his hair on end.

"Your boy will make the burny-burny go 'way," he said, just like a little child. "Your boy will be so careful of his Puddykins." She smiled hard back at him from the bed, trying to put into her face that she thought he was so sweet and so wonderful to her; to put it in so that it would show. Of course she felt it. But she knew her face didn't show things enough. It was a horrid, small, pale face. Morton would say, sometimes in the evenings, "Put your love in your face, little love. Show your knight that you just love him!" And she would try, actually push, make herself tense all over to show him that she was everything he wanted.

Morton pranced off to the bathroom down the hall, with a little glance over his shoulder to show her that he was prancing to cheer her up. She could hear the water running in the new shower-bath, hard; splashing. Two months ago they had had the shower-bath put in, above the regular tub. New, modern, splendid things all the time.

Four months ago Dr. Palfrey said she couldn't. One year ago they had come home from the wedding-trip—six wonderful months in Europe—and moved in with Mamma Gorton, into her big stucco house that looked like a little palace, with a tower and red tile roof and broad verandas, not for sitting on, but impressive as you came up Tomkins Street. The elegant Gorton house.—A year ago in Europe. All the pictures she had longed to see all her whole life, the Louvre, the Uffizi. Morton was so good to let her go so much when he didn't care for pictures. "Real masterpieces," he would say. "I can't believe my little Puddy *really* knows such a lot. Such a wise Puddy!" Those were the days when they had made up their secret, little language together. It was the way innocent, lisping children might talk to each other. He called her his Puddy, and she called him Teddy-bear, and Baby-boy. Once or twice she had wanted to slip off and go and really look at the pictures, just alone, not talking or even making sweet jokes—only looking and really seeing. But darling Morton had been so hurt. He hadn't understood at all, and had looked at her like an injured little boy one time, and the other time his other way, when he looked like the manager of the Royal Rug Co. So of course she hadn't gone alone. It had been unwifely of her in the first place. Morton wanted his little wife close, close to him always; when he was in the office of the Royal Rug Co. was the only time they had to be separated. And that had been their honeymoon, the time for being terribly close; all day and all night, together like two little playing children. Europe one year ago.

It was funny how when she was alone nowadays she kept putting things in their place in time. This so many months ago, that so many years. It was as if she was measuring her distance from all the events in her life. One year and a half ago they were married. In the city, with her aunt from Newark there to represent her side, looking dingy and like nobody against Mamma Gorton in her brocade and jet, and the pointed cap with the long black veil that she wore in faithful mourning for Papa Gorton, whose picture hung on the wall of the staircase. Laura wondered if Papa Gorton would have been any different; he had been dead ten years.—Different from what? she asked herself sharply.

And two years ago she had been living, quite alone, in two little rooms in the city, going out and giving drawing-lessons to children, at people's houses, and making just enough money to see her way clear. An orphan, with nobody but the Newark aunt, and no prospects. Just hoping to get more drawing pupils so that she could save a little for her old age. Of course there had been Jeff. Jeff. He had been in her class in advanced painting, long, long ago, and he had stuck by her and come to see her always, and brought her bunches of flowers although he was even poorer than she was. She couldn't have married Jeff, that was clear enough now, although in those days she used to wonder if perhaps some day he wouldn't get started towards success. Where was Jeff now? Maybe he's beginning to make a good living, a little voice said obscurely inside her.

Oh but then the great day had come when she had met Morton. At the house of Mrs. Grayson, the one with the three daughters who were beginning water-color. He had come in to look at their progress, and been very kind and polite to the drawing-teacher, and it had been so terribly exciting when he asked if he could see her home. And then everything had begun, the calls and the boxes of violets and red roses, and going to the theatre, and then the evenings on her little sofa discussing Morton's ideals—surely it was quite proper with her landlady, dear Mrs. Fay, like a mother and in the very next room. And then they had become engaged, and the whole world had changed. She had left her poor little teaching life and met Mamma Gorton and the aunts and uncles, and put her savings, such as they were, into a dress to be married in and two other nice dresses, and they were married.

And Jeff had congratulated her. "You struck it rich, all right. I wouldn't have thought it of you." She didn't like the way he said it, or his choice of words, but Jeff always meant well and couldn't have intended to be rude. What had happened to Jeff since? He hadn't come to the wedding. She would never know, now, what became of Jeff.

Old days, old friends. She had been like a sleeping princess, whom the prince had awakened with a kiss to a whole new world of elegance and comfort. Morton had suggested that lovely picture too. Lucky, lucky, lucky. And all in the space of two years.

Two years in the other direction, forward—she would still be here, right here in this huge bed, with everything still there, not a dream, not spirited away; no, just the same. The weeks would pass each with its Sunday, the months, the years, and she would be here, Morton Gorton's wife, growing older with him and loving him just as hard as she could. She would have forever the love of a good man. She ought to express her gratitude somehow.

"Thank you, God," she said out loud.

When Morton came back from the bathroom she got up and washed and dressed for church. She wore her new blue poplin, with a white jabot. Her yellow hair was hard to comb and hurt when she pulled the brush across it. The romping that Morton loved in bed was very tangling to her hair. She made it neat and pinned up the back so that one fat curl stuck out from the knot the way he liked it.

He waited for her so that they could go down together to breakfast. It was one of their little rites, every day. He put his arm around her waist and they walked along the upstairs hall past the photographs of European churches, and down the stairs with their heavy carved rail, to the big front hall and into the dining-room. Mamma Gorton was already there, sitting in her high-backed chair at the end of the table.

Laura took her place at one side. Morton came behind them and laid one hand on his wife's shoulder, one on his mother's. They bent their heads. Morton's voice was very rapid and devout. Laura had never been able quite to make out the words.

"Oh Lord bless us and lave us to this thy bountitory use in cane to thy loving service for Christ's sake."

Then Laura and Mamma Gorton both said "Amen" reverently and with a great deal of cheerful noise Morton sat down at the head of the table. He stretched out his hand along the table for Laura to take.

"Little wife; little mother," he said.

"Hm," Mamma Gorton said. Her head was long and oval like a large egg. She had very bright, small eyes. Her iron-gray hair was thin and drawn straight up to the top of her head in a small bun. There were hairs growing out of her chin, but they in no way diminished the impressiveness of her appearance. Today she was dressed in a dull black satin dress with white net ruchings at the neck. A jet and gold cross hung from a ribbon around her neck, over the deep folds of loose skin at her throat's base. On her old hands were three diamond rings, large and sparkling, and they glittered in the Sunday morning light as the hands moved incessantly over the top of the table, picking up crumbs if there were any or making the gesture if there were not. Mamma Gorton would moisten her forefinger-tip with her tongue absently and then tap it about over the table, and the crumbs it picked up she would eat.

Because it was Sunday morning breakfast was an even heavier meal than usual. There was melon first and then creamed chipped beef, pancakes, three kinds of bread, and boiled eggs. The eggs were brought in in a silver bowl of hot water and set with the coffee service that stood before Mamma Gorton. She asked them each how many eggs they would like, and cracked them into cups which were handed to Morton and Laura. Laura took one egg. Morton took three. Mamma Gorton poured out the coffee from an immense urn, into cups that were decorated with blurry pink roses. They were passed by the maid.

Laura stirred her coffee round and round. For no particular reason she was thinking of the cup she used to drink her coffee from where she lived in the city and worked. It was an old cup that she had bought from the window of a second-hand store. It was white and very thin, with a picture in clear black of a country-house surrounded by ancient trees. She was very fond of the cup, and she used to make her breakfast and put it on the little table by the window and drink her coffee. The picture was repeated on the bottom of the inside of the cup, and she enjoyed like a child drinking up her coffee and coming upon the picture. The cup had been left with the rest of her paltry things when she left her rooms for the Gorton house.

"My little wife must eat more," Morton said. "We need flesh on those little chicken-bones."

Mamma Gorton looked at Laura with her bright strong eyes, and it seemed to Laura that the old lady could see her straight through her clothes. Laura felt herself shrinking. The bright eyes travelled over her and there was nothing that they did not see and know about.

After breakfast Mamma Gorton went into the red parlor and

read her Bible. Laura went to the front door, and opened it. The autumn air came in from Tomkins Street, smelling of Bleecker. The street was empty and decorous, redolent of Sunday. She went out and closed the door behind her. The veranda ran around the whole front of the great stucco house, broad and empty, with a stucco wall and, at one corner of the house, a swelling that made a large circular place. Laura walked along the veranda. The trolley-car passed along its track with a melancholy sound, the brakes grinding as it started down the grade. Across the street was the Rainer mansion, of brownstone, huge and with many turrets and small pointed angles of roof. Further up a house was being built of concrete for some new people.

It made her start when Morton spoke beside her. He was a good deal taller than she, such a big man, with heavy shoulders; his neck was short and went up straight in the back from his shoulders to the top of his head where his hair stood up boyishly.

"Meditating?" he asked. "I want us to share our meditations. Shall we walk a little together and put our thoughts in order for God to read?"

They walked up and down the long veranda, in and out of the circular place. Another trolley-car came laboring up the grade with a whining noise. There were no carriages or automobiles about, since it was not yet church-time. They walked up and down, up and down. Now that she was trying so hard, Laura could not meditate at all. There seemed to be nothing in her mind, nothing but little jerky thoughts about the things she saw: a hop-scotch game marked out on the slate pavement, the queer bare places where the barrels had stood over at the new concrete house.

When it was time to go to church Morton put on his gray hairy felt hat and went out to back the automobile into the street for the ladies to get in. Laura and Mamma Gorton came out of the house together. Laura walked a little behind her mother-in-law. Why did she feel so shy, so frightened, so like a child, going to church each

Sunday? She felt small and vulnerable, unequipped to endure the grandeur of what lay before her.

They got into the back seat of the automobile and Morton drove them at a good pace down to St. Martin's. Carriages were being driven up to the church door before them and they went slowly behind to let Laura and Mamma Gorton off before Morton put the automobile over to one side. The ladies stood silently on the church steps waiting for him. There were other Bleecker people arriving, but now was not the time for greetings; now one stood silent, about to enter the house of prayer. Laura held her kid-gloved hands pressed close against her coat; Mamma Gorton wore already her religious expression, sad and disapproving and somehow ominous.

It was a magnificent new church, built only a few years before by St. Martin's parishioners fitly to express their devotion. It was Gothic, made of stone, immense, with flying buttresses and stained glass windows. From inside the sound of organ music stole out, bringing the sacred atmosphere into the fresh air. Morton joined them on the steps, and all together they walked on hushed feet into the dim and imposing place, into the richly colored dusk, the omnipresence of organ-music and God.

Up the aisle with humbly bowed heads, and into the Gorton pew, well up forward on the center aisle. Mamma Gorton first; Morton stood back for Laura to pass before him into the pew. In a row they knelt on the prayer-stools covered with red damask cushions. Mamma Gorton held her nose between her fingers, and her lips moved. Morton's head was deeply bent. Laura supported her head like Mamma Gorton. But what did they pray in this moment? She could never think of any prayer, exactly. Little thoughts of no importance trickled through her mind, and she braced herself against her triviality. "Oh, God, forgive me for coming into this sacred place." At a certain moment, decided upon mysteriously, Mamma Gorton and Morton sat back upon the seat, and Laura sat up too. She felt a briskness about them on either side of her, as if they had successfully attended to something. Morton looked straight before him. Mamma Gorton fanned herself, as she always did, with the palm-leaf fan that was kept stuck in the prayer-book rack.

The organ music swelled and the service began. Morton found the places for Laura in the prayer-book and handed it to her each time, with a sad smile. In a row they knelt and prayed, in a row they stood and sang; they and the rest of the congregation, the church-goers of Bleecker, dressed in fur and broadcloth, proudly humble and gratified and experienced in the service. The choir-boys sang; the rector moved mysteriously back and forth before the great golden altar, with his curate; genuflecting, pressing their palms together, raising a hand towards God: with holy nasal accents gabbling the service: in their white garments and the colored and golden scarfs about their necks. And always the music behind everything, going and then coming again, eternal, inescapable, accusing, mournful, triumphant, the congregation held its hymn-books before it and sang with sad, reverent voices.

"Oh Jesus, thou art standing
Outside the fast-closed door.
With humble patience waiting
To cross the threshold o'er."

Beside Laura, Morton's voice rose strong and true, a tenor. She sang too, but she was never sure whether her voice came out audible or not. She could not hear it herself. Oh, Jesus! So humble, so patient. She saw the figure with its soft brown beard, the white long garments, the bare feet, the hand raised with two fingers extended. Humility; subjection; devotion. Laura felt the curious hot stirring inside her that she always felt here every Sunday in this church, and that must be the welling up of her love for Morton, and her gratefulness, and her unworthiness. She pressed her feet closely together. It was like a hot stream let into her veins. Oh, Jesus, meek and mild. Make me meek; make me mild and wifely. All over her, as hot as liquid fire.

There was the little break, and Morton slipped from the pew and went to the back of the church. There was, all over the church, the discreet rustle of paper, the subdued clink of money; Laura's money and Mamma Gorton's was in the small white envelopes that were a sort of badge of St. Martinshood. And then the four dark-suited men, Morton second from the left, marched softly, reverently, but nevertheless firmly, up the aisle in step. Their heads were raised, their eyes ahead. From the altar they received the large silver plates. They moved amongst the congregation and the little rustle and clink went on as they worked back through the church. Morton stopped at the Gorton pew and the plate was passed to Laura; upon its pad of crimson velvet lay all the little white envelopes, the bills, the pieces of silver. Laura added her envelope after Mamma Gorton, and looked up at Morton's face. But he looked at her blankly.

Then the four marched up the aisle again with the laden plates, which were received and consecrated. The four men came back to their pews. The congregation settled down to the sermon. Morton laid his large hand on Laura's knee. This was not an ordinary caress; this was a holy caress: we are here, it said, together before God; we are one in His sight. In sickness and in health, until death do us part. The rector's voice had changed. He was reading his own words now, and his voice was no longer nasal; it droned on and on. The smell of peppermint came faintly through the church.

This was the strange time, the time when, each Sunday, the interior of that church came closer and closer into Laura's soul, so that it was as much part of her as her emotions, or more; more acute. It seemed to tear at her; it reproached her, it chastised her, it made her want to prostrate herself and weep helplessly in fear, because all of it seemed to say that she was wicked; and all the faces of the people were sad and religious and reproached her too.

Straight before her was the vast and terrible altar, shining with gold, with the great golden cross, elaborate and curled, standing in the center. The white-covered tables; the rows of silent choir-boys; and, above everything, Christ on the cross made in the deep glowing colors of stained glass, hanging there in eternal holy torment, and in a smaller panel on either side, two women—Mary the Mother, and Mary Magdalen.

The whole interior of the church except for that shining end was made of dark and costly wood. Along the high sides were the arched stained-glass windows, depicting saints, with Latin words written below them: they let in rich light, purple and deep green and a crimson that was the color of new blood. The droning voice went on and on. Everything here was blessed, everything was sacred. The hot feeling had dropped away from Laura and she felt chilly now, almost shivering, and afraid. She was obsessed by the feeling of helplessness. Morton's hand lay in religious love upon her knee; she belonged to him until death did them part. And she belonged also to all this, the richness and the holiness and the crimson blood, to the humility of Jesus and the tears and the remorse. She was possessed by this sacred grandeur, forever, after death too.

Then the sermon was briskly over and there was another hymn and another kneeling upon the cushioned bench, and the choir-boys marched down the aisle by twos, bearing at their head the golden cross, with their eyes raised towards it. Behind walked the rector and the curate, with downcast faces. There was a reverent pause; then as if at a signal people began to move out of their pews, and the religious look was gone from their faces because they had attended to their spiritual needs, and they pushed down the aisle in a crowd towards the rector who stood at the doorway shaking hands. Beyond the doorway the blue sky glared, incongruous with the light of church. The sky outside was a blasphemy upon the light inside. Laura followed Mamma Gorton down the aisle with Morton's hand under her elbow, and shook the rector's hand, and went out into the church-yard where people were chatting in groups.

Their spirits were well-fed and they looked like people after a big meal. They looked nourished and confident and rich. The Gortons joined group after group and discussed the sermon, the weather, personalities. The rector was very popular. In every group it was said "Such a good man. Speaks so clearly, doesn't he? I quite agreed with every word he said. So different from poor Mr. Reed."

The burning was so in Laura's feet and ankles that she could hardly stand. It seemed interminable, the standing and talking, the exchanging smiles, the occasional introduction—"Haven't you met my new daughter? This is Morton's bride of a year." But there were few introductions now. She had met nearly all of them, the people of Bleecker, the communicants of St. Martin's, the people with whom she would spend the rest of her life. It was as if the burning in her blood that she had felt in church, that had to do with giving herself to Morton forever, with being humble and loving Jesus, had sunk, now, into her feet. They were like fire and there were terrible pains in them.

Finally the crowd thinned out and the Gortons got into the automobile and drove away home for dinner.

At this time of day the sun came flooding into the dining-room. The shades were drawn half-way but still the sun fell hot and yellow through the lower half of the windows and made squares upon the floor. For Sunday dinner there was pea soup, with toasted croutons floating on top, and filet of sole with cucumber, and a great roast of beef with red gravy and brown gravy; browned potatoes, peas, vegetable marrow, and watermelon pickle. There was orange and grapefruit salad; and for dessert there was vanilla ice cream with chocolate sauce, and a chocolate layer cake. Morton was the talker at the Gorton table. After he had said the grace between his mother and his wife he kept up a barrage of jokes. Laura laughed and pushed the appreciation she felt into her face. Mamma Gorton said "Hm," and dampened her forefinger and with it picked up the crumbs within her reach and ate them.

It was long, Sunday dinner, and there was something about it reminiscent of church. The light was different, but rich, too. It was a big room, panelled in dark wood. The long, broad table stood in the middle covered with a vast white cloth, and the food upon it loaded it down. There was a little gravy on Mamma Gorton's chin; she ate a great deal, methodically. Morton loved ice cream like a child. He took three large helpings, with plenty of chocolate sauce. After their great dinner they walked out of the big, shaded, but sunny, room into the hall and through to the red parlor. There were white and pink peppermints on a glass dish that stood on a high base. Mamma Gorton put two in her mouth. Morton sat down in the biggest red chair and lit his Sunday cigar.

Laura stood swaying before the chair with a brocade seat.

"I think I'll go up and take a little nap," she said.

"Sunday dinner makes you sleepy," Mamma Gorton said. She put two more peppermints into her mouth.

Laura climbed the staircase and went into the bedroom. She let herself drop across the bed and stared stupidly before her. The sun came in here too, hot sunshine like blood. She was shaking all over; there was something the matter; inside her head she heard a voice shrieking, as if from far away, shrieking and shrieking.

She heard a step in the room and Morton's arms were all of a sudden around her, tight, his bear-hug.

"My darling little soft wife," he mumbled. "Did you plan so that we could sneak away together and be alone?"

"I thought you had to smoke your cigar," she stammered.

"You know your baby boy isn't old enough for cigars," he said into her ear. "Your baby boy just wants to romp in his crib, with his baby girl. Oh-h," he groaned luxuriously, leaning over on her and rubbing his face slowly, deeply, against her cheek.

In her mind little jumpy words hopped up and down, foolishly: 'He loves me so, he loves me so, he loves me so. . . .' She put her arms around his neck and squeezed just as hard as she could. She would hug back, yes she would, and play the way he wanted to.

With all her strength she clung to him, holding him to her with crazy force, trying to make her mind stop jumping by the exertion she put into her muscles.

"Oh-h, oh-h," Morton moaned. He was enormous; he seemed to be all over the whole bed; she had the feeling that she was frantically embracing something vast and growing vaster, bigger and bigger within her arms.

"Oh-h, my little wife, my soft little wife, my plump little . . ."

He was hot, and moist, and smothering her, overwhelming her. Still she clung to him wildly, giving as hard as she could the enthusiasm he wanted. Then he began to stroke her hair with his big damp hand, putting hot, quiet kisses on her cheeks, her hair, her forehead.

"There, Puddykins, there. . . ."

But she could not stop the wildness now, she was shaking as if with a chill all over. She pulled her hands away from him and they shook and were rigid and she was still straining, straining. The voice was screaming inside her head, screaming. . . .

"Baby! Laura! Stop that!" Morton sat up on the bed and shook her by the shoulders. "Stop that screaming this instant!"

But she couldn't stop, and it was out loud, terribly loud; she was screaming, screaming, screaming.

"I can't have a baby!" she screamed. "No, I can't! Never, never! I can't ever have a baby!"

There were hurrying steps and Mamma Gorton was there. She had a sponge from the bathroom and she pushed it into Laura's face. It was icy cold. Laura shuddered and twisted her head away and threw herself around on her bed. She was not responsible for anything; she was being thrown about the bed, a voice was screaming out from her head where she could not stop it.

"Stop that instantly!"

"I can't stand it!" she screamed. "I'm going to break! I'm going to snap! I can't stand it, I can't stand it, I can't . . ."

"This is a disgrace," Mamma Gorton's voice said somewhere.

But now there was a kind of luxury, a release, in going on screaming. Laura hurled her body from side to side and screamed. Oh, screaming and screaming! Slowly she felt her strength ebb away and there wasn't anything left to scream with and finally she lay still, absolutely exhausted, on the bed with her eyes closed. Now she did not dare to open them.

"I've never heard of such a performance," Mamma Gorton said.

"Go out, Mamma, please," Morton said. "I'll talk to her."

She felt him sitting there, in a chair near the bed, and she did not dare open her eyes. She lay perfectly still. The minutes went by slowly in the sunny Sunday afternoon. She felt the terrible remorse creeping back into her mind, and the fear, and the wanting, the humble wanting, to be good. To be good, so good. The remorse crept in like worms, and at the same time the burning began slowly again in her feet, not very much, but a little, a reminder. And all the time that she had been screaming they hadn't burned at all. But she mustn't think about her own feet.

"Laura."

"Yes," she said.

"You must have been overtired, I know. But you know your Morton only wants to love you with all his heart, don't you?"

"Yes, Morton."

"You know that God has made us one person, so that it is right for us to be always close, don't you?"

"Yes, Morton."

"I know you must be deeply sorry for the wicked thing in you that made you treat your Morton so badly, frighten him like that. Laura?"

"Yes, Morton."

"I want you to kneel with me, now, beside our bed, and pray to the dear Jesus to help you be a good girl, and my good loving wife."

She was so utterly tired that it hurt her to struggle up and off the bed and on to her knees. Morton knelt beside her and put his arm around her, holding her two hands within his two.

"Oh, God," he said. "Hear the repentance in the soul of this Thy loving servant, who has erred and is sorely in need of Thy guidance. —Now tell God what is in your heart," he said to her. "Pray to him and to Jesus to forgive you."

Her mind was a dark and empty place where little white pinwheels spun round and round.

"Jesus, make me good, Jesus make me good," she said inside her head. The words spun round and round on the pinwheels and white sparks flew off into the dark.

Morton's arms were close around her holding her on her knees for a long time. Finally he got up. She stayed quite still on her knees.

"My little tired wife," he said, and picked her up and laid her on the bed. "Perhaps you had better spend the rest of today in bed," he said.

"I'm so tired," she said.

"Would you like your little husband to take your clothes off and put your nightgown on for you, so that you can rest?"

"Oh, no," she said hastily. "I just want to lie still and not move. I'll put my nightgown on later. Tomorrow perhaps I'll rest in bed."

"But you'll be all rested tomorrow."

"But you wouldn't mind if I rested, just one day?"

"Of course not. I'm not a brute," he said stiffly.

He drew all the shades down nearly to the bottom so that it was very dim. Then he tiptoed away and left her. At first she did not think or see. The only thing was the little burning in her feet, not bad, just a reminder that it was there.

But then she opened her eyes and stared, absently at first, at the highboy across the room. Slowly her mind began to focus on it. It was such a beautiful highboy, very simple, of maple wood, made long ago, with plain, lovely lines, and only one carved shell in the front for decoration. She looked at it and looked at it and it seemed to rest and nourish her whole being. She felt as if she would like to lie, quite still, and look at that highboy for years.

1941

WHO LIVED AND DIED BELIEVING

It was a strange, hot summer. The days throbbed and the nights were exhausted and melancholy. In August the temperature rose over ninety and hung there; the heat shimmered over the buildings and the streets of the town. Every afternoon at two Elizabeth Percy came down the steps of the house that was made into apartments for nurses. She walked along the burning pavements, around the corner, past the newsstand where the magazines hung fluttering on lines of wire, to Massey's Drug Store.

Her hair was very dark and as smooth as dark brown satin; it was combed back from her calm forehead and fell curving under at the back behind her ears. She wore plain uniforms with small round collars close about her neck, and she was all white and fresh and slender and strong.

From the heat outside she would walk into the dim coolness of the drugstore that smelled of soda and candy. There was a faint sweat upon the marble of the soda fountain; Mr. Massey and the other clerks stood about in their light tan linen coats, and they smiled at her without speaking. Dave was behind the prescription counter wrapping up a small package; first the white paper and then slowly the thin bright red string. He lifted his head as she walked down the center of the store to where the tables were, and his eyes met Elizabeth's. She sat down at the small black table and one of the boys from the fountain came and took her order of Coca-Cola. Several electric fans whirred remotely, high on the ceiling. The door opened again at the front, and three internes from the hospital came in. They leaned together on the marble counter in their whites. Their faces were young and pale with heat.

Dave came around the corner of the counter, and sat down beside Elizabeth. Mr. Massey walked slowly up towards the front of the store; he smiled absently at them; he always smiled at them as they sat together between two and three.

They never talked much. Elizabeth sucked the drink slowly through a straw, and lifted the glass and let bits of crushed ice drop into her mouth; they melted on her tongue. She loved to look at Dave. He was very thin and tall and he had straight yellow hair that fell forward in a lock on his forehead. His eyes were restless. He would glance at her suddenly and smile.

"How you doing over there?"

"She's just the same."

"Long case."

"Unh-hunh. Going to be longer."

"Tough you have to nurse one of those cases. Beckwith have any idea how long it'll be?"

"One afternoon," Elizabeth said. "Grainger told me yesterday he said he was going to use shock. Maybe."

"Insulin?"

"No, I don't think so."

Dave raised his eyebrows and shook his head. The damp yellow lock trembled against his forehead. He had finished the second year of medical school and was working at Massey's during the summer months.

"Oh-oh. That won't be so good."

"Grainger'll have it, in the mornings."

"No, no fun," he said.

"I'm so sorry for Mrs. Myles."

Dave shrugged his shoulders.

"Don't get tough," she said. "You're not a doctor yet. Beckwith's sorry for her, too. It's not the usual thing. She's gone through plenty."

"Sure," he said.

"Oh, real doctors have pity, you know; it's just you little boys."

She smiled at him, and he smiled back after a minute. He looked restless and impatient. He reached one hand under the table and put it on her knee, and looked into her long, calm, dark blue eyes.

"Meet you at eleven?" he said. Elizabeth nodded. He took his hand away.

"She wants to see you again."

"Oh, God."

"It doesn't hurt you any. Just go up there to her room for a minute and say good night. She gets so much out of it."

He gave a sort of groan, and shifted in his chair.

"She's got those damned eyes. I don't *mean* anything. I don't like her looking like that."

"It's just because we're going together," Elizabeth said. "It's the only thing outside herself, you see, like the only thing that's outside and ahead, and she likes to think about our going together."

"Oh, God."

"She asks me about you every day. Lots of times. I don't know whether she forgets she's asked before or whether . . . Come on, do it again once. It doesn't hurt you."

"All right. All right. Eleven."

"Eleven."

She got up and walked to the counter and laid the check down with a nickel. She went out into the heat, crossed the street, and walked up the wide steps of the hospital entrance.

In Copperthwaite Two the corridor was dim and hot. Elizabeth stopped at the desk and turned over the leaves of the order book. Dr. Beckwith had ordered the shock treatment for the morning; no breakfast. Elizabeth drew in her breath. Miss Grainger came out of the door of 53 and down the hall, without her cap.

"Hi," Elizabeth said.

"Hi."

"See you've got it ordered for tomorrow."

"Yeah, man."

"Does she know about it?"

"I'm not sure. He came up and went over her this morning, heart and all, before we went out. Told her, but not exactly; said they were going to give her a treatment and there'd be acute physical discomfort. I love Dr. Beckwith. Discomfort. I don't look forward to it, I tell you. Seems like there's some things you don't get used to and I don't like shock."

"What have you all done?"

"About the same. Walked. This walking miles in this weather does me in. I'm going home and go to sleep."

Elizabeth flipped back the pages of the order book.

"What is this stuff, anyhow? We didn't have it, then."

"Oh . . . camphor derivative? . . . something. Reckon I'll know plenty in the morning. How's Dave?"

"Fine," Elizabeth said. They parted and went along the long corridor in opposite directions. Elizabeth pushed open the heavy door of 53.

Mrs. Myles sat beside the open window and in the vicious heat observed passing back and forth outside (along the pavement?) back and forth from Hell the doughy and grimacing faces of the damned. And a little part of the rotted grapes that rolled about within her brain watched the faces with an abstracted care; each of the faces was forever familiar, a face seen before (where?), seen before and seen again, and where, where, had been the face before? In her brain the fruit gave out a stench that she could taste in her mouth, and with it came the horror; no, no, those faces she had never seen before; it only seemed that she had; and the seeming was wrong and she could not send it away, the seeming stayed, shaking its tattered locks and grinning; yes, these faces had been seen before. The faces passed, and none of them was his. Watch,

watch, observe with shrinking but insistent care each hideous face that comes nearer and nearer with death in its eyes and the unbelievable humanity, the bigness, in the coming-nearer mouths, until each face passed and was not his, was never his.

Her heart that was no longer her friend beat frantically one two three four five six seven eight eighty is a normal pulse for a woman seventy for a man but this was—hundred and forty . . . MAD.

The heavy-strained tension split with the scream of silk. The door opened and Miss Percy came in. So cool so calm so bright. With calm brow, with dark hair, and eyes like dark blue water. Cool as the little leaves that tremble in the tree. What thou among the leaves hast never known. This she has never known, with her calm eyes. Oh reach to me, thou among the leaves, reach down to me in Hell with your cool hands, reach down to me.

She sees it all clean. The same world, clean. It is just me. I must remember that, it is just me; the world is cool and calm and bright. Not this. It is just me. Not mad, he said, just an exaggeration of your understandable state of tension, just an exaggeration of a normal point of view, just an exaggeration but not mad.

"Poor old Mr. Duggan next door's making quite a lot of noise," Miss Percy said, smiling. She stood before the mirror of the yellow-oak bureau and took her cap from the bureau post and pinned it to the back of her dark head. "I hope it doesn't bother you too much. Anyway, we'll go right out."

"Poor Mr. Duggan," Mrs. Myles said. "Is he getting any better at all?"

"I think they're going to give him some treatments that will make him all well."

The nurse glanced quickly at the patient.

She didn't mean to say that. She doesn't know if I know it, too. They are coming.

"You'd better wear your wide hat," Miss Percy said. "The sun's real hot this afternoon."

Obediently she put the hat upon her head and tied the ribbons that held it on under her chin.

"Put a little lipstick on," the nurse said. "It's so becoming to you to have a little color in your lips. Don't you remember what Dr. Beckwith said when he met us outside the steps yesterday, how pretty you looked? You've put on a pound and a half in two weeks. It won't be long before we have you weighing what you ought to. Before you know it you're going to be right strong."

Now to smile. Now widen the corners of the mouth and look straight into Miss Percy's eyes and hold it for a moment. But no! This is no smile. This is the terrible and tragic shape of a comic mask. Thus grimace the damned, who burn in the fires, and looking upward to the cool hand that is stretched in kindness and impotence to meet their torment, try one last time and achieve the horrible stretch, the grin, of the comic mask.

They walked down the hot dim corridor and turned to the right.

"Can't we please go down in the elevator?" Mrs. Myles said.

Miss Percy's face looked troubled.

"I know," she said. "Only he wants you to walk through the hospital."

"All right."

So once again. Endure, endure. Endure to the end.

First they walked through the children's ward. Once it had not been bad; the universal slime had not had time to foul this too; she had seen them as children, delicate and pale and sweet. But then the tide of the slime had mounted here too, and ever since it had been this way. Student nurses, nurses, internes passed them. "Afternoon, Mrs. Myles." They all know me. Can they see it in my face? . . . In the little beds the children lay or sat, with their sick faces. Sickness was everywhere. This is the great house of sickness. The children's faces were greenish with the heat. Which among them is mine? He is dead. He is not dead; which among them is mine, not well and laughing, but sick, which among them is my sick, corrupted child, infected from me all its tiny beginnings with the worm of sick sick sick. I am sick and all of mine is sick.

And she smelled the sharp recurrent fear. Fear, that clawed at the ruin of her mind; fear that rattled in her chest about the flabby palpitating boundaries of her heart. This fear is wicked, she thought: I am not afraid *for* the children, I am afraid *of* them. I am afraid of everything. I am full of poison of wickedness and fear; cold poison.

"He wants you to face things," Miss Percy said as they passed through and beyond to the men's ward. "You know. Not get so you think you couldn't do something, special."

"I know."

In the beds the men lay, with sickness floating in the pools of their eyes. They passed on through the women's ward. A woman looked up. One side of her face was swollen out to huge proportions, and covered with bandage through which leaked sticky, yellow stuff. There was the long ominous smell of sweet ether and they passed suddenly across the hall of the hospital and their feet sounded sharp and loud on the stone flagging, and they went out into the loud sad heat. They descended the steps and started to walk down the road away from the town.

Suddenly from behind in the sunshine blared a loudspeaker, carried on a truck painted silver, with huge letters advertising an air-cooled movie house downtown. Slowly, slowly, the truck crept along the hot street. The enormous screaming music shook the atmosphere:

> "Fall in love, fall in love, says my heart. . . ."
> *Fall in love*, FALL IN LOVE. . . ."

It swung slowly around a corner, out of sight. From far away in the afternoon the idiot voice still screamed:

"Fall in love, fall in love, says my heart. . . ."

They walked steadily on, the nurse with a secret little smile; the woman, with a stiff and empty face.

The hours passed in gross and threatening procession. And with the hours the woman felt the always coming on, the rising walls, of the enclosing fear. Like sound-proof glass, shutting her away; the terrible pawlike hand fumbling with the cork to stopper her finally into this bottle of aloneness.

She sat beside the window in the decline of the afternoon, and her hand was too sick with fear to stretch out to the shade and pull it down against the sun. She did not dare to move her hand. And soon the sun had bobbled behind the dreadful mountains of the west.

The nurse spoke to her several times and at last in her closing bottle she heard the voice from far away and turned, and it was supper being put before her on a tray. In the bowls of all the spoons were faces, that grinned at her and twisted their mouths into screams.

She ate, and then she was sick and the good food left her body in protest and she sat again by the window where the evening light now ran in around the edges of the shade like liquid poison, wet and lying on the floor and on the furniture of the room. The nurse put a table before her and laid out cards for a game upon its surface.

She looked down and saw the ferret faces of the kings and queens, the knaves; pinched and animal-like faces that whispered until the whispering was like a whistling in the room; and she turned her face away, but there was only the faraway flapping shade with the night running in around the edges, and she looked again at her hands but they were vast and swollen and she turned away and closed her eyes but within her was nothing but fear.

"How do you feel?" the nurse said in the evening room.

"How do you feel?" the nurse said.

"How do you feel?" the nurse said.

"HOW DO YOU FEEL?" the nurse said.

The nurse said, "Mrs. Myles, is there anything the matter?"

"It's as if," she said, "all the human things had been taken out of me and it left holes, like a cheese with great empty holes. And the holes have to be filled with something and they are all filled up with fear. So that where I had all sorts of things now I haven't got anything but fear in all the holes."

But that wasn't it at all, not only that; there was the bottle, how to tell some one of the bottle, glass and soundproof, where the stopper was being pushed tight home with her inside; not like a moth, no, not so clean, not like the souls in bottles, *animula, vagula, blandula*. No, like a festering purple lump of tissue.

Hell is not heat or cold, it is banishment to the ultimate ego. And in a few hours I shall be stoppered forever, she thought, I will not be able to speak, I will not be able to hear. I will be *mad*.

She asked for a pencil and paper. She wrote, and her handwriting was not her own; it was strange and inchoate like the sawings of the line of a fever chart. She looked at it with desperation. Will I scream? Will I groan? Will I grimace and mouth meaningless words? What will I do, with all of them watching me, crawling loathsomely inside the bottle, the face plastered on the purple stinking tissue like the fearful little faces in the spoons; while they watch, with their cool, well eyes, dressed all in white.

She tried to explain about the bottle on the paper with her failing handwriting, and then she folded it and wrote the doctor's name outside.

"Put it somewhere," she said urgently. "I want you to give it to Dr. Beckwith tomorrow if . . . if I . . ."

If I can no longer communicate what I feel, if I am mad.

"You're going to be fine," the nurse said. "You're going to be fine. Nothing's going to happen to you. Don't be afraid."

She thinks I mean die. No. Only the bottle. Or die?

Or die? For they are coming in the morning with something in their hands. For they are coming in the morning, footsteps measured, slow, down the corridor to me, bearing . . . the cross? . . . in their arms. No. No. You can still endure a little, do not think of Christ, that's the beginning. When the stopper is jammed at last deep into the neck of the bottle, then it will all be thoughts of Christ. Just with the last resisting inch, I can avoid the thought of Christ.

But Christ. So cool, so calm, so bright. O Jesus thou art standing outside the fast-closed door. Jesus with his mild face, his mournful eyes, the bright brown beard, the suffering. Oh, no!

The minutes, the hours passed in ever-gathering procession. Miss Percy ran water and opened the high, narrow bed and helped the woman into it.

"Dave is coming to say good night to you," she said above the bed.

"Dave is coming to say GOOD NIGHT TO YOU," she said.

Oh . . . Dave is coming to say good night to me. . . . Dave? I don't know what is that word: Dave. Something; once; better; but not now. Only the bones of ego smelling of fear and dirt.

"Mrs. Myles."

"Mrs. Myles."

"Mrs. Myles."

"MRS. MYLES!"

She turned her head and in the doorway, unreal, remote, beyond hell, they stood, the nurse, white and slender, and the young man—he was Dave. They stood there, down a tiny vista beckoning, the last reminder. For they were love. It still endured, somewhere, upon the fading world. It was a flickering candle point upon the dark; flickering in the waves that even now, like the great winds of Hell, blew the candle flame, tiny, tiny.

The woman on the bed strained towards what she saw. Upon these bones of ego hangs one last shred of flesh, and as long as it hesitates there, gnawed by the mouths of cockroaches, so long that shred of flesh shall reach, shall strain towards what it sees, towards love. The shred is hanging by a nerve, and the candle point flickers and grows far, far away at the end of the cone-shaped darkness.

"Good night, Mrs. Myles."

"Good night," she said. "Are you going out somewhere together?"

"Unh-hunh," Miss Percy said. "Reckon we'll go for a drive in the country to find a breeze."

"Yes," the woman said. "I hope it'll be cool, in the country. I hope you have a lovely time. I hope you're happy."

She turned her head away from the door and closed her eyes, struggling to maintain that point of light somewhere in the darkness that was growing. As long as I can see it the bones will not be wholly bare, and the world not gone. I hope they will be happy. They love each other. Here I lie: in my sepulcher, and the stopper hovers, and the smell of brimstone everywhere. But while the candle flickers I will remember. When it gutters and goes out, I will go out, and the shred of flesh shall drop at last and the paw that reeks shall push the stopper down. . . .

"Well, if you need anything, you know you just have to ring and Miss Perley will get it for you, dear. Good night," the nurse said.

But that, the woman did not hear.

After eleven the hospital was quiet and the lights along the corridors were turned out, so that only the light over the desks of the nurses in charge shone. The wards were dark and still; along some corridor could be heard occasionally the rattling trundle of a stretcher being pushed in a hurry, the stifled coming and going of a night emergency.

Elizabeth Percy went out through the hospital to the main entrance with Dave. A yawning nurse behind a desk raised her eyes and said "Hi!"; a doctor came hurriedly along the passage, wriggling his arms into a hospital coat as he went; his head was down and as Elizabeth passed he glanced upward from under his brows, nodded, and said, "Miss Percy. . . ." They came out on to the open stone flagging of the entrance hall where lights burned behind the admittance desk, and went down into the melting, melancholy night.

Elizabeth put her hand through Dave's arm and squeezed it; he glanced down at her and smiled.

"How you, babe?" he said.

"A little whipped. . . . That case is so hard, you can't do anything for her much and she's going through something awful."

"Forget it," he said. "You're off now. Climb in. Reckon it'll hold together a little longer."

She got into the old Chevrolet parked by the curb in the darkness.

They drove through the subsiding lights of the town, past the movie theatres with their electric signs turned off, now; the few people in light clothes dawdling before the doors of ice-cream parlors; there was the faint occasional hoot of a motor horn, the slam of a front door. As they passed into the outskirts of the town, the smell of the honeysuckle met them, drifting in from the country, and from far away the small sweet sawing of the crickets in the fields. They crossed a bridge and drove out along the country road, like a tunnel of darkness covered over with the branches of the trees. Their headlights made a white passage down the center of the tunnel. The smell of honeysuckle grew stronger, filling the whole night air, and sometimes they would pass a spot where the honeysuckle smell grew suddenly sharper, sweeter, bursting like fresh fountains into scent.

"My, this is nice," Elizabeth said. Her head was leaned back against the back of the seat.

He pressed her knee with his right hand and drew it toward his.

"Heat like we've been having can't last much longer," he said. "Registered over a hundred outside the store this afternoon. Got to crack sometime. May Leeds says her father and all the farmers are praying for rain."

"How's May?" Elizabeth asked in her low, quiet voice.

"Oh. . . . I just took her to a movie while I was waiting around for you. She just dropped in while I was finishing up. . . . I've got to do something with the evenings, haven't I?"

"Of course, darling."

"It was a lousy movie."

She said nothing.

Far out along the road Dave stopped the car off to one side, under the boughs of the trees, and switched out the lights so that nothing could be seen; only the wide dark; the smell of the honeysuckle quivered through the darkness, and in the field beside them a whippoorwill called. Dave lit a cigarette and put his arm around Elizabeth.

"God, it's good to get out of that hellhole," he said.

After a moment Elizabeth spoke.

"I can't get Mrs. Myles out of my head," she said. "She just doesn't get any relief at all."

"Oh, skip the hospital when you're out of it."

"I know. Only I keep thinking that's what love can do to you."

"Inability to adjust."

"Yes, I know. But I guess it isn't so easy to adjust when you're too much in love, and then everything sort of came on her. I can't help picking things up. She was just mad about him and apparently he never cared much about her and she knew it, and that must be just . . . awful. And then when she got pregnant he went off with this other woman, and when she had her baby it died right away. Placenta previa. It would take quite a lot of adjusting."

"Well. . . . Skip it. You can't go stewing about patients' problems. Leave that to Beckwith. How about kissing me?"

"You'd think she'd be through with love, wouldn't you? But she sort of hangs on to the idea of it. Like about . . . us."

"Yeah. Listen, I'm sorry, but I can't go up there any more and represent something for your patient. It just makes me feel too God-damn gummy."

"You don't have to. You never had to, only she seemed to get so much out of seeing you and it's awful seeing her every day, so lost. Anyway, she's getting shock in the morning."

"She is?"

"Yes. I hope it'll do the trick."

"How about skipping the hospital, baby? You're supposed to be a nurse, not an angel of mercy. Quit brooding about work out of hours. Kiss me."

She put both arms around him and kissed his mouth. His arms came around her and she felt the restlessness, the impatience in his body, and the eagerness, the searching.

"Oh, darling," she said. "I guess I'm pretty much in love with you."

"I don't mind you one bit myself," he murmured.

She started to speak, checked herself, and then spoke.

"Dave, darling, you wouldn't hurt me, would you?"

"Mmh-mmh."

"You could hurt me so easily. I'm so wide open to you."

"That's just the way I like you," he said, and he put his mouth down on hers, and his hands passed down her arms. Now they were close together, closer and closer in the satin darkness, and in the field the bird called at intervals and the smell of the honeysuckle came down in waves of shuddering sweetness. Over the country where they were the night sky seemed to brood, hanging soft and thick and vast over the land. Far away a train passed in the darkness and across the fields Elizabeth heard its whistle cry three times, three times—ah, ah, aaaah.

When they drove back into town it was very late and the air had a false coolness; there was a little breeze that would go away with the dawn. Elizabeth leaned silent against the seatback. Dave sat up straight and drove, and talked about the coming year of work.

"We get Parsons in surgery and will that be something. You remember Jim Jencks from down Eliza County, he was a real nice guy, I used to see a whole lot of him; he just had one run-in with

Parsons after another, and that's one reason, I guess, he isn't going to be able to come back this year. Hope I don't get fixed up wrong with the old bastard."

"What's Jim Jencks doing now?" Elizabeth said.

"He just went on home. The damn fool, he got married. That finished him. Reckon he'll be raising pigs the rest of his life."

"I didn't know he got married."

"Yeah. Lehman, Lemmon . . . ? Married a nurse, anyway. Never had good sense."

Elizabeth made a small noise with her lips.

"Oh! . . . Beg your pardon! Only *you* know, the business of guys marrying nurses, the way they do. . . . You know just as well as I do."

"Yes."

He left her in the dark and empty street before the apartment house where she lived. In the silence of the town the car sounded noisily as he drove away. Elizabeth looked after the car for a moment and then she walked slowly up the brick steps to the house full of nurses asleep.

The woman in Room 53 was awake, passing from unconscious to conscious horror, as soon as the phlegm-gray dawn had filled the corners of the room. There was the relentless metronome beat of doom rapping everywhere. It could not be slowed, nor stopped, nor avoided, but beat faster minute by minute until at last the beat would fuse, would *be*, the footsteps coming down the corridor outside, bearing the thing that would be borne. The woman turned her head in an old and useless reflex against horror and stared out of the window into the gray light.

On the bank opposite the hospital window there were a number of little things, moving about and pecking, and she knew that they were birds; but they were not birds, they were frightful lumps of mud, mud-birds, that jerked about the dirt. She turned her eyes away from them in loathing, but there was nowhere else to look.

She closed her eyes upon the horror of outside, to meet the inside horror.

The chorus sang the evil hymns. O Jesus, thou art standing outside the fast-closed door. O, Jesus, thou . . . the bright brown beard, the promise that is stained and filthied with corruption, and where is there to fly to lose this wickedness? Abide with me; fast falls the eventide. The awful sweetish dripping of the notes in chorus; that seems to be a promise, that asks for comfort.

The panic grew and the metronome beat, a little faster; the tentacles within reached out in frenzy and there was nothing there to grasp, only abide with me; fast falls the eventide; the dim valley of sin, echoing in the shadows. Though I walk through the valley of the shadow of death, I shall fear no evil; for thou art with me; thy rod and thy staff. . . . Were those what they would bear? The rod and the staff? Though I walk through the valley of the shadow of death. . . . I shall fear this evil, spreading like phlegm along the valley, everywhere, and all is evil, abiding with me. . . .

Oh, no! she cried inside herself with one last straining, no! But where was there to look? And in the ultimate necessity there flickered far off the pale point of the candle flame.

And then the footsteps down the corridor. And then the footsteps, am I dreaming them? The door opened and the priests and the acolytes came in—no, the doctor and the resident and the internes and the nurse—no, the white-robed priests of this obscene observance, this sacrifice, and I am the sacrifice that lies quite still upon the altar, and they bear the weapon in their hands: the huge, brutal, long syringe lying upon a bed of gauze, and I am Christ to meet their sacrifice, to give my life. Six people in the room, and the sacrifice.

"Good morning, gentlemen," the woman said.

The nurse, by the head of the bed, laid her hand upon the patient's hand. The three internes stood grouped at the foot of the bed. The doctor stood on the right of the bed and looked down into the patient's face. The resident stood halfway down the left side of the bed, and in his hands he held the syringe.

She looked up into the doctor's face and upon it lay his eyes, flat, like gray, wet, cold oysters laid upon a plate.

"Listen," the woman said hurriedly. "Tell me, quick. Does it matter what thoughts I am thinking? I mean will this fasten them permanently this way? Because my thoughts are so bad, and I can't seem to think any good thoughts. . . ."

"It doesn't matter, kiddy," said the doctor. The eyes like oysters swam at her, and spun a little round and round. He laid his fingers on her wrist. The resident took her left arm and felt with his fingers along the veins on the inside of her elbow. She closed her eyes. Now let me think one good thought, that my brain may be embalmed in this sacrifice with a good thought held in it like a fly in amber. Oh, stay with me, flame, the point before the eyes, the one last point. . . .

A wave from the outside of sick; of liquid; of shuddering horror ran up her veins.

"Thrombosed," the resident said. "We'll have to try another."

"Steady, kiddy," the doctor said.

Oh, flame, abide with me in the moment of dissolution. . . .

Then crashingly a thousand carmine circles spun in her brain and there were crashes and mad carmine and the dark.

"Look at that," the leftmost interne said as the figure on the bed sat straight up, clenched in convulsion.

"Patient down on G Ward fractured three vertebrae in one of those," the resident said, watching.

"You'll have your good days and your bad days." The nurse's voice came to her. "You'll have your good days and your bad days, Mrs. Myles."

She was eating lunch off a tray and it was lettuce that she was putting in her mouth. It was thin and crisp and very cold. The world around her was hot and the sun beat through the window beside her. Everything was fatigue, and pain in her back, but the lettuce on her tongue was cool, and the nurse's voice; her name was Miss Percy and she was always there, in the revolving mist, speaking to her out of the wilderness, cool and clear.

"You'll have your good days and your bad days, Mrs. Myles."

She was walking through the jungle of the world, and she was lost. She did not know where she was. It was an utterly strange, green jungle. Only the nurse, Miss Percy, was there beside her and so she continued to walk through this land.

They came to a brook that ran through a shady hollow and they sat down on a large stone by the margin of the brook and the nurse took off the woman's shoes, and she put her tired feet in the brook. The water was warm and fresh and ran softly past her feet. Beside the brook stood tall green trees that she had never seen before. She kept her feet in the soft running water and listened to the rustling in the leaves of the strange trees.

"How did I get here?" she asked. "Where have I been?"

The nurse's voice came with the sound of the brook, cool and clear.

"You're taking a walk in the country. You're staying at the hospital for a while."

"I don't remember. . . ."

"You'll have amnesia for a little bit. It's all right."

It's all right. . . .

Miss Percy stopped the doctor in the corridor.

"Dr. Beckwith, may I speak to you for a minute?"

The doctor stopped on one foot in his hurrying walk. The two horns of the stethoscope stuck up from the pocket of his white coat.

"My patient isn't getting hardly any sleep, doctor. I wondered if you could order something."

"Can't give sedatives, you know, with the treatments. Has a counteractive effect."

"She just seems so terribly tired."

"Well, she didn't even feel tired before. . . . I'll order insulin tonight, Miss Percy. See whether that'll put her to sleep."

"Thank you, doctor."

"You don't look as if you'd got much sleep yourself," the doctor said.

"Oh . . . it's just this heat."

"Got to break soon."

"Yes."

They were in a bowling alley, that was what it was, although she did not know where the bowling alley was or how she had got there. But the nurse was sitting on one of the wooden theatre seats behind her. She herself was standing, facing the alley with a bowl in her hand.

She continued with the action that somehow she had begun. She neither felt the bowl with her hand nor felt the floor under her feet when she moved forward. It was like moving through air. She willed herself to make the gestures that somewhere inside she knew should be made now, and her body carried out the commands, but without sensation, without seeming to touch anything at all.

It just shows what you can do by will power, she thought, surprised. I can do anything I will myself to do, even though I am moving in air.

She let go the bowl and watched down the long straight alley where the bowl rolled, and heard the rumble of the falling pins.

She watched as the three black bowls came rolling up the wooden trolley to the side, and came to a stop. She picked up one of them and although she had picked it up she felt nothing against her palm.

It's almost fun, she thought, seeing what you can do by will power.

It was night, and suddenly she could not bear to lie in bed any longer. Since the nurse had stuck the needle in her arm the strangest energy and slow hope had begun in her.

In the dim spaces of this room the nurse was moving about. She was taking off her cap.

"I want to get up," the woman said. "Can I get up? I want to talk."

The nurse turned and smiled.

"All right," she said. She pulled forward the big chair that was by the window, and helped the woman into it. The nurse sat down on a small straight chair and smiled at the woman.

"But were you going away . . ." the woman said, puzzled. Something stirred in her head, faintly remembered.

"No," the nurse said. "I haven't anywhere special to go. I'd be glad to stay a little later, Mrs. Myles."

"You don't know," she said, "what hope can feel like. It's like running water. I mean freedom. Oh, you don't know what it's like! to be able to see freedom. Even just a little bit."

"You're going to have all the freedom in the world."

"I keep thinking of the loveliest things—long straight roads and driving along them fast in an open car. You don't know what hope can feel like. It's like the wind beginning to blow. Am I really going to be free?"

Suddenly the words of something whose origin she could not remember came into her head and she began to repeat them aloud: "That this nation, under God, shall have a new birth in freedom, and that government of the people, for the people, by the people, shall not perish from the earth."

Shall not perish. . . .

"That's what I mean," she said. "That's the way it feels. I can't remember but it wasn't that way before, it wasn't for the people, by the people, I mean as if I were the people, as if I were a nation. A woman like a nation."

"Yes," the nurse said. "I know. Instead of under a dictator, you mean. It's awful to live under a dictator and not belong to yourself any more, isn't it?"

"Yes," she said impatiently, pushing that part away from her, for now there was hope, forming like a five-petaled flower, like a star. Sitting forward on the edge of the chair in her excitement, she repeated the words again, whatever they were: "This nation under God shall have a new birth in freedom, and that government of the people. . . ."

And after some time the nurse went away and came back with a tall glass that was filled with sugared water, flavored deliciously with lemon, and the woman drank it.

And on some mornings the doctor and the resident and the three internes came into her room, and the resident carried the large syringe. He was always the one who inserted the needle into her vein. It was a thing that came suddenly on some mornings and it had to be faced, once more; endure, she thought, endure to the end. And always at the last she summoned to her the vision, with her eyes closed, of the candle flame, that companioned her through the darkness, through the bad days, through it all. It did not leave her, it remained to fortify her in the last extremity, when they came and the needle went into her arm and in her head spun the carmine circles and the world crashed, and then the dark. . . .

"Don't think she'll have to have another," the doctor said, as they watched the figure in convulsion on the bed. "This stuff certainly is magic in some cases."

On an afternoon in the yellow sunshine, suddenly she was sitting under an apple tree in the yard beside the hospital, and the nurse, Miss Percy, was sitting on the grass beside her. Mrs. Myles turned her head slowly and smiled. The heat had gone; it was a cool and lovely afternoon; the leaves rustled in the tree above her and from its branches came the smell of apples.

On the grass further away some internes were playing baseball. Their voices shouted to one another, and the ball could be heard smacking their cupped palms. A breeze trickled along the air. The shadows were beginning to lengthen from the wall of the hospital, and in that light the internes, in their white clothes, ran and shouted. From a grass bank on the other side of the road from the hospital a bird called, suddenly, sweetly.

"Hello," Mrs. Myles said.

"Hello, dear. You're feeling much better, aren't you?"

"Yes," she said. Things were swimming back into her memory, the buildings here were taking their places in the world. And everything was very calm, very peaceful; there was no hurry. It doesn't matter.

She looked at the nurse, who had been there all the time. In the darkness and the long confusion, in that strange land where she had been, the nurse had been with her all the time. She studied the dark, smooth hair, the oval face, and the long, dark blue, quiet eyes.

"How is Dave?" Mrs. Myles said.

"You're remembering, aren't you?" the nurse said, without looking at the patient. "I think he's fine. I haven't seen him for a while."

"But . . ."

That did not fit. She stayed silent for a little time, while the remembrances slowly rearranged themselves within her head.

"But you're in love with him," she said slowly. "It was you both. You are in love with each other."

"Well. . . . You see, we aren't going together any more."

Something was wrong. Wait while the sifting memory slowly settled. Her own life was dead, somehow she had learned that, some one had taught her that in the strange, twilight land. She knew that she had been reborn and that this was a new life. She could never have the things of her own old life, for they had gone and they were dead. But one thing only . . . a candle burning down a vista, some constant star that had companioned her through the dark valleys of the land she had left. . . . She remembered two figures standing in a doorway.

"You're not?"

"No," the nurse said. She looked tired. They stared at each other and then a new and curious thing happened, a wave swept upward and from her eyes the woman felt tears falling. It was not despair. It was only deepest sadness. The last thing had gone out of the old life. Now the past was wiped black and she was all alone and beginning a new life, reborn alone. The purest, quietest sadness swept her and she could not halt the tears that fell and fell.

"You mustn't mind at all, dear," the nurse said. But their eyes kept meeting: the nurse's quiet and dry, the woman's full of tears.

The baseball game had broken up and a young interne came strolling by the apple tree, and looked down at the two who sat upon the grass. His face Mrs. Myles knew. It had looked at her on many mornings.

"Afternoon, Mrs. Myles, Miss Percy," the interne said, and then stopped in embarrassment at the tears on the woman's face.

"Well . . ." he said. "Seems fine to have a good cry, doesn't it?"

"Yes," she said, crying quietly, for all that was dead, now, forever, and could never be brought back. And it was fading fast. Fade far away, dissolve, and quite forget what thou, among the leaves, hast never known. It was all over; it was finished; the fight with death and sin, the wandering in the strange lost land. It was all gone, and love was gone too, and the candle flame had silently gone out. Above their heads where they sat upon the grass the little leaves in the apple tree whispered. It was all gone, and from now on the world was new, a page unwritten.

1942

SOME DAY I'LL FIND YOU . . .

ROUTINE AT THE Desert Sanatorium started at seven-thirty in the morning. The trays of breakfast came down from the big house on metal trucks with a heater inside, to the adobe courts where the patients lived. Each court was built around a patio with grass and a fountain, and was named after a tribe of Indians—Apache, Papago, Comanche, Yavapai. Miss Cecil came on duty in Papago just as the breakfasts came trundling down. She carried them in to the patients and took their temperatures. In Papago there were four arthritics, three sinuses, an acute asthma, and Mr. Burt.

Miss Cecil took Mr. Burt's breakfast in to him in the big corner room. All the shades were drawn down against the bright desert sunshine, and Mr. Burt was lying with the covers up over his head. Miss Cecil pulled the shades up after she had set the tray down on the bed table. She advanced on the bed with the thermometer in her hand.

"I know you're awake," she said.

"You're wrong," Mr. Burt said. "How about we have a nice bath, hm?"

"You can give yourself a bath."

"The pronoun is yours, not mine, dear," Mr. Burt said. He peered up from under the sheet, his hair on end. "Strictly the property of the nursing profession. Okay, we'll take our temperature."

Miss Cecil stuck the thermometer in his mouth and left the room. When she came back he was wandering around the room in blue silk pajamas. She took the thermometer out of his mouth and glanced at it, shook it, and stuck it back in the glass vase full of alcohol. Mr. Burt climbed back into bed and pulled the breakfast toward him.

"How's my temperature?" he asked.

"Normal. You're just as healthy as a buck."

"You think so, Gretch?"

"My name isn't Gretch."

"I know. You just make me think of a girl named Gretch."

Mr. Burt ate his breakfast and lit a cigarette to smoke with his coffee. One of the colored orderlies came by with the morning papers. Mr. Burt lit another cigarette and began to read the papers. He read them thoroughly, the three of them: New York, Los Angeles, and Tucson.

He was finishing the sporting page of the Tucson paper when Dr. Millis knocked and came in on his morning rounds. He was a well-set-up young man, a little stout, with yellow hair. He wore a Sigma Xi key hanging from his watch chain under the open white laboratory coat.

"Well!" he said. "You look pretty chipper."

Mr. Burt put down the paper and snuggled back into bed.

"I bet you're beginning to itch to get back to the old grind, eh?" the doctor said.

"No," Mr. Burt said.

Dr. Millis laughed and sat down in a wicker chair in the midst of a flood of sunshine that came in from the small screened porch adjoining the room.

"I guess you writers are just professional sour-pusses."

"I guess."

"Seriously, though. You're okay. We've been all over you and you haven't got a thing to worry about. Just watch the liquor and the cigarettes. When you came in here you were pretty well shot, granted."

"Granted," said Mr. Burt.

"But you'd been hitting the bottle and the nicotine pretty hard, you know. That Hollywood life . . . But now you're in fine shape. Got a good tan to show your wife. You look like a different man."

"Do I?"

"You really do. We're quite satisfied to have you leave us any time now. And although you like to have your joke, I know you're beginning to find it a trifle dull here."

"I find it lovely here," Mr. Burt said. "I'm staying."

"Well." The doctor laughed heartily. "We're flattered that you like us so much. And naturally we can't exactly throw you out. But, man to man, you ought to get back to work; get back into your regular life."

"Heaven forbid."

"I realize you felt pretty terrible when you came to us."

"Don't forget about the buildings falling in on me."

"I know. You were right on the edge of a collapse. But if you'll just observe the general health rules I've told you, you'll find the old grind won't get you down. I know the routine is pleasant here—we've tried to make it so—but it's not normal for a man, you know. It's not life."

"That's what I like about it."

"I'm going to talk quite frankly to you. The way you're letting yourself think now, you're in full flight from life."

"Okay," Mr. Burt said. "Call it my private little Waterloo."

The doctor laughed.

"Once you've smelled the smoke of battle you wouldn't change it for this quiet place on a bet. You should have let Mrs. Burt come on last week when she wanted to."

"I would rather you put a live bushmaster in this room than Mrs. Burt."

"I know you don't mean that. And I know that, underneath, you're missing your youngsters. Aren't you?"

"No," Mr. Burt said. "I dislike them."

"You just can't be serious, can you?"

"Oh, yes I can. I can be serious as all hell."

"Well, look at it like this. The world's in a bad way, these days. You've got a duty to perform. You've got your work to do. You ought to get out there and observe life as it is. The proper study of mankind is man, you know."

"I disagree," Mr. Burt said. "I know better. The proper study of mankind is me. How do you like that? It just came to me. I'll give it to you. The *Medical Journal* would snap at it."

"Very witty," the doctor said. "You're a clever chap. Too clever to be here when you ought to be out in the world, working. Introspection won't do you any good. In fact, as your doctor, I'd like to warn you against it. Don't think about yourself. It's dangerous. Think about the problems of the world and what you can do to help solve them."

"Oh deary me."

"It's easy to laugh."

"Not so easy as you might think, Doctor. Okay. So I'm defeated. What are you going to do about it? *I'm* not going to do anything about it. I'm perfectly happy here. I like it. I'm going to stay. I like the desert, and the plant you've got here, and the people, and I like the food, and I like this room and my nice comfortable bed. And I like Miss Cecil. When she doesn't talk too much."

"It's going to run you into money, this room. And you're not pulling down a salary, remember."

"Don't you worry about your dough, Doctor. I've got enough. It'll last quite a while. You'll get your dough. Mrs. Burt will get her dough. All I want is just to be let alone, see? I'm happy, and I feel healthy. Nothing hurts. I love it."

"I must warn you that it's a very unsound point of view to take. It isn't a healthy state of mind."

"I think it's a lovely state of mind. Now go away, will you? I've had about all I can stand for this morning."

"I'll have to discuss your case with Dr. Jarvis."

"Just go away. Just go quietly away."

Dr. Millis got up and went out and closed the door after him. Mr. Burt lay still, comfortably relaxed, in the bed, crooning softly to himself. After a while he put out his hand and pressed the bell. Miss Cecil came and stuck her head in the door.

"I'm going to take my sun bath," Mr. Burt said. "I just thought you might like to warn the ladies."

"Of what?" Miss Cecil said, and went away. Mr. Burt laughed softly. He got out of bed and put his feet into straw sandals and wrapped his cotton dressing gown around his thin body. He examined his teeth in the mirror over the bureau. Then he smiled at himself.

"Hello, Burt," he said to the face in the glass. "How you doing?—Doing just fine, thank you, Burt."

He went out across the soft, watered green grass of the courtyard and through the men's door to the sun-bathing terrace at the back of the building. There were several large screens dividing the men's side from the women's side. There was no one on the high, narrow cots lined up in the men's side. On the other side of the screens women's voices were talking. Mr. Burt pulled one of the cots into position so that the shadow of the nearer legs to the sun fell directly on top of the shadow of the farther legs. Then he dropped his wrapper and lay down on his stomach under the rays of the desert sun.

After twenty minutes by his wrist watch he turned over and lay on his back, with his arm thrown over his eyes. The women on the other side were discussing obstetrics.

"He told me I had the damnedest pair of ovaries he'd ever encountered," a voice said.

"Ooooo," Mr. Burt said.

There was a flurry of laughter.

"Hello, Mr. Burt," the voice said. "I didn't know you were there."

"Don't you mind," he said. "I'm just a little ghost."

"The Papago Clinical and Drinking Club is meeting before lunch," the voice called. "I hope you'll join us."

"Delighted."

After Mr. Burt had finished his forty minutes in the sun he went back to his room and took a warm bath in the tub. Then he put on fresh silk pajamas, a red-and-white-striped dressing gown, and another pair of sandals. When he came out into the courtyard there were five people sitting on the grass in the sun, wearing dark glasses and holding drinks.

"Hello, you pretty things," Mr. Burt said. He got a glass from the pantry next to the nurse's room, and made a drink for himself from the bottle of Scotch that was being passed around.

One of the five was a man who had been at the San for six months with a bad sinus. He had been operated on three times. The others were women.

"Mrs. Grimes had an attack last night," one of them said. Mrs. Grimes was the asthmatic.

"She did?"

"Couldn't you hear her? Millis and Jarvis were down here in the middle of the night, and they had an oxygen tank in there, and the whole works. It was awful listening to her. She's resting up today."

"It's amazing, she'll be as strong as a horse tomorrow. Just when the attacks get her," another woman said.

"She's got an allergy to rain, that's what it is, Cecil told me."

"An allergy to what?"

"Something or other in rain. Remember how it rained a few minutes yesterday?"

"How are you feeling, Mr. Burt, dear?"

"Bearing up," he said. "Bearing definitely up."

"You're such a fake," one of the women said, smiling at him. "Aren't you, darling?"

"It's just that he loves us so much," another woman said. "He just loves being with us."

"That's it," he said.

"And we love you, too. I don't see how the Clinical and Drinking Club ever got on without you."

"How about we all have another?" the man with the sinus said.

"Can you drink all you want now?"

"Two before lunch and two before dinner."

"Mr. Hallowell in Yavapai can't drink anything any more. They think it's his gall bladder."

"Do you know whether they made him eat a gall-bladder meal? That awful stuff you have to swallow and it makes you sick as a dog, and they don't know any more afterward than before?"

"Mrs. Leeson in Apache went out in a wheel chair this morning. I saw Alphonso pushing her down the walk."

"How long's she been here?"

"Nearly as long as I have. Must be a good eight months."

"Oh, my," Mr. Burt said. "I'm so happy."

The trays of lunch came trundling down on the metal truck, and Miss Cecil came out of the nurse's room and began to distribute them. Mr. Burt had his out on the porch of his room, where it was shady now. There was jellied soup and chicken livers on toast and asparagus and tuna-fish salad. The orderly brought in the ice cream with butterscotch sauce just as Mr. Burt was finishing his salad. When he was through, Mr. Burt went back into the bedroom and drew the shades. He lay down on the bed and went to sleep.

From one-thirty to three-thirty was rest period at the Desert San. Cards attached to the inside of the bedroom doors requested that no noise be made during this time, no radios or victrolas played, as patients were trying to sleep. It was the hottest part of the day. Just after three-thirty Miss Cecil came into Mr. Burt's room with a tall glass of grapefruit juice. She set it down on the bedside table. Mr. Burt turned over in bed and yawned luxuriously. Miss Cecil pulled up the shades.

"Hello, Gretch," Mr. Burt said.

"My name isn't Gretch."

"I know, but I like to call you Gretch."

Mr. Burt drank his grapefruit juice and got up and took a warm shower. He dressed in a pair of flannel trousers and a linen coat, and put his money in his pockets. When he went out into the courtyard everyone was sitting around.

"Hello, Mr. Burt, darling. Where do you think you're going?"

"Going into Tucson. Want to come?"

"Don't taunt me. I suppose you're going to get drunk."

"Mrs. Lawson, what an idea."

"Well, come back to us, won't you?"

"I'll come back. With my shield or on it."

He got into his car with the California tags and drove along the wide, flat, straight roads into town. After he had parked he walked slowly down the sidewalks looking into the shopwindows, at the displays of cowboy clothes, of sunglasses in opticians' windows. He went into Porter's and wandered around its wide aisles. After a while he bought two wide tooled leather belts studded with pieces of colored glass, and had them sent to his children in Santa Monica.

He came out and crossed the street and went into the Pioneer bar. After the afternoon sunshine it was cool and dim in there. Mr. Burt sat down on one of the stools in front of the bar and ordered a Martini. At the other end of the room a tenor in cowboy clothes was singing "South of the Border." Mr. Burt sang softly with him as he began his Martini.

"'I was a picture in old Spanish lace,'" he sang.

The bartender grinned at him.

"Haven't I seen you before somewhere?" he said, wiping up the bar with a cloth.

"Probably," Mr. Burt said. "I get around. I'm in a whole lot of bars. All at the same time. Here and other places."

"Yeah?"

The outside door opened on the sunshine and a girl came in. She was tall, and she was wearing a pair of long close-fitting copper-colored trousers, and a leather shirt that matched, and a dark-brown Stetson with a flat crown, on the back of her head. She walked with a long-legged, energetic stride. She was beautiful. Mr. Burt glanced up at her face as she passed and glanced quickly down again at his drink. It was a face he had never expected to see again. He took a swallow from his glass and waited for her to pass. But she had seen him.

"I leave you seven years ago sitting at a bar and here I find you again and you're *still* sitting at a bar," she said. She was smiling all over her lovely face.

"Why, it's Mrs. Wilkinson, as I live and breathe," Mr. Burt murmured. He got up and stood with his Martini in his hand, thin, stooped, and smiling a little.

The girl leaned over and kissed him.

"Darling, I'm so damned glad to see you," she said. "I've missed you so."

"I've missed you, Gretch. It appears."

"I want a Martini," she said, smiling at the bartender. "It seems so funny to be having a Martini with you, Andy. As if we hadn't moved away from a bar. As if we were still sitting at it. In Louis'."

"Oh, Mrs. Wilkinson," he said as they sat down. "You've got such a sinister little memory."

"I've missed you," she said. "I've missed it all."

Mr. Burt held up his fingers for two more Martinis.

"And what," he said, "would you be doing in Arizona? Besides disturbing my peace of mind?"

"I'm staying at a ranch. J6. Out toward Benson. Where are you staying?"

"I'm staying at a ranch, too. Sort of."

"What's the name of it?"

"I can't for the life of me remember."

"Darling, you haven't changed any, not a bit."

"I don't still have little pieces of paper sticking to me, though, do I? You could always make me feel like a God-damned commuter."

"Aren't you rich, or something? In Hollywood?"

"I've had my little fling," he said. "I made my pile, as they say. But I don't work any more. Not any. Too rich."

"Huh," she said. "I bet you have your typewriter with you."

"Oh, yes, I have it. To remind me I don't have to write anything any more."

"Darling," she said. "Couldn't we go and sit at one of those little tables?"

They went over to a table in a corner and a waiter with a long horseface brought them two more Martinis.

"How is Mr. Wilkinson?" Mr. Burt asked. "And all the little Wilkinsons?"

"There aren't any little Wilkinsons," she said. "And I don't know whether there's any Mr. Wilkinson, either. I'm trying to make up my mind."

Mr. Burt lifted his eyebrows.

"You make me wonder what the hell," he said.

"I wish you'd understand. The thing is, he bores me."

"Mrs. Wilkinson, you bore so easy."

"He certainly used to bore you."

"That's different. I always thought he was an old horror. You were the one who didn't. I seem to remember all the things you thought he was that I wasn't. Like large, and male, and dominating, or some such. He bored the hell out of me, but I wasn't in love with him and I didn't ditch me for him, if you follow me."

"I know you were right, now. My God, I've had to be so serious about love. You don't know."

"I can imagine."

"I can stand just so much maleness, I find."

"I never could see," Mr. Burt said, "this getting a toe hold on a girl, and then proposing to her. I belong more to the Gibson girl school. You under an apple tree in a peekaboo waist and me in a straw boater, down on one knee. But we can't get away from it, dear, you certainly did ditch me."

"The thing is, I didn't know anything."

The cowboy had stopped singing ballads, and his place was taken by a young woman with blond hair, in a red dress. The small orchestra began to play very softly, and she began to sing.

"Oh, dear," Mr. Burt said. "Why did they have to dig this song up?"

The girl with him put her hand out palm up on the top of the table, and he put his hand over it.

"Darling," she said.

"That was a sweet idea of yours," he said, "sending me the record of it after you'd consented to be Mr. Wilkinson's. I used to play the God-damned thing. I was pretty desolate, my darling."

She looked at him and sang a little under her breath with the music.

"'Some day I'll find you. . . . Moonlight behind you. . . . True to the dream I've been dreaming. . . .' Do you remember the words?"

"Of course I remember.—You were a ruthless girl, my darling. Not that you'd admit it. It seemed so foolish to me that the only time I'd ever gotten outside myself and wanted to see someone else have fun more than anything I could think of—that I couldn't do a damned thing about it."

"Oh, darling. But you did go on and marry Miss Butterworth, didn't you, and you've had children, and everything. . . ."

"What the hell," he said. "I didn't stay in that awful little room on Tenth Street playing Mr. Coward's record, no."

"I know it serves me right, that now I'm the unhappy one."

"I've never been able to get you out of my mind," he said. "Not ever. I've been vague about how you look, because in the state I was in about you I had no detachment at all. But I knew you were the loveliest-looking person in the world. With special reference to your legs, your hands, and your bosom. Then there was your mind and your morals, too, although they kind of got me laughing now and then. Do you remember coming down to my apartment the first part of the night you went away? And lying on the sofa? That, of course, was the way I wanted to spend about fifty percent of the rest of my life."

"Darling. . . ."

"I used to sit and make up lists of the things that weren't going to be any more—no more having you walk into bars, mostly legs, to meet me for lunch, no more taxi rides when I could kiss you, no more little bed that falls apart in the night. There ought to be an Indian word for that. Not any more of anything. I used to think that you'd come back to me. For a while I didn't get drunk because if I had it would have been very drunk, and no good if you suddenly had wanted to see me again. I did a lot of work, because I didn't want to go anywhere especially, and there wasn't any place to go that we hadn't been, together. My God, we'd been together in almost every place in the city except the subway. I used to think I could at least take long subway rides to Jerome Avenue, wherever the hell that is."

"Darling. . . ."

"Look," he said. "Would you mind if I kissed you?"

"I'd love it," she said.

"You're such a beautiful girl," he said after the kiss. "Don't you suppose there is any God?"

"Listen," she said. "Does it really have to be over?"

"I don't know," he said. "Does it?"

"Seeing you makes me know Mr. Wilkinson isn't any good for me."

"I was telling you that," he said. "Quite a while ago."

"No, but do you suppose it's fair? I mean about your wife, and everything?"

"I don't know. I honestly don't know."

"I was surprised when I heard you'd married her. I always thought she had shifty eyes."

"You told her that one night in Louis'. I don't think she liked it."

"I suppose you never heard the last of it. She's rather a grudge-bearing girl, isn't she?"

Mr. Burt looked into his drink.

"Well, no," he said. "I don't think she is. I guess she's had kind of a hell of a time with me. She doesn't say much about it."

The girl shrugged her shoulders.

"We all have hells of times," she said. "But I think it's silly to make a fuss about it."

"Just how do you mean?"

"Well, you had a hell of a time, and I'm sorry. I've had a hell of a time with Mr. Wilkinson. But then things pick up, so why stew about it?"

"I'd forgotten," he said, "just how ruthless a character you were, my sweet."

"All I want is to have F-U-N," she said, spelling it out.

"I have the queerest feeling," he said, "that we really are back in Louis' with me holding your hand. Not knowing about all the horror you can get yourself into. All the God-damned suffering."

"Couldn't we be as if we really were back? I don't feel any different."

"You aren't any different. I think you're beautiful and invulnerable beyond our generation."

"Darling."

"It's just people like Miss Butterworth who get different. It's just people like me."

"You aren't any different either."

Mr. Burt looked at his hand, holding hers.

"Look," she said. "I'm supposed to be having dinner with these people. I could call them up. I don't have to do anything. I don't have to be anywhere."

"I can't imagine you," he said, "not having to be somewhere else with somebody else."

"I'll go and telephone," she said. "Shall I? I'll go and tell them I can't come."

"All right," he said. He was looking at his hand and hers.

She got up and walked out of the bar. He watched her go, and she disappeared into the lobby of the hotel. Mr. Burt reached in his pocket and got out an envelope and a pencil. He wrote on the envelope, "I guess maybe it isn't fair or something," and lifted his finger to the waiter.

"You give this to the lady when she comes back," he said. "And look. Here's for the check. You can keep the rest."

"Thanks a lot," the horse-faced waiter said. "Was there anything the matter?"

"Not really," Mr. Burt said. "'One more such victory and we shall be undone.' Pyrrhus."

"Yeah?" said the waiter.

Mr. Burt went quickly out of the bar and down the street in the gathering dusk. He got into his car and drove out over the wide straight roads to the San.

When he walked into Papago it was very quiet. The doors to the patients' rooms were closed and lights shone behind them. A nurse came out into the twilight.

"Hi, Mr. Burt, honey," she said. "Where you been?"

"Horsin' round," he said. "Where's Gretch?"

"Who?"

"Miss Cecil."

"Honey, you know she's off in the evenin's."

"I forget things," he said.

"Supper's been over for ages. You had anythin' to eat?"

"No."

"I could get you some orange juice. And some milk."

He went with her into the pantry and came out again with the two glasses in his hands. He stood in the middle of the courtyard alone, on the soft grass. In the large desert sky the stars were bright and yellow and he picked out the Big Dipper and Orion. From the patients' closed rooms there came the low mingled murmur of radio voices talking and singing. Far out on the desert suddenly a few coyotes barked, making the hullabaloo of a whole pack.

He set the empty glasses down on the concrete edge of the fountain and went across and into his room and shut the door. He took off his clothes and got into pajamas and a dressing gown. Then he began to wander around the room. He sang softly to himself the chorus from the old Coward tune.

When I draw near you
You'll smile a little smile;
For a little while
We shall stand
Hand in hand. . . .

Suddenly he went over to the bureau and peered at himself in the mirror. His face was long, thin, and narrow, with full lips and green eyes under thick eyelids; the hair was ruffled. He put a finger up to one of his eyes and wiped it; then he examined the tip of the finger, and shook his head. It was barely damp.

He went and bent over and pulled a portable typewriter out from under the bed, and slung it up on the small table opposite the bureau. There was yellow copy paper stuck under the lid of the case. He pulled the paper out and laid it beside the machine and drew up a straight chair. He fed a sheet of paper into the typewriter and then sat down and pecked at it with the middle finger of his left hand. He looked critically at the capital *M* that he had made. Then he jerked the chair closer, lit a cigarette, hunched his shoulders up, and went to work.

1945

ON THE BEACH

THEY CAME to the beach early, in triumph at the perfect morning. It was as if, Mary thought, after all the rain and the two cold days, they had a vested interest in the weather, as though they had invented today themselves, and a great improvement it was.

She was sure Mac, her seven-year-old boy, felt just the same way, that the blue, crystal perfection of the morning was their private production, because they always felt the same way about everything. He was wandering off down the beach now, weaving up toward the dunes and down to the edge of the water, inspecting everything like a proprietor. Ever since he was a tiny baby, their instant sympathy had been astounding. He had used to look up even from his play pen, the light in his face reflecting her exact mood. It was wonderful to have one person in the world who felt along with you, without words, as though by an electric communication.

MacNeil, her husband, was not so, she thought as she began to arrange herself for the morning on the sand; and she did not care if he was not, since one person in the world, her child, was always with her; it made it more interesting to have another member of your family quite different from you, introducing new and foreign matter into the sensitive blend that was the domestic atmosphere. Together she and Mac would absorb the new elements MacNeil brought home on weekends and come up with the identical laugh or the identical wrinkling of the nose. And it was not as if she could reproach herself for a minute with having tried to possess the child; it was not that at all; it was only that things took him as they took her, as though in parturition a whole strain of her own humor and tastes and imagination had not become separated from her, but ran through them both, side by side.

But today was a Wednesday, the middle of the week, and there was only the wide blue glittering morning to receive together. Taking her time, consciously enjoying each second of being alive, Mary spread out the big striped beach towel to lie on; set her beach bag and the canvas back-piece conveniently to one side; took out the bottle of baby oil. She sat down and spread oil all over herself until her skin gleamed. Then she lay down flat on her stomach facing the ocean, with her chin propped upon her hands, and looked out to sea. The life she felt so full of today seemed to flow like a stream out into the vaster water and on toward the edge of the world, the pale-blue horizon, whence it gently turned with the turn of the world and came back, still fluid, into herself again, in as unbroken a flow as the circulation of the blood.

How happy Mac is, she thought. She twisted her head to see him. He had settled down on the heap of glacial boulders at the end of the beach, and she thought he was sailing his boat in the rock-pool they called the Bathtub. She could see part of his tanned, smooth back, still plump with puppy fat, and part of his red jersey trunks. Without a break she turned back to the enormous blue in front of her.

And here face down beneath the sun, she thought. Two sandpipers stalked along the margin of the water. The morning was young and a blue haze hung lightly over the water. Far out on the water a sailboat sat, apparently motionless, but the sail did not flutter and after a time she realized it had moved along, in relation to the headland. The sun was so tranquil and hot that the heat seemed to her to purr; she could feel it scratching at the edges of her back. *To feel the always coming on, the always rising of the night. And now at Kermanshah the. . . .* The night was a long, long time off, and this was morning, blue and virginal.

All at once the sailboat was no longer there. It must have moved, in the crystal timelessness of the day, beyond the headland, on into unseen waters. While she was here, still, as though forever, herself opposite the ocean that spread enormously over the curve of the globe, not falling away from it, forming a part of the roundness of this world until it met another shore, thousands of miles from here, another beach. She and the sea, and, somewhere comfortably near, her child. She wondered whether the sun had purred for him.

All under her she felt the world, the globe, a round mass pursuing its course in space, wonderfully ordered, punctual as a chronometer. All things were in their places—the world going privately around, and going around the sun, and the sun participating in the galaxy, and the galaxy belonging in some vaster dance. Mary stretched out her hand and sifted the dry hot sand between her fingers. When I was little, she thought, I used to think of the world as ending at the horizon. Right here where I am was the center, and the stars were only there to look at.

But perhaps because of the scientific facts mixed in every bowl of oatmeal nowadays, Mac had apparently never felt that medieval, center-of-the-universe way. One day she had felt the sense of the globe upholding her in space so vividly that she had wanted to share it with him, and yet was conscientiously afraid of rupturing some concept more natural to childhood. She said, cautiously, "Did you ever think of the world being round underneath you?" They were walking home from the beach, on the narrow path between bayberries that scratched their legs. He looked back at his mother with surprise. "Of course. It *is* round underneath me."

Everything hung together, the oceans did not fall off the world, the world did not desert the sun, and the sun danced in its appointed figure. *And here face down beneath the sun. . . .* She stirred and turned her face sidewise upon her folded arms. This way she saw the ocean at an angle. Into her frame of vision slid a gull, coasting along the currents of the air high over. . . .

At the same moment that she noticed the sound of the planes, she felt again that new, unpleasant jerk in all her nerves, like the jerk that pulls the sleeper back into consciousness in the early hours of the night.

She sat up, sharply, on the towel and peered at the three planes flying out to sea. At some distance behind the first plane could be seen a white object, somehow reminiscent of a hornet's egg—which was the target which the planes, from the Navy base down the coast, towed out to sea on clear mornings to shoot at.

And she had seen them on many mornings before, so why, she thought, crossing her legs under her and following the planes with her eyes as they flew out into blue space, did she today feel this sick jerk, this dreadful sort of awakening, which was like a wound that altered the calm course of the blood?

Feeling disrupted and cheated she lay down again, and again let her eyes find the knife-edge of the horizon, now standing sharper and clearer out of the haze. *And now face down* . . . , she began to recite to herself, like an incantation to restore something which was lost. But she could see it was not coming back, the life did not any longer flow out of her to the world's edge freely; but remained hesitant, questioning, on the inside of her eyes. She rolled over on her back and shut her eyes to answer the question.

Well . . . the answer was not hard to find.

They were playing bridge last weekend and before pivoting to new partners at the table, were talking about the H bomb and the new site in South Carolina for an installation.

"They're not going to make the actual bombs there," the other man said.

And then MacNeil dropped the thought.

"It's the chain reaction I mind the idea of," he remarked casually.

The others seemed to understand, but Mary had never heard of it.

"The what?"

"It's not so much the blowing us to pieces," the other woman said in an explanatory way. "Civilization or anything, because I suppose we'd eventually build a new one. Maybe it would be a better one anyway. It's the having the atmosphere gone."

"*What?*" Mary said.

MacNeil took it up again.

"Nobody seems to be able to assure us that there might not be a chain reaction," he said. He was beginning to shuffle the cards, and the other woman to deal. "To put it in an elementary way, if there was, the atmosphere surrounding the earth would ignite. Blow up."

And it was when he said that, over the card table, that Mary had had the first of these jerks. It was not a conscious reaction at all. It was, on the contrary, like losing consciousness, at the same time that it was like being brought sharp awake out of the beginning of sleep. In fact, consciousness made her say only "How horrible!" The reaction was not connected with anything that was conscious; it belonged to her nerves and to the mysterious centers of life that were responsible for those miraculous reflexes that saved one from falling down when one lost balance, that made one throw out a hand and save one's eyes.

Now she lay quite still with her head buried, waiting for the answer to her question to settle her, to settle whatever the sources were that could send up that awful, primeval jerk. If you know what a thing is, she explained to herself, you can accept it and go on from there. Now I know what the jerk came from. The idea of the end.

Not the end of me, or the end of civilization, or the end of man even, but the *end*. The *isn't any*.

So the planes must have made the jerk come back because they are going to shoot at the target to practice hitting targets, and planes drop bombs on targets, and bombs can cause chain reactions. And chain reactions etcetera etcetera, and that's the whole of it. The full circle of destruction. So let me get back to the living circle of the globe under me and its place in the eternal circles of space, *please*. Because the other has not been, is not, and perhaps never shall be.

She turned over again, cautiously and superstitiously, and took a small quick look at the horizon to see how things were.

They were all right. The life, the energy, of herself in this lovely and pristine morning now swelling to full noon, flowed out once more quite free toward the edge of the world, returned, and again drew out from her with the softly ebbing tide, like healthy blood. She drew a sigh, because it was all right, and her fancy began once more to play upon the sea.

The beaches are the edges of the sea. I lie on the edge of the sea, and beyond the sea are the beaches of the world, the broad white beaches and the stony shores, and the sinister beaches where the smugglers climb at night without lights.

The palm-bordered beaches of the lonely islands in the South Seas, Stevenson's islands, Kon-Tiki's islands, all alone in the Pacific. And the pink beaches of Bermuda where Miranda walked. And the beaches of the Carolinas where the pirates' gold is somewhere buried still. All the beaches edge the sea and hold it down to earth like clamps along the thin outside, while the sea swings back and forth, clamped down at its edges only, hugging the globe, and the earth quakes at intervals and shudders, and the volcanoes spew up the earth's insides in molten rivers, and the whole thing hangs together and nothing falls off.

Even the waterspouts, in the far-off tempests that only sailors see: they strain up from the world and meet the sky, but they come down again, and sometimes split a ship. But they come down.

A safe world. A safe, centered, maternal world that draws its own to it. I will not hear an objection to that, she thought. It *is* a safe world, and I love it, and it spins under me on itself as it also circles the sun, and the sun is always there. . . .

Her eyes rested upon the stretches of water in peace.

She began to realize that she was hungry, and sat up to put her hand on the lunchbox, in her beach bag, that they brought down every good day. She brushed off the accumulation of sand crusted along her arms where she had flung them outside the towel.

She stood up and stretched. She became aware of how well her body felt, and how young she still was; she shivered a little and flexed her legs at the knee. She caught sight of Mac far down the beach digging, and called, "Hi! Mac, I'm going swimming."

When he came back they proceeded down to the water with the delaying anticipation of a dog approaching its food, and felt the water with their toes. "Cold!" they both said at the same instant.

Mac held out his little finger crooked, and she linked hers with it.

They thought.

"What goes up the chimney?" he said.

"Smoke."

"May your wishnmywish never be—*broke*!" he chanted as they pulled apart.

They walked into the water. Mac was brown all over except for the red postage stamp of his trunks. He kept turning his head and grinning at his mother, each time a little wave smacked against them. When the water reached his ribs under his outstretched arms, he suddenly shrieked and dived into the sea. Two steps farther she followed him in.

When they were cold from swimming they came out again into the now blazing sun of midday. They walked up the slopes of the beach toward their little encampment with the sand making boots around their feet and ankles.

"That heat," Mac said. "It purrs like a cat, doesn't it?"

"It certainly does," she said, and laughed out loud because he had felt it, too.

They chased each other up the beach for a bit until they were partly dried off, and then settled themselves on the big towel and unfolded the little waxed-paper packages that contained hard-boiled eggs, and crabmeat sandwiches and lettuce sandwiches. There was milk in a thermos bottle; peaches, and sugar cookies.

"We know how to enjoy the good things of life, don't we, Mother," Mac said, crumpling up his pieces of waxed paper and putting them back in the box. It was an expression his father used sometimes, and he looked like a small-size caricature of his father, with his light hair standing up in spikes.

"We sure do!" Mary said, and jumped up to shake the crumbs off her bathing suit; sitting down again, she leaned over and dusted crumbs off her child's round, brown stomach. "Now for naps."

She arranged the reclining canvas back-piece to cast a shadow on Mac's face as he lay down on one side of the towel; then lay down herself beside him with her face buried in her folded arms.

"Aren't you going to kiss me goodnight?" he said.

"I most certainly am," she said, and sat up again.

She looked down for a minute at the round, tanned, glowing face and started to lean over to kiss the peach-bloom cheek.

There was a tearing, ripping sound in the heavens, a kind of whizzing like a length of silk being split. Mary sat up sharply.

Mac got up, too; he jumped to his feet with his head thrown back, peering up into the unbroken blue whence the piercing sound had come.

"Jets!" he cried joyfully. "Pr-r-r-r-r-r-r . . ." and he began to imitate the sound of a machine gun, doubling himself over and holding an invisible gun to his hip.

The jerk came then, in her innermost, uncontrollable foundations. Sick, draining, both startling her out of the dream of the day and blacking consciousness, the jerk came and went. She sat quite still, letting the sensation pass.

"Weren't they lovely jets?" the child said happily, lying down and lifting his face for his kiss.

But she felt no impulse to give it to him. He seemed too far to reach.

When she bent over anyway to kiss the round cheek, nothing went out to her child. All her life and her love seemed to shrink behind her eyes and mouth, gathering themselves around some other focus, as blood and fluids rush to a wound.

But the child was satisfied, and rolled over on his side, heaving a great sigh.

She started to lie down beside him, but her body did not want to stretch out. She felt the need of sitting up, hugging her knees, staring sightless at the sea. Something against nature had happened to her.

For a moment, there had been a clean break in the feeling which had always united her with Mac. Something unseen and awful was stronger than her love for her child. She had always known that there must some day be a break between them; when the break came, it would naturally come through his moving away from her, toward the world. But she had moved away from him. It had not been conscious. But it had been so.

What had divided them was not any ordinary fear, for love was stronger than fear, and in any real danger her first response would have been, she knew, toward Mac; like the time when he was four and fell off the pier and she had been in the water after him with no memory of having dived. But this was not a real danger. This was the danger of utter unreality, of the end of existence for everybody.

And there it was: the unreal danger, present in the world. Ten years ago, even, a mother could have lain all summer on a beach with her child, and nothing under the canopy of the heavens could have come between them.

She moved, stiffly, and lay down on the towel beside the boy. She propped her chin on her fists and stared out to sea. The life began to move out of her again, slowly, sluggishly, over the broad blue waste.

She thought of its deep strata, the green, the blue, the black layers underlying one another; and moving along the strata, and from one stratum into another, silently, the billion elemental creatures of the sea. And each of these was a center in itself, for itself, a cell or more of responses either reaching out like tentacles or shrinking in to the cell's mysterious core. In her sadness and isolation, she felt she was, at bottom, no different from those silent creatures. She was dark, and alone, and unrelated. All things had fallen from her, her child, her love, and the day she had greeted with such triumph. This, she thought, was what the threat of extinction did to one.

She dropped her head down in her arms. *To feel the always coming on, the always rising of the night. . . .*

She knew that the shock of those jerks would lessen and disappear for her. One could forget any danger that failed to happen. She would forget it, and forget the primitive, subhuman isolation it had brought her. Perhaps by tomorrow she would forget. It had been like exploring a region not meant for human eyes, something people were not supposed to know about.

"Mother," Mac said.

"Yes, darling."

"I've got something in my eye."

She sat up. "Close your eyes," she ordered. "Don't rub them. It'll come out."

She bent over him and again kissed his cheek; it was sweet-smelling with health, soft, and with the bloom of velvet on it.

She moved the canvas back-piece to cut off the sunshine that had begun to creep across his face, and went on looking down at the drowsy child, her love moving steadily across the deep water that separated their two existences.

Then she lay down again, relaxing, her cheek laid on her arm, and felt the sun burning her bare back. She looked athwart the broad sea that curved far, far away to the other side of the world, where another shore would meet it, and felt the heat of the sand coming up into her body through the towel. There was no sound anywhere, only the heat and the air and the water lying blue before her to the horizon, and gradually she began to imagine the world revolving underneath her in its predestined place, humming as it spun.

1952

INSIDE

I don't like superhighways, I realized a few weeks ago when I was driving down from New England to Virginia. It is the country through which they run, I thought—something to do with its atmosphere, at once of frantic commercialism and of total unreality. As I entered the New Jersey Turnpike, I felt that the sense of unreality was perhaps to be expected of the Jersey flats, for those low, misty lands stretching for melancholy miles are so precisely like the marshes that surround one in illness. I drove at fifty-five; someone had set the speed limit at sixty, and all the grim-faced drivers who passed me were clinging to their sixty as though they had an obligation to meet the speed limit—a compulsion in which free will played no part. There was nothing human about any of it, the sad swamps or the driven drivers or the signs that said, "Service Area 27 Miles." At least when one is ill the voices calling across the lowlands of one's feverish mind do not use the word "area."

At the end of the Turnpike, I saw ahead of me the great, fantastic arch of the Delaware River bridge, as preposterous as a giant's toy. I told myself that the hills one approaches when driving are never so steep as they appear to be from a distance, but this bridge *was* precipitous and my car seemed to climb it like a child's bug car being pushed up a table leg. I saw that the only way to manage the thing was to leave it to those hidden reflexes set at the age of fourteen, when one first learns to drive. The arch turned and came down, and at the bottom I was again conscious of the rush, the push, the concerted drive all around me of speeding cars, and I wished I had picked a slower, more winding route than this—one lined with real houses in which real people lived real lives.

I hadn't stopped to buy any gas on the Turnpike, and soon after I left it, I drew up at one of the stations where my credit card is honored. The man who waited on me had criminal ears, shifty eyes, and four fingers on one hand. None of this surprised me, but when I asked for a package of the cigarettes I smoke, he said they didn't carry that brand. I followed him into the office while he wrote out the slip for my gasoline and oil, and as I waited, I found myself facing a cigarette machine with my brand prominently displayed.

"Oh, you *do* have my kind of cigarettes!" I exclaimed.

His eyes flickered. "So I do," he said.

I felt almost frightened as I put my twenty-five cents in the slot.

Later, I stopped for a midafternoon snack at a super snack bar, where I paid thirty-five cents for a hamburger and twenty cents for an ice-cream cone to a brittle waitress with abstracted, inhuman eyes. Then back into the car again, to press down the road toward Baltimore, passing trucks on the upgrade, being passed by them again on the downgrade, eyes straight ahead, and the tail of one eye or the other glimpsing nothing more rural than shabby billboards and the promise posted of more and bigger motels to come.

In the late afternoon, I stopped for the night at a motel a few miles north of Baltimore. I chose it because it had a tree growing in its front yard and because, just beyond, there was a small house with a sign in front saying, "Chicken Dinners." An old man with one eye and a limp showed me to a cabin and collected six dollars from me. I did not like him; he, too, looked inhuman—like everyone, I suspected, who would choose to live on a superhighway. And after I had paid and showered and changed to a clean dress, I realized I had not picked my motel well, either; it was at the top of a long grade, and the trucks were laboring hard.

The sound of the traffic was overwhelming. It whistled, it

whined, it roared by. That incessant noise was the one immediate fact. As I locked my door and set off across the strip of grass to the house next door for dinner, I wondered whether I would be able to get any sleep that night.

The little house had its very threshold on the highway. I opened the door and walked into a semi-Victorian parlor, much like the one my Irish nurse used to have when she retired to spend her old age in Dorchester, Massachusetts—overstuffed horsehair chairs, gilt-framed photographs on the walls, a carpet with cabbage roses, a calendar hung on a hook. It smelled like my nurse's parlor, too. At one end of the room, there were four tables set with silver on old-fashioned white tablecloths.

A lady of perhaps sixty, with a curly fringe dyed dark brown, rose from one of the horsehair chairs as I came in.

"I would like to have dinner," I shouted, above the scream of the cars.

"The regular?" she shouted back. I nodded. When I had sat down at one of the tables, I read the menu, printed on an orange card:

Chicken Dinner	$1.50
Half a Chicken	
two peices of bread	$1.00
Coffee and cake	.25

The lady had gone out into the kitchen, which I could glimpse through maroon plush portières, but it was impossible to hear any sound of getting a meal; it was impossible to hear anything, even a fork lifted and set down upon a plate before one.

There was no one else there. It was almost as if I had invented the place—this comfortable, ugly parlor like my nurse's in Dorchester long ago, this homey, slightly smelly, human habitation set down on the edge of the nightmare road.

In a short time, the lady brought in a round platter on which were the fried pieces of half a chicken; a plate of cole slaw; a plate of sliced tomatoes; dishes of three different kinds of relish—spiced crab apples, mustard pickles, and peach preserve—and six hot rolls.

"Do you want I should shut the windows?" she asked me, her voice still raised. She had dark, snapping eyes.

I nodded, and she closed them. After they were shut, the noise was still overwhelming.

"It must get on your nerves," I yelled at her.

"Oh, you get used to it," she said, and went and sat down in her horsehair chair at the other end of the room.

I did well by that platter of chicken, and the cole slaw was delicious, with a mustard dressing I have never tasted anywhere else. I ate three of the hot rolls, and when I had finished, the lady brought me a big slice of chocolate layer cake and a cup of excellent coffee.

"Did you ever see an orange tree?" she called across the room at me suddenly as I was drinking my coffee.

"Have you got one?" I called back.

"Two. And a lemon tree. My son brought them to me. He goes to Florida winters."

"I'd like to see them," I said.

After I had paid her the dollar and a half for that huge meal, she led me out the front door and around the side over the soft grass. There, at the back of the yard, were three sturdy little trees bearing large green fruit in clusters.

"And that's an angel-trumpet," she said, pointing to a plant. "Do you know anything about angel-trumpets? I've had this one a year and it hasn't bloomed yet."

"Oh, it takes at least two years," I said, to be encouraging. "What beautiful dahlias!" I was looking across a low picket fence at a bed of autumn flowers in front of a cottage.

"Those are my son's. He built that house when he got back from Japan after the war. He was a prisoner of the Japs. They had him in that camp two years, and you should see his legs—all cigarette burns. And they had him in irons." She pronounced it "ahns."

"It's a nice little house," I said, thinking of the wonder of returning from the wide and various world to build a cottage on the highway. "Is he living here now?"

"Yes. He just goes to Florida winters. That's his son." She nodded toward the highway. A boy of fourteen or so was slowly pedalling along by the side of the road, his head bent. "My grandson. He's been out doing his chores, cutting folks' lawns."

I watched the bicycling boy pump slowly up the grade in the early twilight of his home. The lights were being turned on over at my motel. "Do you know the man who keeps the motel?" I asked her.

She looked a little surprised. "John? Why, yes. He's First Reader at our church."

"What happened to his eye?"

"Kicked out by a horse. John used to keep the livery stable around here."

The twilight was deepening in the yard. Outside, the cars and trucks were roaring by, their lights on now. She walked toward the road with me as I turned to go.

"It must be tiring—never any letup in that noise," I shouted as we stood at the edge of the yard.

She shrugged her shoulders. "You get used to it," she said again. "I forget about it. Sometimes it don't seem quite real, those folks in their cars, or like they had real lives of their own."

1953

THE EMPRESS'S RING

I WORRY ABOUT IT STILL, even today, thirty odd years later. I close my eyes to go to sleep at night, sometimes, and I am back at the old, disintegrated sand pile where I lost it, digging in the dirt-mixed sand with my fingernails to find my little ring.

It was tiny, a little girl's ring that was said to have belonged to the Empress of Austria. I suppose that would have been Elisabeth, the beautiful one who climbed mountains. It was given to me, I think on my eighth birthday, by a family friend whom I called Aunt and who was herself so erect, so blond, so high-voiced that I thought of her privately as a princess. I was told that she had bought the ring in an auction room in Vienna and brought it home—all for me.

The ring was gold, with a curly banner across the top which was set with five little turquoises. The gold setting of the stones was etched or engraved; it gave a delicate and lacy effect. I thought it was the most beautiful ring, the most royal ring.

"Far too good for a child to wear," my nurse said firmly. I can see her entwining her fat red fingers as she said it. "You won't be wearing it out to play, that's one thing."

But the thing was that I did. I was compelled to after her saying that. For nobody—certainly not she—could understand the love I had for that ring, and the absolute impossibility of my ever losing anything so precious. I wore it when I went out to play in the shed that adjoined the old barn and connected it with the abandoned milkhouse that was now called my playhouse.

Getting a playhouse, even a makeshift one, had been a sort of victory a little while back. Our only neighbors, the Wilkinsons, had a daughter named Mimi, who had a real playhouse, one built for the purpose: a tiny model of a cottage, with little green shutters at the windows, a shingled roof, a door with a shiny brass knocker engraved "Mimi," and, inside, miniature chairs and a table upon which Mimi, a girl with natural ringlets, set out tea parties with real Dresden china made for children's use, china with pink rosebuds which were unendurably thrilling—pink rosebuds and gold rims.

Ours was not the place for that kind of thing at all. We had nothing that was modern, nothing that was fascinating like rosebuds on little new china teacups. Our big white house seemed to settle down deeper into the ground with every spring freshet. The barn was red. The place had once been a working farm, but all that was left of that now was the stanchions in the lower barn; the horse stalls in the upper barn, where one could stand and look out of the little horse windows over the swamp at the melancholy woods beyond and imagine that one was a horse; the market garden of rhubarb that came up doggedly year after year, no matter how many boxes of furnace ashes were dumped upon it (the rhubarb ended by coming up out of the ground at least six feet higher than the original garden had been); and the little house at the end of the woodshed, which had once been used to prepare the milk for marketing. There was a sort of slot at the front of this milkhouse, and the cans had been shoved out through it into a big box with a lid, where they could be picked up by the men who took them away. But of this I had only been told. Now there was no activity on our place. The pines in front of the house sighed and whistled in winter, the dandelions came up like little suns all over the lawns in springtime, the swamp turned from gold to crimson to purple as the summer passed sadly by, and in autumn the pumpkins lay rotting on the ground down below the lower barn.

I had to have a playhouse. I wept. And so the abandoned milkhouse was swept out, some of my nursery furniture was moved into it, and an ornate Victorian knocker was screwed on to the weathered board door that would not quite close, and it was officially referred to as my playhouse.

What was it that was wrong? It was not really a playhouse, to begin with—but I had imagined far wilder excursions than this required. I made the effort; I imagined that the too high shelves inside, where cans had been stacked, were really shelves for my own needs, to put books and toys and tea-party china on. I imagined that the bulkhead which contained the slot for pushing out the cans was really a window seat.

My mother gave me some china to use for my own efforts at tea parties. Rosebuds were what I yearned for, rosebuds were what I dreamed about at night. Small, neat rosebuds on a field of glistening milk-white china—*little* china, made for children. What I got was probably much nicer. It was the odds and ends of an old broken-up adult tea set—orange-and-white china with gold arabesques. I set it on the too high shelves—the plates on edge against the wall, the teacups in a row, the saucers in a pile, the teapot turned so that the broken spout did not show. It was probably very beautiful. But there was nothing, there could have been nothing, that would take the place of pink rosebuds.

Then I was given my little blue ring. It was a ring meant for a little girl to wear. It was real gold, and real turquoises. It was beautiful, and it had belonged to an empress.

It belonged to my hand. It was just the right size. In the morning sun, when I went out to play, its five turquoises shone in a curly row. Even all these years later, I can remember looking at it and feeling satisfied, complete, and happy.

It was probably not the first day I wore it that I lost it, but I did not have it very long. I went to play in the old sand pile that moldered away in the inner corner of the shed nearest to the barn. The sand pile was the remains of several cartloads of sand that had been dumped there, but since there was no frame to hold the sand (such as Mimi's sand pile had) it had sifted, filtered away, become mixed with the dirt of the woodshed, disintegrated, spread out; it was another of the things I had that had something the matter with them.

I don't know why I went to play in the sand pile at all. I was too old, and this was my playhouse stage. But sometimes I did go and play in it, in the scattered remains of my babyhood, just as sometimes I went and slid into the hole under the foundations of the barn that I had discovered when I was four—not to hide any more, not for any game, just to be in there and feel it around me again.

I went to the sand pile again, at the wrong age, and, whether the first time or a later one, I lost my little ring playing in it. The loss did not strike me all at once.

I came in to lunch, and my nurse said, "There. Will you look? You've lost your beautiful gold ring with the stones in it, just as I told you you would."

I said nothing. I looked at my horribly bare hand and looked back at her, not showing anything. I didn't want her to see anything. Because I was convinced it was because she had told me I would lose my precious possession if I wore it out to play that I had lost it. I didn't want her to know this.

"I know *exactly* where it is," I said. "It's not lost at all."

And in a way I did know exactly where it was. It was in the sand pile somewhere, and the sand pile was not more than ten feet wide, even in its disintegrated condition. It had to be there. I looked and looked—that day and other days, too—with a hollow, painful feeling inside me because I had lost my precious possession. At some point, I must have given up.

But I never completely gave up, because years later, in my teens, I would suddenly remember my ring, the one I had lost, and would go out to the sand pile, by now almost obliterated but still a definite area to me, and dig and dig. It had to be there. I never found it, but it was there just the same, somewhere in the mingled sand and dirt, within a definite space about ten feet square.

Once, I dreamed that I had found it. It was when I was a young girl going to dances, and the dream was about the most irrelevant to my life that could be imagined. But when I woke, with the clear memory of finding the ring and seeing it lie in my palm with its banner of five little blue stones, my excitement and the verisimilitude were so great that I went out to the woodshed—in a beige crêpe-de-Chine dress, I remember, that reached my knees; high heels, and my hair shingled—and began to dig once again. Then the telephone rang for me, or someone drove up in a car. But after the dream it was not finding it that seemed unbelievable.

Even now, in another part of the country, I sometimes remember my ring and wonder why I could never find it. Today, for example, I took a walk in this Southern springtime, filled with the sound of the persistent mourning dove and the occasional thrill of the wood thrush. I passed the brook, which is called a run, and the thicket of bamboos that grows beside it, and mounted the gentle rise that leads on past the Lambeths' house. The Lambeths have a lovely house—old, built of pink brick, but all made fresh, all charming and inviting; inside, their floors gleam, their chintzes are trimly fitted to the chairs, and they drink their whiskey out of silver tumblers with gadroon edges. I would love tumblers like that, but they must cost a fortune. As I rounded the curve just before the entrance to the Lambeths' house, I thought I would stop and pay them a call. It would be fun to sit before their crackling fire and drink their whiskey from one of those enchanting tumblers, and perhaps come to know them better. But as I came abreast of the drive, I saw that two cars were parked near the door. The Lambeths already had callers. I felt a little hollow, and passed on.

When I made the circuit that brought me home, I felt thirsty and got myself a drink of water. My glasses are a sorry collection, the odds and ends of a number of broken sets. I went upstairs then and into my room, where I tidied up a little before lying down to take a nap. I don't know why it is that Mrs. Hildreth, who makes my slipcovers, can never make the arms fit properly; the cording lies unevenly upon the frame of the chair and gives a sloppy appearance.

I lay down, and as soon as I closed my eyes, there I was again, years and years later, back in the old woodshed of the place where I grew up, scratching and clawing at the sand pile, trying to find my little blue ring. I'm sure there is not as much sand, nearly, left there any more as I see when I close my eyes. There may not be any sand at all; the place is sold, and the new owners may have fixed everything up, torn down the shed, perhaps even put up a new, properly fenced-in sand pile somewhere for their growing children. I don't know.

Perhaps if the old sand pile *is* still there, one of the new owner's children will one day really find my ring, for it is there somewhere. Perhaps the child—a little girl—will be poking about with a tin shovel and will turn up that scrap of gold with its five little blue stones. I wonder what she will make of it.

1953

THE BUBBLE

Now when Eric was born in Washington, D.C., I was eighteen, and most people thought I was too young to be having a baby.

I went down there two months before it was going to come, to stay at my mother-in-law's house. She was crazy for the baby to be born in Washington, and I was just as glad to get away from New York. My father had been divorced from my mother, and she had gone abroad, and he was getting married to Estrella, so I couldn't go *there*, and I had got so I couldn't stand that first awful little apartment, with the ivory woodwork and a red sateen sofa; I didn't know how to make it look attractive, and it depressed me. Tom, Eric's father, stayed on in it after I went to his mother's; I remember he used to work in a bond house.

It felt strange, staying with my mother-in-law. She had a big house, right opposite to the old British Embassy. That makes you realize how long ago this was, and yet I am still, all these years later, wondering about why it was the way it was. Mrs. Tompkins' house was a real house, with five stories and four servants, and meals at regular times and a gong that the colored butler rang to call you to them. I had never lived in a real house. My father always had apartments with day beds in them, so we could open the whole place up for parties, and we ate any time. My father was an art critic on the *Tribune*. Nobody remembers who he was any more; everybody forgets things so fast.

My room in Washington was in the front, on the top floor, looking out at the rambling, old, mustard-yellow Embassy. Sometimes at night I would lean on the window sill and watch the cars draw up and the people in evening dress get out and walk up the strip of crimson carpet they rolled out across the sidewalk for the Embassy parties. And I would weep, up there on the fourth floor, because I was so big and clumsy, and I felt as if I would never, never go dancing again, or walk along a red carpet, or wear a low-cut dress. The last time I had was one night when I went dancing at the old Montmartre with Tom and Eugene—I was in love with Eugene—and I had seen myself in a long mirror dancing and realized how fat I looked, and that was another reason I wanted to get away from New York and go and have it in Washington. I had two black dresses—one plain wool and the other with an accordion-pleated crêpe skirt—and one velours hat, and I wore them and wore them and wore them all those last weeks, and I swore to myself that when it was born I would burn them in the fireplace in my room there. But I never did.

I used to live in a kind of fever for the future, when the baby would have come and I would look nice again and go back to New York and see Eugene. I took regular walks along the Washington streets—N Street, and Sixteenth Street, and Connecticut Avenue with all the attractive people going into restaurants to lunch—in my shapeless black dress and my velours hat, dreaming of the day when I would be size 12 and my hair would curl again and I would begin to have fun. All those days before Eric was born were aimed frontward, hard; I was just getting through them for what it would be like afterward.

My mother-in-law was the one who was really having the baby; she was full of excitement about it, and used to take me to Washington shops to buy baby clothes. Looking back all these years later, I remember those sunny afternoons in late winter, and the little white dresses and embroidered caps and pink sweaters spread out on the counter, and stopping to have tea and cinnamon toast at the

Mayflower, with the small orchestra playing hotel music, and they seem beautiful and tranquil, but in those days I was just doing any old thing she suggested, and I was living to get back to New York and begin having fun again.

I remember she gave a ladies' luncheon for me, to meet some of the young mothers she thought I would like to know. I suppose they were a couple of years older than I, but they seemed middle-aged to me and interested in the stupidest things; I wanted to cry because nobody was anything like me.

But now I remember that the luncheon was really beautiful. The dining room was big and long, and on the sideboard was Mrs. Tompkins' silver *repoussé* tea service. The table was laid with a huge white damask cloth, and the napkins had lace inserts. It was a real ladies' lunch party, with twelve ladies and a five-course luncheon; I had never been to one before in my life, and I seldom have since. I remember the first course was shrimp cocktails in glasses set in bowls filled with crushed ice. And for dessert there was a special confection, which had been ordered from Demonet's, the famous Washington caterer; it was a monument of cake and ice cream and whipped cream and cherries and angelica. But all I could think about was how food bored me and how I wanted to get back and begin living again. I felt in such a hurry.

Later that day, Mrs. Tompkins gave me a lot of her linens. It was before dinner. We used to sit in the small library and listen to *Amos 'n' Andy* every night at seven. And this night she brought in a great armful of linens to show me, and everything I admired she would give me. There were damask tablecloths with borders of iris and borders of the Greek key, and round embroidered linen tea cloths, and dozens and dozens of lace and net doilies to go under finger bowls, and towels of the finest huck with great padded monograms embroidered on them. "Dear child," she said, "I want for you to have everything nice." I ended up with a whole pile of things. I wonder what ever became of them. I remember imagining what my father would have thought if he could have seen me with a lot of tablecloths and towels in my lap. "The purchase money of the Philistines," he might have said. But I have no idea what happened to all that linen, and my father is dead long ago and nobody remembers him any more. I remember when I went up to my room to change into my other dress for dinner I wept, because I was so big and ugly and all surrounded with lace doilies and baby clothes and Eugene might fall in love with somebody else before I could get back to New York.

That was the night the baby started to come.

It began about ten o'clock, just before bedtime, and when I told my mother-in-law her face lit up. She went and telephoned to the doctor and to the nurse, and then came back and told me the doctor said I was to rest quietly at home until the pains started to come every fifteen minutes, and that the nurse, Miss Hammond, would be right over. I went up to my room and lay down. It didn't hurt too much. When Miss Hammond arrived, she stood by my bed and smiled at me as if I were wonderful. She was tall and thin with sallow hair, an old-maid type.

About one o'clock, Mrs. Tompkins telephoned the doctor again, and he said to take me to the hospital. Mrs. Tompkins told me she had wired Tom to take the midnight down, but I didn't care; I was having pains regularly, and the difference had begun, the thing I have always wondered about.

We all got in a taxi, Mrs. Tompkins and Miss Hammond and I, there in the middle of the night, and drove through the dark Washington streets to the hospital. It was portentous, that drive, significant; every minute, I mean every present minute, seemed to matter. I had stopped living ahead, the way I had been doing, and was living in right now. That is what I am talking about.

I hadn't worn my wedding ring since I fell in love with Eugene. I'd told my mother-in-law that I didn't like the feeling of a ring, which was true. But in the taxi, in the darkness, she took off her own wedding ring and put it on my finger. "Dear child," she said, "I just won't have you going to the hospital with no ring." I remember I squeezed her hand.

I was taken at once to my room in the hospital, where they "prepared" me, and then almost immediately to the delivery room, because they thought the baby was coming right away. But then the pains slowed down, and I stayed in the delivery room for a long time, until the sun began to stream through the east window. The doctor, a pleasant old man with a Southern accent, had come, and he sat in the sunshine reading the morning newspaper. As I lay on my back on the high, narrow delivery cot, the pains got steadily harder, but I remember thinking, There's nothing scary about this. It just feels natural. The pains got harder and harder.

There was the doctor, and a nurse, and my own Miss Hammond, whom I felt I had known forever; occasionally she would wipe my forehead with a cool, wet cloth. I felt gay and talkative. I said, "I know what this pain feels like. It feels as if I were in a dark tunnel that was too small for me, and I were trying to squeeze through it to get to the end, where I can see a little light."

The doctor laughed. "That's not what you're doin'," he said. "That's what that baby's doin'."

But that was the way it felt, all the same.

"Let me know when you need a little somethin'," he said.

After a while I said, "This is *bad*." And instantly he was at my side with a hypodermic needle, which he thrust into my arm, and the pain was blunted for a time.

"Let me know when you need a little somethin'," he said again.

But I was feeling very strong and full of power. I was working my way down that long, dark tunnel that was too tight for me, down toward the little light that showed at the far end. Then I had a terrible pain. That's all I'm going to stand, I thought calmly. Deliberately I opened my mouth and screamed.

At once, they put a mask over my face, and the doctor's voice said, "Breathe deeply."

And I was out.

I would come back into the brilliant sunshine of the room and the circle of faces around me, and smile up at them, and they would smile back. And then a fresh pain would approach, and I would say, "Now."

"Bear down," the doctor's voice said as the mask covered my face and I faded away from the room. "Bear down."

So I would bear down, and be gone.

Back into the sunny room and out again, several times, I went. And then, on one of the returns, to my astonishment, I heard a small, high wail that I nevertheless knew all about. Over to one side of me stood a crib on stilts; it had been standing there all along, but now above its edge I could see two tiny blue things waving faintly.

"It's a boy," I heard my darling Miss Hammond's voice saying. "You've got a beautiful boy, Mrs. Tompkins."

And then I felt a fearful pain coming. They put the mask over my face for the last time, and I went completely out.

When I woke up, it was in my own room. Mrs. Tompkins was there, and Miss Hammond, and Tom. They kissed me, and beamed at me, and Tom kept pressing my hand. But I was immune from them all.

I was inwardly enthroned. Seated on a chair of silver, sword in hand, I was Joan of Arc. I smiled at them all, because I might as well, but I needed nobody, nothing. I was the meaning of achievement, here, now, in the moment, and the afternoon sun shone proudly in from the west.

A nurse entered bearing a pale-blue bundle and put it in my arms. It was Eric, of course, and I looked down into his minute face with a feeling of old familiarity. Here he was. Here we were. We were everything.

"Your father's come," Mrs. Tompkins said.

My father's head appeared round the door, and then he came in, looking wry, as he did when people not his kind were around. He leaned down to kiss me.

"Brave girl," he whispered. "You fooled 'em."

That was right. I had fooled them, fooled everybody. I had the victory, and it was here and now.

Then the nurse took the baby away, and Miss Hammond brought a big tray of food and cranked my bed up for me to eat it. I ate an enormous dinner, and then fell asleep and did not wake up for fifteen hours.

When I woke, it was the middle of the night, and the hospital was silent around me. Then, faintly, from somewhere down the corridor, although the month was February, someone began to sing "Silent Night." It was eerie, in my closed room, to hear singing in the darkness. I looked at where the window showed pale gray and oblong. Then I realized what the tune was that was being sung, and felt horribly embarrassed. I could hear my father saying, "These good folk with their sentimental religiosity." Then the sound of the singing disappeared, and I was never sure where it had come from, or, indeed, whether I had really heard it or not.

Next morning, bright and early, a short, thin man with gray curly hair walked into my hospital room and said, "What's all this nonsense about your not wanting to nurse your baby? I won't have it. You *must* nurse your child." He was the pediatrician, Dr. Lawford.

Nobody had ever given me an order before. My father believed in treating me as if I were grown-up. I stared at the strange man seating himself by the window, and burst into tears.

"I tell you what, my dear little girl," he said after a few moments. "I'll make a bargain with you. I believe you have to go back to New York and take up your life in six weeks. Nurse your baby until you have to go, and then you can wean him."

I nodded. I didn't know anything about any of it—only what

older women had said to me, about nursing ruining your figure —and all of that seemed in another life now.

Flowers began to arrive, great baskets of them from all Mrs. Tompkins' friends, and they filled up my room until it looked like a bower. Telegrams arrived. A wire came, late one day, from Eugene. It read, "AREN'T YOU SOMETHING." But Eugene no longer seemed quite real, either.

I would lie in that hospital bed with the baby within my arm, nursing him. I remember it with Dr. Lawford sitting in the chair by the window and tall, old-maidish Miss Hammond standing beside my bed, both of them watching me with indulgent faces. I felt as though they were my father and my mother, and I their good child. But that was absurd, because if they were taking care of anybody, it was Eric.

I stayed in the hospital ten days. When we went home to Mrs. Tompkins', it was spring in Washington, and along every curb were barrows of spring flowers—daffodils and hyacinths and white tulips.

Miss Hammond and Eric had the room next to mine on the fourth floor. Miss Hammond did what was called in those days eighteen-hour duty, which meant she slept there with the baby and went off for a few hours every afternoon. It was Mrs. Tompkins' delight, she said, to look after the baby while Miss Hammond was out. Those afternoons, I would take a long nap, and then we would go out and push the baby in his father's old perambulator along the flower-lined streets, to join the other rosy babies in Dupont Circle, where the little children ran about in their matching coats and hats of wool—pink, lavender, yellow, and pale green.

It was an orderly, bountiful life. Breakfast was at eight, and Mrs. Tompkins dispensed the coffee from the silver *repoussé* service before her, and herself broke the eggs into their cups to be handed by the butler to Miss Hammond and me. We had little pancakes with crisp edges, and the cook sent up rich, thick hot chocolate for me to drink, because I had not yet learned to like coffee. In those days, a thing like that did nothing to my figure. When we had gone upstairs, I would stand in front of the mahogany mirror in my bedroom, sidewise, looking at my new, thin shape, flat as a board again, and then I would go in to watch Miss Hammond perform the daily ceremony of the baby's bath—an elaborate ritual involving a rubber tub, toothpicks with a cotton swab on the end of them, oil, powder, and specially soft towels—and the whole room was filled with the smell of baby. Then it would be time for me to nurse Eric.

I used to hold him in my arm, lying on my bed, and it was as though he and I were alone inside a transparent bubble, an iridescent film that shut everything else in the world out. We were a whole, curled together within the tough and fragile skin of that round bubble, while outside, unnoticed, time passed, plans proceeded, and the days went by in comfortable procession. Inside the bubble, there was no time.

Luncheon was at one-thirty, *Amos 'n' Andy* was at seven, dinner was at seven-thirty, bedtime was at ten-thirty, in that house. The servants made excuses to come up to the fourth floor and look at the baby, and lent unnecessary helping hands when the butler lifted the perambulator down the steps to the street for our afternoon walk among the flowers. The young mothers I had met came to see the baby, and Mrs. Tompkins ordered tea with cinnamon toast served to us in the drawing room afterward; they talked of two-o'clock feedings, and the triangular versus square folding of diapers, and of formulas, and asked me to lunch at the Mayflower, early, so that I could get home for the early-afternoon feeding. But the young mothers were still strangers to me—older women. I did not feel anything in common with their busy domestic efficiency.

The spring days passed, and plans matured relentlessly, and soon it was time for me to go home to New York with the baby, to the new apartment Tom had taken and the new nurse he had engaged that Mrs. Tompkins was going to pay for. That was simply the way it was, and it never occurred to me that I could change the plans. I wonder what would have happened if a Dr. Lawford had marched in and given me an order. . . . But after all, I did have to go back; New York was where I lived; so it's not that I mean. I really don't understand what I do mean. I couldn't have stayed at my mother-in-law's indefinitely.

I don't remember starting to wean Eric. I remember an afternoon when I had missed several feedings, and the physical ache was hard, and Mrs. Tompkins brought the baby in for me to play with.

I held him in my arms, that other occupant of the fractured bubble, and suddenly I knew that he and I were divided, never to be together again, and I began to cry.

Mrs. Tompkins came and took the baby away from me, but I could not stop crying, and I have never again cried so hard. It never occurred to me that anything could be done about it, but we were separated, and it was cruel, and I cried for something. I wish I could remember exactly what it was I did cry for. It wasn't for my baby, because I still had my baby, and he's grown up now and works in the Bank of New York.

After that, time changed again for me. It flowed backward, to the memory of the bubble and to the first high moment in the hospital when I was Joan of Arc. We left Washington on a morning with the sun shining and barrows of flowers blooming along the curb as we went out the front door and the servants lined up on the steps to say goodbye. Eric was in a pink coat and a pink cap to match, with lace edging. But he didn't really belong to me any more—not the old way. I remember Mrs. Tompkins had tears in her eyes when she kissed us goodbye in the Union Station. But I felt dry-eyed and unmoved, while time flowed backward to that night we drove to the hospital in the middle of the night and she put her ring on my finger.

Of course, when we got back, New York looked marvellous.

But even while I was beginning to feel all its possibilities again, time still flowed backward for me. I remember when it was that it stopped flowing backward. I was in someone's room in the St. Regis, where a lot of people were having a drink before going on to dance. I sat on the bed. A young man I had never seen before sat beside me. He said, "Where have you been all my life?"

And I said, "I've been having a baby."

He looked at me with the shine gone out of his eyes, and I realized that there were no possibilities in a remark like mine. I laughed, and reached out my glass to whoever the host was, and said something else that made the young man laugh, too. And then time stopped flowing backward and began once more, and for always, to hurry forward again.

So that is what I wonder about, all these years later. What is it that makes time hurry forward so fast? And what is it that can make it stop, so that you can live in now, in here? Or even go backward? Because it has never stopped or gone backward for me again.

It isn't having a baby, because I've had four, God help me—two by Tom, counting Eric, and two by Harold, not to mention that miscarriage, and although I hoped it would, time never did anything different again, just hurried on, hurried on.

It isn't, as it occurred to me once that it might be, getting free of men in your life as I was free of them long ago with Mrs. Tompkins. Here I am, rid of my husbands, and the younger children off to school now, in this apartment. It isn't big, but I have day beds in the bedrooms so that every room looks like a sitting room for when I have a party. I'm free, if you want to call it that, and my face isn't what it was, so that I'm not troubled with *that* kind of thing, and yet, when you might think life would slow down, be still, time nevertheless hurries on, hurries on. What do I care about dinner with the Deans tonight? But I have to hurry, just the same. And I'm tired. Sometimes I imagine that if Mrs. Tompkins were still alive, or my father, even . . . But they're dead and nobody remembers them any more, nobody *I* see.

1954

MISS AUGUST

Mrs. Harley sat at the open window of her bedroom at Hardpan Farm, in a flood of morning sunshine. Her door stood open, so that she could see when the Doctor passed. She had finished going over her dreams of the night before, which she had recorded in a painstakingly relaxed hand in her dream book—a flat loose-paged notebook like those used by students. She was now working at reading a novel in the morning; she came from a rigid Boston background and this was part of her analysis. It *was* work; she had to struggle with guilt and the nagging urge to go downstairs and help somebody do something.

There was the clatter of footsteps hurrying down the hall, and, looking up, relieved, she saw the little Doctor passing. He was followed by the new nurse, a Miss August—a German, it was said. Her hair was cropped like a man's, and she had a round bullet-head, which she stuck out in front of her as she hurried. They went on toward Miss Parsons' room.

Mrs. Harley felt happy that there was a new nurse. But changes were so difficult; one felt unsteady on one's feet. Her happiness slipped into worry: Would the new nurse be an understanding one, with that queer bullethead thrust out?

Do not let yourself be a host to such fantasies. Trying, in vain, to take hold on the happiness again, Mrs. Harley resolved her dilemma by going back to trying to read a novel in the morning.

The door to Miss Parsons' room opened, in the gentle way that the Doctor always opened the patients' doors. His head came round the edge. "How's my girl this morning?" he asked of the young woman lying in bed.

She watched with fearful eyes as her precious Doctor was followed into the room by a strange woman with deep, ominous eyes.

"This is our new friend," the pink-faced, round little Doctor said distinctly. "Miss August. She knows all about the things we talk about; she has insight."

The patient, however, cowered under the sheet.

"I'll be along this afternoon for our hour," the Doctor said. He vanished out the door, and Miss Parsons could hear his footsteps—those footsteps that always brought hope down the hall—trotting away in their usual hurry. Her soul seemed to go away with those footsteps.

The new nurse approached the patient with a fixed and dreadful smile.

"I am going to be your friend," she said menacingly, in a German accent.

The Doctor was catching a cup of coffee in the dining room before starting his rounds of an hour with each of the eight patients at Hardpan Farm. He was always in a hurry these days; he had the patients and, in addition, the endless complications of running a sanatorium so far out in the country. Beautiful as it was here, the nurses would not stay. The last one, Miss Spurgeon, had been perfection; English, quiet, serene, her manner made everyone breathe easier. But she, too, had left after two months. Following her departure all the patients had been worse for a couple of days.

Even with her limitations, there was always Mrs. Martin, who had just brought the steaming cup of coffee to the Doctor. She was a practical nurse, and ran the household affairs—was in charge of the linen, supervised the servants, planned the meals. . . . Damnation! Now Mary and Alf had given notice from the kitchen.

Mrs. Martin, a big woman with a pile of white hair, sat down by the Doctor while he had his coffee.

"Three patients in bed on this beautiful morning," she said. "If you ask me, they'd be a lot better if you got them up and set them to work. There's nothing in the world ails them; they're just rich and spoiled."

"I didn't ask you," the Doctor said.

Mrs. Martin was never daunted. "Good old-fashioned melancholia, that's what's the matter with most of them," she continued. "Nothing better for it than to wash a few dishes, scrub a few floors . . ."

If he advertised in the newspaper of the nearest town, in addition to the New York papers, he would surely be able to find another couple. Perhaps a better couple. The Doctor was positive everything would, in the end, turn out right.

". . . to take Mary and Alf in for their Thursday off," Mrs. Martin was saying.

"Yes," the Doctor said automatically.

"Well, is she going to?"

"Who?"

"Miss Hughes, I *said*," Mrs. Martin said impatiently.

"No," the Doctor said. "Miss Hughes wasn't well at all yesterday. She can't drive them in. You'll have to take a man off the farm."

"I never heard of such a thing," Mrs. Martin said, although she had been at Hardpan Farm for three years. "Can't do this, can't do that. Get them up and make them forget about themselves, *I* say."

"Oh, be still!" the Doctor said. He finished his coffee and wiped his white mustache. "These people are not to be relied on, I've told you."

"Doctor," Mrs. Bethel said pleadingly.

"Yes," the Doctor said gently. He sat by the window in the chair he always sat in, and Mrs. Bethel, in a fresh wash dress, sat opposite him in the chair she always sat in.

"Doctor, please tell me the truth."

"I always tell you the truth," the Doctor said.

"I can't get it out of my head," Mrs. Bethel said apologetically. "Doctor—am I crazy?"

The Doctor gave a tiny sigh.

"No," he said. "I've told you. You are regressing. You are looking for something in the past, and when you have found it, you will come up again. You feel strangely because you are not living in outer reality."

"But I want to live in reality!"

"There are two realities," the Doctor said.

"I feel so full of fear," the patient continued.

"That is because your energy is not running outward, freely—as it will," the Doctor said, one more time.

But the patient was particularly distressed this morning.

"I am so full of fear," she said again. "I am so afraid of hurting you with my fear. What would I do if anything happened to you?"

"I'm a tough old bird," the Doctor said. "Don't you worry about *me*. Think about yourself, and then you'll be able to think about other people rightly. If I let the worrying you all do about my health affect me, I'd be dead now."

The word was unfortunate, and the Doctor regretted it. Even after all these years he was learning to remove himself still more from the picture. There was a pause while Mrs. Bethel visibly struggled with herself.

"Doctor—that Miss August—" Mrs. Bethel gave it the German pronunciation. "Is she *all right*? I mean, is she *kind*?"

"Oh, for pity's sake," the Doctor said in his positive way. "She seems an excellent nurse. She's even had some psychiatric nursing experience, she says. It's almost impossible to find a psychiatric nurse today."

"Oh, forgive me!" Mrs. Bethel cried penitently. "I *know* how hard you work to take care of us. I know what a struggle it is for you."

"Rubbish," the Doctor said. "Now let's get on with that dream of yours."

Mrs. Bethel opened her dream book. She had written her dream down in the middle of the night, right after having it, and the handwriting was uneven and jagged. It frightened her. Summoning her courage, however, she began to read it aloud.

What she wanted to ask was "Is Miss August crazy?" That cropped bullethead, those deep-set eyes, glimpsed at one of the breakfast tables . . . But she did not dare ask it. For there was always projection. . . .

Under the big maple trees on the back lawn, they sat shelling Lima beans in the lovely breezy shade—Miss Hughes, Mrs. Harley, who had finished her hour with the Doctor, Mrs. Bethel, and the new nurse.

"I was for a year with the yogi in Carmel, California," Miss August said in her guttural accent. She bent over the beans, shelling them, as she did everything, violently and as if her life depended on it. "For a year I was with him, and he taught me everything he knew. He sayed to me, 'Go now. I can teach you no more.' So I went next to the yogi in New Mexico."

"How long were you with him?" Mrs. Harley asked. She had read the Bhagavad-Gita back in the days before her analysis, and felt a combination of interested and guilty at being interested in anything in the past. She also felt guilty at being repelled by Miss August's personality. "Be serene; be positive," she told herself, and then felt a little worried because that was a combination of the past and the present, the Bhagavad-Gita and the analysis. But the Doctor said, "There's good in everything." Remembering his voice, Mrs. Harley came out of her tangle and was able to say again, "How long were you with the yogi in New Mexico?"

"I was for a year with the yogi in New Mexico," Miss August replied. "Everything he knew I learned from him, everything. It was then, with the yogi in New Mexico, that I discovered my ambition—the ambition of my life—to go to India and found—you say 'found'?—my own ashram."

Miss Hughes plugged away at her pile of bean pods without looking up or speaking. She was very unsteady this morning. It was like swimming, to move around; or like motion in some even denser element than water. And she had been doing so well. . . . The Doctor said, yesterday, "Well, there is just another piece of the puzzle that has to be found, that's all." But sometimes Miss Hughes wondered if the Doctor was always right—and then smote herself for wondering. The Doctor *had* to be right, or it was the end of the world—not to be contemplated. The thing was—this new nurse. Hadn't Miss Hughes perhaps *known* beforehand, by extrasensory perception, what the new nurse was going to be like—this *awful* person, this *bad* person? Extrasensory perception explained so much. The Doctor always said, "Don't you worry about extrasensory perception. Just leave that till you get well. You've got all you can do concentrating on common or garden perception." But Miss Hughes couldn't help feeling sometimes she *knew* things—things that hadn't arrived yet. . . .

"I will not rest until I have achieved my ambition," Miss August was saying, and all the while a breeze whispered peacefully in the maple leaves; but she never looked up, just tore the naked beans from their pods and cast the ravished pods from her into a paper bag on the grass. "I will not rest until I have my ashram. I have chosen my guru, my holy man, for the ashram. I am in correspondence with him. Weekly I write to him—I tell him all I feel, all I long for. But he writes me, 'Do not come yet. The time is not yet.' So I must work, I must wait. The time will come when the time is ripe. The jewel is in the lotus. *Om mani padme hum*," said Miss August violently.

Mrs. Bethel's hands trembled as she tried hard to shell beans—something she had never done before coming to Hardpan Farm. Somebody is crazy, she thought, but is it she or is it I? I feel so sure it is she. "But I am always wrong," spoke the familiar voice in Mrs. Bethel's mind. "You're always wrong. You're always wrong," chanted a multitude of voices from Mrs. Bethel's childhood and from her marriage. But this yogi business—Alfred had always said it was sheer nonsense. Pure malarkey. "There's good in everything," the Doctor's voice said. "You stand on your own feet and never mind what Alfred said. You're a person in your own right." "But I don't know what I *do* think!" Mrs. Bethel cried inwardly. "I only know what I feel, and I feel somebody is crazy; there is something crazy here. But the Doctor would know if anything was wrong?" she said, more as a question than as a reassurance, as it turned out. That is, he had to know; it was unthinkable if he didn't know.

"I *will* have my ashram," the bulletheaded nurse insisted in her deep voice. She took her eyes for an instant off the rape of the beans to stare defiantly at the little circle of faces around her. "I *will*. I always get what I am determined on. The yogi in New Mexico sayed it; he sayed it just before I went away to the yogi in New York; he sayed, 'Do not fear. You will get what your atman is set upon. Come it today, come it later, you will always get it.' I went, then, to the yogi in New York. Now he has taught me all he knows. And so I feel the time is nearly ripe; that I shall leave; that I shall sail for India. My yogi waits. The time comes near."

Mrs. Martin stepped out on the back porch overlooking the lawn and looked with satisfaction at the little group seated on the grass. This was more like it. Good woman, that new nurse. Get them up, get them out, get them at some kind of useful work and they'd all be well before you knew it. Nothing the matter with a one of them except thinking about themselves too much. She sniffed loudly, so that Mrs. Harley heard her and looked round; then she vanished into the house again.

After lunch, all the patients who had been up went to their rooms for a rest. Miss Diggs, who was staying in bed, had this hour with the Doctor. She was morose; dark and depressed and critical of everything the Doctor said. "I think I have undulant fever," she said. "I think that's what's really the matter with me. You don't have the cows inspected often enough, Doctor."

"Don't you worry about the cows," the Doctor said, from his chair by the window. "The cows are all right. You worry—no, I don't mean worry, Heaven knows—you think about what's the trouble with you. I want you to talk more about your father."

"I don't want to talk about my father," Miss Diggs retorted. "My father's dead. I want to talk about undulant fever. I read a magazine article last night, and it said that Bang's disease—"

"Don't you worry about Bang's disease," the Doctor said, a little wearily. "You let me do the worrying about Bang's disease."

"I want to talk about that new nurse you've imported into this place," Miss Diggs went on, unshaken. "What was the matter with Miss Spurgeon? I liked her."

"Nothing the matter. Just she left," the Doctor said.

"I don't like the new nurse. I don't trust Germans. I don't trust her."

"What ails you people?" the Doctor said. "Have you all caught something, or what is all this rubbish about Miss August? She seems to be performing her duties adequately."

"She is untrustworthy. I can tell. I always know."

"You don't," the Doctor said flatly. "You can't tell me a thing I don't know about what goes on around here. What I want you to do is stop fretting about *my* affairs and get down into your own unconscious and *find* something. That's why I put you to bed. Don't you want to get well?"

"Of course I want to get well," Miss Diggs said irritably. "I have undulant fever, that's what I'm telling you. I am interested in real matters in the real world."

"Oh, bosh!" the Doctor exploded. He didn't need to be gentle with Miss Diggs; she had a skin like elephant hide. "I'm the only one who's living in reality around here. You leave the real world to me."

All afternoon the infinitely fragile, delicate atmosphere of the sanatorium was shaken, trembled, with invisible currents of disturbance—fear and distrust and hatred. The aura that surrounded Hardpan Farm was torn, and waved in shreds in the sweet afternoon breeze.

Mrs. Bethel had gone for a walk down past Goose Farm, in order to be alone and out in the fresh air, and to work out her morning's analysis. She walked in the middle of the gray dirt road, feeling uneasily like a little girl. I must be mature, she reproved herself; I must try hard to be mature. She stopped and stared intently at the weather-beaten board farmhouse—Goose Farm—in order to really *see* it, to be a mature woman looking at an interesting old farmhouse. Goose Farm was a curious name; they must have raised geese at some time, but as far as Mrs. Bethel knew, there were no geese here now. "Goose" was "*Gans*" in German. "*Dein . . . ist mein ganzes Herz*," sang suddenly a tune in her mind: Alfred . . . in love with her . . . long ago . . . in a night club where a young slim German tenor sang "*Dein . . . ist mein ganzes Herz*." Oh God! Alfred . . .

In desperation, she sought about for another association. The Doctor said, "Everything has a good side and a bad side." There must be a good side. Goose . . . *Gans* . . . But all it brought to mind was: German; Miss August. That crazy woman, who was not really crazy, because it was . . . Mrs. Bethel shook her head as though to drive away a horde of gnats and hurried on down the road.

She had not gone very far before she saw it—but it was more as though she started feeling the panic fear even before she saw it. The great ram! Like a god. With that great awful equipment for procreation—oh!

Mrs. Bethel turned and fled back along the country road to the safety of Hardpan Farm. Then for hours she stayed in her room, unable to rid her mind of that terrible shocking sight: that ram, standing beside a fence, in a field. She felt she would never dare go out of the house again.

"Oh, oh, oh!" Miss Hughes cried, weeping, her voice getting higher and higher. "I want to get out! I want my life! I want to live in the world and *do* things!"

"You will," the Doctor soothed her, laying his hand on the arm of her chair. "You will, but you must collect yourself. It takes time. You are doing very well. You can't hurry the mind, you know. It must come. You will."

"But I can't wait! I want to get out of this—this *swamp*. I want to move in the world. I want to do things!"

"Doing things isn't the same as truly moving in the world," the Doctor said.

"But I want to get *out*!" cried Miss Hughes.

The Doctor observed her rising excitement.

"What's stopping you?" he said.

Miss Hughes, deflated, stared blankly at him.

Mrs. Martin, walking with her firm, neat step along the downstairs corridor, passed Miss August hurrying along like a bullet-headed badger, shoulders hunched, head poked out in front.

"Mrs. Martin," Miss August said, stopping short with a jerk. "I must speak with you."

"And I must speak to *you*," Mrs. Martin said, with an agreeable smile. "You certainly have taken hold of things today. Please feel free to call on me, for any help you need."

Miss August eyed her with her deepset gaze. "Help? What for should I need help?" she demanded.

"You *are* a worker," Mrs. Martin said admiringly.

"I must speak with you," Miss August said. "The keys. Where are the keys? I must have the keys."

"The keys? Why, I have them. I do the housekeeping," Mrs. Martin said.

"Give me the keys. I am in charge here," the nurse said in her German accent.

Miss Diggs, who had risen from her bed in defiance of the Doctor's orders, and Mrs. Harley were having a little conference out on the back lawn, far away from the house, under the beech tree, where there was a circular seat around the trunk.

"She won't do," Miss Diggs repeated. "She'll have to go."

Mrs. Harley looked at her with respect. Such strong-mindedness!

"The thing is," she said, "our darling Doctor. He's so overworked, with us and the nurse troubles and the servant troubles and his practice in town three days a week and the farm, too. . . . I'm just so afraid he doesn't realize. I'm just so afraid he gets too tired. I'm just so afraid—" She broke off.

"Well, who's going to speak to him?" Miss Diggs said. "You or I?"

"Oh, *you*!" Mrs. Harley said. "You're so much—" Braver, she meant, but did not say.

"Doctor's put out with me," Miss Diggs said, "because I don't lie in bed on a beautiful day like this, thinking about my entrails the way he wants me to. *I* can't speak to him."

"Well, *I* certainly can't," Mrs. Harley said.

They stared at each other, helplessly.

"Besides—" Mrs. Harley began.

Miss Diggs nodded.

They meant, Besides, we might be mistaken, about everything. The Doctor is always right. Isn't he? their silent voices asked one another, there under the beech tree, with the breeze sighing as the afternoon passed, and a bobwhite spoke up from the meadow beyond the rail fence. Isn't he? they asked each other again, soundlessly.

Miss Parsons lay trembling under the sheet in the late afternoon. Her room was already dim, since it faced the east, but the Doctor did not turn on a light. He sat in the shadow, in the big chair, and said, "Go on. What else did she say?"

"Well," said the little voice. "I don't want to complain of Mrs. Martin—"

"You're not," he said. "You're talking to your doctor. Go on."

"I wouldn't complain for *anything*. Well, she said, as she was taking my lunch tray away, she said, 'Why don't you get up and put your clothes on and take a nice brisk walk instead of loafing in bed all day?' I didn't know what to do. You *told* me—"

"That's right. I told you to stay in bed. You've overstrained yourself. You need rest."

"I felt so—awful. And she said—"

"What now?"

"She said, 'If you ask me, your family's right to think you're being kept here unnecessarily. I don't see anything the matter with you,' she said. Oh, Doctor! I haven't been able to think of anything else all afternoon. Am I a coward? Am I a quitter? Oh, Doctor, I *would* try, but I can't." The weak little voice broke.

"You're a brave girl," the Doctor said. "You've bucked enough to down ten men."

"But she said—"

"Damnation!" the Doctor said very softly. Then he said, "All right, now. Let's get the good out of this. Who said it—her or you?"

"She did—"

"All *right*, then."

Their voices murmured on quietly in the gathering dusk. The Doctor got up, at the end of the hour.

"Doctor—"

"Yes, child?"

"Don't let— Do I have to have *her* come in here?"

"Mrs. Martin? No. I'll deal with her," said the Doctor.

"No, I don't mean Mrs. Martin," the tiny voice said. "I mean Miss August. She frightens me so."

"Damnation!" he said again, softly.

It was the last conference of the day.

The evening was so cool that they had a fire burning on the hearth in the living room after dinner. The five patients who were up (Miss Diggs had been ordered back to bed by the Doctor) sat around the fire with their handiwork. Mrs. Bethel was knitting a pink afghan for her daughter-in-law's new baby. "With every stitch of this," she said to herself doggedly, "I am knitting together a new life." Miss August sat directly beside the fire. Unlike most German women, she did not knit; her hands lay big and latent in her lap. The Doctor, as was his custom, read aloud to the little gathering. It might have been a chilly evening around the fire of any country house; almost.

All the patients, even the ones in bed, by that unspoken, atmospheric grapevine that kept them informed of tensions, of discord, of the least thing awry, knew that something had happened. They did not know what; they only knew it had. Mrs. Martin's face, for one thing; it had been a thundercloud at dinner and when she carried the trays to the patients in bed—to all except Miss Parsons, whose tray Miss August had brought. But Miss Parsons knew anyway. The news came drifting up the staircase with the evening breeze; it came sifting through the cracks in the door. Mrs. Harley and Miss Diggs knew that before dinner the Doctor had given Mrs. Martin a dressing-down about something; she had remained in the kitchen since dinner. Was that it? But Miss August, too, looked even more ominous, more violent, than ever. Something had happened. None of the patients knew what. They never knew what, when they knew things.

But the Doctor continued to read aloud, the only unperturbed being at Hardpan Farm, from Stekel on dreams.

"'Contrary to the learned men, the simple folk have never looked upon dreams as *foam*,'" the calm, aging voice read on. "'Within their soul there persisted a belief in the reality of this psychic experience. . . .'"

"But why am I knitting with only one thread?" Mrs. Bethel suddenly was asked by some inner voice. "Why are there not two threads, Alfred and me knit together?" "Because that garment is fractured," another voice replied relentlessly. "Because I am knitting up my solitary garment, for my sole self; *for a baby, a newborn thing* . . ."

"'Anatole France is justified when he states, "I am firmly convinced that the power of dreams is greater than that of reality." The dream is the bridge between the real and the supersensory world. The ancient peoples knew this better than we. They believed in dreams and through the dream they felt themselves nearer their divinity.'" The Doctor looked up over the top of the book.

"And through the awareness of his divinity," he editorialized, as was his habit, "man is able to apply himself to the development of his own humanity." The patients all looked up eagerly from their work; this way they gathered extra crumbs of the Doctor's wisdom. "Once we are assured of the place in us of divinity, we are free to try to become truly human," the Doctor was proceeding when Miss August broke in, harshly, loudly. "I, too, have dreams," she said. "Terrible dreams."

The Doctor turned his gaze, over the book, on her, politely.

"Yes?" he said.

"Yes. Last night, my first night in my new position here, I have had one of my terrible dreams."

The Doctor looked as if he might be going to interrupt, but Miss August pushed on. The patients looked at her in alarm.

"I dreamed," she said, "that I was in your kitchen here, but of course it was different, I had not yet been in your kitchen. I dreamed I had a great pot, of iron, and in it was my head"—she put her hands to that man-cut hair—"and I was boiling my head in the pot, and stirring it with a big wooden spoon."

The Doctor laid his book down slowly and looked at Miss August with attention. "Is that so?" he remarked.

"Yes," she said abruptly, and was silent.

The Doctor, after a final thoughtful stare, went back to the reading.

"'Divinity is the projection of our ideal into infinity,'" he read. "'But not only is the ideal self projected. The evil self is also refracted outwardly and it reflects back, as temptation or as the influence of demonic powers. . . .'"

The door from the kitchen burst open, and Mrs. Martin, flushed, stout, and outraged, appeared in the room. She paid no attention to the patients, who trembled at her demeanor, but marched straight over to the Doctor.

"Doctor," she said in a loud, clear voice. "I can't go sparing you all the time. I've got to ask you to step in. Will you tell that woman to give me back the keys to the linen closets? I have to make Miss Diggs's bed again; she spilt her coffee all over. That woman's got everything all locked up."

"What's that?" said the Doctor, closing the book.

"Doctor, listen," Miss August hissed urgently. "It is necessary that I speak with you. At once. There iss danger!"

The Doctor looked from Miss August to Mrs. Martin, who continued to stand with her arms akimbo. He got up, slowly, and Miss August got up, and he followed her through the door onto the back porch, where the evening breeze blew in the chilly darkness. After a minute Mrs. Martin, too, went out on the porch.

"Doctor," Miss August's voice was saying. "That woman—that housekeeper—she has been stealing everything. I have checked up on it—I know. The linens, the medicines—all; she has been stealing all. You are being robbed, all the time."

The Doctor did not hesitate for an instant. "Give me the keys," he demanded.

There was a moment's dead silence on the dark porch.

"*Verflucht!*" spat Miss August. She lunged forward. The Doctor felt her large, powerful hands come around his throat, hard; he staggered backward and would have fallen but for the porch railing.

Then Mrs. Martin was struggling with Miss August; she pulled Miss August's clawlike hands off the Doctor.

"What a temper!" Mrs. Martin chided in the darkness. "Aren't you ashamed?"

The Doctor got his balance again. Someone handed him a ringful of keys, and he gave them to the taller shape, Mrs. Martin.

"Make up Miss Diggs's bed," he ordered. Then, to the other woman, he said, "I would like to talk to you, in your room."

In single file, Mrs. Martin, Miss August, and the Doctor passed through the lighted living room and out again toward the bedrooms. The patients followed them with fearful eyes, silent. They had heard nothing but the scuffling of feet outside.

Left all alone in the living room, they looked at one another and at the fire helplessly. Mrs. Bethel continued for a few moments to knit mechanically at her afghan, but soon her fingers felt like rubber. Something terrible had happened—was happening—but none of the patients had any idea of what it was.

Soon the patients—first Mrs. Bethel and then the others in a cluster—all crept off to the safety of their beds, closing their bedroom doors very quietly and stealthily behind them. None of the doors, however, had locks.

Late that evening, when Miss August had been sent off in the farm pickup truck to catch the eleven-o'clock train back to New York, the Doctor and Mrs. Martin sat at one of the dining-room tables drinking the hot cocoa Mrs. Martin had made.

She was bursting—preening herself uncontrollably over the confidence the Doctor had so obviously displayed in her.

"You could have knocked me over with a feather," she said again. "I thought she was such a hard worker—so *practical*. Even this afternoon when she turned nasty—"

"Paranoid," the Doctor said. "Awful . . . awful . . . Poor thing."

"Is that right?" Mrs. Martin said with relish. "Well, you never know."

"*You* don't," the Doctor said.

But even this did not matter, after his display of trust; she was thoroughly appreciated, she knew now. Things like his getting so cross about that little Parsons snip didn't matter.

"The patients have been acting like sixty all day," she continued. "They always seem to know when there's something in the air. The poor things," she said with unaccustomed charity, "helpless and all, being at the mercy, you might say, of that horrible creature."

"She's not horrible," the Doctor said. "She's sick."

They sat in the absolute quiet of the country night, nursing their cups.

"But what's going to happen with her next?" Mrs. Martin suddenly demanded. "Have you turned her loose on the next unsuspecting place?"

The old Doctor sighed.

"There wasn't anything I could do at this point," he said. "I had to get her out of here—as soon as I had the facts."

"Facts!" Mrs. Martin said. "What facts? Had she done something criminal? What did you find out?"

"I didn't find out anything, that *you* mean," the Doctor said wearily. "I'm talking about another kind of facts. You wouldn't know. I told her to go and see Dr. Morris. He's a good man. I hope to God she goes. I told her he would help her to get to India, where it seems she's beside herself to go. And in a way it's true—she certainly can't get to India in her condition."

In spite of all the horror and the fear and the mystery which had convulsed the tenuously balanced atmosphere of Hardpan Farm for those twenty-four hours, after Miss August's departure the patients were all much better for several days. Then they began to sink back into whatever footholds they had found in what was a sort of spiral climbing up.

1954

HOW WOULD YOU LIKE TO BE BORN . . .

FOR THE FIRST TIME since her sister Laura had died the previous Thursday, Miss Florrie Davenant, who was now, alas, Miss Davenant, was attending to the correspondence at Uncle Professor's secretary in the east bay window where the morning sun streamed across the telephone bill ($3.29), the milk bill ($4.18), and the begging letters from a camp for slum boys, a Home for the Blind, and the one from the Lovingston Boys Appeal to which she was replying.

She wore one of Laura's black dresses because she did not own a black dress and never had, no matter what Laura said. Of course, technically she now owned Laura's dresses and the rest of the Davenant sisters' possessions, although it did not feel that way. Laura's cat, a cynical old yellow tom, seemed to know all this and as he wove between Florrie's legs, gave an occasional jab with his claws to her ankles, spitefully. Howard, the cat, had probably been one being who loved Laura; Florrie was sure he hated *her*. The day before, in an effort to sue for his toleration, she had fed him a chicken bone which would have been forbidden by Laura (splinters), but there had been no result of either sort; what did you have to do to make people love you? "What matters is that they should respect you," Laura would have said. Howard did not respect Florrie either, it was obvious; he had probably seen straight through the chicken-bone maneuver. But Florrie had never been quite clear as to what the advantages of respect were, anyway.

The Lovingston Boys request began appealingly.

"How would *you* like to be born into a world where everyone's hand is against you?" it demanded, and went on to outline the case of the Negro adolescents in Georgia who were going to be tried for the murder of a white farmer; it was essential that funds be raised to assure the Lovingston Boys superior counsel, since they would be tried in a white-supremacy state, and to cover the costs of the appeals which would undoubtedly be necessary.

This was the sort of cause to which the Davenants had always responded heroically, via Laura. Florrie had the whole weight of tradition (Uncle Absalom the Abolitionist), habit, and her own easily roused sympathy to push her on, even with the bills lying there still unpaid. She closed her eyes for a moment to bring before them the plight of those poor Lovingston Boys.

She could see them now, in a jail cell, their eyeballs white with fear, abused by a cruel jailer, threatened perhaps by a lynch mob outside; she could even fear with them that awful prospect, the electric chair; at night in their cell they would dream of the chair—"frying" the newspapers sometimes said. Oh, dear!

But no, she did not see, she could not see why they had done what they had done. Without a doubt the farmer had been abusive, unfair, insulting, anything a Georgia poor white might be. But why, why had they drawn that flash knife, when they *knew* . . . If, as the Appeal said, every hand was against you, how could you act to arouse further wrath? How could you kill? How *could* you?

Laura would never have bothered to try to see. She would have said "An outrage," and written her check with a firm, pointed handwriting at once. Florrie sighed, and began her letter.

> Dear Sirs:
>
> I am enclosing a check for $10 as my contribution toward the defense of the Lovingston Boys. I wish it could be more. My sister Miss Davenant, to whom you addressed your letter, is recently deceased, but I know she would have wished . . .

Howard gave an extremely painful jab to Florrie's ankle, and leapt to the writing surface of the secretary, where he strolled across the face of the open letter, smearing the words "have" and "wished." It would be necessary to rewrite the letter. For one awful moment a renegade thought crossed Florrie's mind. With the ten dollars she could buy a heating pad. She had seen one she wanted in Mr. Boyle's hardware store; it had a little light on the switch which burned while the current was on; how exquisitely cozy, when one awoke in the night, to see that friendly little light burning, company in the dark. . . .

But the voice of Laura spoke loudly in her hesitating mind. "The Davenants have always stood for high thinking and plain living," it said. "We *always* give to worthy appeals. That is the sort of people we are. We expect it of ourselves, always." And Howard, as though he were a living emissary of the dead, drew his claws down Florrie's wrist, sharply. He certainly did not like her. She drew another sheet of writing paper to her and began again.

Howard was clawing at the door now, giving that frightful miaow of his to get out, and Florrie rose dutifully to open the door for him. She returned to attend to the rest of the correspondence, but almost at once Howard was scratching to come in again. She had always thought he did it to plague her, this in-and-out gambit, since it was she who had been deputed to open the doors and since he knew, clearly, that it hurt her old legs to get up and down.

"You did it on purpose," she said as she let him in. He gave her a baleful stare, as though to say "Who are you to complain? I am the master of this house, now that She is gone."

He went in and out four times more while she was finishing the morning's letters. She was quite weary, although it was only half-past ten. But now was the time when the Davenants did their shopping, and true to the rule Florrie went to her room to prepare to go out.

But she did something sinful. She put on one of her two blue dresses, the one she loved. "If I wear mourning, that makes me belong with Laura," she thought hurriedly, explaining to her conscience which sat inexorably behind a curtain, reserving judgment. "Perhaps . . . in my blue dress . . . they'll know that makes me different. They might . . . they might . . ."

They might like me, she meant. For always, in the back of her obedient mind, there had been the unquelled hope that they *might*—the people outside, the non-Davenants, the non-Davenant-kind. And oh! how merciful to return from a marketing trip carrying a smile, or a word, like a clear blue stone picked up on the beach. Florrie grasped her shopping bag and went out, locking, as was the custom with the Davenants, the front door.

"They might walk in to see what they could find," Laura's voice said now in answer to some old objection, swallowed years ago. "And what leads you to suppose they might like you, or care? We are the class they hate. We have no power, we have no money, we can't hurt them in any way, and so they hate us, because they cannot avoid the realization that we are their natural superiors."

"Then why do we have to give them money?" Florrie implored, as she crossed the street, of her inner interlocutor. But the answer to that came swiftly as if Laura had been still alive.

"Virtue is its own reward," she said, and Florrie could see her straightening her neck, "and its *only* reward."

With hope and fear Florrie entered Mr. Halloran's Market.

"Good morning, Mr. Halloran," she said at the meat counter with a smile in which she hoped was love and equality and the willingness to have Mrs. Halloran to tea any time.

"Good morning, Miss Davenant," he said with his hard, cold, Black Irish civility. He had called her Miss Davenant. She was Laura to him now.

"I would like a beef kidney," she said, subdued. She had had the wild thought of ordering a lamb chop for once, but now she was restored to the realization of the cost of lamb chops. She turned to the vegetable stands.

There was a new boy in charge today, and his unfamiliarity gave her courage to try her smile again. Perhaps he would take to her; perhaps he would come to trust her, she could do something for him; a dream of putting up the money to see him through college began to form itself madly in her head.

"I would like half a watermelon," she said, the season being summer and watermelon a cheap dessert that would last a long time.

He looked at her. He was young, with black curly hair, and bright blue eyes.

"Oh, you'd like *hahf* a watermelon, would you?" he replied grinning.

She wanted to die. There was no use appealing to Mr. Halloran, even if she had been of a mind to complain. But what she felt was the wild desire to cry, now at last, now that Laura was not here to stop her—"I can't help it! I can't help pronouncing it that way! I've done it too long to stop. It doesn't mean anything, I promise you! *Please* like me."

What she said was, timidly, "Yes, please."

For how could Laura have been right, she thought, as she left the store with her heart pounding. How could they see her as "their natural superior"? No; they saw her as a worm, someone they hated for a worm. She didn't mind that, if only they would be kind to this willing worm. Walking down High Street, she really did not see, she could not see, how she was going to go on, with no one, no one at all, being kind to her. Laura had, at least, borne her the sisterly affection that a Davenant considered appropriate. But now who was there? Was she really going to have to live all alone?—because being alone was the one thing that Florrie feared with panic dread. She thought once more, longingly, of that little light that might have winked in a friendly way at her in the middle of the nights. She couldn't even have that.

She bought the necessary oilcloth, the clothespins, the cotton stockings, on her list, and mailed her letters as she passed the post office. She turned to go home, to Howard and the beef kidney. But it was the thought of the kidney, a meat she had always detested, that gave her the crazy impulse. Lunch out! Who was there to stop her? Whose money was it now? Who but she would suffer if the expense were rash? She went into Logan's Drugstore and sat down at the lunch counter. She smiled a little, this time to herself.

"I would like a lettuce-and-egg sandwich, and a chocolate ice-cream soda," she said, with what Laura would have considered utter imprudence. The woman behind the counter, a lush brunette in a big, dirty apron, looked at her without expression. "Egg salad on white," she called to the older woman at the bread board. Have I said that wrong, too? Florrie wondered. The full-bosomed woman began to put the soda together in a cone-shaped paper cup thrust into a metal container. As she ran the syrup in she talked in a bitter, loud voice to the other woman about some occurrence; it *seemed* to be the continuation of a conversation.

"So she says to me, she says, 'I cahn't endure hahf-ripe cantelope.' The nerve of some people! I could have smacked her one. 'I cahn't endure' . . ."

But—*she means me*, Florrie thought with the quick click of doom. She doesn't quite dare make fun of me to my face, but she is putting her hatred into an imitation of somebody else—*not a real person*. The lush beauty, with her thick, untidy hair, pushed the sandwich and the soda in front of Florrie with a look of refined disdain. But what's the matter with me? Florrie thought desperately, and peered at the mirror at the back of the soda fountain. She saw an old woman, a skinny little old maid in a light blue dress. Perhaps if I went out of my way to show my friendliness . . .

"This is a delicious sandwich," she said, after her first bite.

The woman had her back turned, attending to the milkshake machine. Florrie waited until she turned.

"This is a delicious sandwich," she said again. The woman stared at her blankly—or contemptuously?—and did not reply.

It's no use.

The sandwich was not delicious, it might have been made of straw and sawdust. When the time came, Florrie's lunch came to sixty-five cents, forty for the sandwich and twenty-five for the soda. The last time Florrie had had a soda it had cost fifteen cents. But that was long, long ago.

She carried her heavy bundles out into the street and turned to go home. High Street, Village Avenue, Broadway, up Hawthorne Street . . .

Somebody had lighted a fire in the Davenant meadow, the old meadow where once, so long ago, Florrie had ridden her pony, Master, round and round. She knew what the fire meant: picnickers. The Davenant house was near the edge of town, and the meadow was broad and filled with daisies, and people did stop their cars and get out with their vacuum . . . no, thermos bottles, and settle down on a big rug to enjoy a lunch. There was a precise ritual for dealing with that, too.

The Davenant land was all posted; No Trespassing signs, lettered by Florrie under Laura's direction, were placed at unmistakable intervals along the rim of the meadow, where people could be definitely assumed to have seen them. The next step was to go out to the little group laughing on its rug and playing its portable radio, and say, "I'm afraid you have not seen the signs. This property is privately owned. Would you mind moving a little farther? There is a County Forest just beyond here where there are tables for picnickers . . ."

But that step had always been taken by Laura.

Florrie sometimes said, "But they don't do any harm. It's rather cheerful, that music."

"It is not to me," Laura had said. "It is offensive. In addition, there is a principle involved. The land is not public. What is the use of owning anything if you do not control it? I do not choose to have strangers leaving their disgusting litter all over my meadow, which will attract flies, and, furthermore, rodents."

"Howard could kill them," Florrie said. But the point was really irrefutable. They did leave food scattered about, and papers, and tin cans, and, on occasion, gin and whiskey bottles, which particularly incensed Laura. "I shall call the police in precisely five minutes," Laura used to say, when there was any demurral among the ejected picnickers. At that, they always went.

Fire was the worst of all.

"I'm sure they are guarding it," Florrie had said on those occasions.

"My dear Florence," Laura would say. "Need I point out that these people are conspicuously without concern for other people's property, or they would not be here in the first place, and that only a few sparks from that outrageous conflagration would be necessary to set fire to the barn, the outhouses, and the house? Do you wish to have our house, the Davenant house, destroyed by a fire set by irresponsible trippers, including all our furniture and Uncle Professor's papers and the Lexington sword?"

It was all perfectly logical and true.

But Laura, erect and dressed in black, had always been the one to go out and tell them. And Laura always expected people to hate her; it was almost as if she relished it. "Their natural superiors . . ."

Florrie approached the column of fire with a sinking heart.

She stood on the edge of the road and looked across the meadow.

There, so very long ago, she had lain, a little girl, among the thick daisies and had the loveliest experience of her life. She looked up through grasses at the blue sky and all at once she knew that she *was* the sky, was the daisies, and that everything, all the wide and round and shimmeringly beautiful universe, was one. She had never told anybody about that.

And here, when she was eighteen, she had strolled after supper with Mr. Bainbridge, who went to Harvard and wore a Fly ribbon on his boater hat.

"Do you care for tennis, Miss Florence?" he inquired.

"Oh, I know I should love it," she replied with all her throbbing eagerness in her voice, but it was not enough; perhaps if she had learned tennis earlier? . . . for Mr. Bainbridge had not called again.

Here the pony, Master, had been pastured until he died at twenty-eight, and here Cousin Roger, the philosopher, had walked, head down, for hours the year before he had his stroke; all the Davenants had remained respectfully on the veranda, for surely Cousin Roger was philosophizing; here the children of Cousin Elizabeth had played, those beautiful little blond boys who had been killed, one in an airplane in the First World War, the other in Burma, where he was a missionary.

Scholars, ministers, doctors, minor diplomats; no money, no power, nothing with which to hurt anybody, nothing but the tradition which required that they should help people; and Florrie was the last one.

Here, in this verdant, sunny meadow she had walked, at thirty, and thought, I'm an old maid. Why do I have to go on in the track? If I went to New York, if I took employment in a shop, if even I worked in a restaurant, I might . . . I might . . .

I might be like other people.

Because I don't want to be wise and learned! I don't want to be elevated and kind! I want to do what they do, and get mad, and love and hate, and. . . .

But she never had.

As she drew nearer to the meadow she saw that the trippers were ensconced quite far at the end of the field, and that their fire was a big one, sending up large, crackling flames. There was the sound of loud voices, and of a radio blaring.

She stood at the meadow's edge, hesitating, while the battle fought itself inside her.

She set the bags that held the half a watermelon and the beef kidney and the other purchases down on the ground, and started across the meadow, a skinny old lady in a blue dress that hung limply from her bony shoulders over her flat bosom.

Nobody among the picnickers noticed her until she was quite near.

They were Italians, or some sort of South European stock, people with rich black hair; the men had muscular hairy arms and the women were luxuriant. They sprawled magnificently upon the ground around their big fire; a bottle was being passed around from mouth to mouth. All around them over the grasses of the Davenant meadow were spread the remains of their feast—tins, newspapers, the skins of bananas, an empty bottle, scraps of uneaten sausage, and the butt end of a loaf of bread.

"Hey, look who's here," said one of them at Florrie's approach.

She smiled.

"How do you do," she said, because she knew no other words to greet with. "I hope you are enjoying your picnic."

There was a silence; only the radio blared its meaningless chatter. They all stared at her as though across an invisible wall; as though she had spoken Chinese.

Then an old man with white hair on his bare chest held out the bottle they had been passing.

"Hava some grappa," he said.

Florrie had heard of grappa. She replied automatically in the pattern of sixty years.

"Oh, I never touch spirits," she said.

"She don't never touch spirits," remarked a young, hairy man to the girl whose head was in his lap. There was a sort of stirring among the seated group; a resolution of their mood, a gathering.

"I don't want to disturb you," Florrie pushed on. "But I did want to caution you about your fire. It's very dangerous . . ."

"Don't worry, lady," said the same young man, while the others stared with their large, foreign, dark eyes. "We ain't scared."

Florrie smiled again, hard.

"I'm sure you're not," she said. "But you see, if you left it not entirely extinguished, it might start a fire among our buildings."

A fat woman, in whose lap lay a huge bunch of the daisies from the field, laughed.

"This is a free country," said the old man, irrelevantly.

"I *want* you to enjoy our meadow," Florrie said desperately; why couldn't they understand?—"I only wanted to ask you to put your fire out when you go, and to . . . to . . . perhaps gather up your papers and picnic things . . . you see, they attract rodents. . . ."

"Rodents, she says," said the young man. "It's okay, lady, we're enjoying your meadow." He minced the word "meadow."

"I *must* ask you to subdue your fire," Florrie said. "I must insist."

"She must ahsk," the young man said. "You and who else?"

The young woman lying across his lap sat up. She reached for an enormous over-ripe pear and bit into it.

"Ahsk ahead," she said. "We're staying as long as we like, see?"

"But I *want* you to stay," Florrie mumbled, and then turned away, defeated in her life's search. She stumbled back across the field, and could hear the jeering laughter behind her, and a voice say "Snotty old . . ."

She picked up her starveling purchases and went on, and into the house and closed the door behind her. She stood quite still in the little front hall, tears burning at her eyelids, trying not to cry. She felt as if she had closed the door of a fortress, behind whose walls was now forever an enemy. For a moment she wondered if she would ever dare go out again. But then she started, violently, as something flew by her and landed plunk upon the floor.

It was Howard. He emitted a loud "miaow" and clawed at the edge of the front door. Suddenly Florrie was shaking all over.

"I hate you," she said out loud. "I hate you . . . d-darn you . . . I won't have you . . . I won't endure you . . ."

Her whole withered little body trembled. *I want to hurt some-*

thing beat in words upon her mind, so long confined, so recently turned loose. I want to hurt. Why am I always the one to be hurt?

She carried her bundles out into the kitchen and put them on the table; she sat down on the old painted chair, shaking. Howard had followed her at his leisure, catlike, free and unplagued, swinging his tail. He rubbed his sides against the legs of the kitchen table.

Her eyes, as though involved in a plot quite separate from her consciousness, moved slowly and with method from one special object to another in the kitchen. Howard . . . the package that held the beef kidney . . . the oven of the electric stove . . . the switch that turned on the broiler. The disparate objects formed themselves behind her eyes into a purposeful whole.

But when she realized what it meant her thin little hand went up to her mouth in horror. How could she . . . How could she . . . even think of such a thing . . . She felt her real eyes, the eyes that belonged to the everyday Florence Davenant, grow big with fear.

The word was murder, a word that to Florrie had always been written in screaming scarlet, rayed with flames. MURDER! She seemed to feel the presence of all the people of the world, outside the door, staring at her with condemning, vengeful, hating eyes.

And suddenly she remembered the white eyeballs of the Lovingston Boys trembling in their jail cell. So that was how they had felt. So that was how they could do it.

She drew a long, quivering breath. Slowly, into her turmoil of hurt and horror and fear stole the stroking touch of comfort. She had sent the check that would help to save the Lovingston Boys, she had sent it herself—not Laura, but Florrie Davenant. It was the right thing to do. She *knew* now, and knowing was like a friendly little light, burning in the dark.

1955

OUTSIDE

LIFE IN SUMMER at the Lockards' revolved around art, as it did in winter; but differently. In the winters Peter daily left their exquisite pink house in the country and went to his studio in the city, where he took pupils, and although Theodosia did her painting in the north room at home, she made frequent trips to town. There were the new shows to be seen. When the pictures were bad, Theodosia declared on returning home that they had made her feel like burning all her brushes; ripping her own canvases with a palette knife; casting herself into the Chard River. "Oh, darling, I can just feel it," Peter would respond, if he had not accompanied her. "How unbearably depressing bad pictures can be!" But if the pictures had been good, Theodosia, the next day, would throw herself into her painting with new dedication, working quietly, intently, concentratedly. In winter she also went to town for occasional lunches with women she had been to art school with; but the Lockards seldom stayed in town for dinner with their painter friends, because it meant getting a sitter and leaving their nine-year-old daughter Phoebe, whom they madly adored.

In winter, too, there were teas for the opening of exhibitions at the Institute of Art, one-man shows of their friends' or, from time to time, Peter's or Theodosia's work. The tea table was laid in the back gallery—a long narrow table set with a huge shining silver tea urn at each end and, between, plates of elaborate sandwiches made to resemble checkerboards; rolled sandwiches with spurts of watercress out each end; little square cakes frosted with pink, yellow, green, white frosting and sprinkled with a sort of silver shot. In her black velveteen best dress with the gold grosgrain sash run through slots, Phoebe would walk slowly around the table, admiring the food. Behind and around her a steady babel of voices discussed art, praising, extolling, upbraiding, condemning. The women, either very chic like Theodosia or else badly, artily dressed, pinned their conversational partners to the wall with a phrase. The men (and if they were artists they were either small and natty or huge, ungainly, and bearded) stared hard at a picture with narrowed eyes, a thumb lifted, meanwhile detaining a companion with hand on sleeve until the exact word of summation should be found. Against this background of sound and incessant shifting, a small thought would appear in Phoebe's mind as she contemplated a plate of variegated cakes: That one looks nice, she would think. But she had learned by this time that the display of food at the Institute teas was more a work of art than anything materially satisfying. Once in a while she would take a sandwich, a cake, but it always tasted like the flour paste she made to glue paper dolls with, or like simply nothing at all.

In summer the Lockards remained at home in their pink house in the country. Peter rented his city studio to a pair of vacationing women professors and turned to landscape. Theodosia painted masses of zinnias, their rosy colors suffused with a golden bloom; summer squashes; overflowing baskets of tomatoes with grape leaves and tendrils and bunches of the pale-green grapes of midsummer; day lilies and gourds and huge trumpet-shaped datura. In a way, life was nicer—warm and murmurous with summer insects, bees, and the cicada—but it was lonely, too. Phoebe wandered in the woods, pretending she was an Indian: at the cracking of a twig she would stop short, the coppery aquiline features frozen into stoical immobility.

"Don't you think Baby ought to find some sweet little friends to keep her company in her meanderings?" Peter would ask, with a helpless air, at supper.

"The poor, miserable, lonesome little thing!" Theodosia would cry, her pity fired. "But who *is* there?"

"The Bodsworths?" Peter suggested one evening, tentatively.

"Oh, Peter!" Theodosia replied in dismay. "Those horrible creatures . . . 'Well, Mrs. Lockard, how's ort?'" she mimicked.

"Incredibly awful woman," Peter agreed. "But the children might not be too bad. . . ."

"Well, why don't you?" Theodosia exclaimed positively, turning to Phoebe. "Ask them over. Go over there. Do something. Perhaps supper . . ." she trailed off vaguely. Meanwhile Phoebe's mind had been anxiously working on a problem, turning it over and over. She came up now with her findings. "I'm not miserable," she explained. "Really I'm not."

"Miserable" was such a strong word; Theodosia was the one who looked miserable, Phoebe thought, with her furrowed brow and distressed gaze. She was relieved when her mother said, "You're not? Oh, good!" and began to smile again and chatter about ordering gamboge.

"Good girl," Peter said approvingly to Phoebe, as if they were in league. "Theodosia's so sensitive. She suffers frightfully. Few people can appreciate what your mother goes through—least of all the Bodsworths of this world."

"Oh, darling!" Theodosia cried instantly, generously. "*You're* the sensitive one! What Peter doesn't endure," she said aside to Phoebe, "with the callousness, the cold indifference, he encounters all winter in town. . . . A child like you couldn't, I thank God, imagine. These heavenly, blissful, utterly peaceful summers are all that save him, I really think. When we can be together, alone in our adorable house, with no un-understanding outsiders to spoil things . . ."

And then, as if jointly they realized that they were leaving somebody out, they turned to Phoebe. "Precious!" Theodosia cried, leaning out of her chair to kiss her child. "My own blessing! Mother's little medium-girl!"

This epithet referred to a family story, an anecdote often told to sympathetically amused souls: When Phoebe was four, Theodosia, hugging her at bedtime, had declared, "You're the most adorable, precious, wonderful child in the whole world," and the little girl, with infant literal-mindedness, had said, "No, I'm not. I'm just medium." And so nowadays Theodosia or Peter would often cry, as Theodosia did now, "Who is the most darling, adorable little medium-girl in the world?"

Two or three times during the summer the Lockards gave a party—generally a cocktail party, so that it would be daytime and the guests could see and admire the beauty of the garden. The guests, of course, were friends from town, painters and a few sculptors, who drove out jammed six or eight into a five-passenger car, or took the train and walked up from the station, arriving dusty and outstandingly thirsty. Some obscure sentiment of *noblesse oblige*, however, always made the Lockards dilute the guest list with a few people from the surrounding countryside, some Bodsworth or Capen—not many but just enough to ruin their pleasure in their own party.

"Oh, *God*," Theodosia cried at breakfast that day in August, "Capens and Dr. Lawson *and* the Alfred Allinghams." She put her head in her hands. "And they hate us. My head aches," she added, "as if it were a tooth. I'm incapable of thinking. Throb, throb . . ."

Peter gazed at her with understanding eyes as he finished his egg. "It's given *me* a stomach-ache," he said. "They have about as much idea—I know what they're saying now: 'We've got to go to cocktails with those crazy artists.'"

"The falseness of those people!" Theodosia stormed. "It's we who are simple and basic and good. It's they who have the wild parties, the lack of any conception of a true morality. . . . 'Crazy artists'! Sometimes I think it is people like us who hold the world together, who believe in the true basic principles that keep everything from falling apart. *They* have no core of truth, no dedication to anything beyond their immediate advantage. . . ."

"They hate us because we have," said Peter.

Phoebe looked from one of them to the other.

"I honestly don't think I am going to be able to endure this appalling, splitting headache," Theodosia said. "I don't think I'm going to be able to paint this morning."

"Lie down," Peter advised.

"I'm afraid I'm going to have to. It makes me feel defeated."

"*My* stomach feels as if I'd swallowed broken glass," Peter said. "Pain every few moments, like a knife being turned in my vitals."

"I've got a pain, too," Phoebe said.

"Precious!" Theodosia cried in her anxiety. "Where? Is it frightful?"

Phoebe laid her hand on her side. "No," she said. "It's just sort of a pain."

"Growing pains," Theodosia said, with relief. "I remember having agonizing growing pains."

Phoebe's forehead knitted with her problem.

"It isn't agonizing," she said a moment later.

"Oh, good," Theodosia said.

"Well, mine is," Peter said. "I'm going out and see if I can't paint it out of my system."

"You're so sporting," Theodosia said. "*I've* simply got to give in. If I endure this agony another second I can't answer for the consequences. I can set the glasses out later."

Phoebe wandered down through the deep, murmurous, gold-and-purple swamp. Great hummocks of burned marsh grass, clumps of goldenrod, loosestrife, and joe-pye weed melted their colors into each other under the soft and melancholy late-summer sun. A cicada in the upper, hotter meadows sent up at intervals its shrill high note. Down in a pool of swamp water beside where Phoebe was stepping from hummock to hummock a big bullfrog suddenly ejaculated "Clunk."

Phoebe went on as far as where the sluggish stream wound through the middle of the marsh. She sat down on the humped-up roots of a tree that bordered the stream and took her shoes off and put her feet in the dark, slimy water. The coolness made her feel better. Her pain was still there, and it was not nice. Staring down into the opaque depths of the dark stream she considered: What kind of a pain was it, exactly?

Well, she decided, it was not agonizing, and it was not frightful. She couldn't think of it as torment; it just hurt. It just kept on hurting.

She wriggled a little to put it out of her mind, and fell to poking in the mysterious dark depths of the stream with a long stick. Great chunks of cohesive mud came up, and then a dirty beer can. Phoebe wondered how a beer can ever came to be here, far away from habitations. She assumed the other people had thrown it here, the outsiders, the ones who were brutal and callous. Their children, whom she saw at school in the winters, often seemed silly and even mean, but not brutal and not callous. They probably got to be that way as they grew older. Phoebe threw the stick on top of the water and watched it move by infinitely slow degrees down the stream deeper into the morass.

After a while she got up and wandered out of the swamp again, back up on to the hill, where it was golden and sunny. The brightness and clarity of noon filled the atmosphere, the shadows of early morning had shrunk up to nothing, and the cicada loudly celebrated the height of the day. Over on the side of the further hill Phoebe could see Peter painting, a little spot of white shirt and yellow straw hat behind the shape of his canvas set on the folding easel. He saw her, too, and waved. Phoebe lifted a limp arm and waved back.

She wandered through the alleys of the little garden and up to the house, where she found Theodosia happily arranging a still life on the old carved black-oak chest. She threw Phoebe a quiet, abstracted smile; her being seemed centered on what she was doing, as she inserted a stalk of long grass into the arrangement of zinnias in the gray pottery jug. "Isn't it nice?" she asked, her voice soft and concentrated. "I'm going to paint it tomorrow morning, and it'll look lovely for the party. Killing two birds with one stone."

Phoebe lingered a little longer, but her mother did not look around; she stood off a moment from her arrangement, and then dived back to readjust a huge ragged pink bloom. Phoebe went slowly upstairs to her room and got out the book in which she kept her paper dolls. She stared at them distantly for a moment; the pain still hurt. But it would probably go away soon. Theodosia's headache, which had been worse than any pain Phoebe could have, seemed to have gone, Phoebe thought. She bent to push back an unstuck corner of the wallpaper with which she had covered facing pages of the blank book; each spread made a room for the paper dolls, with furniture cut from magazine advertisements pasted on the wallpaper. She had made a living room, a dining room, a kitchen, and three bedrooms thus. But the rooms now looked ugly, forsaken; the dolls thin and papery and so insubstantial. They looked up at her, their maker, with little faces sharp as the jeering stoats and weasels in *The Wind in the Willows*. They rather frightened her, but she continued patiently, doggedly, to try to play with them.

Theodosia came to call her for lunch.

"Wash your hands, precious," she said, smiling, in the doorway.

"All right," Phoebe said, getting up. "But I don't feel very hungry. My stomach hurts."

"Oh, darling!" Theodosia cried with compunction. "And I forgot! Is it frightful, darling? Are you suffering?"

Phoebe considered.

"Not exactly," she said. "It just hurts."

"Do you think you want the doctor?"

Phoebe looked back, puzzled. "I don't know," she said.

"Well," Theodosia said, "if it doesn't feel all better soon, you tell me, won't you? I can't bear it to have my darling little girl in agony, you know," she added.

"I'm not in agony," Phoebe said, conscientiously.

"I'm so glad," Theodosia said. "I don't feel as if I could bear it if you were. Those ghastly people," she continued as they went out of the room together. "After I've made those exquisite flower arrangements, I know what they'll do. They'll just stalk in and snatch a drink without noticing anything. People like that just don't *see*. Well, there'll be the others—darling Frankie and Beth and Clarissa, anyway. . . ."

By five o'clock people had begun to arrive, climbing the picturesque winding stone staircase that led from the road up to the pink house; two cars from town had parked and debouched their occupants, and now somebody from nearby had come—Mrs. Capen and her daughter, Mrs. Fellowes. "I'm so thrilled to meet you, Mrs. Lockard," Mrs. Fellowes said to Theodosia. "I've heard all about your art work."

Theodosia was rigid; she felt, she always said, like a little girl at school when she was confronted by such large, hearty, normal people. "Won't you have something to drink?" she offered, in a small voice. Peter, passing with a bowl full of popcorn, gave her hand a squeeze. A gentleman had just appeared at the top of the steps. "Dr. Lawson!" Theodosia exclaimed in unnaturally social tones, and hurried away to greet him. "Isn't it an exquisite day?" she said.

Dr. Lawson regarded his hostess gravely, as she stood, trembling with excitement, in front of him. “Exquisite,” he agreed.

Phoebe passed peanuts among the steadily enlarging crowd. Sure enough, the pain had gone, quite suddenly a few minutes ago, but she felt funny; rather as if she was floating. This, she thought, must be sort of the way Peter and Theodosia felt all the time, for now she saw everything in the most heightened terms: the stone crock of meadow grasses at the top of the steps, for instance, shimmered with beauty. It was not just nice, it was achingly beautiful. Everything—the colors of the ladies’ dresses, the flowers in the garden, the view—shone with an unearthly brilliance in vivid tones of acid green, glittering red, and piercing purple. Maybe I’m going to be an artist, Phoebe thought, doubtfully.

On the terrace five of the artists were engaged in a hot dispute about Picasso. “Eternal . . . classic . . .” said a woman in a kind of neigh, quite extraordinarily like a horse.

“But he can’t *draw*,” said a young man, running his fingers through his yellow hair.

“Draw? Why, nobody even started to draw before Picasso!” somebody else fairly screamed.

“Why do we discuss antiques?” asked a fat man impatiently.

Mrs. Capen interposed her broad-brimmed blue straw hat between the yellow-haired young man and the horse lady. “Are we talking about art?” she inquired eagerly.

“Dear lady,” began the fat man. The group disintegrated, drifted away.

Mrs. Allingham, trying to be more than just a wife and mother, had cornered a live artist, a very tall young man with a skull-like face, and had him pinned down on an iron love seat. “I want to hear all about your work,” she said, flashing her large, lustrous eyes at him, from under her little hat made of yellow and orange flowers. “What is it you are trying to *say*?”

The tall young man squirmed on the hard iron seat and said something unintelligible that sounded like "Waxworks."

"But what is it you are trying to *prove*, I mean, in your art?" Mrs. Allingham persisted, flashing her eyes and scooping up a handful of the peanuts that Phoebe was passing her.

The gentleman named Dr. Lawson came strolling up with a short squat man, who stared into the skull-like man's eyes and said, "Jesus Christ, you here?"

They found seats facing Mrs. Allingham. "I was just asking Mr.—Mr.—" said Mrs. Allingham urgently.

"Cobb," the skull admitted.

"—Mr. Cobb just what it is you are all trying to *say*, in your work," she said.

"I am trying to say something very definite. Shall I tell you what it is?" said the short squat man loquaciously. Mrs. Allingham turned her full liquid gaze on him with relief. "Brace yourself," the short squat man said.

Dr. Lawson was paying no attention. He had laid his hand on Phoebe's forehead. "This little lady has a high fever," he remarked, rising. "Has anybody seen her mother?"

Phoebe swam sickeningly back into consciousness in a strange room in the middle of the night. The room was ambiguous, unexplained: all dark except for a very strange small blue light that burned on the wall low down near the floor. Why should a light, and blue at that, be there? A hard object pressed against her cheek, and, feeling of it with her fingers, she realized it was a sort of bowl and remembered that at some unidentified time earlier she had thrown up into it. She thought it possible that she might do so now. She was all alone.

In a rising fog of fear she made an effort to assemble the few facts she possessed about her situation. It came back to her that this was the County Hospital, and that she had had an operation. Dr. Lawson had made a joke—it seemed a long time ago—about sprinkling talcum powder in her insides.

Dr. Lawson must have gone away. He must have gone to bed. Theodosia and Peter must have gone home—they were here once—and gone to bed, too. Phoebe was all alone in this place, with nobody but outsiders anywhere near her, and even the outsiders had gone away and left her. From her chest down she could feel nothing; her body was threateningly numb. The queer blue light burned steadily. Suddenly she had to throw up, and did. Her chin was all wet afterward. She could not see what to do with the bowl, which felt crescent-shaped.

I feel horrible, she thought, the words passing through her mind like gray shapes; I am suffering terribly.

"I feel awful," she mumbled out loud in the empty room. But nobody heard, and nobody ever paid attention if you said things quietly. Phoebe turned her face away from the side the basin was on and began to scream at the top of her voice. Scream followed scream.

The nurse, who had slipped downstairs to catch a cup of the midnight coffee served to the night nurses, had just come back on the floor. She came hurrying down the corridor and pushed open the door of Phoebe's room; her skirts made a rustling of starch in the darkness. Phoebe screamed again.

"Now you look here, young lady—" the nurse began with the approved brisk callousness.

When the nurse came out of the now silent room, the supervisor, Miss Percy, was sitting under the single light at the desk in the angle of the corridor, bringing the charts up to date.

"What was all the racket in Twenty-seven?" she asked without looking up.

"Hysteria," said the nurse. She settled down in the other chair and bent over to loosen the shoelaces of her white buck oxfords; her feet were tired. "Nothing was hurting her. Just no control. What can you expect? Sadie Poole lives over near the parents, up to the old Tompkins place. She says they live it up, all right. Wild parties. He has a *studio*! Nude models, I bet. The parents go wandering around the fields, she says. It's no life for a child. Crazy artists, Sadie calls them, and I see what she means."

1956

A SLOW BOAT TO CHINA

At Gettysburg, familiar to them as the halfway point between home and St. David's, Elvira Wilson and her son, nicknamed Pete, paused for lunch before turning south into Maryland and Virginia. Something was missing; this was the first time in five years that Pete's father, Jimmy Wilson, was not along to make of the return to school a gay, triumphant, almost riotous occasion; Jimmy had had to go to Detroit. They were rather subdued, Elvira felt anxiously, as they went into the short-order joint Jimmy always stopped at, and ordered hamburgers and milk and coffee. This would never do. Next year Pete would go away, in a more final sense, to college; how degrading to have his last return to school a depressing one alone with his mother. Elvira placed one teaspoon behind the other, on the counter, and with her fist pounded the rear spoon sharply, so that the front one jumped bowl first into the glass of water. Pete's face broke into a grin; the counterman laughed. Jimmy's old trick was always a success.

After lunch they turned south on Route 15 and tore down through the increasingly green, increasingly lush landscape. It was almost like being granted something normally forbidden—the page turned back to summer, a chance to live over again time that was actually finished. Thick green willows wept over the gingerbread balconies of brick houses deep in the country. Town by town the countryside became more Southern, relaxed, yearning. Elvira drove at a steady sixty-five, with style, the way her father had taught her to drive long ago in an old red Jordan roadster. She sat erect, her neat, smooth head held very high, but Pete slouched, like all the young today, his head back against the seat, one foot propped on the dashboard. As they left Frederick, Maryland, he began to whistle an old haunting tune.

"What's that?" she asked.

He sang: "'I'd love to get you . . .'"

But her attention had been distracted by the appearance of the Blue Ridge Mountains to the west of them, running along parallel to their rapid passage. Heavy, looming, inscrutable, they abruptly appeared to her, for the first time, frightening. She stepped the car's speed up to seventy and tipped her chin higher.

"Hey," Pete said mildly, taking his foot down off the dashboard.

She gave a little laugh and continued to hold the speed. It was a pretty pass, she thought, when one became afraid of inanimate objects. She supposed it might have something to do with what people called a resistance to Pete's leaving her; a dread of losing him. But she had *never* been that kind of sap. Jimmy always phrased it that one held one's child solely in trust, against his becoming a man. When she thought how her own father had trained her for independence—the target practice, the flying lessons, the full allowance at sixteen . . . But in the meantime the mountains traveled along beside them, high, perilous, and somehow terrible.

It occurred to her that perhaps the Blue Ridge really did look different today.

"Them there hoary pinnacles are quite something, aren't they?" she asked cautiously.

"Aw, shucks," Pete said. "Them ain't no hoary pinnacles. Them's just some little old country mountains."

But she thought it helped the way the mountains made her feel, to keep talking.

"Does anybody ever go skiing in them?" she continued, as she took a curve with a smooth turn of her thin wrists.

"Too forested," Pete said. "Some of the guys go climbing in them, though, with their families, week ends."

"I've never been attracted to mountain-climbing, have you?" she inquired conversationally.

"I don't know. Never gave it much thought."

"I read somewhere," she said, "what some mountain-climber said when he was asked why he climbed—Everest, I guess. He said, 'Because it's there.'"

"Seems kind of a dumb reason," Pete said. "You mean he didn't even want to?"

He went back to whistling. To their right the mountains marched along southwards, in somber, mysterious ranks, the higher and the lower. They were more purplish than blue; they seemed almost to topple, but the mists sustained them. In the foreground the rich country ran, raw red and bright green, over the rolling hills, and the road ran over the country like a white tape laid down ahead; but lift your eyes higher and there stood the mountains, waiting; threatening with an ambiguous eloquence. Elvira looked away at her wrists as they controlled the wheel; from one of them hung a gold bracelet; the cuffs above them were heather-mixture tweed; she wore a white silk blouse with her suit, and the collar was pinned with a gold horse's bit.

"Hey, Mom," Pete said. He shifted his weight and recrossed his long, straight, skinny legs.

"Yessir," she said.

"Look," he said, and paused.

"Looking," she said.

"Pop said something," Pete said hesitantly, "about giving away some of my stuff to the Welles brat. I mean, I didn't want you to exactly clean out my room so I would hardly recognize it when I got home Christmas, or anything."

"I guess you'll have no trouble recognizing it," she said lightly. "You don't want us to leave it totally untouched by mortal hands, do you? Or you want it should be a shrine—James Wilson, Jr., slept here?"

Pete laughed.

"Heck no," he said. "I'm saving that."

They were crossing the Virginia line.

"But I was just thinking," Pete said.

"An excellent practice," she said.

"I was thinking about that Erector set you gave me way back. The thing is, I just didn't want Pop to give it to the Welles brat. That always was a super Erector set, Mom. I'd sort of like to hang on to it."

She glanced sidewise at him and, catching his eye, made a humorous face.

"You plan to clutch it in your hot little fist as you arrive at Dartmouth?" she said.

He shrugged his broad, flat, skinny shoulders.

"I guess it is sentimental," he allowed.

"*Un tout petit peu*," she said.

"Which being translated?"

"You'll get it in first-year French," she said.

Pete put his head back against the seat again and, after a moment, began to whistle, the same old, haunting tune that had followed them all the way down from the higher, more autumnal states. She knew that she associated it with something and was unwilling to plumb what.

"'I'd love to get you . . .'" Pete sang softly to himself.

As she listened, the car whirled past a weathered, paintless Virginia shack; two scrub pines in front, and a desolate old Ford pickup truck. The front door of the shack stood open on darkness, and, in the instant they swept by, a hen came wandering, pecking, out of the door. They tore on down the long road to school. To the west the mountains still ranged, purplish, demanding, and inescapable.

It was with relief that Elvira took the turn into the narrower road running east, that led to St. David's and left the Blue Ridge behind them.

"It won't be long now," she remarked cheerfully.

"That's *right*," he replied in a nasal, mock-radio accent.

Soon the school appeared, crowning a low hill off across the rolling countryside like a minor Acropolis, with its classic buildings—the gymnasium, the Great Hall, Anderson Hall, and the white-columned dormitories.

"That's a fine sight," she said.

"Not half bad for a salt mine," he agreed.

They drew up with dash in front of Number Three dormitory, where most sixth-formers lived. Pete continued to lounge back, squinting speculatively at his future living quarters.

"Brooding, my good man?" Elvira inquired briskly. "We've got to get cracking. Get this crate unloaded before we go into Mr. Harrison's office. Front and center," she ordered.

Pete's abstracted expression broke into a grin.

"Right," he said, and, jumping out, began to pull the bags out of the back of their station wagon.

"Put your back into it," she encouraged. She could hear Jimmy saying the words, in other years; gaily, inimitably.

A tall boy with red hair came around the side of the dormitory.

"If it isn't Wilson. I'll be switched," he remarked, approaching.

"Higgins, you old horror," Pete said.

Higgins reached out and snatched Pete's arm into a half-Nelson.

"Hey," Pete said. "If you're all that energetic you can just help me get some of this junk into the dump."

Smiling to herself, Elvira got out of the front seat and stretched her legs, shaking her skirt out; a tall erect woman in a good tweed suit, who looked all wiriness. She kept on smiling; Pete was so obviously a success at school.

Seated, alone, in the anteroom to the headmaster's office, Elvira undid her jacket, leaned back, and lit a cigarette, surveying the other waiting parents, some with their boys, some without. It was easy to tell the parents with new boys—the anxious brows, the whispered, ignored admonitions, the impatient glances thrown toward the closed door to Mr. Harrison's office. There was such a family just opposite to her.

She herself was an old hand at this. She had had her two minutes or so, together with Pete, in Mr. Harrison's office, while the broad, ruddy headmaster read off Pete's schedule and asked if there was anything she particularly wanted to speak about. "Not a thing," she had replied, conveying in the tone of her voice—gay, she hoped, resonant—the satisfaction the Wilsons felt at what St. David's was doing for Pete; her full confidence in Mr. Harrison's judgment. He had given her what she was sure was a relieved smile. Not every mother was so reasonable; some behaved year after year like wild cows whose calves are being taken from them. Elvira had been able to recognize, unaided, the moment when a mother became definitely *de trop*, the moment for Mr. Harrison's little man-to-man talk with Pete. She knew the ropes, the system, and could sit here in a green cotton brocade chair without twitching or looking worried, in this square, stiff waiting room with its green cotton brocade curtains and its copies of old school yearbooks.

The thought of the mountains waiting crossed her consciousness like a cloud; lifting her chin, she gave all her attention to the family opposite her.

The father was handsome; of a sanguine complexion, close-shaven, dressed in a well-cut Glen plaid suit. The mother had been a beauty—a Southern belle, Elvira guessed—and now was a soft-skinned, pretty, but ravaged brunette, unwisely made up. They must have been known after their marriage as a handsome couple; but no longer. Between them sat a boy of about fourteen who resembled his father. He was obviously a new boy, excited and impressed and covering it all up with a touching imitation of his father's self-assurance. There was, in addition, a wriggling little girl, perhaps eight, brought along for the thrill of seeing Brother start boarding school.

But in vain did the little girl squirm for attention against her mother's knees; the faded beauty had great, once-lovely eyes for nothing but that wonderful, that thrilling son—her pride, her delight, her beloved. She kept whispering to him. It was perfectly clear that she was unmoved, unimpressed, by the brisk masculinity that St. David's exuded like an aura; indifferent to its fine buildings and first-rate playing fields; she had obviously not been fooled for one instant by all the talk they had given her about building manhood, inculcating character, developing a sense of honor. What she knew, with animal sureness, was that this was the place where they took away your son from you.

She continued to lean, her elbow on the arm of his chair, and look longingly into the boy's impatient face. Just so must she once have leaned, years ago, toward some favored admirer, perhaps her future husband, when she was a young, beautiful, sought-after, indulged debutante at a Richmond German or, perhaps, a Bachelors' Cotillion.

Nobody now, however, paid the slightest attention to her. The boy ignored her whispers. He spoke occasionally to his father, who nodded and smiled with an air of masculine complicity. The mother might as well not have been there, except to the little girl, who rubbed pleadingly against her mother's knees and was, in her turn, ignored.

The door to Mr. Harrison's office opened and Pete came out. The headmaster's secretary stepped into the anteroom from her own office. She beckoned to the family of four, who rose and went into the headmaster's.

Elvira started to get up, but Pete came across to her and said:

"Got to get my classroom card checked through with Mr. Elkins. Mind waiting here? I won't be long."

He disappeared, and Elvira leaned back in her chair again and lit another cigarette. A new family entered the room, an extremely chic woman in black, with a much-older husband who looked as if he might be a diplomat. They had with them a small, timid-looking boy.

After a bit the door into Mr. Harrison's office opened again and the well-groomed father was to be seen shaking Mr. Harrison's hand. The mother was just beside him. She was looking back into the office where her son must be sitting. Her expression, the turn of her head, was so tragic that for a moment Elvira thought she might be going to make a scene.

Then the system took hold and the preparatory-school machinery, especially designed for separating mothers from their sons, went into action; you could almost see the synchronized meshing of gears. Mr. Harrison took the woman's tragically uplifted hand and shook it. The husband, with mechanical gallantry, put his arm around his wife's shoulders and led her to a sofa. The door into the headmaster's office neatly closed, leaving the boy inside. "Mummy . . ." the little girl repeated. The woman's large, pretty eyes held an expression of primitive suffering. As Elvira watched, the husband said something soothing to his wife. When she turned her face to answer him, it wore a look of real hate.

Pete popped back into the room.

"All set," he said. Elvira got to her feet, and together they went out, and down the steps of the Great Hall into the warm September afternoon.

Pete's new room, on the ground floor of Number Three dormitory, was empty; his roommate had not yet arrived. Elvira went around the room doing all the appropriate maternal things: feeling the springs of the bed, inspecting the closet space, looking severely into drawers for signs of silverfish. She examined the view from the single window; this year it was of the main lawn, with two oak trees and a maple included in it. "Well," she said gaily, "no use prolonging the agony."

"That's *right*," he said, doing his nasal imitation.

She took his young face between her hands and gave him two kisses—firm, official, unemotional, affectionate; the kind of kisses a boy could endure being caught getting.

"It's been nice knowing you," she said.

"Likewise," he replied, looking down at her. He must be a good two inches taller than she, nowadays. The year he had first come to school, she thought, she had had to bend down to kiss him good-by.

He strolled, long-legged, beside her out to the car, and, when she got in, slammed the door after her. They smiled at each other. She started up the motor.

"See you soon," he said.

"Not if I see you first," she replied. It was an old family joke; Jimmy Wilson always made it.

Elvira looked back through the rearview mirror when she was halfway down the drive. Pete had joined a group of boys and was walking rapidly toward Anderson Hall, gesticulating. She settled down to drive.

But instead of fear, the view of the mountains dead ahead which she had dreaded filled her with sudden, unexpected, remorseless anger.

She was disconcerted to find herself boiling mad at the silliest things: at the school for giving Pete a room with only one window; at the garage at home for not properly fixing the tail gate of the station wagon, which had squeaked and rattled all day long. As her rage found its scope, it took wings. She found herself feeling—as she looked angrily ahead at the long, undulating line of mountains, blue in the gathering dusk—furious at those absurd men, those mountain-climbers, with their idiotic philosophy: "Because it's there." What a damned silly reason for climbing a mountain! She could just see them, jaws set, ropes and picks in hand, scaling their preposterous summits like insects driven by instinct, with no will of their own. She began revengefully to feel angry at the mountains themselves—large, purple, ponderous, monotonous, boring.

Her anger seemed to catch on anything in its way, like a dazzling light glancing off polished surfaces. The strength of her anger was so towering that she felt a sense of power toward the landscape, as though she could stride into those mountains, knock their heads together, topple them with a blow like ninepins.

She drew up with a jerk and a squeal of brakes at the red stop sign before turning back on to Route 15. When she was straightened out on the main road, she sank her foot into the accelerator and let the car leap without glancing at the speedometer.

The car swept up toward a scene that, in its instant of visibility, struck her like a sharp, painful note in music: a weathered, paintless Virginia cabin, two tall scrub pines in front; an old, dilapidated Ford truck. The front door stood open upon darkness. Hens wandered, pecking, about the bare dirt yard. A hen ran out. . . .

There was an awful squawk and a bump, and she had jammed on the brakes without consciousness of doing so. She jerked the car door open and walked around to the back where the hen lay spread in blood and feathers upon the road.

Elvira stared blankly at the mess. She had often agreed with Jimmy when he expressed himself on the subject of people who would kill an animal like an insect, sweep on uncaring, leave poorer people to wipe their livestock up off the road. She knocked on a board at the side of the open front door and waited. Nobody came. She walked around, a tall fine-drawn woman in a tweed suit, to the back of the cabin. A corrugated tin wash tub was tipped on its side against the back step. The place was deserted.

She went back to the car and got in; shut the door with a slam beside her; put her hands on the wheel, stared straight ahead down the long straight road north, and burst into tears.

With her tears and as if a part of them, the memory she had resisted earlier erupted; like a damned subterranean stream, like an abscess breaking. Pete was in bed recuperating from measles. His thin little neck stretched up eagerly like a bird's, his shoulders under the pajamas were narrow, a child's; his eyes were bright after the glaze of illness. The new Erector set lay scattered over the bedclothes, bits of it put together into an angle, a support.

"Is there anything you want before I go downstairs?" she asked. There were PTA envelopes to be addressed.

"Turn on the vic. I want—" But she knew what he wanted, the new record; the new tune. He began to sing it along with the record, in his high, clear voice: "'I'd love to get you . . . On a slow boat to China . . . All to myself, alone. . . .'"

As she stood beside his bed he reached out for her hand and pulled at it coaxingly.

"Don't go. Stay with me. Read."

"I've *been* reading. And I've got so much work to do."

"Read some more. I would love to get you on a slow boat to China, Mom," he said. "Wouldn't it be fun. Sailing along, for a long time. Mom, let's take a slow boat to China. I'd *love* to get you. . . ."

Looking down into his lively shiny eyes she felt dizzy; frightened. It was like standing high above a deep, shadowy valley, through which a river, slowly, ran down to the sea. What she felt was a kind of vertigo.

"Can it, kid," she said. "I can't spend my whole day lally-gagging around with the likes of you. Got to get cracking."

A car passed with a whine of the tires, and Elvira became once more aware of her surroundings, the motionless car enclosing her, the road, the cabin. The memory and the tears sank behind her eyes, out of mind. She waited for a moment, uncertainly, questioningly, with the feeling that something was expected of her.

Then she blew her nose briskly. It had been years, in her well-adjusted life, since she had cried and blown her nose and smelled that special smell that went with tears. It reminded her of her childhood. She thought of her mother, languid, with Pre-Raphaelite nasturtium-colored hair, who always said, "Don't ask me. Ask your father. He'll know."

Elvira took a long breath. It was lucky, she thought, that she had never let herself go off the deep end, about Pete, the way some mothers did; she was rewarded by the knowledge that he was a great success.

She got out of the car again and walked back to the cabin. It wore an air of desertion, chilly, damp. But you couldn't really think of something as deserted, she thought, when there was still activity about it; and the hens ran busily, senselessly, about the dirt yard pecking. Somebody must live here; there was the truck. Elvira walked around to the back again and stood in the desolate yard staring past a board privy, set at a crazy cant under a redbud tree that dripped big yellow leaves, at the thin woods behind. She went over to the back door. "Hello," she called. "Hello?" But nothing from the house answered her. "I killed one of your hens," she called. But the deserted house gave out only a breath of mildew.

She walked around to the front and stood fumbling in her purse; took out two dollars and laid them on the floor just inside the open door. She returned to the car, got in, and turned the ignition key; the motor came back to life.

Though it was a little humiliating to find that she was, after all, the sort of mother who cried over her son's childhood, the experience seemed to have done her good. She felt drained but calm, as she let the car's speed mount to her accustomed dashing rate, and she saw with relief that her tears had washed the mountains clean of the dark conflict of emotions that had soiled them for her all day. Now they had resumed their acceptable aspect of beautiful and majestic. Letting her eyes stray west from time to time into the late afternoon shadows settling in the deep places where mountains and valley became one, she imagined what it would be like to climb the mountains: up narrow trails, between thick green walls of forest, until the top was attained, from which the lovely and still sunlit valley could be overlooked. It was an academic reflection, since brisk sets of tennis were the Wilsons' game, but she found herself thinking, as the car tore northward toward Gettysburg, that mountain-climbing would be a wonderfully rewarding sport, if you had the time and could choose.

1957

FLOTSAM

THROUGH MOST of a long, sunny September afternoon, grandmother and grandson strolled past the tourist-trade shops along the streets of Rockport. The season was practically finished. A few vacationers passed—stout middle-aged women in shorts and halter, usually surmounted by a Jazz Age shingle or an imposing pile of marcelled hairdo. Several children of less than school age ran, on little bare brown feet, down to the beach in summer-ragged, summer-faded bathing suits. Here and there an artist had pitched his easel near the sidewalk and stood scowling past his canvas at the cobalt waters of Sandy Bay.

The shops were holding their sales. Their windows were crammed with seashell-trimmed compacts, handmade silver jewelry, enamel earrings, tiny ship models inside bottles, small, purposeless pieces of delft china, miniature oil paintings of the sea set upon miniature easels, dolls' tea sets of imitation Dresden, green pottery in modernistic, lopsided designs, marked-down seersucker sun suits, straw coolie hats from Korea, cork-soled sandals, a pile of sneakers tied together in pairs by the shoestrings with the sign "Your Pick—75¢," nutcrackers in the form of a red lobster, toy lobster pots, real fishermen's nets on sale for decorative purposes with bluish glass floats like bubbles, reels of fishing line, children's yellow oilskins complete with sou'wester, orange life preservers in small sizes—all of it insubstantial as bits of spindrift blown off a summer wave.

Carolyn Moss and seven-year-old Marcus had only yesterday

been driven down to Rockport by Marcus's mother, Mary Bentley; so it was all new to them. They passed slowly from window to window, inspecting everything with interest. From time to time Carolyn caught a glimpse of how they looked—like the mirage of a tall slender woman with a little boy floating, transparent and ghostly, among all those concrete objects. She looked into the dark glass of what she had thought for a moment was the window of the package store she was looking for, and touched her hair. Its streaks of gray seemed only a lighter blond in the short locks that stood up from her forehead like plumes. She had never, she reflected thankfully, lost her ability to adapt to fashion, and, aware of that crêpiness that creeps within the elbow, the knobbiness of aging knees, the flabbiness of bared backs after forty, she wore such dresses as this pink chambray with its flowing skirt, round white collar, and three-quarter sleeves.

She was certainly an extremely young-looking grandmother. No doubt many of these passers-by mistook her for Marcus's mother. She could almost have *been* his mother, too. She and Marcus were so congenial that sometimes Carolyn, confused, would say, "Let Mother hold your coat while you run," or "Tell the little girl your mother says you must go home now."

Marcus would correct her: "Not my mother. My grandmother." He was not in any sense putting her in her place, merely explaining reality to her.

She would never have dared to tell Marcus how very young *he* looked. His fair hair, crew cut, looked like fuzz on a baby duckling. His little white neck rose straight out of the collar of his clean blue-and-white cord suit; he hadn't much tan because of spending the summer with Carolyn in her Boston apartment. Under a saddle of freckles, his nose turned up as if asking questions of the world, and his expression, as he surveyed the window displays, was serious and judicial. Carolyn loved him so much that it was an effort sometimes when he was explaining automobile engines or jet planes to her not to lose track of what he was saying in her adoration of his little white teeth, like pearls, or the way his skin was grainless, like a baby's.

"See that snorkel, Grandmother," he said, pointing. "Gee."

"What do you do with it?" she asked, only half ignorant.

"You put the rubber piece in your mouth, and the top sticks up so you can breathe while you're swimming under water," he said, turning away from the window and looking up earnestly into her face.

"Suppose it tips over sideways—why don't you drown?" she asked.

"You can't. That ball inside—see?—keeps the water from coming in."

"Really?" She loved to feel stupid and respectful before him.

"*Can't* I go swimming, Grandmother?" he asked once again. "If I could go swimming, maybe I could swim under water, if I had that snorkel."

"Not till you get over your cold, darling," she said. "Remember what Muddy said when she left this morning. Perhaps day after tomorrow," she added, unauthorized, because she hated so to see him look cast down. Then she remembered this morning's joke. "What's your dame?" she demanded.

"Barcus," he replied. They laughed again. Actually, during the day his nose had cleared up considerably.

"Barcus is widding," Carolyn said, looking down into that face, so confident, so filled with information, so indeed willing. She was, as ever, poised with longing to get him anything he felt he needed; to buy the snorkel. But instead of asking for it again, he pulled her on to the next window, one filled with Mexican ruffled shirts, huarachos, and tapered black trousers.

"*Why* did Muddy have to go right away again when we just got here?" Marcus asked, in a slightly different tone.

"You know." Carolyn kept her own voice exactly the same. "Mr. Proctor telephoned he needed to see her once more about the separation agreement thing. She felt she'd better spend the night and make sure everything got attended to, because she doesn't want to have to go back to Boston before you drive to Idaho."

"Oh," Marcus said, although it had all been explained to him before. "But I don't see why Muddy has to get a divorce from my father. *Why* does she have to get a divorce?"

Carolyn's fingers tightened involuntarily on his hand. He asked the question over and over, usually at bedtime. And Mary wanted him to be told the truth. The truth, she said, was always best, and it was a mistake to think that children couldn't understand it. Carolyn could only hope Marcus would understand it soon.

"Gerald wasn't true to Muddy," Carolyn said. Her heart sank.

"What's *true*?" he asked.

"True means keeping the promises he and Muddy made when they got married, to stay with each other and be good to each other," Carolyn said.

"*I* think he was good to Muddy," Marcus observed.

"Another kind of good," Carolyn said. "A kind of grownup good. Gerald wasn't nice to Muddy. He took things that belonged to Muddy and gave them to other ladies."

"Oh," Marcus said. This explanation, too, had been given him before. It was a fact that talking about the divorce did not seem to distress him unduly; on the contrary, what Carolyn and Mary told him did not seem to sink in at all. Each time he asked about it, it was with completely fresh puzzlement. "I wish he hadn't," he said now. "Anyway, I wish Muddy didn't mind the ladies having her things."

"Oh, but poor Muddy!" Carolyn cried instantly. "Muddy is so brave and so fine!" She hesitated, searching for an image that would make Marcus see the thing she felt in her daughter. "Remember when she drove away this morning and waved good-by to us? Didn't she look lovely, like a—like a young knight in armor? Muddy always looks like a boy, to me. Sort of a brave little boy."

"She doesn't to me," Marcus said.

"She was the darlingest baby," Carolyn continued as they walked on, swinging Marcus's hand and essaying reminiscence, of which he was fond. "Such a serious little thing. Grandfather used to call her his little Daniel, when she'd plant herself in front of him—that fat-legged little girl—looking so worried, and tell him he shouldn't smoke so much."

"What's Daniel?" Marcus asked.

"Daniel was a man in the Bible who knew what was right. Grandfather was just making a joke. He meant she was perfectly right, he *shouldn't* smoke so much."

"But she was Grandfather's *child*," Marcus objected.

"They seem to swing back and forth," Carolyn said. "The generations do. *We* were the rebels. . . ." But she was not attending to what she said. She had stopped walking and was looking into the open door of a grocery painted bright sticky red. "Let's go in here," she said. "Just for a minute."

Inside they were confronted across the counter by a tall thin man wearing a hard straw hat, who wiped the palms of his hands on his butcher's apron. "Do," he said.

"Can you tell me where a package store is?" Carolyn asked. "I haven't seen any yet."

"Ain't none," he said. "Nearest's Gloucester."

"Oh," she said. She hesitated. The little boy had let go of her hand and was looking into the glass front of a big square tin biscuit box tipped at an angle to display chocolate marshmallow cookies within. "Then I'll have a carton of Schlitz, please," she said.

"Don't carry beer," the man said. "Rockport's dry town. 'Sbeen a dry town for hunderd years."

"Oh. Thank you very much," Carolyn said. She and Marcus walked out again into the sunshine. They stared at the window of the shop next door to the grocery, which was full of children's clothes for going back to school—cheap sweaters, plaid flannel skirts, corduroy pants, felt beanies. "I tell you what let's do," she said to Marcus. "Let's go to Gloucester on the bus. It'll be like a little adventure. I don't think Muddy would mind your going to Gloucester. We could come right back."

"*All* right," he agreed, looking up at his grandmother, as ever ready. They turned and went back up the street to where a sign on a stationery store said "Bus Depot." Carolyn inquired inside. A bus had just left.

They went to wait for the next one, under the horse-chestnut trees on the opposite side of the street, sitting on a slab of granite at the base of a rise on which stood a square white house. The sun was already well down on its westward course. Long golden rays fell shimmering through the leaves and lay across the quiet village street. All at once a number of men carrying folded newspapers came walking down the street.

"They're the first of the commuters, home," Carolyn told Marcus. "They just got off the train from their offices in Boston."

Marcus sucked in his breath. "How did you *know*?" he said.

"That's how they always look when they come home," she said. "In their suits. With their hats on. Grandfather used to come home like that and I would meet him at the station."

Marcus gave a hitch nearer to her on the stone slab. "Here?" he asked.

"No, but it was quite a lot like it. I mean it was at the seashore, too. At Manchester. It was terribly different, too," Carolyn added.

"How different?" he murmured, his eyes already bemused.

Carolyn settled herself and put her arm around Marcus. "Well, I would drive to the station in our brown-and-tan Chrysler roadster—we thought it was terribly snappy, but I guess *you* would think it looked funny, darling. I'd have the top down; I used to tie a bandanna around my head so my hair wouldn't blow to pieces. I'd tear into the station yard, and there the other people would be, waiting for the train—other wives, and the people expecting guests. We'd all speak to friends on the platform, and everybody would be all dressed up—white accordion-pleated skirts up to your knee, and broad-brimmed hats that came way down over your eyes. People were starting to wear brown-and-white shoes. And big huge pearls."

"And bananas," Marcus said.

Carolyn laughed. "Ban*dan*nas," she said. "Big handkerchiefs. It isn't like that any more, somehow. That kind of people don't seem to take trains any more, or maybe they just don't meet trains. And all the stations seem to be falling down. . . . Anyway, we'd see the train coming down the track from Boston, and some of the husbands would be hanging from the railing to the steps of the cars, ready to drop off. And on the car platforms would be all the bags of the people coming to visit—terribly snappy bags with canvas covers on them. The people who owned them would get off, in their city clothes—the ladies in their linen suits and their cloche hats, and the gentlemen in their straw boater hats with club ribbons. Then all the husbands would find their wives and kiss them and go off arm in arm to their cars; and all the hostesses would find their guests and kiss them, and take them off to *their* cars—oh, Marmons and Locomobiles, with chauffeurs."

"And then what?"

"Well, and then we'd all go home to the parties. And over the week end there'd be dances," she said. "At Myopia and at people's houses. I remember one with a black glass dance floor and a big artificial moon up in the trees. The people who gave it were from New York. The ladies always looked beautiful, in their chiffon dresses, and there were millions of stags."

"Stags, Grandmother?"

"Extra men. So that the ladies would have plenty of people to dance with. Because in those days we used to like to have fun and dance with lots of people. And afterward we'd get in the cars and drive all the way to Providence for scrambled eggs. My, we were wild!" Carolyn smiled, as at some secret reminiscence. "Grandfather danced the best, though," she went on. "He was very tall and thin, and we would simply *fly*—skim in and out through all the other couples on the floor, and do complicated, difficult steps like the Lindy Hop. The banjo player in one of the orchestras wrote a song for us called 'Carolyn.' People used to sit down to watch us dance. . . . Grandfather would have just loved you, darling," she said, as she so often did. "He always wanted a little boy, and he would have loved to have *you*."

"I would have loved to have *him*," Marcus replied cordially. "If he just hadn't got killed."

"What it shows is that we *must* not speed," Carolyn replied instantly. "There is nothing dashing or romantic *about* it. It's just suicide, that's all it is. The speed limit is plenty fast enough for anybody, that's what the speed limit is *for*. I hope when you grow up you will never, never go too fast, now that you know what can happen to people when they speed. And I hope if you ever do start to go too fast you will just remember your mother sitting here beside you telling you not to."

"Not my mother," Marcus said. "My grandmother."

They sat still, waiting dreamily for the bus to come. A brown, ribbed horse-chestnut leaf came drifting down to rest beside Carolyn's hand. The last one of the newspaper carriers walked along the other side of the street now; he was followed at some distance by two little girls, up from the beach, with wet blonde hair hanging in their eyes, and behind them strolled a dark man in an undershirt.

"I remember when I was young how my father gave me my tractror," Marcus said.

Carolyn looked down into his face, with its serious narrative expression.

"We were all getting up early because it was Christmas," he continued. "And first we had the stockings, and we had the horn with the buttons on it, and the buttons got broke. And the barley candy. It was a fire engine and two lions, and one of the lions was red. And the fire engine was red. And we had the sailboat. And tangerines. And then we went down to breakfast, Grandmother," he said. "And when it was the tree there wasn't any tractror, because that was the surprise. And I thought there was not going to be any tractror. And my father said, 'What is in the coat closet, do you suppose?' And it was. It was the kind I asked for and it wasn't the baby kind and it was the kind you pedal. And I sat down on it. It was big," he explained.

"I remember," she said. "That's a very nice story you told."

He heaved a great sigh from the prolonged effort. "But why did my father have to go to England?" he began again.

The man in the undershirt had crossed the street and was sauntering toward them under the trees, with his hands in the pockets of his black trousers. He seemed to be Italian or Portuguese, with a tanned face, a smiling mouth, and a great beak of a nose. "Hello," he said, coming nearer.

Carolyn looked away.

Marcus said, "Hello," in tones of pleased surprise.

The man held out a card. "Boat ride?" he suggested.

Carolyn hesitated, and then accepted the card before Marcus's outstretched hand could take it.

The card was somewhat greasy. It bore the picture of a motor launch and, printed underneath:

LEO DA SILVA
BOAT FOR HIRE
DEEP-SEA FISHING
EXCURSIONS

"No, thank you," Carolyn said, holding it out to the man.

Marcus said in a small voice, "Grandmother. A *boat* ride."

The man caught the words and grinned. He took the card from

Carolyn and gave it to Marcus. "Nice boat ride," he said. "Take you anywhere you want to go. Thatcher's Light? Eastern Point? Norman's Woe?"

"We were just going to Gloucester," Carolyn heard her voice explaining. "We were about to take a little bus trip."

"I take you to Gloucester, lady," the man said. "Cheap. For five dollars I take you to Gloucester and return." He said "ree-turn."

"The bus is cheaper," she said helplessly.

"Five dollars is cheap for a nice boat ride to Gloucester and return. I bring you back the other side, all around Cape Ann for five dollars. You come with me, I got my boat at the wharf."

"*Grand*mother," Marcus said.

"We haven't got our coats with us," Carolyn protested. "And this child has been having a cold."

The man looked at Marcus and Marcus looked at the man. "I got stuff in the boat you can put on," Leo Da Silva promised. "I spotted you out in front of Oleana's. I knew you was the type lady would appreciate a nice boat ride."

At the personal note Carolyn shrank further, inwardly. But Marcus said, "Grandmother! It's so cheap! All around Cape Ann for five dollars!"

"It's very late," she said. "It will be dark before long."

"Nice moonlight boat ride," the man said. "I got stuff you can put on. Keep nice and warm. Hah?"

"Grandmother," Marcus said. "A nice *moon*light boat ride?"

Carolyn bent down to Marcus. "It's only because the season is over," she whispered feverishly. "They'll do anything when the summer rush is over. They'll take anybody. . . ." But she did not really know what she meant. Her heart gave a lurch, a plunge, and she wondered if she were having a heart attack. If she were having a heart attack, they could not go on any boat trip, they would have to find a doctor. "We can't stay out late," she said to the man. "This child must go to bed."

The man looked at Marcus and Marcus looked at the man. "Sure," he said. "I get you back fine."

The bus, gray and chunky, came rumbling softly up Rockport's main street, facing her with the decision. Either . . . Or . . . The reason she needed to go to Gloucester was to buy a bottle of whiskey. Mary had accidentally forgotten, she had explained later, to bring the liquor Carolyn had left out on the hall table of the apartment. Carolyn wondered, for an instant, about the reason Mary had selected Rockport—a dry town for a hundred years—to take their holiday in. Suddenly she was struck, appalled, by the nature of this alternative to a little boy's wanting to take a moonlight boat ride. It seemed unspeakable.

"All right," she said. She hoped the severity she put into her voice made up for all the flaws she felt in her decision.

She followed Marcus and the man from the sea down the main street, keeping her eyes fixed on the two backs ahead—the broad, tapering one in the undershirt and the small one hurrying alongside. As she watched, she saw Marcus put his hand in the man's. At the foot of the street they crossed Dock Square and proceeded toward the wharf on the right. Carolyn was increasingly oppressed by a sense as of impending doom.

When they reached the neck of the dock, Da Silva strode ahead and Marcus came back and took Carolyn's hand. He seemed much excited. "He looks exactly like my father, doesn't he?" he said.

The idea was preposterous to the point of surrealism. Nothing, Carolyn thought wildly as she stepped down the inclined, barred-off walk leading to the float, nothing on earth could have been more different from Gerald's gay, urbane personality than this man with seamed neck and sunburned arms, taking her elbow to assist her over the gunwale and into the dirty white launch tied up alongside.

Da Silva picked Marcus up underneath the arms, and transferred him into the boat. Carolyn and Marcus stood side by side watching as the man cast off and jumped into the boat, kicking it adrift from the float. He went forward, rummaged in the decked-in space under the bow, and returned with oilskins. One coat he put on himself. He helped Carolyn into a second, and threw the smallest one at Marcus. When the little boy put it on, it proved absurdly too big. The sleeves drooped like flippers.

"Look at me!" Marcus cried, dancing about. He looked from Carolyn's face to Da Silva's, and flapped his arms. "I haven't any hands!"

"You siddown," the man said. He smiled a large, Mediterranean smile.

The drifting, meanwhile, of the boat toward the boats moored in the middle of the harbor suggested to Carolyn that she had herself in some way cast off from land. She sat down on the very edge of the seat rimming the cockpit, holding on tightly to its edge. It seemed a relief when Da Silva started the engine to hear it burst at once into a loud, spluttering roar. The boat wheeled, took direction, moved out with purpose toward the cut in the granite breakwater and the ocean lying outside of it.

Carolyn felt impelled to call out something that would sound restraining—something definitive of herself as mistress of this voyage. "I hope we can get to Gloucester before the shops close," was all that came to her tongue.

"You wanna buy something?" Da Silva raised his voice over the noise of the engine. He stood, half turned around, at the wheel in the forward part of the cockpit.

"We're going to the package store," Marcus remarked, standing close to Da Silva and looking out to sea.

"Is that right," Da Silva said.

Nobody spoke for some time. They threaded through the jumble of moored craft, and then steered straight out between the high gates that the breakwater made. Once they were outside, Da Silva sat down sidewise to the wheel, and continued to steer with one hand while he reached into the locker space under the seat and brought out a pint bottle that was nearly full.

"Have a drink," he said, offering it.

"Oh, no, *thank* you," Carolyn replied instantly.

The bottle, of dark-brown glass, appeared to her in itself menacing and fateful. And Da Silva certainly had no business offering it to her. Yet it struck her now that, since he knew she had been planning to buy liquor for herself, refusing his might offend him. It was suddenly obvious that it would never do to offend the conductor of a vessel containing the life not only of herself but of the being most precious to her. She reached her hand out for the bottle and tipped it to her lips. The first sip of whiskey, as ever hot and restorative, ran down her throat.

Marcus, sitting between them now, wriggled with pleasure and looked from one of them to the other. "Seems like old times," he said cozily. "When my father was home."

Da Silva laughed, altering their course so that, instead of heading straight out, they ran at an angle to the land. "Where *is* Papa?" he asked.

The smile left Marcus's face. "My mother's getting a divorce from my father," he said.

"Yeah? That a fact, hah?" Da Silva said to Carolyn.

"Oh, I'm not his mother," Carolyn felt it necessary to explain. "I'm his grandmother."

The Italian, or probably Portuguese, stared at her with his pleasant smile. "Don't give me that," he said. "Some grandmother."

It was impossible not to feel gratified. Carolyn accepted another drink from the bottle and smiled at Da Silva with the beginnings of relaxation. Was he a good man or a bad man? Impossible to tell. Was it necessary, even, to speculate? He was in the business of taking people on boat trips; his card attested it. The feeling of impending doom seemed, drop by drop, to be merging into pleasure. Carolyn let herself enjoy the boat's long gliding sweeps up the smooth waters and down again.

"At least you must let me pay for your whiskey," she said.

"O.K., now," he said.

The boat drove southward, engine muttering, and left a neat triangle of wake in the darkening water. Back on shore a white church tower thrust its verdigris dome up through the green, red-splashed treetops over the town, which looked like the port in some old ship print—perhaps an Asiatic port, Hong Kong, Carolyn thought, since against a golden sky two Japanese pines leaned southward on the crest of a hill toward a squat standpipe with a pointed roof. The descending sun stretched fingers of light out over the ocean's glassy swells.

"My son-in-law was a very lively sort of person," Carolyn remarked. "Always on the go. Too much so, I suppose."

"I guess you like a good time yourself, once in a while," the man said.

Carolyn considered. It seemed a reasonable conjecture. "Yes," she replied abruptly. "I do."

"You musta been two of a kind," Da Silva said. "Why the divorce, hah? Or shoon't I ast?"

Marcus, kneeling up on the seat and leaning out over the rim of the cockpit, said to his new friend, "My father wasn't true. That's why my mother has to get a divorce."

"Yeah?" the man said. "Have a drink." Once more he proffered the dark bottle to Carolyn.

She tipped it to her lips and away again. "He never set himself up as perfect," she observed. The idea struck her as funny, and she laughed out loud. Then a sense of outrage invaded her whole being, and with it the confusing thought, as brilliant and almost as independent of her as an exploding rocket, that if Mary could only once in a while laugh at something, Gerald Bentley would be here at this moment, and it would be unnecessary for Carolyn to have embarked with Marcus on this sail at all. "Gerald liked to drink, too," she added.

"Why, sure," Da Silva said. "Who doesn't?"

"I do," Carolyn said. "I like a drink."

"Sure you do," the man said. He said to Marcus, "Your mother is one good-looking lady."

"Not my mother," Marcus said. "My grandmother."

But no one paid any attention to him. Marcus didn't care. "We're going far, far away," he murmured, telling himself a story. "Maybe to England. . . ." The others were having a good time laughing and talking, and he was having a good time, watching dusk fall over the real, the open sea.

1959

RICH PEOPLE

After the shock of seeing that face in San Francisco, it is no wonder my recurrent, dreamlike memory of Clam Harbor, and the days when I was growing up there, enveloped me once more as I lay last night in my narrow bed, awakened by the ghastly laughter of coyotes out in the Arizona desert. But, this time, it seemed to come out differently. . . . I lay there, worrying about the ailing children in my charge, and gradually, instead of them, I seemed to see the old dock, of silvery, splintered boards supported at the corners by the weathered posts called dolphins.

Remnants of last night's fog drift across the dock in gauzy streamers; it is the middle of the morning and everybody has gone sailing except me. But I am nineteen and I would rather be caught dead than out in a boat with those great hearty brutes in their blue jeans, laughing at their wholesome jokes. I am sitting on the edge of the dock with my feet hanging over the edge, and beside me sits the idol of my life, dressed in a dark-red French jersey and tweed skirt, with a string of Chanel pearls around her neck. Mrs. Bogden! She is gazing out to where vignettes of brilliantly blue ocean are framed in the garlands of the mist, and telling me about Paris, Saint-Moritz, and Brioni.

Suddenly—as always in this remembered half-dream—she remarks, "The way to be happy is to be always in love, don't you think?"

I nod, and swallow hard, thrilled. Mrs. Bogden lights another of her Balkan Sobranies and turns, toward me, her face with its delightful nose and dark-red lips, bordered by exquisitely arranged gray hair. "Don't you?" she repeats. She seems actually to want to know what I think. "Don't you think it is?"

I could never, before last night, reply; either in real life or in the memory. What could such as I tell a Mrs. Bogden about anything? Mrs. Bogden, on the other hand, had everything to tell me. I was, at that period, desperately in love, myself; and while the condition was making me anything but happy, this present seemed, for me, perpetually on the point of breaking forth into a radiant heaven complete with Vionnet angel-wings and harps that played "That Certain Feeling." I had fallen in love with a Harvard boy from New York, whose family owned a house in London and a château in Newport, who had presented me with a bottle of Guerlain's L'Heure Bleue. Glamour was what I needed to cope with my situation. Glamour was what Mrs. Bogden was compact of.

She was exactly what I wanted—what I needed—to be; down to her long, dark-red fingertips. Sitting within her aura I thought how wonderful it would seem to be my old Winsor schoolmate Carola Bogden, and have such a stepmother; someone who could with easy grace lead the way along the paths of the great world and into the courts of sophistication. My own family seemed to me unsophisticated to the point of imbecility.

A person who never visited Boston in the old days cannot imagine the degree to which simplicity could be cultivated in families like ours. And the sightseer from South Bend who did, perhaps, stare studiously up at our house on the water side of Beacon Street could never have realized that its two bathrooms contained zinc-lined tubs about fifty years old, in which all of us Eliots took cold baths before breakfast straight through the winter; that even the grownups made their breakfasts of whole oranges, whole-wheat porridge, and whole milk; that decisions about the day's subsequent menus were based entirely upon nutritive, not gustatory, values; that such entertainments as we might attend (Symphony and Shakespeare) were selected upon a comparable basis; that for school we girls were dressed invariably, like our mother, in serviceable Scotch tweeds, worn over long woollen drawers, to which we gave a twist before pulling up our cotton stockings and lacing our brown boots. A Fair Isle sweater might constitute the sole lavish note in our daytime wardrobes. For Foster's Dancing Classes at the Somerset, we wore, with inevitability, pink taffeta with a tinsel rose at the hip and low-heeled silver slippers.

All this high thinking and plain living carried with it a faint but definite religious tinge. To Bostonians like us, living in the way that people from New York did—worldly people, rich people—was Wrong. Not that my family was churchy. They were fully liberated Arlington Street Church Unitarians, which meant that they subscribed handsomely and went seldom. But, as good Unitarians, they believed they best served their faith when they were following their private spiritual convictions.

For my mother, these involved mountain-climbing. Almost from our infancy, she had hauled my older sister Betsey and me up the slopes of assorted White and Green Mountains. Generally she left us far behind, climbing steadily with her measured but energetic step. Many is the time I have come, panting and puffing, upon my mother, after she had been long seated on some summit and was gazing off at the magnificence of its surroundings with an austere and serene expression which—years later in the catalogue of a museum—I recognized as akin to that of a sculptured Boddhisattva, an Enlightened One. When she became aware of my arrival, Mother would turn her faint smile upon me: calm, detached, compassionate. "Sit down, Lucy," she would say, "and try to practice realizing that ourselves and the rest of the universe are of one substance."

I would sit down, but I was never able to get interested in the topic she recommended. My thoughts, as I moved into my teens, ran to formless yearnings for clothes, to fantasies about what the world beyond Boston was like, and to boys. I was well aware that my mother's reflections were worthier ones than mine; I was even, dimly, aware that what animated her was something very remarkable; was, in fact, pure love.

My mother's feeling about all of nature was strongly mystical. At our cottage at Clam Harbor, where we spent the greater part of every summer, Mother taught us to swim and dive by principles a woman from another city might have reserved for dealing with her love life. I can see Mother now—long, spare limbs clad in a gray bathing dress, standing beside the diving board on the raft moored off the beach. She has put on a gray rubber bathing cap, but between it and her long, erect, sunburned neck some loops of sandy hair emerge. "Give yourself to the water!" she cries, as we hesitate before the plunge. When she herself comes to dive, her narrow face, freckled and innocent of make-up, wears an expression of bliss in the instant before she dedicates herself to the sea.

To Mother, there was something Wrong about being separated from the outdoors any more than was necessary. At Clam Harbor we slept out on one long sleeping porch, all four of us, in beds that had tarpaulins for the nights when September equinoctial storms drove pelting rain across them. Our three meals were served on a screened porch that possessed an elevating view over Clam Harbor to Clam Point, and, beyond it, of the Atlantic. Our Irish maids, down from Boston for the summer, viewed this latter custom with a sour eye. It was, of course, nothing to them that our food was cold by the time it reached us, but they did not care for waiting on table mornings when a fresh westerly breeze had sprung up, or evenings when the fog insinuated clammy streamers between the meshes of the screen. Sometimes they asserted their point of view by appearing in some old, raveled sweater, worn over black uniform and white Hamburg-edged apron.

My mother would raise sandy eyebrows. "Bridie," she would say in her ringing voice. "Surely you aren't cold, this splendid day?"

"No, Mum," the maid would always mumble.

Our maids might quit, but they never talked back, for my mother carried about her an aura, unmistakable to everybody, of being in the right. Bridie, or Norah, or Teresa, would appear in another minute or two bearing muffins and sans sweater. But sometimes I would hear her when she thought herself alone, washing dishes after the meal at the copper-lined sink out in the bare, matched-board pantry. "Ah," she would be muttering in exasperation and sheer Irishness. "Aaaah. . . ."

My mother *was* in the right; almost always. She made a study of it. To her it would have been foolish and unintelligent not to. She had trained herself to consider the various aspects of her life in order to determine what in them represented the true, the good, and the beautiful, and then to choose that and follow it up with assiduity. It seemed clear to her that there was always a better and a worser side to things; a higher and a lower. To choose the best of everything was only what one owed to oneself, one's family, and one's God. Outdoors was more beautiful than indoors; Nature was vaster than man; love was superior to more transitory emotions; thrift was wiser than waste; life was short, and there was little enough time for good music and great books without wasting any of it on the trivial or the frivolous. I remember my sister Betsey, aged about twelve, making one of our rare stands against the claims of the superior. "But I don't *like* Brahms!" she is insisting. Her face is red, her hands are behind her back, pressed for support against the walnut door of the library in the Beacon Street house. "I can't help it if I don't like him, can I?"

My mother, who sits on the Chippendale sofa, which had come down in her own family, closes the book she is holding, over her thumb, and replies without heat. "You can help giving way to nonsense," she says. "You know Brahms's music is great. You can, at least, try to feel what you ought to."

My mother was able to admit when she had been wrong, and,

by making a fresh assessment and a fresh judgment, arrive once more at a position of rectitude. "Coming out was not a success for you," she said in early June of the summer of which I write, looking down at me from her unusual height, with the reasonable gaze that had become to me particularly exasperating. If only Mother could be unreasonable once in a while! "You would better have begun Radcliffe at once, after all. I misgauged the matter. A pity. Now, for Betsey, coming out seemed to be almost too *much* of a good thing."

I muttered something. No more than any maid could I have talked back to Mother.

But what a coming out mine was! I suppose Mother would never have countenanced a convention so foreign to fresh air and early bedtimes at all had it not been for some concept of her own about a time of innocent gaiety, meeting jolly boys; a little girlish merriment before settling down to the realities of womanhood. Her own debut, forty years before, seems to have been along such lines. She and my father met first at a dinner at the Crowninshields' house on Marlborough Street. Later they became engaged at the Country Club in Brookline, on the basis of a shared interest in butterflies, sailing, and climbing mountains. I visualize them on that momentous occasion, sitting out on the glassed-in porch at the Country Club so long ago—their two serious faces, which by the time I knew them had grown to look curiously alike, turned enthusiastically to one another. What my mother's dress that night was like I don't know, but in her wedding photographs she wears a trailing white gown trimmed with lace, with a boned collar that comes all the way up her long neck to her ear lobes.

By the time Betsey and I came out, however, enthusiasm and shared interests were simply not enough for a girl to get by with at a dance. Betsey, who came out the year before I did, broke out of the confining circle of our bringing-up by becoming "wild"—one of the wild girls. I doubt whether Mother ever knew how wild; I'm not even sure myself. I know that she danced cheek to cheek, and went out to parked cars during dances to neck. I shared the secret that it was routine for her to spend the night with some old school friend so that she could evade the home ordinance about not coming home alone with a boy after a dance. At the period of which I speak, Betsey's solution was a fairly typical one with Boston girls for whom the boiling point of high-mindedness had been reached. In any coming-out year there was always at least one girl who was suspected of having "gone the limit."

"Health" was the word we used to sum up the whole unbearable repression against which such as Betsey rebelled. I can see her now, one night early in her coming-out year; she had come into my room, where I was doing my next day's homework for Winsor, dressed in a pale-blue chiffon dress, with silver beading at the hip to match her slippers. I said something about her looking nice.

"In *this*?" she asked; her voice cracked with fury. "I hate it! *Look* at this healthy neckline, for Pete's sake! Look at these horrible health shoes! It's all so S.S. and G.!" This was the term for sweet, simple, and girlish in our day. "Look at my hair!" she continued. Hers was the same fine, straight, sandy hair as Mother's, done up in crossed bands at the back. Suddenly Betsey started snatching out the pins that held it. She seized my desk scissors and began to slash.

"Betsey!" I cried, aghast.

"I don't care," she said, hacking away. "Now she'll have to let me get it shingled. I will *not* have a crown of glory."

All that was very well for Betsey. Whether because of the necking parties or not, she turned out a great success at dances, and had dozens of invitations to Harvard football and ice-hockey games. But nobody even tried to neck me. The memory of my coming-out party still brings cold sweat to my brow in the night.

It was described in the invitations as "a small dance," and small it certainly was. There were two other dances the same night, and not enough stags turned up at the Women's Republican Club, where mine was held. The decorations were russet chrysanthemums, the season being October, and the orchestra Ted Groves's—not Bert Lowe's or Billy Lossez's—because Father saw no point in putting money into things that did not matter. It would never have occurred to me to argue about it. His attitude toward expense was as much a part of Father as walking every day, rain or shine, across the Public Gardens and the Common to his office on Milk Street, or his espousal of Women's Rights. Or his attitude toward Shakespeare. I can see Father as he used to stand before the fire in the library. He lifts his sandy eyebrows and remarks, "My father always told me, 'My boy, never let anyone persuade you otherwise than that a scholar and a gentleman—Bacon, in short—could have written the plays.'" Father coughs, and the Adam's apple in his long, loose-skinned throat jerks. He glances toward Mother for support of what he has said. She usually did agree; she agreed about Ted Groves's orchestra when Father remarked that it seemed to him to play very jolly music.

To its jolly music I, the debutante, danced round and round with a succession of dutiful partners. I was dressed in white tulle, of course, with healthy neckline and low-heeled white-and-silver brocade slippers. That South Bend sightseer might, next day, have been impressed by the far greater prominence given to my picture and my party's guest list in the public prints than to the other, bigger dances, but my father was put out because, by an inadvertence, the picture had got into the paper at all. Betsey expressed her own and my reactions to the whole affair when she said, "At least nobody could say it wasn't a nice, healthy evening."

What I felt myself to be, during that winter, was unequipped, unprepared, unaided, helpless, and suffering. What my contemporaries thought of me as was something known as a pill. The attendants in the dressing rooms of the hotels grew well acquainted with me through those hours when I cowered there, assuming chattiness, rather than let some wretched boy be stuck with me any longer. After the first month of it, I stopped even bothering to invent excuses to the attendants about needing to mend my dress or my stocking. I simply fled to them.

In February, just before the dances stopped for Lent, I fell in love. It began as if it were a mutual rescue of and by two kindred sufferers. I had retreated to the fireplace in the long room at the Country Club when the music stopped at the end of an interminable circling in the arms of the son of one of Mother's friends, whose stiff face softened when I said I had to speak to somebody across the room.

There, leaning against the mantelpiece, stood a slight, wistful-looking young man with red hair. When he moved as I approached, I saw that he was lame. I had intended to stand there for only a moment, to gauge my position and decide whether to beat a retreat, once again, to the familiar upstairs dressing room or to join the hostess's group along the wall. But the strange young man put out his hand and touched my arm. "I say, do you mind talking with me?" he said in an English accent. "I don't dance, you see, and I do feel most awfully solit'ry." He smiled a shy, crooked smile.

I smiled, too. "I'm Lucy Eliot," I offered.

"What a nice name," he said. "'Lucy Locket lost her pocket.' My name's Giles Wall." We shook hands. He shifted his position with a cripple's clumsiness and went on. "Music is what I'm mad for. Music and ballet. What are you keen on?"

"I think I like pictures the best," I said, struggling to reveal the truth about myself. "But I like music, too." We could almost have been Mother and Father, all those years ago, exchanging enthusiasms.

But before I even so much as left the Country Club that night, the situation I had got myself into was revealed to me. "You were certainly hitting it off with Giles Wall," Betsey said to me as we put our evening wraps on. Betsey still went to some of the debutante parties, as an L.O.P.H., or Left On Papa's Handser. She had managed to screw a white bunny-fur jacket out of the family this last Christmas but my own wrap was that ultimate Bostonian degradation, the family Chinese robe, worn over a sweater for warmth.

"He asked me to have tea with him at the Copley, Friday," I said. I am sure my eyes shone. Inside me a river of stars seemed softly to be flowing.

"Good going," Betsey said. "You'll end up with millions yet, old dear."

"What?" I said, only slightly distracted from the contemplation of the heaven which consists of the cessation of being rejected.

"You know who he *is*, don't you?" Betsey said. "Giles *Wall*. Wall and Wall, in New York. Bucky Sturgis has the room next to him in Claverly, and he told me Giles went to school in England. And his mother ran away and married a Duke. And his father is married to a ballet dancer. And they own about ten houses. Just rolling. Giles isn't a bit popular at Harvard, though. He isn't even in a club. So he's just the thing for you," Betsey added with sisterly candor.

The stars in my river were all exploding. By the time I came down the stairs to the hall, where a milling crowd of stags in tails or black tie waited to say good-by to somebody or to take someone home, and saw Giles—his face greenish-white against his red hair—leaning against the further wall, I could feel the first stab of an agony which was to pierce my growing love like the golden arrow that pierces the red-velvet heart.

There was never again to be, for me, the feeling of easy communication we had had when we leaned together against the fireplace, talking. Only my adoration continued to grow; and, along with it, the conviction of my utter inadequacy.

Giles used to come to see me, parking his Lancia at the curb on Beacon Street and limping up the steps, while I watched, hidden behind a glass curtain in the bow window, my heart thumping. I would go down to meet him in the reception room to the left of the front hall, and we would sit on the stiff sofa there while Giles talked about ballet and music; Betsey and her beaux would more than likely have pre-empted the living room, and I never liked to take Giles to the library because Mother was usually there. Giles talked about how fabulously beautiful his mother was, and how his father had never cared for him, and how his leg was broken playing rugger at preparatory school in England and set improperly; how he had later hated Eton, and about the symphony he was writing now. "But *nobody* understands what I am trying to do," he would insist. "Nobody at all, actually."

My heart bled. "I *want* to understand," I cried.

"Do you?" he would say, turning his bemused eyes on me. "Sweet. Sweet Lucy Locket. I say! Couldn't you get your family to let you come abroad this summer, p'raps? I'd adore to have you meet my mother. I'm sure she'd ask you. She's living in France, you know, with that beast Fallchester she married. She's divine, my mother is. Very fair, with a face like an ill white lily. Quite, quite different from Mona." Mona, I had learned, was his father's present wife, his fourth. "Mona's divine too, of course, in quite another way from my mother. Dark, with the serene sort of brow a woman has to have if she's to do her hair in smooth bands. Mona has the perfect ballet face, actually. I wonder how long my father will love her."

"I'd love to go abroad!" I cried when he seemed to wait for a reply to his suggestion. "Maybe Mother *would* let me . . ."

But of course Mother wouldn't.

"I think not," she decided. "This would not be a wise summer for Europe, Lucy. I admit my judgment was off about coming out, for you, but this winter was to have provided your time for gaiety. It's certainly provided nothing else. You must learn to seek a balance, dear. Radcliffe, next year, will give you the intellectual discipline you have lacked the past several months. I think of Europe, too, when you do go, as a place of study; you will, of course, thrill to the masterpieces of art there, as well. But the coming summer should be a time for vigorous exercise after your winter within doors—Besides, Giles's mother hasn't invited you."

"She would, if you'd only say I could go. . . ." But I knew it was no use. Mother's logic and her sense of the fitness of things seemed always irrefutable. She liked Giles. She thought of him as that poor unloved young thing who was, moreover, lame. But she was simply unconscious of those elements in his life that made me feel, underneath all my longing and desire, a sort of terror lest Mother might, after all, let me go to visit the Duchess of Fallchester. I was too unequipped for it. Once again, but differently from in the dark days before the meeting with Giles beside the Country Club fireplace, I felt myself unprepared, unassisted, helpless, and suffering. I had been to good schools, I had learned what my mother had tried to teach me, but I did not know anything that I needed. My need seemed as infinite as the sea.

In late May we moved as usual from Beacon Street down to our huge, gray-shingled house at Clam Harbor, cold as a cave at this time of year. The change that had occurred in me was reflected by my realizing, for the first time, that my childhood's summer home was perfectly hideous. Our healthy summer routine began: a dip in the ocean before breakfast at seven, reading and letter writing till ten, swimming or tennis till luncheon, or sailing for the whole day; and for gaiety, a frequent tea party in somebody's garden to view how beautifully the cosmos and the sweet williams and the calendulas were coming along. My father, home from town by that time of the afternoon, would accompany us, in boater hat with club ribbon and white flannel trousers. Sometimes there was square dancing in the evenings, when we pranced back and forth until the house shook. We had a neighborhood tradition at Clam Harbor, which had come down from the last century, of playing a game of beanbags. Two sides were chosen, their members alternating with each other down two long rows. The beanbags were thrown crisscross by members of each team, and the team that got its twenty beanbags down to the end of the line and back to the start again, won.

Giles was in France with his mother, and wrote me a few short letters: "Sweet Lucy, how is America? We had dinner under the pergola last night and I wished you could one day see the moon rise over the Rhône. My mother is suffering terribly, of course. . . ." Her suffering was nothing to my suffering, I felt; his wish nothing to my own wish—my need—to be somebody entirely different, somebody at home in the great world, whom Giles could love; someone beautiful, sophisticated, and like an ill lily. I could visualize all too perfectly how I looked in my actual person, dressed in the old cotton frocks we kept at Clam Harbor; wearing dirty sneakers; my hair unattractively blown about. I was without glamour and inescapably healthy, because I had never learned how to go about being anything else.

Into my need, like a sail on the horizon of a shipwreck, came Mrs. Bogden. Somewhat breathless whispers of her fame had reached me earlier. Mr. Bogden, a Boston widower, had met the former Mrs. Hurst in London the summer before, as he was starting on the Little Tour with his daughter Carola, who graduated from Winsor the year before I did. After sending Carola home in September to continue her work at the School of the Museum of Fine Arts, he had remained in England to press his suit. In December, he married the American divorcée, and in spring, after a honeymoon in North Africa, brought her home to Boston.

Later, when we had become fast friends, Mrs. Bogden used to tell me about her flat on Half Moon Street, where she was living at the time of Mr. Bogden's advent—tiny, terribly amusing, really, and not at all expensive as such things go. Nicky Eritsoff had sublet it to her for twenty guineas only. How I could visualize that flat! My ravished imagination supplied color to the French furniture she described, the brocaded armchairs. I could see the delightful little suppers after the theater, before a small coal fire, and breathe in the atmosphere, permeated deliciously by Houbigant's Giroflée—the scent which I came to know so well and which seemed the essence of my idol. Perfume was another of the elements in that unknown life to which I fearfully aspired. No one in the Eliot family had ever come any closer to perfume than 4711 Cologne. But, for my birthday in May, Giles had presented me with a bottle of L'Heure Bleue. I concealed it from Mother, who I knew would not have let me accept it. All alone, in secret, I would take the big crystal bottle with its handsome stopper out from under a pile of sweaters in my bottom drawer, and sniff the scent, which, more than words and images even, could suggest the atmosphere of another world. Sometimes I wept.

The first time I met Mrs. Bogden was early in June, after a day out racing my Lightning, with Carola Bogden crewing for me. A squall had overtaken us in the afternoon, and we had been successively wet through and dried out again by the sun and the chill east wind that followed the rain. By the time we walked up to the Bogdens' cottage, carrying the oars and the sailbag, we must have looked a sight. We went into the house, familiar to me from childhood, and suddenly it was unfamiliar. A Russian icon was hanging on the matched-board wall at the foot of the stairs, a fur rug lay on the hall floor, and in the air was a curious, dry fragrance. We walked into the living room, where a woman with beautifully arranged gray hair was crouching before the fire holding the fire shovel out over the flames.

"Uh—*Maman*," Carola said. "This is Lucy Eliot."

Without rising, Mrs. Bogden turned toward us and smiled, with dark-red lips. "Howd' you do," she said in the same sort of international-British accent Giles had. "So nice. . . . Trying to take the awful damp out of the air, darlings, by burning a bit of me perfume. An old London trick—Dare we try for some tea? Life is so difficult," she added, making a face in the direction of the kitchen door.

Perhaps I make her sound vapid. She was not. She was intuitive and had a gift for understanding, or if not understanding, for a kind of sympathy; putting herself wholly in one's place and surrounding herself with an indignant loyalty that became, for me, like an oasis in the desert. After the first of the times I was invited up to Mrs. Bogden's bedroom I was never again to feel alone in my aspirations, my longing, and my pain. "But of *course*, my darling," she had said earnestly, bending the gaze of her intelligent gray eyes upon me. "Of course you must find a way to attract Giles! I know so exactly your feeling. It must all have been *too* frustrating. We must arrange something."

We would often sit in that bedroom to which she had brought, from the other world, a touch of richness, a sense of luxury. The chairs we sat in were low, square, covered in pale satin, without arms; one sank into them. On one table stood Mrs. Bogden's perfume bottles—square, round, tapering, or chunky. On the other were placed signed photographs of her friends abroad. *Violet Rutland* was, I learned, the signature of a Duchess. There were pictures of Carol and Madame Lupescu; of Leopold of Belgium; of Otto of Hapsburg; and one signed *Edward P*. These two tables were, to me, like altars to the new god I worshipped.

"But of *course* you must visit his mother next summer," Mrs. Bogden would agree. "We must make you utterly enchanting for her. I used to know Marna slightly when she was Wall. I know she'd adore you, with your pretty eyes and divine skin. We must arrange something that will make a little *more*, p'raps, of your looks." Her eyes would move—not in judgment, I felt, but in compassion—over me, and then across the room that she had made so cozy to the window. They would rest, briefly, on the scene outside—the roofs of the Sturgis cottage next door, the bare rocks of Clam Point in the sunshine, and, beyond, the cold blue sea. Her eyes would return to me. "This fall, p'raps, we must run over to New York? Stay at the angel Carlyle, don't you think? And have a bit of fun in the shops?"

"Oh, yes!" I would reply. Hope had been born again in my heart, and trust where there had been despair. It was Mrs. Bogden who had saved me.

I realize now thirty years later, that, with the egotism of youth, I never tried to turn the talk to any other subject but me. Possibly I would not have thought myself worthy to bring up such a sacred topic as Mrs. Bogden herself. Certainly, in those days, I believed her to be invulnerable. Though I never thought consciously about it at all, unconsciously I must simply have assumed that anyone so wonderful as she must be happy. Her philosophy, as it reached me in its application to my problems, was one of happiness. "But, darling, I know so well!" she often cried. "Life *is* so difficult, and all one wants is to have f-u-n, isn't it?" It occurs to me now that she always put these beliefs of hers in the form of questions, as on the morning when we sat together on the dock in the dissolving mists and, to something I must have said about how unhappy I had been before I met Giles and her, she said, "The way to be happy is to be always in love, isn't it?"

I remember, as well, how she would get to her feet after one of our sessions, and walk away from chair or weathered board step, singing; tall, exquisitely thin, dressed with quite another sort of simplicity from our Boston simplicity—the simplicity of perfection. I think of her in that crimson tweed skirt and jersey, with a string of chunky pearls clasped with a fake ruby; pearls in her ears; on her feet shoes made for her at Hellstern's in Paris, and sheer lisle stockings "for the country," with openwork clocks running up the ankles. Her gray hair made a delightful shape, her large gray eyes were clear and lively, her mouth was painted dark red. "'Love—may—come—to—anyone!'" she sang as she walked away. "'The best—things in life—are free. . . .'"

Needless to say, my infatuation did not pass without comment from my family. For example, at supper out on the screened porch, one stormy evening when the candles flickered and guttered in their blue-and-white china candlesticks, Betsey said, "How's your crush, Lucy? Taught you how to make your fingernails look like claws dipped in blood, yet?"

I flushed. "That's disgusting!" I said. "You always take the most ignorant, stupid, *Boston* attitude to Mrs. Bogden. She's just above your comprehension, that's all."

"You can have her," Betsey said. "Joe Worthington says she was known all over Europe as an adventuress."

"It's a lie!" I cried. I threw my napkin down on the table beside my plate. "She's wonderful, and beautiful, and understanding, and kind! Which is more than—more than—" But I could never express myself with the violence of the words that spoke in my head.

"Lucy! . . . Betsey!" Mother was like a moderator, calling the meeting to order. "Control yourselves. Betsey, even if a person in our midst seems neither what we should call wise nor distinguished, that is no excuse for repeating defamatory tales. Both of you! Be still!"

We sat, after our family custom of calling for a silence to put an end to discord, while the salt air of evening slapped the backs of our necks and our bare arms; we saw the light on Badger's Island flash, at regular intervals, through the dusk. Mother, at the head of the table, sat erect as ever; Father sat at the other end, his long back hunched over, crumbling a roll between his fingers. Betsey had turned her gaze away from me onto her plate. Suddenly she cried, "Mother! How can you be so unfair? Mrs. Bogden is just the sort of person you disapprove of most, and yet you won't let me say anything against her!"

"You may express your disapproval if you like," Mother said. "Only you're not to condemn anyone. Or spread scandal. And if you should ever find me taking an uncharitable attitude toward anyone, I hope very much that you will call my attention to it."

"I don't think Mrs. Bogden is *worthy* of charity," Betsey said. "She's a hard-boiled baby, if you ask me. You don't imagine she gives you all this famous understanding for your own sweet sake, do you, Luce? She's simply trying to get to know us."

"Mother! Do I have to listen?"

"Betsey, you're displaying an unwarranted vanity, it seems to me. The person in question *is* ordinary, but she may have sincere affection for Lucy. My hope is that Lucy is not so in need of affection that she will settle for that brand of it for very long. But you are not to malign the person."

"Mother!" Betsey said, disgusted, "Why must you always be so Godlike?"

Mother smiled and shook her sandy head. Then, I remember, she expressed one of her most characteristic ideas—the sort of idea, I suspect, upon which she meditated at the summits of those mountains she was always ascending. "None of us need to worry about being too much like God," she said. "But if you're talking about charity, it has always seemed to me that God is charitable not because people are in any way worthy of it, but because if he wasn't, he wouldn't be God."

It was in August—an unusually hot day—when the letter from Giles came, in the morning mail. I read it, and then hurried over to Mrs. Bogden's house.

She was sitting on the grass of the front lawn—none of our nineteenth-century cottages had modern terraces—on a big plaid steamer rug, doing her toenails in the sunshine. I knelt down on the rug beside her, sank back on my heels, and held my tongue while she finished the infinitely careful application of deep crimson varnish. Against the black knitted *maillot* she wore, Mrs. Bogden's legs and arms were beautifully brown and smooth.

At length, she put the brush back into the bottle of polish, twisted its cork tight, and smiled at me. "What troubles you, my sweet?" she said.

I thrust the letter at her, and at the same moment divulged its contents in a burst. "It's Giles! He wants to come *here*! He had some terrible row with his mother's husband. I think the Duke knocked him down. And he left, and wrote this from London. He wants to come and stay with *us*, before college opens, and what shall I *do*?"

Mrs. Bogden gazed at me earnestly, took the letter from my hand, and read it. She ran the ball of her thumb absent-mindedly over the address at the top of the first page, and put the letter slowly back into its envelope.

"What a beast Fallchester is," she remarked. "The boy really *is* in a jam, poor child. Life is so difficult, isn't it? I think it'd be good for him to come here. There are times when one does need utter, utter rest."

"But he *can't* stay at our house!" I cried. "Freezing to death at meals out on that horrible porch? Playing *beanbags*? With Betsey always snooping around? And Mother preaching at us all the time?" I swallowed hard. It was the first time I had ever criticized Mother outside the family, and my words sounded profane to me. I hurried past them. "Giles has never seen anything so absolutely awful as the way we live! He won't know what to make of it. He'll never want to see me again."

My idol smiled. "I'll put him up," she said, and as she spoke it was as if honey and bliss were dropping from her lips. "I'd love to have the poor child. I'll give a little party, for one of the nights he's here. Something a little amusing, p'raps? And plan an evening at the Magnolia Casino? Take lunch to Queen's Island, and a bit of champagne? And when there's nothing more diverting, dine down at the fisherman's dive in Clam Depot, just for fun, don't you think?"

"Oh, yes," I breathed, once more resurrected. "That would be *wonderful*. . . ."

We come now, in this string of old memories, to a scene which my mind always tends to avoid, but which I force myself to face. We are all on the beach at Clam Harbor. I am sitting on a huge, emerald-green Turkish towel, beside Mrs. Bogden, who has on one of her French *maillots*; pale blue, this time, against her radiant tan. I suppose I myself must have been wearing some dreadful Annette Kellerman. We are both looking up at my mother, who stands on the sand just at the rim of the emerald towel.

She is speaking about our plans for Giles's visit. She wears that baggy old gray bathing dress with its rows of rust-stained white braid; her hair is inadequately tucked under a gray rubber cap. She must have paused to speak to us on her way down to the water's edge; perhaps I even called to her. Plain, austere, unmodified in any way by fashion, her appearance is simply overpowering.

"I don't feel that it is suitable," she is saying. "Since you say Mrs. Bogden has never seen Giles. It is not as if he were already her friend. He *is* a friend of ours. We have, Lucy, guest rooms and to spare. If he's asked to stay with us here before college opens, do by all means tell him to come. But he must stay at our house, and fall in with our normal occupations and amusements as any visitor might."

I realized that there was nothing more to be said. But Mrs. Bogden didn't. She said, "Simply, dear Mrs. Eliot, I've so much time on my hands, as I'm sure you've not. It would give me enormous pleasure to arrange little amusements for the children—*quelques petites divertissements*; something to accustom them to gaiety—"

"Lucy," Mother said, "is accustomed to simplicity."

"But don't you feel," Mrs. Bogden insisted, "that when one is young and, so to speak, on the verge of the great world, one needs the little helping nudge, the outstretched hand? In short, something a little *different* from this rather—simple—life? Life is so difficult, actually." But Mrs. Bogden had made a fatal error.

"Very," my mother said. "And so there can be no question of

having someone who is coming to pay us a visit staying with neighbors. However kind their intentions," she added politely.

Above the burning yellow beach that ran for miles around the curve of Clam Harbor into Graniteport and so out again to Badger's Point, the sun seemed suddenly put out. Within a private night I got to my feet, shaking all over.

"Then I'll tell him not to come!" I cried, stone-blind, to the people still out in the sunshine. "I don't want him here! I won't *have* him come, that way!"

There is no record in my memory of any answer to my words. That is the scene's end. But I remember well what came of it. I wrote to Giles that we were going to be driving around in the White Mountains after the middle of August, so we could not have him to stay beside the sea; but that I looked forward to seeing him at Beacon Street after college began. Nobody told me, or forbade me, to do this, or advised me how to go about doing it. It was my solution to my own problem, like a lid shutting on a particular time in my life.

I never saw Giles again. He never returned to Harvard, but stayed in England. A year or two later, after I had already moved to Arizona, I read in a Los Angeles paper that he had been married to a Lady Honor Wilkes; a cousin of his, the paper said. In the news photo she had one of those sharply chiseled British faces with short fair hair parted on the side. I have no idea whether they are still married.

Today I know nothing of the world in which people like that live, nothing; I left even the world of Boston when I came out here. I have only been back for Father's funeral. Every winter, of course, Mother pays me a visit on her way to stay with Betsey and the grandchildren in Seattle; it is odd how both Betsey and I have moved to the corners of the country farthest away from Boston. But distances don't faze Mother. She travels by jet, and arrives serene with a copy of the Upanishads in her hand. She is amazing.

She it was, for example, who after that year of my hopeless struggle to keep going, ending with my flunking my freshman exams at Radcliffe, found me this job of mine, to which—although I don't mean to sound boastful—everyone agrees I am so exactly suited. I have moved up over the years, and in spite of not possessing a degree, to being assistant director of this school for delicate children—children who are sent to us from all over the world—from Japan and Antibes and London, from New York and Middleburg. They are places, often, that are healthy enough in themselves; there has been only one lack in these children's fortunate lives to have made their eyes hollow and their coughs hacking.

The school is lodged in what was once a hospital, in the desert outside Tucson—a series of adobe blocks, constructed around small patios, each with a fountain in the middle and a colonnade, off which open eight to twelve rooms. I live in the one named Saguaro, with seven of the children and two of the younger teachers. In the daytime the sun is blazing, and the children take carefully supervised sunbaths, spaced into their schedules so that they will get them before eleven, when the sun becomes dangerous. In the evening the sun sets behind Tucson and T Mountain. Night in Arizona has a large, a sterile quality—clear black air and stars like arc-lights. It is then, after I have gone to sleep, that I am sometimes wakened by coyotes out in the desert, like a band of mad nightmare phantasms howling and laughing, and cannot go back to sleep, but lie here and remember the years of my own youth, which was such a sheltered one and passed among people who loved me.

My wholesome background had, of course, everything to do with my being allowed to try out at this job, untrained for it as I was. It is an axiom of the work that if you have never known emotional security in your childhood you cannot possibly impart it to others.

I am one of those lucky ones who are able to say, My mother loved me, always, always. Mother produced the opportunity, in fact, that time when I was at my lowest ebb, just the way she always did produce whatever was needful—as though out of the air; as though by the Indian rope trick. She arranged for my interview with the then director, Miss Alden, who was in the East, through one of her myriad associations with worthwhile people in philanthropy, social betterment, and child welfare.

She saved me, at a time when Giles had disappeared forever from my life, and when I was ashamed to see Mrs. Bogden any more—embarrassed to; as if, by bungling the Giles business, I had let her down too badly. I was turned back on, reduced to, my own dreary, unappealing, unrewarding, lone self. Even then, I realized I was being saved from something, and that it was Mother who was saving me, after all, not Mrs. Bogden. Sometimes in the early days I used to feel that, by working at this job, I was helping the little boy whom Giles once was—the unloved, the forgotten, the suffering child of this century. It hadn't taken me long to realize, once it was too late, that Giles would have *loved* the life in our Clam Harbor house. It would have been the very life he had always been starved for. Any rebellion I'd ever felt toward it seemed to expire as though with a little sigh of relief as soon as I was settled in Arizona.

It had been Mrs. Bogden, it would appear, not me, who was building up a head of steam against Boston in the course of those long tête-à-têtes of ours. She never breathed a word to me about what must have been her rising fury, but less than three years after the summer of which I have been writing, she kicked over the traces, as people put it in the letters I got from Boston. Flew the coop. Bolted. She divorced Carola's father and married a Honolulu Hutchinson—immensely rich; as, indeed, Mr. Bogden had been. But, I realize now, Mrs. Bogden could not possibly have understood, when she married Mr. Bogden in London, about Bostonians and their attitudes to money. For them it is not something to lavish, or even to spend. It is something to nurture, like a plant. It is a sacred trust. In any case, it is nothing with which to have, as Mrs. Bogden would have said, f-u-n. I used to have a vision of how she must have looked as she boarded the Boston section of the Twentieth Century, Reno-bound. I saw her close the door of the compartment behind her, pull the little hat off her gray hair, take a handful of bills from her Hermès purse and throw them up into the air, stretch her arms out, throw back her lovely head—so like the powdered head of an eighteenth-century king's mistress—and exclaim, "God!"

But I had never actually seen Mrs. Bogden since I left Boston, until I went to San Francisco last week to meet the boat the Aylesworth child was sent to us by, from Hawaii. The Aylesworth child is typical of our pupils—stiff with tension from the violent emotions rich parents seem to spill around them like largesse: desire and hate and jealousy and malice and anger and more desire. If they could only see, if they could just grasp, that their conflicts are all their children have to use as nourishment! What can a child know of feeling but what it feels? The Aylesworth child was sent to us alone, which again is typical. The reasoning would be: Nothing could possibly happen to her on that nice, safe ship; if she's sick the stewardess can look after her, can't she? And, besides, the child's not a baby, she's eight. . . . Not a baby, just a child who has begun obscurely to realize that it is facing life—*life*—with absolutely nothing to face it with. We here have come to feel that unloved children are often living out their parents' conflicts in a sort of pathetic attempt to offer some little solution. At school we rage against such parents.

I had gone on board to fetch her, and was walking up the promenade deck toward her stateroom—the Aylesworths would never spare expense, of course—when suddenly I saw Mrs. Bogden. She was coming along the deck very slowly, on the arm of, I suppose, her husband. I've said already that I know nothing of the world in which rich people navigate; nowadays, I know no world except the world of sick children; so it's possible that many rich people look the way this couple did, and that if I were more used to them I wouldn't have felt so shocked.

But the aging couple were as frightening to me as figures out of Hieronymus Bosch. They came toward me, not seeing me—I am not a person anyone notices—he in white trousers with a pencil stripe and navy blue blazer, she in a cream-white, knitted costume and a white, broad-brimmed straw hat. Rich, they looked; rich, irritated, fussy, with eyes as bright as jewels; cynical, bored, unhappy. But it wasn't any of all that which shocked me, for I have often enough read such descriptions of worldly people in the pages of novels. What I never read about in any book, what gives me the knot in the pit of my stomach, was the look in Mrs. Bogden's face; the look far behind it.

I'd thought for a moment of going up to her, holding out my hand, and saying, "Mrs. Bogden, it's Lucy Eliot." But the look in the still-beautiful, pleasure-loving, powdered old face stopped me while I peered, hesitating. The look I am talking about was a double look, really; it was two things at once. Part of it was fear, under the cream foundation—fear like a smart whip to brighten up the tired eyes; and part of it was the even deeper-hidden thing the fear was of: death, holding the whip and looking at me, right there out of her face. I don't know what manner of death. Just death.

I was too shaken to do anything but hurry on along the deck. But last night, back in Arizona again, I woke in the middle of the night and heard the coyotes howling and laughing crazily out in the sterile desert; and once more, as so many, many times before, my mind went back to Clam Harbor and the days when I was young. Once more I seemed to be sitting on the silvery splintered boards of the old dock in the morning cool, talking to Mrs. Bogden, who is dressed in her favorite dark red. Her face is turned away toward the sea, but—lying in the Western darkness—I could hear her voice asking me, as I have so often heard her ask, "The way to be happy is always to be in love, isn't it? *Isn't it?*" She turns her lovely face toward me, and this time her face is full of death.

Suddenly, for the first time, I realized what it was I should have answered her. Within my narrow, schoolmistress's bed I felt my whole body strain as I imagined crying out, "No! No, it isn't! Feel what you ought to feel! Practice unity with all creation! Give yourself to the ocean!"

Because Mother was right, of course—about Mrs. Bogden as about everything else. Today, at the age of eighty-three, my mother's face has no death in it. Her face is filled with that life she has believed in all along; which always has existed and ever shall exist. For a while I lay there, awake in Arizona, thinking with pride and absolute acceptance of my wonderful mother, but then—such is the unregenerate human ego—I had to turn my face to the pillow and begin to cry.

"What about me?" I kept blubbering as I squeezed the pillow around my head so that the children should not hear me, and smelled the curious scent that tears always have. "What about all those years? Where is my *life*?"

1960

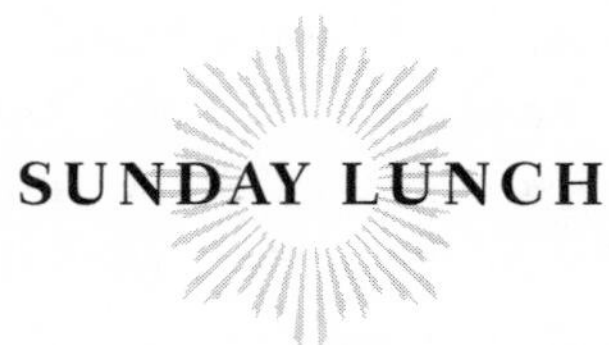

SUNDAY LUNCH

THE JOYFUL YOUNG clergyman followed his hostess, and his hostess's son and wife, through adjoining sitting rooms and out a door onto an open terrace. The terrace was round in shape and fitted into the angle of a wing to the main house. Its pink bricks were laid in a concentric pattern, and in the middle of it rose the curved-over rim of a brick well, topped by an arch supporting a well sweep. Between terrace and lawn stood willow oaks and mimosas, whose branches made a feathery awning overhead, pinned everywhere with pale-pink mimosa blossoms. Bees were going about their murmurous business in the masses of roses—pink, red, and yellow—that climbed the walls of the remarkable old Maryland house, and a delicious scent drifted through the warm June air.

"Just time for a cozy confab before the others arrive," Mrs. Beneker remarked. She seated herself gracefully on a white iron chair. Pretty and chic, she had the figure of a girl of twenty—a far better figure than her daughter-in-law's—and was dressed in gray linen with white touches. On entering the house after church, she had removed a broad-brimmed gray straw hat before a mirror in the hall and, turning, threw her guest a most complicated smile, compounded of flirtatiousness, recognition of his cloth, and a pretty acceptance of her inability to do other than flirt. "I do think Sunday lunch is a divine institution," she said. "Oh! I've made a sort of joke, haven't I, Mr. Watson?"

He nodded happily. With his dark, shining eyes and graying hair close-cropped to his round head, he looked like a small, friendly animal. Since he had been learning to practice his secret ability, he could hardly wait for people to say things—any things—because he loved them so and they couldn't hurt him anymore and they were so wonderful, with their crazy reserves and their touching braggadocio, their determined frustrations and their self-inflicted suffering. His eyes rested on Mrs. Beneker, and he prayed for her to go on talking. He could hardly come right out and say, "Go on, go on, I can hardly wait to hear the awful things you say." He couldn't come right out and say, "You are my mother and my brethren."

"We've just time to all make quicky friends," she said.

Her beautifully coiffed reddish-tinted hair rose from her pretty neck, around which hung a string of pearls. Mr. Watson's eyes strayed innocently about other visible furnishings of Mrs. Beneker's life—the iron chairs, with their springy wire-mesh seats; the glass-topped bar table set under a willow oak and loaded with bottles, etched glasses, and a silver bucket of ice; the sheer curtains that billowed out through the open French doors; the huge, brilliant-blue pool just beyond the row of trees; the well-tended borders of flowers against the walls of the house; the marble benches. The young clergyman hadn't the faintest conception of what all of this cost; it simply looked nice to him and it was a beautiful day.

The son, a hulking blond fellow, threw himself into one of the iron armchairs and sat blinking up at the sun through baggy lids. He and his wife hadn't been in church; they were coming down the wide front stairs as the others entered the house. Under his jacket he wore a white silk shirt, its neck left open, with a printed silk scarf instead of a tie. He made Mr. Watson feel violence.

Mrs. Beneker's daughter-in-law was big-boned and gawky, with a sulky young face. Her polished chestnut hair swung against her cheek whenever she turned her head. She sat on the opposite side of the well from her husband, staring down, as though with interest, at the concentric brickwork.

"Alec! Make us drinks, please," Mrs. Beneker said crisply. "The wherewithals are on the table."

My! thought Mr. Watson. When people spoke that way to each other, it was like a bump to his consciousness. Often they made his consciousness hurt before they even said anything. Before he had begun to understand that he was a mirror to them, this reflecting had made him so uncomfortable in society that he had been on the verge of becoming a recluse.

Young Beneker got up and lounged heavily across to the bar table. "What'll it be, Reverend?" he asked. He gave Mr. Watson a disarming smile.

Mr. Watson smiled back. "Bourbon-and-water, please," he said in his gentle way.

"Don't *I* get a drink?" the girl said.

"All in good time is soon enough, Audrey," her mother-in-law said without turning her head.

Oh! Mr. Watson thought. He looked placatingly from one woman to the other. "At least they don't let clergymen into the lifeboats first," he said, as a little joke, to the girl. He received from her a reluctant smile.

While Alec was making and bringing the drinks, Mrs. Beneker resumed charge of the conversation.

"We're so glad you're attached to St. James's, Mr. Watson, and we hope to see you often here at Rosemont!" she said, in her perky, challenging way. "Dr. Beecham—such a friend. He married Alec's late father and me. Did he tell you?"

"Not yet," Mr. Watson said.

She smiled. "He surely will! It was Dr. Beecham who went up to marry Alec and Audrey, too, you know. That, of course, was not one of Rosemont's weddings." Mr. Watson listened entranced to Mrs. Beneker's speech. "We are regular communicants at St. James's, except in the winter season, when we go for two months up to be near the Great White Way. There it's dear old St. Thomas's for us!"

It was not just Mrs. Beneker's language, so like a boarding-school girl's, that fascinated Mr. Watson. Underneath, she herself—this shy, stiff, tense little person who was driven to communicate in catchwords—was all the while hiding something. What was she hiding? She was hiding it from everybody. And . . . the secret was not exactly shameful, Mr. Watson felt, groping. Mrs. Beneker's secret was something precious to her, which she sat on like a hen an egg.

Mr. Watson knew it would come to him. All he had to do was let himself go and *be* her. Sometimes he had the most amazing visions of people's inner lives. Until he understood it, he had often made himself ill this way. Once, visiting his cousin Eric, he had felt sicker and sicker, until all at once it was Eric who came down with pneumonia.

"Occasionally when Mother is up near the Great White Way, she goes even farther north and visits Beantown," Alec Beneker said. Instead of being entranced by his mother's girlish speech, he was sneering at it. "Beantown's where I wooed and won Audrey, Mr. Watson," he said, spitting the words, "and brought her back to Rosemont a bride."

"One more in a succession of lovely Rosemont brides," Mrs. Beneker said, not tumbling at all.

"Oh, God," Audrey said.

"Audrey. Dear." Mrs. Beneker inclined her head toward the guest. "Remember where you are."

Mr. Watson smiled blissfully. He didn't care if Audrey did swear. He didn't care what she did, she was so lovely with her glittering hair sweeping her still-childish cheek, so young that even her anger seemed young and almost sweet: fierce, indignant anger—nothing cold about it.

She's cooking up something, the young clergyman thought. She's in the midst of some plot. Is she going to leave him? She feels that way. Go ahead and say anything you like, he thought, at Audrey.

Swear all you want. The more you say, the more I know you, and I love to know you.

Audrey Beneker let out a long-suffering sigh and cast her eyes up into the boughs of the willow oaks.

How long, O Lord, how long, Mr. Watson thought along with Audrey.

All this time Alec had not even glanced at his wife but gazed steadily at his mother, smiling faintly and mockingly.

Why is he so venomous? Suddenly, out of the venom, a hint of something new sprang up in Mr. Watson's mind—a feeling full of light and grace. He felt that the two of them were going to be very close, soon.

He asked himself if it were merely the original prenatal relation between them that he sensed, for his faculty always needed this kind of checking. He was pretty sure not. Experience at the hospital psychiatric clinics, when he was in seminary, had taught him to recognize and discount regressiveness. His visions about people always seemed to have to do with the future.

"Mother," Alec Beneker said, eyes never shifting from the graceful little lady in the gray dress, "tell Mr. Watson about this historical old house."

Audrey's eyes jumped to find her husband's. "Hysterical old house," Mr. Watson heard her murmur. It must be some old joke between them. But Alec didn't even glance back at her.

Mrs. Beneker took charge of the conversation again as though it were a refractory horse. Ignoring her son's suggestion, she said, "My old nurse" (Mr. Watson was struck by a wave of hatred from Alec) "—I know that nowadays one isn't supposed to have *had* a nurse, but there it is," she added. "My old Aunt Lucy used to tell me, 'There's a different way fittin' for each and all. What's fittin' for this one ain't fittin' for that one.' That's all I was trying to say to you, Audrey dear, about the presence of Mr. Watson," she said lightly, as to a little girl.

But the young wife wasn't being treated like any little girl. She continued to look away.

"It's fittin' to offer the preacher the first drink, Aunt Lucy would surely agree. But it sho ain't fittin' for the preacher to go first into the lifeboat! Isn't that right, Mr. Watson? The clergy is supposed to be up on deck organizing the singing of 'Nearer My God to Thee.'" She laughed, tinklingly. Mr. Watson nodded. "A crisis is the very time we depend upon our spiritual leaders," Mrs. Beneker went on with wide-eyed earnestness. "I did think it was atrocious a couple of years back—or was it longer?—when some priest—not one of us, praise the Lord—made that pronouncement about fallout shelters. Do you recall it? He said it was a man's duty to own a gun and use it to fight off intruders into his fallout shelter, comes the day of the Big Bang. I suppose he himself would do likewise. That's not very fittin'! Or Christian, either. Is it?"

Alec went on gazing at his parent. The young wife sulked. Mr. Watson smiled and smiled.

"Isn't it nice; you don't hear much about shelters nowadays, do you?" Mrs. Beneker went on, with unshakable social poise and small talk. "I always thought it such a mistake when President Kennedy allowed himself to be quoted—in *Life*, was it?—saying everyone ought to have his own fallout shelter. I can't agree. How about people in cities? How about the poor? That didn't seem very Christian to me, either."

Mr. Watson, accustomed to any number of Sunday irrelevancies from parishioners, smiled some more. Audrey, who had come to the bottom of her drink, held it out mutely toward her husband to be filled. But his eyes never swerved from his mother.

The bees still hummed in the climbing roses. The terrace was deliciously shaded from the midday sun by the awning of tiny leaves. Far beyond the row of sheltering trees, the summer fields could be seen, golden in the sunshine. Audrey held her empty glass, balancing it.

"My own feeling is," Mrs. Beneker said with pretty diffidence, "people should spare time from their busy lives to consult their consciences. Ask themselves what is fittin', when and if the awful day of the Big Bang should arrive. As we pray it will not, of course. The pundits tell us that the danger has become *so* great that there *is* no danger anymore." She blinked, and Mr. Watson, like a mirror, blinked with her. "I mean, people need to ask themselves are they worth saving. Then what are they worth saving for? *I* have come to the conclusion," Mrs. Beneker said, "that the value old people have in a post-Bomb world must be twofold."

She paused, but nobody spoke. The clergyman was struggling with an influx of mystifying impressions. These are what pass for Great Thoughts to her, he thought, groping.

"Twofold," Mrs. Beneker repeated. "After the cataclysm will be a new world. If there is any world left at all! And youth must inherit. The use of the old, in such a world, will be twofold."

"Oh, stop saying 'twofold,'" Audrey murmured.

"Shut up," her husband told her.

"What was all that?" Mrs. Beneker asked.

Audrey got up and walked into the house.

Mrs. Beneker lifted her eyebrows minutely and went on. "A twofold value," she said. "Both necessarily in relation to the youth. First, to care for them. They will need those with wisdom and tenderness to care for them in their terrible hardships. Second, to teach the youth. It is us oldsters who must pass on the torch of civilization."

Mr. Watson's eyes, moving to Alec's face, drawn by a barrage of dark emotion, winced. She's making him feel . . . murderous.

He hoped he was exaggerating. He often did exaggerate. There was the time when, driving with John Nichols in John Nichols's car, he suddenly had the perfectly clear impression that John was going to push him out of the car, at sixty miles an hour. Instead, in a minute John turned toward him and said, "How can you believe in such rubbish as God?"

"Mother," Alec Beneker said. He peered down into the wavery depths of his drink. "Why don't you tell Mr. Watson about this fabulous old house?"

"What you want me to tell?" his mother said tartly.

"Oh, anything at all. I'm sure he'd be interested in its history. Its quaint ins and outs. This is a truly venerable mansion, as you can see, Mr. Watson. Three Presidents have set foot on these thresholds. Innumerable brides—none more beautiful than my mother—have been carried across them."

"Go find Audrey and tell her to come back," Mrs. Beneker ordered. "People will be arriving."

"In a moment, Mother," he said lazily, turning his glass around and around.

"Why can't you ever do something when I ask you to do it?" she snapped.

Alec gave her a blank, artificial smile and made a couple of hitching, straining movements as though trying to get up out of his chair and unable to. But it was too late now anyway. Giving little cries and salutations, a man and a woman in Sunday-lunch attire came pushing through the French windows, hands outstretched.

"How pretty all this is!" the woman exclaimed. She pressed her cheek to that of her hostess, who had risen.

"Vera! Dear!" Mrs. Beneker turned to the husband. "And Raymond! Have you met Dr. Beecham's new assistant at St. James's? Mr. Watson, Mr. and Mrs. Pugh."

Mr. Watson jumped at hearing his name spoken. He had been rapt in a vision—sudden, radiant—that fulfilled the earlier hint, that explained everything between Mrs. Beneker and her son. One of the miracles of reversal-into-the-opposite was going to happen to them.

His vision was of them together, as though for eternity, in a tiny, secret place, a place not a bit grand but humble rather—only the barest shelter, such as a stable was. "Silent Night, Holy Night" sang itself joyfully in Mr. Watson's head. At the bottom of everybody's life, no matter how hateful, he thought, persisted the same age-old symbol, the same right relation, that needed only time to work itself out. That time was not far off for the Benekers. No matter what base motives drew its parts, neither fire nor flood could keep love apart.

More and more people were arriving, and in no time at all the young clergyman, with his shining eyes, was being tossed about like a little boat on a sea of chatter about the stock market, jet travel, politics—subjects he knew nothing whatever about. But, with the key to everything in his heart, he smiled and smiled, listened and listened, as he practiced being all things to all men.

Mrs. Beneker, for her part, was relieved to be greeting new arrivals. It made her so uneasy when Alec kept bringing up the house in that annoying way of his. As she greeted two more newcomers, she looked over their heads and saw that Alec was making drinks, and Audrey, praise the Lord, back on the terrace where she belonged, speaking to people, fulfilling her obligations. Mrs. Beneker hoped she'd have the grace to pass canapés.

She didn't know why Alec had to keep asking her to tell about the quaint ins and outs of this old house, unless it was simply because he saw it annoyed her. Why must he be so harsh, so grim? She'd endured his unsuccessful growing up—the poor marks, the undesirable friends, the debts—always looking forward to having a tall grown-up son to lean on; but all she'd got in the end, it seemed, was an enemy.

Simply to be annoying must surely be why he did it, because she was almost positive that he couldn't have the faintest idea of the truth. She had had it put in long after he was married and gone away. She had sent to New York for the plans. Nobody but two workmen, to each of whom she had given a hundred dollars, knew that it existed right here under her feet as she stood talking.

She couldn't think it unnatural not to have told Alec. Telling him would have been the unnatural thing, what with his unpleasantness to her. As a grown-up man with a wife—furthermore, as a rich man—it was certainly his own responsibility to provide for himself and Audrey.

The fact was, she thought, even as she pressed Tom Hyde's hand and said, "How awfully good of you to come! How *is* your poor leg?"—the actual fact was it felt heavenly not to share her secret. Not with Hobart, her husband, dead for years; not with Alec; not with anybody. It made her happy just to think of it there, underfoot, cozy and snug, ready and waiting. When she walked into it, as she occasionally did to check on supplies, being enclosed made her feel as though the place itself embraced her—almost like being Aunt Lucy's baby again; back in her arms and loved. It was so nice there—the tidy shelves of canned goods, the neat bunks against the wall. She'd had two bunks put in, because she had this silly feeling that, even at her age, love might come to her. Even at her age, you never knew what strange encounter might still occur!

Her thoughts made her give Tom Hyde a sudden flirtatious smile. "Alec!" she called in her pretty, high voice. "Ask Mr. Hyde what he'll take. Quickly!"

Alec nodded. Make another round of drinks. Meet another round of people. Get through another of Mother's Sunday lunches. . . .

What Mother didn't know was that he knew. When—as it amused him to do—he called people's attention to the antiquity of this house, he could see it set up doubts in her mind about whether he possibly *could* know. Of course he knew! She was the one who was too silly to know anything.

Since he was about eight, he had been aware of the secret passage in Rosemont. He had never discussed it with her, but what had he ever discussed with her? Imagine not knowing more about a boy's nature than that! During his childhood he had not only stolen off into the secret passage but had made his own additions to it—nailed up a shelf here, scooped out a cranny there, even once constructed two steps. She'd never known it because she'd been too busy with her flirtations to know anything about the skinny, unpopular boy he had been.

On a weekend three years ago, when he and Audrey had been visiting just like this and he couldn't sleep, he had, just for the fun of it, after so many years, gone down the passage that began in the attic, wound around the drawing-room chimney, and went down two steps—*his* steps—to a shorter passage, then down the side of a stone wall that was part of the cellars. The passage used then to end up in an outlet into the terrace well. There he had encountered something strange, something new. She had built it without telling anyone. Not even him!

It wasn't locked. He had walked about in it, catching his breath after the squeeze through the passage, viewing the tidy rows of cans, the neat bunks, the water tank. She'd made it very snug, cozy. In the three years since then, there had been other weekends here, and another thing his mother didn't know was that in that time her precious secret had received a slight alteration. He had taken out a square lead-lined wooden panel backing on the passage and fitted it with nylon strips so that it could easily be removed. Then he replaced it.

If the ultimate escape ever did become necessary now, she could go down into her secret place to sit it out, to wait for the day when she would come out and start caring—caring!—for all that youth she talked about, start teaching whatever in the world she thought she had to teach. There would be time then. Plenty of time for her to reflect on all the ways she'd failed life, failed her child.

And just in case she needed reminding, why, it would be a surprise to her, wouldn't it—a real surprise—to see the end of her precious shelter begin to move. And who would come crawling in? None other than her own beloved son, if he had to come through fire and flood to get there.

1965

THE MOST ELEGANT DRAWING ROOM IN EUROPE

"The Contessa doesn't seem entirely real, she's so exquisite," wrote Emily Knapp to her friend and fellow-librarian Ruth Patterson, at home in Worcester, Massachusetts. "I wish you too might have seen her in her tiny jewel box of a palazzo yesterday, as we did! She'd lent us her gondola for the afternoon. (I can't tell you how super-elegant we felt, or how much attention we attracted on the Grand Canal.) Persis Woodson, the artist I wrote you about meeting on the Cristoforo Colombo coming over, remarked that all over America next winter people will be showing home movies with us prominent in them, pointing us out as aristocratic Venetians lolling in our private gondola!

"It is Persis that Mother and I have to thank for this wonderful opportunity—this unique experience. Her older brother, Tim Woodson, who was American consul here after the war, wrote to the Contessa about her. The Contessa can't seem to do enough for Persis, and even for us as Persis's friends. Do I sniff a romance in the dear dead days? We ended the afternoon having cocktails at the palazzo. Never in my wildest dreams did I think I'd catch a glimpse of quite such high life! Strange to relate, Persis seems more irritated than charmed by the Contessa. But Art is all Persis lives for, and besides, through her brother she is more accustomed to such grandeurs than we."

Emily paused and looked around, taking conscious pleasure in her surroundings. She was sitting at a table in the grape arbor at the end of the terrace of the *pensione*, where she was sheltered from a hot September sun. Through interstices of the grapevines there was a view of a short stretch of the Grand Canal, framed by two tall palazzos, one pink, one yellow. Up the little San Trovaso Canal moved coal or garbage barges, ponderously putt-putting; more rapid launches; and an occasional, palpitatingly leashed-in speedboat. As each boat passed by, waves were created that slapped for a moment against the marble steps to the *pensione*, then subsided. Wooden planks, nailed together, leaned against the stone entrance post, ready for use as a bridge to arriving boats. On the main, flagged terrace the sun still struck robustly at five o'clock in the afternoon; between the terrace and the shade of the arbor, monstrous big dahlias raised flaming faces to the sun. Everything was very quiet right now. Older people were resting. The servants were busy in the kitchen. Persis Woodson was off seeing a Bellini Madonna at the Church of San Zaccaria. Emily was saving her strength for the concert tonight. She felt a little nervous about venturing out at night in Venice; but Persis, whose judgment she deeply respected, told her that was nonsense.

Suddenly a launch backfired, out in the San Trovaso Canal, and Emily leaned forward to see. A young Italian was tinkering with his trouble-making engine, very handsome in profile, his neck round and brown and strong. In a moment more he got his engine going and was moving out toward the opening into the Grand Canal; in another moment he was gone.

Once more all was quiet. All of Venice seemed to subside into its omnipresent waters, to be a mere illusion of iridescent bubbles that floated on the bosom of an ageless, maternal sea.

"The Contessa's gondola was a marvel to behold," Emily resumed. "All the *pensione* help dropped their work and dashed out to have a look at it. It was enamelled black, with brightly polished brass sea horses and dolphins. And not one but two magnificent gondoliers, all in white, with broad red sashes. As we boarded it, the *signorina* who runs the place said to us, 'That is a most beautiful gondola.

There are not many such left in this day of launches.' You could see her opinion of us soar!

"To help one, the younger gondolier standing on the steps offered a positively rocklike elbow to put one's hand on—instead of grasping one's arm the way the public gondoliers do. From inside the craft the older, fat gondolier supported one with a proffered elbow equally rocklike.

"Inside, instead of the worn black leather seats the public gondolas have, they were slipcovered in white linen, piped with red and yellow, the Contessa's colors. Even Mother was impressed!"

Emily paused again. Her mother—small, indomitable, highly critical of what she didn't like—was never abashed by her surroundings, never ashamed to say she preferred Massachusetts to Italy. She had, Emily reflected, twice her daughter's character. At the memory of the disgraceful way she had behaved to her mother that morning, she licked her lips and tried to close them over her teeth. Her awful teeth. . . .

"Everybody on the Grand Canal stared as we made our progress down toward the Rialto Bridge on our way to view the Church of Santi Giovanni e Paolo (in Venetian dialect, San Zanipolo)," she continued, turning with relief to the pleasure of writing the letter. "The passengers on the vaporetto all rushed to our side, and people even came out on the balconies of palaces to take a look!

"Persis, who knows more about Venice than I, having paid a visit to her brother here when she was a young girl, said the public gondoliers would recognize our gondola by its colors, and by the coat of arms on the gondoliers' silver arm brassards. Isn't that impressive?

"One young gondolier yelled something at us, and Persis, who knows some Italian, said he said, 'You got American *miliardi* there?' And our man said, 'Oh, sure, sure.' So while we may have deceived the tourists, you can be sure we did not deceive the professional gondoliers into thinking us Venetian aristocrats! Still, I did enjoy lolling back like a lady. Loll is what you do, in a gondola."

Emily thought of her mother again. Mother hadn't lolled! Mother was, perhaps, incapable of lolling. She'd sat upright in the reclining seat, looking about her with calm curiosity as they turned off the Grand Canal into a very narrow one. Up this they had slowly progressed, squeezing past barges moored along the *fondamenti*. The marble water steps here were moss-grown and slimy. The overhanging houses and decayed palaces could not have changed to any extent in four hundred years. Emily turned to smile up at the gondolier behind her—the young, slim one—to show her appreciation. When he saw her looking at him, he smiled back. She turned around in her seat again, as always aware as soon as her eyes met another's of how her teeth looked.

"Hoh!" the old gondolier shouted as they slid up to an intersection, hesitated, and swung into an even smaller, more obscure canal. Black tidal waters lapped against moldering palace portals and underneath the sills of square windows, crossbarred like those of the prison. They passed a tiny baroque church standing in a little stone-paved campo. Medieval stone arches and crooked *calli* led back on either hand into the secret inner places of Venice. "Unsanitary? I hope to tell you," Mother remarked.

"We drew up before marble steps the full width of the campo," Emily wrote. "They call them campos in Venice, not piazzas as in the rest of Italy. It was so thrilling! Because there right in front of us stood the Verrocchio statue of Colleoni! The Scuola San Marco with its marvellous Renaissance façade was on our left, and the church was straight ahead across the campo."

Emily paused again. She did not intend to tell Ruth the way she'd felt inside the Church of San Zanipolo. It was the way she so often felt inside these Italian churches: almost in tears. She, who'd gone to a Unitarian Sunday school, to nothing at all since she grew up! She had the feeling she would give anything to share whatever all those kneeling figures with kerchiefed heads were experiencing.

"We did San Zanipolo—doges' tombs, and a notable Bellini and a Veronese. Then we started back, to wind up at the Contessa's for cocktails. The gondoliers had been consorting in a nearby café, and came bounding across the campo to assist us into the gondola. A whole crowd of people were assembled on the steps to watch us embark. We slid off, and made our tortuous way back to the Grand Canal. The Contessa lives up near the mouth of the Canal.

"Such swank! The Contessa's butler came out to the water steps to receive us, dressed in a tail coat and batwing collar. He led us into a little walled courtyard with black-and-white marble paving, said something in Italian, and disappeared. Persis told us we were to go up to the balcony, via the marble outside stairs. After we got up there, we felt in a bit of a quandary as to where to go next—whether to stay on the balcony or go into a drawing room we could see through open French doors. It all seemed very European and intimidating, at least to me.

"We were tentatively approaching the drawing room when our hostess put in an appearance, looking absolutely stunning. What is it women of fashion *do* to make them look so different? The Contessa simply has everything!

"*She* made the drinks, not the butler. He only brought out the plates of things to eat. I'd thought of course he'd make the drinks, but somehow it seemed even more sophisticated her doing it. Mother and I sat down, and Persis walked round peering at the Old Masters that hang on the Contessa's walls, looking stony-faced. Mother, of course, was perfectly at ease. Far more so than poor me! You can't faze Mother.

"The drawing room had an air even the grandest rooms in America don't have. There were little armless, satin-upholstered chairs and sofas; little tables with, set out on them, the Contessa's collection of jade. The Contessa herself sat draped at one end of a sofa. She kept urging us to take the food the butler had brought in and left on the tables. There were hot cheese things over a flame, and tiny hardboiled eggs. I asked what they were, and the Contessa said they were quail's eggs! She didn't hop up and hand things the way you or I would. Just sat there waving a hand and saying, 'But doo . . . You must . . . Please . . .' I've written you what I remember, but I can't catch what that extraordinary air of hers is. I guess one just can't understand someone like that. She's too different.

"Her hair, like everything else about her didn't seem real. It formed an enormous aureole around her head. I got my nerve up at one point and asked her to recommend a hairdresser in Venice. The Contessa said, as nearly as I can reproduce it, 'For your hair go to Carlo, darling. He is the best hairdresser in all Italy.' I can't explain how foreign and sophisticated it sounded. I glanced at Persis, but she just looked black, as she does when things become sophisticated. I couldn't help feeling maybe the Contessa rather took to me, although I know people like that say 'darling' to everybody.

"She had on a good deal of makeup; she has some skin trouble that has pitted her skin. She wore a brilliant yellow-and-orange flowered silk shift—you have no idea how fashionable! And wonderful little delicate slippers of yellow lizard! I couldn't help exclaiming—you know me, always gushing—'What a beautiful dress! Isn't it, Mother?' Dearest Mother, who is nothing if not frank, said, 'A nice dress for the morning.' I happen to know she doesn't approve of shifts—I shouldn't have asked her. But the Contessa, of course, could handle it. She said, 'I'd hardly wear it in the morning,' but with the most charming laugh. It's all so obvious that she's always at ease and has been everywhere and speaks quantities of languages and knows everybody and is rich and does exactly as she pleases!

"While we were there, she answered the telephone that stood by her sofa, and had a conversation with someone in Italian. You could tell it was a man. Her face got all eager and her voice softened and you could tell she was using pet names. She seemed almost pleading, but, of course, I didn't understand a word. When she hung up, her face came back to its chic, hard composure, and she said to Persis, 'Now, tell me more about Tim, and darling beloved Monica.' What I'm trying to say, Ruth, is that that kind of utter perfection *defeats* me. It's hard to believe that I belong to the same race as the Contessa, she's so exquisite.

"She said goodbye to us on the balcony; the butler saw us to the boat landing. This time we were helped into the launch. The Contessa told us she only keeps the gondola out of sentiment (quite an expensive sentiment, I feel sure!) and that she goes everywhere in the launch. 'Where?' I asked, and she said, 'Oh, to the Lido, darling, in the morning, for my swim and lunch in my cabana, and to parties, and to friends. . . . And to things like tomorrow night.' I had a glimpse of her life, like an exquisitely designed work of Venetian glass art.

"The launch was as smart as the gondola, with white linen slipcovers in the cabin, also piped in red and yellow. How do you suppose it feels to have your own colors? The Contessa told us about tonight's concert at the famous Scuola San Rocco, decorated by Tintoretto. We would never have known about it otherwise. It will be an all-Vivaldi program by the Virtuosi di Roma. She said she'd take us home in her launch afterward. Doesn't it all sound like a movie? Not a bit what I expected when Mother and I boarded the Cristoforo Colombo!

"I tell Persis she is a perfect angel to ring us in on all this, but Persis says she wouldn't have gone at all if she'd had to go alone. In the launch, as we sped home, I said, 'The Contessa certainly couldn't do more for us,' and Persis said, 'I know. But in another way, she doesn't know we're alive.' 'But that's sort of fascinating,' I said, and then, because dear Mother gets offended when she is left out of the conversation, I said, 'Didn't you think the Contessa was fascinating, dear?'

"You know Mother! She said, 'I thought her hair looked like an African bushman.' All I could do was hope the man running the launch didn't understand English. . . ."

"Well!"

The voice was Persis's; she had entered the arbor, broad-brimmed hat in hand. Instantly Emily's being, which had been flowing into her letter, shrank back into an awareness of herself. She had an abrupt picture of how she looked, bending over the table, teeth hanging down like a silly fringe. She looked up and, helplessly, smiled at Persis, knowing that whatever she did, anywhere, her teeth always preceded her—splayed, jutting out, a fool's teeth—while around them she smiled and smiled merrily. "Did you enjoy the Bellini?" she inquired.

"Yes, it was a superb one," Persis said. She stood leaning against the post of the grape arbor, fanning herself with her hat—a bulky, jolly-looking woman in her late thirties, like Emily. Her gray hair was clipped short. "There was an Andrea del Castagno in a side chapel. They have to light it for you. Afterward I went back to the Doges' Palace for another look at that Bellini, to compare them. I came back on the traghetto. Do you realize the fare is less to be ferried over if you stand up than if you sit down?"

They laughed together, with the pleasure they took in local detail and in laughing. Persis sat down.

"I had a *caffè cappuccino* at Florian's," Persis went on. "To comfort myself after having looked across from the Doges' Palace at the prison again. I agree, the terror still clings to it. Sitting at Florian's, I found this in Morris." She flipped open a guidebook she carried and read aloud, "'Sometimes the stranger, passing by the Doges' Palace, would find a pair of anonymous conspirators hanging, mangled, from a gibbet, or hear a whisper of appalling torture in the dungeons of the Ten. Once, the Venetians awoke to discover three convicted traitors buried alive, head downward, among the flagstones of the Piazzetta, their feet protruding among the pillars.'"

"Oh dear!" Emily said. "Right where we were *standing*!"

They stared, half pleasurably aghast, at one another.

"Was it wonderful in the Piazza?" Emily asked.

"It was all right enough. Too many Germans, as usual. But at least it's no longer the absolute sink of high society it was in my youth! If Florian's would just lower its prices, it might belong to the people some day."

"But all those grand dukes," Emily couldn't forbear saying. "And Cole Porter and everybody. . . . It must have been awfully glamorous."

"Glamorous enough," Persis said. She smiled indulgently at her little friend. "You never actually saw it, as I did when I was young. The young sense so much, they know everything—But I don't need to tell you about being sensitive! The trouble was, Venice was wasted on those people. They just came to look at each other. They'd just as soon be in Palm Beach. They don't care about the true Venice."

"Didn't you think the Contessa's pictures were good?"

"Certainly," Persis said indifferently. "She probably got Perseoni to select them for her. In fact, I think Tim said Perseoni did select them. Anybody who's rich enough can get good pictures."

"You were so angelic to ring us in on the Contessa," Emily began once more. She couldn't seem to help saying it over and over.

Persis smiled and didn't reply. She would never have gone to that ghastly woman's at all except for the treat she knew it would be for the New England Knapps. She was attracted by little Emily Knapp, and was sorry for her—so pretty and gentle and sweet, crushed by that old tyrant of a mother. The morning when the *valet de chambre* had called her downstairs to the *pensione* telephone, where the Contessa was holding on, she had taken a positive satisfaction in saying that she was travelling with friends. She said "old" friends. She said she couldn't leave them. Might she bring them, she asked briskly. There was a moment's silence. Then the Contessa said, in that husky voice, "But of course." Although, while she was standing at the telephone in the *pensione* lobby, Persis hadn't yet met the

Contessa, she knew just how she would look. And sure enough, she looked exactly that way.

Here, in the grape arbor, Persis was visited by a fleeting memory of herself, long ago, on that visit to Tim in Venice. She giggled now. "Remember I told you Italian men seem to have changed since the old days? Because they don't pinch one and call out '*Bella signorina!*' the way they used to do?"

Emily nodded, all receptiveness.

"Well, at Florian's it came to me why. It's not that *they've* changed. *We've* changed!"

Emily began to giggle, too. They looked at each other and laughed some more. It was the kind of joke that drew them together—a joke on their own old-maid state. Together they scampered companionably over the bridges of Venice, in and out of galleries, through the vast rooms of palaces, like girls together whispering and giggling.

Emily began to put her writing things away. "I must go and help Mother get ready for dinner," she said. "If we leave for the concert about eight-thirty, it's time enough, don't you think?"

"How is your mother this afternoon?" Persis asked politely.

"She's very well," Emily replied, politely.

But when she got upstairs to the large room the Knapps shared, Mother was still looking for that wretched comb.

"Darling. *Please* let me buy you another," Emily said.

The bedroom had a chandelier of inferior Venetian glass, each spoke forming a different-colored flower, three tall French windows that opened on a narrow balcony over the San Trovaso Canal, and an odd little closet that had been converted into a lavatory. The toilet was down the hall. There were twin beds, and on one of them Mrs. Knapp sat holding in her lap the overnight bag in which she kept her curlers. She had been going through its contents yet once more. Now she paused in her search to regard her daughter.

"What's the use of that," she said, "when it has to be somewhere in this room? I'm not in the habit of taking my comb around with me in my pocket, the way I know you young people think it's smart to do."

Emily tried to close her lips over her teeth. What her mother *was* in the habit of doing, she wanted to retort, was using her daughter's things when she mislaid her own. She mislaid them with increasing frequency. But Emily was determined she would not disgrace herself as she had done this morning, when, opening her eyes, she had found her mother sitting before the mirror combing her hair with Emily's comb. The most awful rage had leapt up in her and she'd cried, "Why must you use my things? I loathe sharing my things!"

Mrs. Knapp had turned full around in her chair. "Well! Now we know," she said.

Eight hours later—all this time since—the anger was still there. "I never mind sharing my things when there is some reason for it," Emily said very gently, going right on with the morning, "but all I would have to do is go round the corner to the *farmacia* and buy a comb. There isn't any reason why we have to use the same comb."

"A waste of good money," her mother pronounced. She went back to rummaging around in the overnight bag. "It has to be somewhere right in this room."

Emily sighed. "Time to dress," she said.

"Dress for what?"

"Well, for dinner, dear. And we're going to this wonderful Vivaldi concert at the Scuola San Rocco that the Contessa told us about."

"You can count me out," Mrs. Knapp said. "I have to find my comb."

"But it's such an opportunity! And we're coming home in the Contessa's launch. Think how exciting *that* will be! Didn't you enjoy yourself yesterday?"

"It was all right," Mrs. Knapp said. "Your Contessa seems to deny herself nothing. But I can't spend my whole life in pleasure, the way you seem to do."

It was so unjust! "Darling. We only came to Europe to enjoy ourselves," Emily said.

"Pleasure doesn't have to cost so much money," Mrs. Knapp bore on, licking her lips easily. "Take soft drinks. You young people think you have to have soft drinks all the time. When *I* was young, we might make a pitcher of lemonade and carry it under the walnut tree and sit and drink it, after the chores were done. But we didn't think we had to drink soft drinks all day long."

It was so unreasonable! "I planned our trip just in order to give you pleasure," Emily said softly. "And we haven't had any soft drinks since we left home—"

"Hah!" Mrs. Knapp said. "I never wanted to come—you know that. I said so enough times."

Emily took a firm grip on herself. "But you didn't mean it, dear," she said. "All my life I've heard you say you wished you could see Europe and its treasures. That's what you really want. I'm only thinking of *you*—"

She broke off, for her mother had whirled around on the bed and was sticking out her tongue at Emily. "'*Only thinking of you!*'" she mocked, like an antique little girl. "Always perfect, aren't you?"

Emily's mind seemed to explode. Fragments of outrage came drifting down from above. Her teeth, her teeth . . . So far from perfect; so always in the wrong . . . unbearable, unbearable. In the end, as ever, the debris of Emily's thoughts settled down as into a smoking ash heap, soft, growing cooler. The only thing to do was bear it. Sometimes she had the feeling that her whole life was spent waiting for her mother just once to say she was sorry that she had not had Emily's teeth fixed when Emily was a little girl. But it would have to come from her. The accusation was too appalling to be made, and grew more so.

"You have to realize that from now on your mother's bound to fail," Persis said soothingly, as during the concert intermission they stood together downstairs in the Scuola San Rocco, smoking cigarettes, two women wearing hats and carrying the raincoats they hadn't dared leave in their seats. "She *is* getting like a child. But of course she still has flashes of great wisdom," she added politely.

"It just makes me feel guilty, not to be kinder," Emily explained. "She can't help it if her memory is failing."

She had told Persis enough of the scene in the bedroom to make her see what it was like, dealing with Mother about things like the comb—not enough, she trusted, to disgrace her parent. She hadn't mentioned the sticking out of the tongue, for instance, or her own violent reactions.

"It is true, she *didn't* want to come, once we'd made up our minds," she went on. "I suppose the truth is I made her come. Perhaps I did the wrong thing. Perhaps I was selfish. Maybe I should have let her—oh dear!"

"You did the right thing," Persis told her firmly. "You're giving your mother a wonderful trip, and don't ever forget it, no matter what happens." They gazed into each other's eyes, thinking of death. "Let's go back, shall we? . . . Aren't the Tintorettos superb?" she said as they began climbing the flights of broad, shallow steps, looking up to either side and ahead at the pictures.

"Have you spotted the Contessa yet?" Emily asked when they had regained their original seats along the side of the enormous chamber that was lined, walls and ceiling, with the huge, dark Tintorettos. They stuffed their raincoats behind them to make the pewlike seats more comfortable.

It had been raining, although not hard, when they took the vaporetto down the Canal after dinner. They scampered through the drizzle from the *pensione* to the Accademia, bought their shoddy paper *biglietti*, and nipped onto the waterborne covered waiting room, which had a central rail to separate those embarking from those coming ashore. In a moment a vaporetto crashed up to the waiting room with, as usual, a stupendous bump. It had been fun sailing down the Canal, seeing the lights of the palaces through a blur of rain. Disembarking at the Frari stop, they scampered up through dark *calli* and over little bridges with a sense of adventure, at last gaining the Campo San Rocco, with its lighted Scuola and the people streaming in for the concert. There was no question but that it would have been most unwise for Mrs. Knapp to come out in such weather. In Venice, there was no way to escape rain.

"No, I haven't seen her," Persis replied to her friend. She looked about the hall, which was filling up with a seemingly all-Venetian, or at least all-Italian, audience. The only light was furnished by huge striated Venetian-glass lanterns, standing along three sides of the room. This flickering and glancing radiance fell on handsome, archaic faces—old, proudly beak-nosed men and beautiful red-haired women like those in Titians. One such Venetian beauty sat just in front of them with her blond little girl, who rested a lovely, oddly mature face against her mother's shoulder.

"There she is. Look," Persis said, poking Emily and nodding across the hall. "Over on the far side, this row, talking with an old gentleman with white hair. See?"

"Do you suppose he's her lover?" Emily whispered.

"I don't think so," Persis said.

"I do so appreciate your giving me this opportunity to see so many wonderful—" Emily began once more.

"It's a pleasure to me to do something that will give you pleasure," Persis declared. Then, for the violins were tuning up, "Sh-h-h!"

After the concert, feeling bemused with Vivaldi, the two women moved slowly down the great stairway with the push of the crowd. At the bottom they took up a stand facing the stairs, to await the Contessa.

She was an unconscionable time coming. At last, after almost everyone had descended, she appeared at the top of the lowest flight of steps, talking to a man with sleek black hair, her huge, *cotonata* head tipping one way as she spoke to him, tipping the other as she turned away to take another deliberate step down. She wore another silk shift like the one she had had on the day before—this time a purple-and-blue flowered print with a long blue silk stole she held wrapped tightly around her shoulders as she continued to descend the stairs one step at a time, stopping entirely now and then to reply to the man or to free one hand and gesticulate. She spied the two women waiting and tossed up her chin in recognition. "Ah!" she said, coming up to them. "You are here. You have enjoyed the concert?"

"It was wonderful," Emily said. "I was simply carried away."

"Yes," the Contessa said. "I have told you I will take you home. We go this way. My man is at the campo steps with the launch. Follow me." Her vivid, erect form swept forward, the ends of the silk stole floating behind. At the main door of the Scuola, some young Italians seemed to be waiting for her; she held out her hands to them, then swept them into her entourage so that they, too, were following. She did not introduce Emily and Persis, who stood awkwardly waiting while she spoke to the young people. By now the Contessa's companion of the staircase had disappeared.

Her group of guests followed her through steadily falling rain across the campo to steps that led down to a narrow canal. The launchman of the day before, now in oilskins, helped the Contessa first into her boat. Then the young Italians got in—two men and a girl. Last of all, Persis and Emily were helped aboard.

"I love your white slipcovers," Emily chattered nervously as she took her seat inside the cabin. "Isn't this snug here, out of the rain?" The launch had started up, and was moving very slowly along the dark canal, which was clogged with moored boats.

"Yes, very," the Contessa replied. "Have you all met? Countess Lieto, Count Morosini, Prince Fenna, Miss Woodson, Miss Mmmm. . . . All these young people live on the Giudecca, where the launch will take them after it has dropped us off."

With that the Contessa fell silent. The young people talked to each other in Italian, laughing and exclaiming with extreme gaiety. The launch, which had moved so very slowly, now turned into the Grand Canal and picked up speed.

Persis, no doubt, could feel at ease, Emily thought, but for herself she felt most uncomfortable with no one speaking to her. She peered out through rain-streaked cabin windows at a Canal like black velvet. Only a few lights were left burning in the palaces they passed. Emily held her wristwatch up to the faint glow from outside and saw that it was now twelve-fifteen. The launch drove steadily, strongly, through the midnight waters.

"Why, there's our canal! That's where we live!" she exclaimed, pointing, to the Contessa, who sat in the shadows wrapped in her stole.

"Yes," the Contessa said.

Emily looked toward Persis, but Persis was peering out of the window beside her. Everything must be all right. The Contessa could hardly be abducting them! She spoke such good English she must have understood just now. Perhaps they were to be asked into the palace for a nightcap.

Past the black bulk of the Accademia, past the still lighted-up grand hotels they swept, and at last made the turn into the Contessa's canal. At the landing the launchman jumped ashore and stood holding the boat to the water steps, extending one crooked elbow to support the ladies as they got out.

"Here is where we leave our young people," the Contessa observed, going ashore.

"*Arrivederci!*" cried all the lively young Italians, not stirring. "*Arrivederci, Leonora! Arrivederci, signore!*"

"Goodbye, my darlings," the Contessa replied, and stood waiting for the two women at the top of the steps, under the faint light shed from the windows of her palace.

They followed her into the paved courtyard. The Contessa

opened a door underneath the balcony and led the two women into a dining room, all white, through which she passed to a square white hall ringed with short columns on which stood the busts of doges. Then the Contessa opened another door onto the night.

"Here is the street," she said in her husky voice. "Your way leads straight ahead. You need only keep going in a direct line and you will arrive at your *pensione*."

"Good night," Emily heard herself say as she stepped out into the rain.

She heard Persis, too, saying, "Good night."

"Good night," said the Contessa, and closed the door.

In the street they stared into each other's eyes.

"Well!" Persis began.

Suddenly the rain began to descend very much harder.

"Come on, we have to dash," Persis continued. "Fortunately, I know this part of Venice well. Not that she knew that."

It was thundering massively out over the Grand Canal. Flashes of jagged lightning revealed pitch-black alleys opening on either hand and the oily waters of the small canals they crossed over humpbacked bridges. All around, inscrutable dark façades looked down.

"This is scary!" Emily panted, hurrying along.

"Nothing bad seems to happen in Venice nowadays," Persis threw back over her shoulder. "Small thanks to the Contessa."

"I don't know how people ever dared live at all, in the old days!" Emily cried. Not a soul was visible abroad on the streets, but every turning, every archway suggested an assassin.

They had just entered a deserted campo when the sky all at once burst and rain came down in a deluge. The two women shrank back as far as possible into the doorway of a church facing into the campo. Emily kept hoping that the church door they backed up against would not suddenly, horribly, open.

"Never," Persis began. "Never! In all my life! Have I ever imagined anything so unspeakable, so insufferable! I told you people like that are appalling, but this is the worst. I never dreamed anyone could *do* such a thing! And those damned young Italians being taken all the way home."

"Why would she do such a thing?" Emily asked. "Why would she want to?"

An earsplitting crash broke overhead, silencing them. Each wondered, as she huddled back into the comparative shelter, what she had done to deserve being treated so at the hands of the Contessa. It seemed to each imperative that there be a reason for tonight, and that she should discover it.

"I am very angry," Persis announced when she could once more be heard. "I never want to hear of that woman again."

"I'm afraid it was I who let you in for this. You said you wouldn't have gone—" Emily began.

"Don't be absurd," Persis said. "It's not *your* fault she's a monster. I shall certainly write Tim about this—every word of what happened."

"Maybe that's what she wants you to do," Emily said, coming up with one of her solutions. "Maybe she used to be madly in love with your brother and he jilted her. Maybe this is her way of getting even—doing this to you."

"I doubt it," Persis said. She smiled grimly into the rain. She was fairly sure the reason for this outrageous performance was that the Contessa hadn't liked having the little Knapps brought along yesterday. Well, let her not like it! Persis didn't for one moment regret bringing them.

As suddenly as it had increased, the rain now decreased in volume. The two women ventured forth, and scurried the rest of the way home in silence. Downstairs in the *pensione* the light was on, and the *signorina's* brother lay on the sofa in the entrance hall, asleep. Yawning, he rose politely as they came squelching past him in their soaked shoes, their saturated raincoats. They could hear him putting out lights behind them.

"Mother'll be so upset," Emily whispered as they climbed the stairs to the bedroom floor. "She can never get to sleep till I come in."

"Just tell her what was done to us," Persis whispered back.

"Oh dear," Emily sighed, beginning to rehearse it all. They crept down the corridor, past closed bedroom doors, past the door marked "Toilette," to the turn in the corridor which separated their rooms.

"Good night," Persis whispered. "Dry yourself off thoroughly."

"You, too. Good night. . . ."

Emily opened the door upon a dark room where a breeze stirred, and tiptoed in. She was astonished to realize, from a faint snore, that her mother was fast asleep. Rather than risk awakening her by turning on a lamp, she tiptoed to the converted closet and, closing its door softly after her, switched on the light inside. She had begun to run water in the basin when Mrs. Knapp called, "Emily? That you?"

"Yes, dear." She opened the door again. "I hope you haven't been too worried."

"Worried? Why should I be worried?" Mrs. Knapp, aroused, sat up in bed. "You were with that friend of yours, weren't you? Miss What's-Her-Name, Miss Woodson. The bully."

"Well, dear, you do worry at night, you know," Emily began, but it was too late to engage in argument. She turned back to the basin. "We got wet," she said. "It's been raining hard."

"I thought your Contessa was bringing you home."

"Well, that's it, she was, but . . . I'll tell you about it tomorrow," Emily said, too tired to face the explanation. "It's very late."

"How late?" the old lady demanded.

Emily looked at her watch; it was half past one. "After midnight," she said.

"Mercy!" said old Mrs. Knapp. "I thought it was about ten. I found my comb!" she announced, triumphantly. "Guess where it was."

"Where?" Emily asked faintly.

"Right here in my bedside table!"

"Oh, good," Emily said.

There was silence. When at last Emily jumped into bed, she said softly, in case her mother had fallen asleep, "Good night."

"I hope you enjoyed your evening of pleasure," her mother said.

It was too much. Emily's body—as though even an instant's rest had refreshed it—seemed to rally. "I'll tell you all about what happened," she said. "It wasn't pleasure at all, not a bit." She swallowed indignantly, and began her tale. "Wouldn't you think anyone as fortunate as the Contessa—with as many gifts from the gods," she went on, "would be above base motives and acts? After all, surrounded as she is by a life like a work of art—"

"Poor thing. Face all pitted," Mrs. Knapp said. "I don't see what's such a gift of God about acne."

"But I barely noticed her acne!" Emily exclaimed.

She hesitated, contemplating the idea of the Contessa with a complex. But it was impossible. In all the blazing crown of the Contessa's perfections there was only that one tiny flaw. Emily brooded. Suddenly she was struck by the implications of the compassion her mother had expressed, and sat up straight in bed, furious.

But a snore informed her that her mother had already lost interest.

1966

SOURCES

"The Earliest Dreams," *The Earliest Dreams* (New York: Charles Scribner's Sons, 1936), originally published in *The American Mercury*, April 1934. Copyright © 1934 by Nancy Hale.

"The Double House," *The Earliest Dreams* (New York: Charles Scribner's Sons, 1936), originally published in *Vanity Fair*, May 1934. Copyright © 1934 by Nancy Hale.

"Midsummer," *The Earliest Dreams* (New York: Charles Scribner's Sons, 1936), originally published in *The New Yorker*, September 8, 1934. Copyright © 1934 by Nancy Hale.

"To the North," *O. Henry Memorial Award: Prize Stories of 1937*, edited by Harry Hansen (Garden City, NY: Doubleday, Doran & Company, Inc., 1937), originally published as "All He Ever Wanted" in *Redbook*, March 1937. Copyright © 1937 by Nancy Hale.

"Crimson Autumn," *Redbook*, November 1937. Copyright © 1937 by Nancy Hale.

"That Woman," *Between the Dark and the Daylight* (New York: Charles Scribner's Sons, 1943), originally published in *Harper's Magazine*, April 1940. Copyright © 1940 by Nancy Hale.

"A Place to Hide In," *Between the Dark and the Daylight* (New York: Charles Scribner's Sons, 1943), originally published in *The New Yorker*, December 14, 1940. Copyright © 1940 by Nancy Hale.

"Book Review," *Between the Dark and the Daylight* (New York: Charles Scribner's Sons, 1943), originally published in *Harper's Bazaar*, March 1, 1941. Copyright © 1941 by Nancy Hale.

"Those Are as Brothers," *Between the Dark and the Daylight* (New York: Charles Scribner's Sons, 1943), originally published in *Mademoiselle*, May 1941. Copyright © 1941 by Nancy Hale.

"The Marching Feet," *Between the Dark and the Daylight* (New York: Charles Scribner's Sons, 1943), originally published in *The New Yorker*, June 14, 1941. Copyright © 1941 by Nancy Hale.

"Sunday—1913," *Between the Dark and the Daylight* (New York: Charles Scribner's Sons, 1943), originally published in *Harper's Bazaar*, July 1941. Copyright © 1941 by Nancy Hale.

"Who Lived and Died Believing," *Between the Dark and the Daylight* (New York: Charles Scribner's Sons, 1943), originally published in *Harper's Bazaar*, September 1942. Copyright © 1942 by Nancy Hale.

"Some Day I'll Find You . . . ," *The Empress's Ring* (New York: Charles Scribner's Sons, 1955), originally published in *Good Housekeeping*, September 1945. Copyright © 1945 by Nancy Hale.

"On the Beach," *The Empress's Ring* (New York: Charles Scribner's Sons, 1955), originally published in *The Virginia Quarterly Review*, vol. 28, no. 3 (Summer 1952). Copyright © 1952 by Nancy Hale.

"Inside," *The Empress's Ring* (New York: Charles Scribner's Sons, 1955), originally published in *The New Yorker*, December 12, 1953. Copyright © 1953 by Nancy Hale.

"The Empress's Ring," *The Empress's Ring* (New York: Charles Scribner's Sons, 1955), originally published in *The New Yorker*, December 12, 1953. Copyright © 1953 by Nancy Hale.

"The Bubble," *The Empress's Ring* (New York: Charles Scribner's Sons, 1955), originally published in *The New Yorker*, July 24, 1954. Copyright © 1954 by Nancy Hale.

"Miss August," *The Empress's Ring* (New York: Charles Scribner's Sons, 1955), originally published in *The New Yorker*, September 18, 1954. Copyright © 1954 by Nancy Hale.

"How Would You Like to be Born . . . ," *The Empress's Ring* (New York: Charles Scribner's Sons, 1955). Copyright © 1955 by Nancy Hale.

"Outside," *The Pattern of Perfection* (Boston: Little, Brown and Company, 1960), originally published in *The New Yorker*, September 29, 1956. Copyright © 1956 by Nancy Hale.

"A Slow Boat to China," *The Pattern of Perfection* (Boston: Little, Brown and Company, 1960), originally published in *The Virginia Quarterly Review*, vol. 1, no. 1 (Winter 1957). Copyright © 1957 by Nancy Hale.

"Flotsam," *The Pattern of Perfection* (Boston: Little, Brown and Company, 1960), originally published in *The New Yorker*, September 5, 1959. Copyright © 1959 by Nancy Hale.

"Rich People," *The Pattern of Perfection* (Boston: Little, Brown and Company, 1960), originally published in *The New Yorker*, July 9, 1960. Copyright © 1960 by Nancy Hale.

"Sunday Lunch," *The New Yorker*, May 8, 1965. Copyright © 1965 by Nancy Hale.

"The Most Elegant Drawing Room in Europe," *The New Yorker*, September 17, 1966. Copyright © 1966 by Nancy Hale.

The text in this book is set in 10¼ point Fairfield, an old-style book font created for the Mergenthaler Linotype Company in 1939 by the Czech-born American type designer Rudolph Ruzicka, who later wrote, "Type is made to be read, and that implies a reader [who] expects nothing but to be left in optical ease while he pursues his reading." The font was revived for digital use by Alex Kaczun in 1992. The running heads are set in Trade Gothic, designed in 1948 by Jackson Burke. The paper is an acid-free stock that exceeds the requirements for permanence of the American National Standards Institute. The binding material is Arrestox, a cotton-based cloth with an aqueous acrylic coating manufactured by Holliston, Church Hill, Tennessee. Text design and composition by Gopa & Ted2, Inc., Albuquerque, New Mexico. Printing and binding by LSC Communications, Crawfordsville, Indiana, with jackets furnished by Phoenix Color, Hagerstown, Maryland.